ALOHA BRIDES

THREE-IN-ONE COLLECTION

YVONNE LEHMAN

BARBOUR
PUBLISHING

Published by Barbour Publishing, Inc., P.O. Box 719, Uhrichsville, Ohio 44683,
www.barbourbooks.com

*Our mission is to publish and distribute inspirational products offering exceptional
value and biblical encouragement to the masses.*

Member of the
Evangelical Christian
Publishers Association

Printed in the United States of America.

Dear Readers,

When I consented to write three historical Hawaii novels, I had no idea there was so much exciting, interesting history. When developing fictional characters, I need to be true to history, such as the first Hawaiian to become a Christian, working around tsunamis and volcanic eruptions, first missionaries, royalty, paniolas (cowboys), annexation, picture-bride era, and World War II.

I sincerely hope these stories will be as intriguing to you as they were for me to write. I appreciate the loyalty of my readers through the years and look forward to hearing from you and any new readers. My desire is that you see how God worked in the Hawaiian Islands and know that He is always ready to work in the lives of we who believe. My hope is that you will be thoroughly entertained by my stories.

I wish God's richest blessings upon you.

Yvonne

ALOHA LOVE

Dedication

To Carmen Leal, my writer-friend who lives in Hawaii and made *paniolo* suggestions that inspired my plot ideas for *Aloha Love* and gave me the idea for its sequel, *Picture Bride*.

Chapter 1

1889, The Big Island, Hawaii

The Little People won't let the Night Marchers hurt me, will they, Daddy?" five-year-old Leia asked as Makana Lalama MacCauley tucked her in for the night.

"You know they'll keep you safe, Leia. And so will I."

Her little pink lips turned into a smile, and her big brown eyes—so like her mother's—held confidence that her daddy would not tell her a lie. "*Aloha au la oe*, Daddy."

Mak bent to kiss her forehead. "I love you, too."

Tucking his daughter in safely for the night was a special time, but he dreaded what would follow. As her eyes closed, his smiled faded. Her words resounded in his mind, but there were places in his heart even they couldn't touch. Reaching over to turn down the wick in the whale-oil lamp was like inviting the chill, beckoning the darkness with its never-ending feeling of loss, that aching loneliness, the unfairness of it all.

When Mak left the room, leaving the door open a few inches, his mother stepped from the doorway of her room. Observing the expression of displeasure on his mother's face, he braced himself for a reprimand. They walked down the hallway and into the kitchen.

He didn't sit, and she didn't follow her usual routine of brewing a cup of hot tea. Instead, she sighed and held onto the back of a chair. "I heard what Leia said, Mak. How long are you going to let her believe in those idols and myths?"

"She's a child, Mother. And the myths of the Little People are fun. The paniolos' children she plays with tell these stories like my friends and I did when I was a child. Besides," he added, "I believed in faeries, brownies, and silkies."

"But you were taught by your dad and me the difference between myth and truth."

"Don't you teach her the truth, Mother?"

"She needs to know what her dad believes, too."

His stare caused her to look away. They both knew his current beliefs were not fit for a child's ears.

He shook his head and walked toward the screen door rather than say something disrespectful to his mother.

But his mother did not allow him the same courtesy. She constantly badgered him about God and letting Leia go to the mission school. His own early education had been at the mission school, so he knew his mother was teaching Leia more than she would learn there—and in less time.

They'd been through this many times. With a deep sigh, he walked out into the calm night. His heart was heavy. How could he keep his little girl safe when he hadn't kept his own wife safe? And how could he give Leia assurance that God would keep her safe when he had stopped believing in the love of the God who had let his young wife die? He and Leia needed Maylea so much.

His mother kept raising the question, "Is your own child never to learn to ride, Mak?"

How could he force his daughter on a horse when her mother had been killed by one? He, who trained horses and bred them for the royal races, would not insist his daughter learn to ride. He had not been able to calm her fear, or his for her, and horses sensed that. But his mother was right, Leia was almost six years old.

Leia had become as adamant about what she wanted as his mother, and it seemed they both were taking sides against him.

He lifted his eyes to the sky, star-spangled with lights of blinking mockery, a sharp contrast to his mind, punctuated with his mother's questions, his daughter's resoluteness, and his own indecision. He bent his head and gazed at the dusty path leading to the carriage-house stables.

This was a lonely time of night. The moonlight wasn't as pleasant as it used to be. The stars not as bright. The quiet was not comforting. His cattle were in the fields; his horses grazing or in the larger stables. His paniolos would have gone home or settled in the bunkhouse.

Strange how a man's life and confidence could take a 180-degree turn in so short a time. He'd thought himself a man after marrying Maylea and taking over the care of the ranch and his mother when his dad died. God was in His heaven, and all was right with the world. But all was not right with this world. His mother was now taking care of him. She and his daughter seemed to question his every move.

He would consider their requests after the race. Leia was young. There was plenty of time.

This was not the time to make such decisions. Next year, he'd be a different man. There was the upcoming race. He must attend to that. He walked into the stable and breathed in the aroma of rich earth, straw, and horseflesh so welcome to his sense of hope.

Hope?

No. More than hope.

Not seeing his jockey, Chico, he assumed the man had retired to his room in the carriage-house part of the building.

Mak strolled over to the great racehorse that only he had trained—that only he and his jockey had ridden. Panai was the most beautiful horse he'd ever seen—midnight black with a streak of white down his face from his ears to his nose. He had the eyes of a winner, one with the desire to just be given the chance. He was almost ready.

Panai would bring Mak the victory he must have, his number one goal: to win.

Then, and only then, could Mak find relief from his grief and anger.

Mother and son. . .racing for the coveted Big Island Cup.

Ill-conceived it might be, but Mak would have his revenge.

Chapter 2

April 1889, Texas

Jane looked out on the range from her upstairs window and saw the cows wandering aimlessly, likely chewing their cud, their only concern swishing away flies with their tails.

What a life.

But would hers be any more exciting?

Realizing she was twisting the impressive diamond on her finger that she'd worn for more than a year, she stopped, studied it, and understood anew what it represented.

Jane Marie Buckley and Austin Price were made for each other. They grew up believing it because their parents told them so. Having heard it repeatedly through the years was probably like cud chewing. She'd had to swallow it. But lately, the thought of being a married woman was hard to stomach.

Realizing she was once again moving the diamond ring up to her knuckle and back again, she stopped. It seemed that right hand of hers was always trying to take the ring off her left.

She had nothing against Austin. No one seemed to know of any fellow more suitable for her. And nothing was really wrong with him. She liked him. Furthermore, she loved him.

The Buckleys were in cattle and horses. The Prices were in oil. Her daddy would throw her the most fantastic wedding Texas had ever seen—that is, if she ever set a date. Things kept coming up. There'd been her daddy's cattle drives and Austin's college education, Matilda's embarking on another excursion, Jane's going off to college—or not wanting her wedding to be at the same time as a friend's.

The wedding part delighted her, but she wasn't too keen on marriage. She'd seen too many friends marry and become dull and boring when they weren't frazzled over what to do with their children.

The men fared well, but the women—that was another matter. Yet what else was there for an educated, marriageable young woman?

As a privileged married woman, at least she wouldn't have to worry about the flies. While strolling over the green lawns avoiding the cow patties, her swishing fan would flick the flies away. Another thought made her giggle. Would a fly dare to land on the likes of Mrs. Jane Marie Buckley Price?

The fast clip of horses' hooves and the clanking of turning wheels on the cobblestone drive broke her reverie. Leaning closer to the window, she saw the fancy coach come into view. That could be none other than Aunt Matilda Russell Buckley—her most exciting relative in the world. With a tinge of sadness, Jane remembered the shocking explosion at an oil refinery several years before that had killed her dad's only brother and had left Aunt Matilda a widow.

Come to think of it, Matilda fared quite well as a single woman. But again, the word *widow* had a more respectable ring to it than *spinster*. Jane cringed at the thought of being married just yet, but she certainly didn't want to be a spinster.

Did she?

She would prefer to be a widow like Matilda. Not that she wanted Austin dead. She just wanted to have an exciting life like Matilda. Seeing her aunt emerge from the carriage, Jane was reminded anew that her aunt was nothing less than colorful in her long green skirt with a matching traveling vest over a white blouse with flowing sleeves. She'd been told by a few friends and acquaintances that she and Matilda were a lot alike, but Jane felt like a washed-out version of Matilda. Her own hair was brown, her eyes blue green, and her skin less glowing. She pinched her cheeks but knew it to be a futile gesture to appear more attractive. Matilda would be stunning.

"Matilda," Jane called from the window. Her aunt looked up, revealing her beautiful peaches-and-cream skin, reddened lips, and copper-colored hair beneath a wide green hat adorned with graceful plumes. Matilda waved vigorously, and her lips spread into a delighted smile. Even from that distance, Jane could see her aunt's green eyes.

Turning from the window, Jane dashed down the hall and sped down the wide, curved staircase to the foyer. Inez had apparently heard the coach and was hanging her white apron on a peg in a closet below the staircase. The meticulous Inez closed the door, then smoothed her black dress and lifted her hand to make sure her black hair was not in disarray before opening the door to a visitor.

"I'll get it," Jane said. "It's Matilda." A dreaded look appeared in Inez's eyes. Nevertheless, she reopened the closet door to take out her apron and return to her duties.

After all, it was only Matilda, whom Inez considered "that worldly woman."

Pilar, the seventeen-year-old daughter of Inez, held a different opinion. The girl yelled from the kitchen, "Did you say Matilda?"

Jane nodded.

Inez warned, "Remember your place, Pilar."

But Pilar's "Ohhh" sounded like she thought royalty had arrived.

Jane shared that thought as she swung open the front door and hurried toward her aunt. Feeling quite plain in a simple cream-colored day dress, Jane nevertheless fell into her aunt's arms for a warm, meaningful embrace while they expressed their joy at being together after a three-month absence.

"Ahem."

The cough from the coachman brought to their attention that Matilda's bags had been deposited on the wide, front porch of Buckley House. Matilda reached into the front of her blouse and withdrew a small purse from which she took a gold coin that widened the eyes of the driver.

"Thank you, ma'am," he crowed exuberantly, bobbing his head of collar-length hair. "Been a pleasure, ma'am."

By that time, Inez stood in front of the open door while Pilar came out to help with the bags.

"Oh, if I'd known"—Pilar's eyes widened, and her chest rose with her rapid breathing—"I would have put flowers in your room, and—"

Matilda waved her graceful hand. Sparkling rings adorned several fingers. "Oh, I'm sure your mother will excuse you long enough to pick some flowers from the garden."

"Yes, ma'am. I know she will."

Inez smiled stiffly, but they all knew if Matilda requested something, it would be done. Pilar rushed to take hold of the largest bag and tug it inside. Matilda was not opposed to picking up her own bags, but allowing Pilar to do it meant a generous tip from Matilda, perhaps a gold coin or two.

Jane stopped at the bottom of the staircase when Matilda did. "I assume suppertime is as usual," her aunt said.

"Of course." Jane laughed. "Nothing ever changes around here except a new bull, the birthing of a few more cows, and Austin's bringing in another oil well."

Matilda lifted her graceful hand in a dismissive gesture and looked toward the great chandelier hanging from the two-story-high ceiling. Then she focused on Jane with widened eyes and a serious tone. "I will fill you in at suppertime."

Matilda grabbed Jane's shoulders and stared into her eyes. With a flourish, she turned, lifted her skirts, and ascended the stairs.

Jane had no way of knowing what Matilda had on her mind. But one thing was certain. Aunt Matilda's appearance meant something momentous had occurred or was about to.

And it could only be disastrous. . .or sensational.

Chapter 3

Buck, I bear news from the paradise in the Pacific," Aunt Matilda said after she greeted Jane's father with an exuberant embrace.

"After grace, we'll look forward to hearing it." John Buckley stepped back from Matilda and smoothed his mustache as if it had been disturbed, although not even the top of Matilda's elaborate coiffure had touched it. He stepped over and pulled out a chair for her from the dining room table.

Jane could hardly wait for his prayer to end. The Hawaiian stories she had heard about for many years were better than any fairy tale. She figured Matilda exaggerated, but she didn't mind.

"It's Pansy," Matilda said as soon as she and Jane said *Amen* after Jane's father asked the Lord's blessing on the sumptuous meal. Pilar would get another gold piece out of this dinner of the choicest beef, mid-April spinach from the garden, canned vegetables from last year's harvest, and the best corn bread that ever came out of an oven. Inez was too proud to accept money other than her wages.

"Pilar, you may remember Pansy," Matilda said, addressing the young woman who stood with her hands folded in front of her white apron as she waited to see if anyone needed anything. Much to the chagrin of Jane's father, Matilda never excluded anyone from her conversations and had point-blank said that anyone who didn't like it was downright snooty. So Mr. Buckley took it on the chin when Matilda gave a thumb gesture for Pilar to have a seat at the table.

Matilda continued her elucidation. Of course Jane and her father knew exactly who Pansy was. Pilar probably did, too, but Matilda had her way of doing things. She looked at Pilar and explained, "Pansy Russell is my brother's wife. Kermit Russell is a pastor in Hawaii. He never liked the name Kermit. Pansy wrote a long time ago that everybody in Hawaii calls him Pastor, Brother, or Reverend Russell, so she started calling him Russ. I need to remember that."

Pilar nodded. Matilda lifted a forkful of mashed potatoes in which Pilar would have included scads of fresh butter, milk, and mayonnaise. It appeared to melt in Matilda's mouth; then she washed it down with sweet tea. "This is an aside," she said, "but I simply must compliment Pilar." She faced the young cook again. "You milked the cow, churned the cream, and made this butter, did you not?"

"Yes ma'am."

"Oh, at a time like this I am so grateful for you." She took another sip of tea. "Now, for my news."

They all waited. Although her dad had cut his meat and popped it into his mouth, Jane hadn't taken a bite of anything.

"Pansy is ill." Matilda took another sip of tea as if needing some libation to relieve her dry mouth so she could get through the announcement.

A sympathetic "Ohhh" sounded from Pilar.

Jane glanced at her father, who simply alternated focus between Matilda and his food. They were accustomed to her drama. But this sounded serious.

Matilda reached into the pocket of her skirt and drew out a sheet of light blue paper. "This is exactly what Pansy wrote." She unfolded the paper and read:

> *My doctors do not expect me to live. I'm ready to go if the Lord doesn't see fit to heal me. I want to be buried on the Big Island that has become home to me. My only regret is that I might have to leave my husband and dear children and friends in Hawaii.*

Pilar's eyes popped. "She has children?"

"School children, dear." Matilda reached over and patted Pilar's folded hands. She stopped talking, as if one act of a stage play had ended and she was getting ready to begin the next. "I'm totally parched from that long carriage ride." She took another sip of tea.

"But this," Matilda said, closing her eyes and shaking her head. "This is what just about sends me over the edge."

Hearing Matilda's heavy sigh, Jane watched her dad respectfully lower his fork to his plate. Jane folded her hands on her lap. Pilar held her hands over her mouth and nose. Anything that could send Matilda over the edge would be colossal.

She took a deep breath and then read each word with great deliberation:

> *Russ needs you, Matilda. He will need you more after I'm gone. You know you're like a sister to me. If at all possible, I want to see you. But I don't know if I can live that long.*

Jane watched Matilda swallow hard. She cleared her throat and continued to read:

> *One of our dear church members, Makana MacCauley, has taken over some of my classes. I wrote to you about the MacCauley tragedy. He has his own problems, so I don't know how long this will last. If at all possible, please come.*

Knowing that Matilda could burst into tears, bellow out an unseemly string of unacceptable syllables, become uncannily silent, or even throw things, they waited.

Mr. Buckley ventured to mumble, "I'm sorry."

Matilda sat with her finger bent against her lips and her eyes lowered. After a long moment, she laid her hand in her lap and nodded. "I thought Pansy had mentioned a Rose MacCauley before. I remembered because she has the name of a flower. Seems there was some family tragedy. Something about her son's wife being in a terrible accident." Her head moved from side to side, and she sighed. "Perhaps I could be of some help to her." She smiled. "We who have suffered loss have a responsibility to comfort others."

She let that sink in. Jane found it amazing that her aunt could say so much without really saying it and leave no room for debate. Matilda had lost her husband. Jane's dad had lost his wife and brother. Jane had lost her mother and uncle.

Her daddy must be thinking they all had a responsibility to others. And she was sure the Bible said so.

Matilda held out her glass to Pilar. "Could you freshen my tea, dear?"

"Oh, of course." Pilar stood and pushed her chair back under the table. She went to the sideboard, dumped the tea into the sink, filled the glass with ice from the icebox, and poured the tea from a crystal pitcher.

"I must go," Matilda said dramatically after the tea was set at her plate and Pilar had moved away to await any further directive.

"Yes, I understand your concern," Mr. Buckley said. "How long since you've seen Pansy?"

"Ten years," Matilda said. "I've been remiss, but of course when your dear brother was alive, I traveled wherever he suggested."

Jane knew her dad would be skeptical about that. Matilda rarely did anything she didn't want to do.

She looked at them again. "I must go to Hawaii. Perhaps Pansy will still be alive by the time I arrive. If not, I need to comfort my brother. Maybe I could help out in that school. As you know, Kermit—I mean Russell—Russell is my only living blood relative."

Jane knew her dad would be thinking that when Jane's mother had died, Matilda had been right there to help in any way. She'd become not a mother, but a wonderful friend and companion to Jane and a big help to Jane's dad. When her husband had died, Matilda had been able to comfort Jane's dad with tales of the wonderful life his brother had lived.

"I understand." Jane saw compassion in her dad's eyes as he looked at Matilda. "When are you leaving?"

Matilda lifted her napkin from her lap to her nose for a moment and sniffed lightly. Her voice trembled. "How can I, Buck? A lady of my position cannot travel that far alone. I must have a companion."

Jane's heart almost leapt from her chest. The glance between her and Matilda before her aunt again slid her gaze to John Buckley spoke volumes. They both knew who that companion must be.

Jane's dad nodded. "What about your friend who traveled to California with you? Would she not accompany you?"

"Oh no, Buck. She fears water. Would barely put her toe in the Pacific

Ocean. She would never step foot on a ship that would keep her on the water for months."

"You might advertise," he said.

"There isn't time." She folded the blue paper, and her lower lip trembled. "And how could I trust a stranger?" She returned the note to her skirt pocket. "I would have to wear my gold pieces taped to my body." She glanced again at Jane, and the lowering of her eyelids seemed to say, "Jane, it's your turn."

"Daddy." Jane turned her face to him. "Aunt Matilda has done so much for us. What if I accompanied her to Hawaii?"

His mouth fell open. After several moments, he closed it. He opened it again. "Jane, you're getting married."

Chapter 4

Jane could say one thing with confidence. "Daddy, you know I can't have anyone but Aunt Matilda plan my wedding. She's been like a mother to me." She lowered her hands to her lap and absently moved the diamond ring toward her knuckle and back again. "We can't expect her to plan a wedding while her sister-in-law is. . ."

Instead of finishing the sentence, she looked down at her food. A sense of guilt washed over her for having felt so excited over the possibility of going to Hawaii when the situation was so dire. But Matilda's phrase *paradise in the Pacific* kept tripping across her mind.

"Daddy," she said, "Aunt Matilda has done so much for us. For me. Maybe it's time we did something for her."

He certainly couldn't dispute that. Matilda kept her eyelids demurely lowered and her napkin pressed to her lips.

Her dad was rarely without words, but he seemed to be searching for some. Finally he said, "Matilda, you don't know how long you'd be away."

She shook her head. "No. There's no way of knowing."

He exhaled heavily. "Jane, what would Austin say about your being away for. . ." He shrugged. "An indefinite period of time?"

"Why, Daddy," she said as if mortified. "Austin spent those years away from me getting his education. Should he have that privilege, but not me because I'm a woman? Would you want me to marry a man so selfish that he wouldn't want me to be a kind, caring person?"

He seemed to be struggling with how to answer. Finally he said, "Well no, of course not."

"Oh Buck," Matilda said, drawing his attention back to her. "Pansy wrote several years ago that the tourist trade has started in Hawaii. By the hundreds, people from all over the world visit each year. It's a paradise, Buck. Why, it wouldn't surprise me if Jane decided to get married there. It's a perfect place for a honeymoon."

Matilda made it sound like everything was settled. She had included the romantic idea of a wedding and honeymoon in spite of her sister-in-law's illness. But looking from her aunt to her dad, Jane recognized that uncertain look in his eyes. He frowned. "I've heard it's an uncivilized place."

"Uncivilized? Why, Buck, it's been seventy years since the missionaries went there and made the Hawaiians wear clothing." Matilda's hand came up and lay against the bodice of her dress, fashioned in the latest style. "And too," she went on. "Pansy said they've almost stamped out those sensuous hula dances. The hula

17

is only done now for parties and special occasions, and the dancers wear clothes." She fanned her face with her hand as if the thought were too heated to discuss.

Jane stole a glance at Pilar. The two of them had seen Matilda's own version of the hula right in Jane's bedroom.

"Why, those Hawaiians don't even square dance like you do here in Texas." Jane could almost visualize Matilda teaching the Hawaiians to square dance. Her dad was probably thinking the same thing.

Matilda must have seen his brow furrow and the slight shake of his head. She moved to another subject. "Besides Buck, from information I've received from Pansy, Hawaii is so civilized they don't let their cows wander off unattended right up in their front yards. Her gaze moved to the wide windows of the dining room, as if seeing a herd of cows.

Her dad's gaze followed Matilda's, and he spoke defensively. "They have to graze."

"Yes Buck, but not so close to the house. Why, Pansy said the cattle and horse ranches there had cowboys before we had them here."

"Hawaii has cowboys?"

Matilda nodded. "Hawaii has huge cattle ranches, and Pansy said the cowboys are called *paniolos*. They send salted beef all over the world. Apparently, their ranchers are as advanced as—or perhaps more advanced than—you are here." She paused, giving him time to take that in. Jane and Matilda knew her dad did everything in the most up-to-date way.

Matilda went further. "Jane and I could check that out and send information to you. Besides," she added, "A spirited girl like Jane needs an adventure before she settles down to take care of a man for the rest of her life. Austin has said he had enough travel during his years abroad. He wants to settle down."

Jane watched her father's face. He seemed to be in deep thought. She knew he loved her, but ever since she had turned thirteen, he hadn't quite known what to do with her except treat her like he would a boy. She was grateful for that and for Matilda's influence on her life. Because they never tamed her wild streak, Jane did not consider herself a drawing room type of person.

"Jane, what about your students?" her dad said in an apparent last-ditch effort to find a reason not to let her go.

"Daddy, they are equestrian students," she said, as if he were the child and she the parent. "The classes are at my convenience and theirs."

His eyes brightened. "Your own equestrian events, Jane. You're becoming a well-established equestrienne."

Jane tried not to show the sudden stab of disappointment that swept over her like a cloud of Texas wind in a dust storm. In the last two events, she'd placed second to Rebecca Cawdell. It was downright embarrassing every time she looked at the trophy or anyone congratulated her.

"Well, if they're advanced in Hawaii like Aunt Matilda says, I could learn even more while I'm there." Maybe she really could and come back to get that gloating gleam out of Rebecca's eyes.

Although he smiled before he said, "I would miss you," he sounded sad.

Jane reached over and covered his hand with hers. "Daddy, you could come there any time. Even go with us, if you like."

His lips tightened, but she saw the slight glimmer in his eyes meaning that such an event was a real possibility.

"Of course you could," Matilda said. "Buck, I couldn't very well have asked you to come along unless Jane agreed first. But that would be wonderful, having Jane and you along on this most important trip to be with my poor, ailing sister-in-law and comfort my brother."

That brought it back around to the seriousness of the trip.

Jane did want to be helpful to the Russells. She expected, however, that she and Matilda would still be able to see the sights of that exotic land. But how much freedom would she have with her father there watching her every move?

Chapter 5

Jane picked at her meal. The delicious aroma had vanished, and the food was tasteless. She could not pressure her father into anything. Matilda was the only person in the world who could come close to talking back to him and get away with it.

And too, Matilda had taught her that more flies are caught with sugar than with vinegar. So Jane sat there being sweet.

"Well," her dad said, "I realize this is important to you, Matilda. And Jane. . ." Straightening his shoulders he leaned back against the chair, a signal that he had decided.

"Jane," he said, "since you will have to wait until your aunt returns before the wedding is planned, and if it's what you want. . ."

Jane nodded and lowered her eyes lest they pop out with anticipation.

"This trip can be a wedding present from me. That way, apart from the sadness of the situation, you may find some joy in your journey."

Her heart hammered against her chest. "I really think it's something I should do, Daddy."

"Yes," he said. "I can tell both you and Matilda feel a great sense of responsibility in this matter." His glance swung toward the high ceiling. She had the feeling he might understand her and Matilda better than she'd realized.

"But with you gone, that would mean changes here, too. Eating dinner alone without my little girl. For a year, at least."

His gaze wandered to Pilar. Was he thinking he wouldn't need Pilar and her mother without Jane around? But how could he in all good conscience dismiss them, even for a year, after he'd saved them from a life of destitution?

Her father seemed to be debating the issue himself. "Matilda will be busy comforting her brother." He smiled at Matilda, then turned his attention back to Jane. "You might become bored."

Bored? Jane could hardly believe that word. The stories from Pansy's letters that Matilda had shared over the years had been enchanting. Of course, Matilda had a way of making a trickle of water sound like an oil gusher.

Matilda slapped both hands down on the table and put on her best smile. "You are so right, Buck. Why not send along a companion for Jane?"

"Wha—" Jane's father stammered. "Who?"

"Why, who else but the one you implied." She lifted her hands in the air. "Pilar."

Pilar screamed, and they all jumped.

She quickly slapped her hand against her mouth, and the gulp of swallowing just about made her choke.

A face peered around the dining room doorway. Jane glanced from Inez to Pilar, whose head began to bob like it might fall from her neck. Her mother's head was doing the opposite, moving from side to side as if the very idea was out of the question.

Jane knew that Pilar was happy just pulling down the bedcovers for Matilda. The thought of going to Hawaii would be as earthshaking to her as it was to Jane.

"Daddy, Pilar has been very much like a companion to me—at times like a younger sister." That was partly true. In earlier years, they had cried together about Pilar's loss of her dad.

"Besides Buck," Matilda said, looking at Inez instead of him. "Inez is capable of running this household without Pilar. I mean, with only. . .you here."

Inez's hand moved to the throat of her high-necked black dress. "But she's only seventeen."

"Oh how lovely." Matilda about came out of her chair. "Imagine Pilar celebrating her coming-out debut in Hawaii."

She'd shocked them all into taking on the demeanor of statues. After a long moment, the unblinking gaze of Inez moved to Pilar. The two stared at each other as if looking at strangers.

Jane wondered if Inez was thinking about a coming-out debut. When Inez's husband had lost his business and killed himself, it had seemed that any hope of Pilar's marrying into a fine family was gone.

Inez turned and disappeared from the dining room. Pilar's head was bent, not bobbing anymore, and her teeth had captured her lower lip.

Matilda sighed. "Maybe I can convince Inez to let Pilar go as a companion to Jane."

After dinner Jane walked with Matilda in the gardens, and they settled on a bench.

"Matilda, what was the tragedy Pansy mentioned?"

Her aunt paused. "I honestly don't recall, Jane. We wrote to each other often, and she told about many events in their church and school. The MacCauley name seems familiar, but I just can't place which tragedy that was." She patted Jane's hand. "We can find out when we get there."

When they got there. Oh, she could hardly wait. And she could hardly believe her dad had given his permission and blessing.

"Matilda, I can't get over how you can get people to do what you want them to. I know why Daddy agreed to send Pilar along." She laughed. "To help protect me. But Inez was shaking her head with that stiff look on her face. As soon as you talked with her in the kitchen, though, she relented."

"Didn't you notice, dear?" Matilda said with an air of superiority. "She didn't have much fight left when I reminded her that she and your daddy would be here alone."

Jane wasn't sure she understood.

Matilda grinned. "Inez used to be very friendly with me. But after your mother died, she seemed to be competing with me for your father's attention. I think she's sweet on him."

Jane's mouth opened in surprise. "I never suspected. I don't think he does, either."

Matilda nodded. "She probably tells herself it's gratitude. The Ashcrofts were never extremely well-off, but they were considered successful and were accepted in society circles. After the bankruptcy and the shame of suicide, that vanished. Inez has, not so graciously, accepted her role as housekeeper and has tried to teach Pilar that she is only working class."

"Takes a strong woman to do that, doesn't it?"

"Indeed," Matilda said.

"Um, Matilda, have you been. . .are you. . .sweet on my daddy?"

Matilda laughed. "My dear, if I were, don't you think I'd have had him proposing to me by now?"

Jane giggled. "Well, yes." She had no doubt that Matilda could marry any man she wanted to.

"He's too much like his brother. So. . .settled, I suppose you could say."

"Weren't you happy with Uncle Wesley?"

"Oh, yes. I livened him up, and we traveled all over. But you don't always know what you want or what you're getting until after you've got it." Her eyebrows lifted. "Don't you worry about Austin." She smiled off into the trees. "You'll liven him up."

Realizing she was twisting the ring on her finger, Jane looked down. Traveling to Hawaii and back would take about ten months, at least. They couldn't just get there and turn around and come right back. Possibly for more than a year, she wouldn't have to be concerned about planning or even thinking about a wedding. Just as Austin's travels had settled him, so would hers.

When she returned, she'd be ready for that. . .surely.

She dared not look at Matilda. Burning deep inside her and making vivid pictures in her mind was that island of paradise. Like a jewel in the sea on the blue Pacific, it seemed to sparkle in her mind with a brilliance far greater than what she wore on her finger.

Chapter 6

Before Mak could dismount at the mission school, Reverend Russell ran out of his house across the street and rushed up to him. Mak's first thought was that Pansy had died. But the reverend wore a wide smile, and his eyes were brighter than Mak had seen in a while. Maybe he was going to say one of those phrases like his wife was now in heaven with Jesus. If he did, Mak would turn Big Brown around and have him gallop back to the ranch.

Although it likely would be true, no man had a right to be glad his wife had died. He braced himself. The reverend waved a pink piece of paper at him. "Mak! Mak! My sister is coming to the island."

"Your sister," Mak repeated for lack of anything more to say.

"Yes, yes. Come on. Get down from there and look at this."

Mak dismounted and took his class materials from his saddlebag. He passed the reins to a schoolboy, who ran out to lead the horse out back and tie him in the shade where he could have feed and water. After giving the stallion a farewell stroke, Mak looked down at the pink paper.

The way Russell was tapping the paper with his finger prevented Mak from reading it, but the man looked up at him above his half-glasses and told him what was in it.

"This was written the week before they planned to leave port. They could be here within a week. Or sooner depending on how smooth the crossing is."

"They, you said?"

"Ah yes. Matilda, that's my sister's name. Haven't seen her in ten years. She's bringing her niece. Oh, how old is that little girl now? Janie was about thirteen, maybe fourteen last I saw her." He looked off, not seeing children at the door of the school but a memory tucked in his mind.

"Janie was a skinny little thing. Orange pigtails. Big eyes and a face full of freckles." He sighed and looked at the ground as if he'd returned to reality. Then he gazed into Mak's eyes. "That was a hard time for her."

Mak could imagine. The description Russell gave left a lot to be desired.

"But Matilda can do anything, Mak. Doesn't matter if it's a business or a school, she can run it. Why, she could even take over the preaching if need be."

Mak stared at Russell as he chuckled. "Oh, and a companion for Jane. A young woman they took in after—" He folded the paper. "But you don't need to know the details."

Mak could agree with that. The most he needed to know was that someone was coming to help at school and he could get back to his business on the ranch. "How is Miz Pansy today?"

Russell's face brightened. "This has done her a world of good, Mak. We can see where her illness is headed, just like the doctors said. But she'll hang on for Matilda." He nodded. "You just wait and see."

Mak nodded, wondering which was easier—knowing your wife was going to die or experiencing the unexpected shock of it. He focused his gaze on a wagonload of children being drawn up to the school, grateful for any distraction from his disturbing thoughts.

With a finger movement toward his hat, Mak left the reverend and walked toward the long, two-story school, as many children were now doing. Lessons would begin soon.

Greeting children while walking across the long porch, he was again reminded that some were as young as Leia. Was it fair to turn his mother into a teacher? She was already a substitute mother. He wasn't sure anymore. . .about many things.

After morning classes, Mak returned to the ranch, and Leia ran out to meet him as usual. After dismounting, he knelt to take her in his arms. He hardly felt her soft little arms around his neck before she moved back and began asking a zillion questions.

"Is Miss Pansy any better? What did you teach? Can you teach me what you teached them? Put me up there and let me ride. You can hold me real tight and I won't fall off."

The last time Mak had tried that at her request, she'd screamed no at the last minute, and he'd visualized the horrible scene all over again and felt the emotion of it. Yes, he understood his little girl wanting something she couldn't have. He had lived that way for three years.

He nodded to a stable boy who came to lead Big Brown to the barn.

Leia put her hands, balled into little fists, on her sides and poked out her bottom lip.

"Watch out. Your lip might get stuck like that."

She snickered.

He smiled at his little girl, aware of her beauty like her mother's. Black curls and eyes so dark they often looked black. Her skin was a smooth, deep, tan color typical of Tahitians.

His mother often said Leia resembled her mother in coloring but was like him in stubbornness.

"I'll tell you all about school at dinner," he said. "I need to check on Panai."

He saw the droop of her little shoulders when she turned toward the porch. He didn't look into his mother's eyes but felt her stare. Maybe someday he could shake that feeling of tension that he didn't measure up to what his mother wanted of him.

After finding out how things went at the ranch and apologizing to Panai for not being around him all day, he cleaned up and joined his mother and daughter for dinner.

His mother gave thanks, and then she and Leia bombarded him with questions about the visitors, most of which he was unable to answer.

"Reverend Russell did say that one of the visitors had orange hair and freckles." He hoped to prepare Leia so she wouldn't be too surprised upon seeing the reverend's guest and blurt out something to hurt her feelings. She'd been raised with people of different nationalities and coloring, so she had no problems with that. But he didn't think either of them had seen anyone with orange hair.

He watched the twitching of Leia's lips as if she wondered how to deal with that. Her little shoulders fell as she exhaled deeply and began to eat. His mother's eyebrows arched, but she changed the subject.

"You seem to enjoy teaching at the school."

Was that a note of pride in her voice? Had he finally pleased her?

"Believe me, teaching horses is a lot easier than teaching such energetic children. They are a challenge. But yes," he said. "I find it fulfilling. I'm glad to be of service to society the same as anyone else." He sighed. "I know you would like to help, Mother. And you could do it better than I. But I need you here with Leia."

Her silence spoke as loud as her words. He, or she, could take Leia along.

"Daddy, what's their name?"

"Who? The children?"

She held up three fingers. "The one-two-three new ones that's coming on a ship."

"Matilda, I think. And Janie. I don't recall his saying the name of the other one."

"How old are they?"

"Well, Matilda is Reverend Russell's sister, so she would likely be about his and your grandmother's age. Janie. Let's see." He looked into his memory. "Reverend Russell said he saw her ten years ago and she was thirteen or fourteen, so she should be twenty-three or twenty-four. The other one is a companion, so she wouldn't be a child. But I don't know if she's young or old."

"This Jane must be single," his mother said, as if she were not thinking of someone for him. But she was always thinking of someone for him. "I mean, coming this far with a companion and not a husband."

Mak shrugged. He wouldn't know. But it's possible that being an orange-haired woman with eyes big as a crocodile's and a splotched face might be reason enough for still being single at that age. He immediately chided himself for the unkind thought. People couldn't help their outer appearance any more than they could help what fate dealt them.

"Daddy, can we meet them at the dock?"

His grimace made the hope on her face wane.

It was a great treat of most islanders—going to the dock, greeting newcomers and visitors, seeing how they dressed, what they brought with them, finding out if they were going to stay.

"These are Reverend Russell's relatives," his mother said. "I can't imagine that we wouldn't go." Her eyes questioned, or perhaps challenged, Mak. But she waited for his reply.

He nodded. "Doesn't everyone go to the docks when ships come in?"

Leia squealed and clapped her hands. Ah, he'd made the women in his life happy. . .for the moment. "Can we make leis for them?" She glanced from him to his mother, looking for approval. "They're coming to help Miss Pansy. And Miss Pansy is my special friend."

"That's a wonderful idea," he said.

For the next several days, they took as much interest in those leis as he did his horses. His mother and Leia were making three leis of shells, beads, seeds, and feathers. Greeters would bring fresh flowers to the dock. Those could be added to any kind of lei the moment a ship appeared as a dot on the horizon.

"You two are doing a fine job," he said. His mother and daughter looked like he'd given them a piece of heaven when he added, "Reverend Russell said his sister has been a teacher and that her niece has finished college, and one or both will probably take over for me in the classroom. Leia, when the new teachers come, I will think about letting you go to their school."

He'd pleased his family and told himself he would seriously consider it. Pansy's sister-in-law and niece would likely have the same sweet, loving, gentle nature that Pansy had.

Chapter 7

October 1889, Hawaii

"Focus on the horizon," Jane and the other passengers were told by the captain. "That will get you accustomed to solid ground again. Just like you had to get your sea legs, you'll now have to get your land legs back."

Jane didn't worry about that. She was ready for land. During those first few days of travel, she had taken care of the others, putting cold cloths on Matilda's and Pilar's heads when they had come down with bad cases of seasickness.

Now she stood at the railing, focused on the horizon for that first glimpse of land. Once it first appeared like a pencil line across the ocean, it always reappeared no matter how high the waves.

"Like oil," Jane said, glancing at the faces of Matilda and Pilar, who looked as excited as she felt. "No matter how much water, the oil keeps rising to the top."

"And often looks like a rainbow of color," Matilda said.

"Speaking of rainbows, look." A rainbow of colors more vivid than she had ever imagined made a halo over the ocean and that speck of land.

So this was her first glimpse of Hawaii. Swept away like an ocean wave was any concern or fatigue of that long, wearisome, boring, sometimes perilous voyage.

A sparkling deep blue sea splashed up against high, jagged rocks. As they drew nearer, mountainsides of brilliant green appeared, then palm trees. Their tall, slender trunks rose into the clearest blue sky she'd ever seen. The tops of the trees were crowned by fan-shaped leaves, reminding her of peacocks proudly spreading their tail feathers.

"Oh, that aroma," Jane said.

Matilda laughed. "It's certainly not of cattle droppings and horses."

Jane and Pilar laughed, too. As much as Jane enjoyed the smell of horses, she was delighted with this mixture of heady yet delicate flower scents. She'd never thought about smelling an island. She supposed travelers to Texas might think it had the odor of cattle and oil.

"Oh look." Pilar said, pressing her hand against her heart. "They're getting into canoes and coming out here. Are they—" Her face screwed up like a tight fist. "Are they going to attack us?"

"Of course not." Matilda scoffed.

Pilar wasn't convinced. "Mr. Buckley said they're uncivilized. And Miss Matilda, in our history lessons on the way over here, you said they killed Captain Cook."

Matilda scoffed again. "You would have failed if I had given you a test on it, Pilar. That was more than a hundred years ago. And the people thought he was a god and couldn't die. I doubt they're going to think we are gods." She laughed.

Jane smiled and looked out at the big brown men, their muscles bulging as they rowed, moving through the water faster than the ship. "Aunt Matilda," she said timidly. "Those men are wearing skirts and necklaces."

Matilda patted Jane's hand that was clinging to the ship's railing. "Those are costumes, dear. Pansy wrote about them. These men are greeters. They don't always dress like that. I didn't tell you because I didn't want to spoil the surprise. And those things around their necks are not called necklaces. Pansy wrote me all about it. Those are. . ." She stood thoughtful for a moment, holding her hat against the sudden swift breeze. "Pansy spelled it l-e-i-s. I suppose they're called lee-eyes."

"*Aloha, Aloha, Komo mai*," the rowers called. The passengers waved and yelled, "Hello and thank you."

"Don't they speak English?" Jane asked.

"Pansy said English is the official language," Matilda said. "But they like to give a Hawaiian greeting."

The rowers escorted the boat to the wharf, where passengers disembarked down the gangway. They pulled the canoes up onto the white sand and formed a border, making a path for the passengers to walk through, each one bowing, greeting. Jane saw then that the "lee-eyes" the greeters wore seemed to be made of shells and what looked like long teeth and pieces of bone.

At first, Jane thought there must be some personage of high acclaim aboard ship, even though she thought she'd met all the passengers. The welcomes and greetings, however, seemed to be for each of them. At the end of the row of men stood many women and groups of children. The women came forward and greeted each of them as if they were long-lost friends.

"Matilda. Is that you?" A man in a suit came up to them.

Matilda screeched, "Russ!"

Jane feared her aunt would break his body with her exuberant hug. However, he wasn't a small man and seemed quite strong. He looked slightly older than Matilda, and his thin brown hair had a lot of gray in it. They broke apart, and she kissed his cheeks and he kissed hers. Both had tears in their eyes.

Matilda stood shaking her head like it was all unbelievable. Finally her brother wiped at his eyes and looked away from her. "Is this little Janie?"

Jane nodded and went into his open arms. Then he held her away by the shoulders. "You're not little anymore."

What could she say? "Ten years does that to a girl."

He laughed. "And it did it well. Ah, this is Pilar?"

She said, "Yes sir," and he opened his arms to her.

Uncle Russ motioned to a group of people. A woman and a little girl hurried up to them. Jane was surprised they wore clothing much like one would wear in Texas. But that healthy-looking woman couldn't be Pansy.

"Matilda," her uncle Russell said, "meet a dear friend, Rose MacCauley."

"Oh I'm so anxious to get to know you," the woman said. She held up a long loop of flowers and managed, in spite of the big hat, to slip it over Matilda's head and make sure it draped equally down her back and chest.

"Jane, this is Leia MacCauley," Uncle Russ said with a big smile. The child reached up for Jane, who bent down and for some strange reason felt like she might topple to the ground. However, as the child was arranging the loop as Rose had done for Matilda, Jane said, "Thank you, Leia, for the 'lee-eye.'"

The girl wrinkled her nose. "What's a 'lee-eye'?"

Uh-oh. Jane felt like an excessive amount of saliva had formed under her tongue. Something wasn't right. The people around her began to sway. "This. . . this necklace is called. . .what?"

"It's a lei," Leia said and snickered. She pronounced it *lay*. To make matters worse, the child turned to a man several feet away, standing with a group of children. "Miss Jane called the lei a 'lee-eye,' Daddy." She put her hand over her mouth.

Children snickered.

Rose MacCauley motioned to the man called Daddy. "Mak, come and meet Russell's relatives."

Jane looked at the ruggedly handsome man, who lowered his gaze to the ground. She resented what she felt was an unsuccessful attempt to keep a grin off his face. But what could she expect from a man holding in front of him a hat with flowers around the band?

The man came closer. But why was he swaying?

She heard the name. "Mak MacCauley," and somewhere in her swirling mind it registered that he had been mentioned in Pansy's letter as a teacher. But the hat? Was that another lei for her?

Just in case, she said, "I could use a hat like that."

He said abruptly without a smile, "Sorry I can't say the same about yours."

Should she laugh? Be insulted?

No, he must be drunk. He couldn't stand still. In fact, he often seemed to be twins. Looking around at the others, she saw that they too became like waves on an ocean.

She had that excessive saliva feeling again, and her ocean waves were not gently rolling but sloshing against her insides. She had to swallow it, but something wouldn't go down. Instead, that something was coming up.

Aboard ship they'd been warned it might take a while to get their land legs back, and if they felt dizzy, they should hold onto something. She extended her hand. Mak did the same. But before they could touch, she withdrew hers and covered her mouth with her gloved hand.

She heard some exclamations and Matilda's voice. "Oh, my dear. We were told that green is even greener in Hawaii, but I didn't know they meant faces. You look perfectly ghastly."

Jane could only focus on what was in front of her, and she stared in horror at the man who stared back, making her feel like the most disgusting creature in the world. She should have kept her focus on the horizon. "I feel. . .I feel. . . I. . .uh. . ."

She turned and ran.

Chapter 8

Jane made it a few feet behind a bench to a grassy spot and felt like a cow heaving in labor. She colored the grass even greener with whatever had been inside her stomach. She wiped her mouth with a. . .silk bandana?

Bent over, the lei swinging in front of her, she managed to look around and up to the side and saw the man with the flowered hat now on his head and minus a bandana around his neck.

"Thank you," she managed to squeak out after wiping her mouth. Looking down she didn't see anything unseemly on the lei or on her clothes. Straightening she accepted the arm he offered and allowed herself to be led to a bench. She took a deep breath but only exhaled through her nose lest he guess what had soured in her stomach.

Leia came over and pulled a little purse from her pocket. "Don't feel bad." She wrinkled her nose distastefully. "People do it all the time."

Jane noticed that several other passengers were doing exactly that. Some had been fortunate enough to find a reasonably private place to empty their stomachs. Matilda and Pilar gave her sympathetic grins.

"This will help," the little girl said, holding out a piece of hard candy.

Although she feared having anything in her stomach, Jane accepted the candy. Maybe it would at least freshen her breath enough that she could again join the others.

"Thank you," she whispered to the girl, who smiled and said, "Are you the new teacher?"

Jane didn't know what Pastor Russell's needs might be, but there was no way in the world she was going to be a teacher confined to a school building. Her hesitation was filled by Matilda coming over. "Can you walk, dear? We need to get you someplace where you can lie down."

"Oh no," Jane said, rising from the bench. She held the soiled bandana in one gloved hand and placed the other hand on Matilda's arm. "I think standing still is what did it." As they walked up to Uncle Russell and Rose, she apologized. Matilda had said her face had been green. She felt sure it had turned deathly white from the way she had felt. Now feeling warm, her face was probably red.

She laughed. "Oh, I must be a sight."

"Oh, you're fine." Rose MacCauley echoed Leia's words. "It's not unusual. A voyage like that is hard on a person. Believe me, I know."

Jane tried to smile, but even that effort felt weak. She was trying to figure out the relationships here. The man, woman, and child were MacCauleys. The woman looked older than the man, but she was quite lovely.

31

She didn't feel it proper to ask. Anyway, Matilda was still discussing her. "Jane was never seasick a moment aboard ship. She had her sea legs the whole time. We decided that must have been due to her being such an avid horseback rider."

"Avid?" Rose MacCauley said as if that were shocking. The woman's eyes widened as she looked from Matilda to Jane and back again.

Jane saw the questioning flicker in Matilda's eyes. Like she, Matilda must be wondering if the woman was asking the meaning of the word.

After a moment of hesitation, Matilda simply said, "Yes. Our Jane is an expert equestrienne."

Mak's mother put her hand to her heart. "Another example that God brings good from the worst of things."

Jane didn't exactly follow her line of reasoning. Perhaps the woman hadn't understood the words *avid* or *equestrienne*.

Rose MacCauley turned to the man who had stepped aside. "Mak," she said. "It might help if Jane rode your horse. She's not ready for land yet."

Jane thought he looked dumbfounded. He snorted, not like a horse, but it was definitely a snort. "You know the horse is spirited. And. . ." He gestured toward her. "Miz. . ."

Jane knew he didn't remember her name. He changed his wording. "She wouldn't know where to go."

"Then perhaps you could give her a ride," the woman said in a low but meaningful tone.

Pushing the candy aside with her tongue, Jane took several gulps of air. "I'll be all right. I don't think there's anything left in me." Looking around at the men in skirts she saw pants legs exposed beneath the flowered material wrapped around their thighs. "Maybe I could go for a canoe ride or something."

Matilda seemed to like the idea. "Oh, wouldn't that be fun."

"No, no," Uncle Russell said, shaking his head vigorously. "I don't recommend that. But Mak," he said to the man, who had stepped farther away from them. "A ride might be a good idea. The schoolchildren are too excited for lessons. You could take Janie to my house, and she could get some ginger tea. You'd be there before our carriages or the children in the wagons."

"It's all right," she said, seeing his frown and knowing the man didn't want her on his horse. Or did he just not want her near him?

As if confirming that, he turned and walked away, past the children toward where a couple of wagons tied to horses were in the shade. Uncle Russell offered an arm, and Jane began to move toward a carriage. "Oh," she said, "this is like walking on marshmallows."

Next thing she knew, a huge brown stallion was right beside her. The man with the flowered hat reached down for her.

"You don't have to do this."

"I know," he said. Uncle Russell put his hands on her waist and helped hoist her up. Oh what she'd do for riding pants right now. However, she squished her billowing skirts around her to keep them away from the horse's head and from being able to fly up and blind this. . .person. . .who wore flowers.

The man had his arms around her, holding on to the reins, looking over her head, and she was breathing the most wonderful sweet air and feeling the cool breeze on her face. They were only trotting, but the movement was similar to being aboard ship. Her shoulder was pressed into his flowered shirt.

She ventured a glance at him. He saw it and said, "Try not to throw up on my horse."

A deep breath of air filled her chest, and she felt her shoulders rise with it. She was well enough to remember someone had called him Mak. That was the name of the person Matilda had said was teaching for Pansy.

That little girl had asked if Jane would be her teacher. Well, she figured she would be as qualified as this aloof man. She would not just sit there and let him make fun of her, even if she did feel much more comfortable and hardly aware of any surroundings other than the strong arms around her and the musky smell of him combined with that of flowers. . .on his hat.

"I wouldn't insult a horse by throwing up on him," she said. Noticing the pocket on his shirt, she reached up and pulled at it gently with her gloved finger. "I could just deposit it right here."

Chapter 9

Equestrienne? That's what the woman had said of this sassy young woman who wouldn't surprise him if she did throw up in his pocket. Perhaps her horseback training made her sit so straight. Or was it his reluctant attitude that rankled her into that erect posture? On second thought, he doubted that. After all, she had accepted the ride.

He felt it best not to attempt small talk. While he kept glancing at her hair beneath her hat to determine just how orange it might be, she kept her eyes on the scenery, which was not too inspiring at the dock.

Whether this would be simply a ride for a couple miles to the area where the mission house, school, and Reverend Russell's house were located would depend upon her reaction. If she began to thank him, compliment him, or any other of that female kind of thing, he'd gallop her right up to the reverend's home and deposit her.

He left the dock area and trotted the horse along the beach where she could feel the motion and see the ocean. She gasped. "Oh, I've never ridden a horse on a beach."

The turn of her head from one side to the other revealed her wonder as she looked at the ocean, smiled, took deep breaths, and looked up at palm trees.

Seeing her enjoyment and hearing her say, "I'm feeling much better," he rode farther and longer than he'd intended.

The carriages and wagons were already lined up in front of Reverend Russell's home when they arrived. Russell must have heard the horse's hooves when Mak rode up to his house. He came out and reached up for Jane, who then held onto his shoulders and tested her land legs.

"I think I'm okay now," she said. "I feel a little weak, but. . .okay." She looked up at Mak. "Thank you," she said softly, but her eyes, which were not big as a crocodile's but were big enough to be interesting, held a guarded expression as if she didn't know what to think of him.

Good.

He didn't want her thinking of him.

At least her face no longer looked green. Not splotched either, although he had observed a few tiny freckles across her nose on otherwise flawless skin. She wasn't bad looking. With that hat he couldn't be sure of her hair, but he thought it more a sun gold than orange. And the few strands of her hair that had blown against his face had not come from a fourteen-year-old with her hair in pigtails.

He touched the brim of his hat and gave a slight nod. "I'd be grateful, Reverend," he said, seeing that his mother's carriage was at the side of the house, "if you would please tell Mother and Leia I'll be at home."

The reverend lifted his hand in response before he smiled at Jane and said, "Come inside. We've made some ginger tea for you. That will make you feel better. Maybe you can eat a soda cracker."

Mak turned Big Brown as he saw Jane put her hand on the reverend's arm and heard the man telling her to call him Uncle Russell. She walked with him up on the porch, where Leia came out.

"Are you coming in, Daddy?"

In a house filled with sickness and women and a preacher? "I need to go and check on Panai, Leia. I'll see you at home, later."

She lifted her hand and waved at him, then reached out to take hold of Jane's free hand.

Mak adjusted himself better in the saddle, which felt rather empty now. He didn't like the feeling of remembering when he and Maylea had ridden like that, nor did he like a woman being so close, the feel of his arms around her. Nobody should have been on this horse with him. It only made him miss Maylea even more.

Of course the feeling had nothing to do with Jane; she had simply brought out emotions that were never far from the surface. He had nothing against her. He just didn't need any woman invading his space.

Mak galloped the horse faster than usual, needing the wind on his face. He longed to feel free, to ride until all the distress was blown from him. It never happened. But he spent the rest of the afternoon tending to Panai, where his hope lay. Later he spent time in the ring with the wild mustang he was in the process of taming. Being in control of something was a good feeling.

Hearing the clanging of the triangle, he had Kolani take the mustang into the stables. After washing up, he entered the kitchen as Coco was putting dinner on the table.

His mother's blessing seemed shorter than usual.

"First," he said, upon seeing Leia's eyes light up and knowing she was about to go into a long spill about the day's events, "before you tell all about the reverend's relatives, how was Miz Pansy today?"

"Oh, so much better, Daddy. She just smiled and cried. She said they were happy tears."

"I'm sure they were, honey."

"Pansy has hung on for this, Mak," his mother said. "She was so happy. But you know she's been getting weaker."

"Miss Jane got better." Leia's eyes widened. "She might could be my teacher if I could go to school. I like her, Daddy." Her little shoulders lifted with her deep breath. "And I like Miss Pilar. She's nice. And Miss Tilda, oh my."

His mother laughed.

Mak glanced from one to the other. "Now what does that mean?"

Leia shook her head, and her gaze traveled around as if she were trying to see an answer. "I don't know," she said. "But I think. . .oh, I know. Miss Tilda is like a volcano."

They all laughed. He had taken Leia close enough to see the fire that continually spouted up like a fountain, lighting up a night sky with red fireworks, literally.

"Oh she is, Mak," his mother agreed. "She is so full of life. I think we're friends already."

"Me, too," Leia assured them. "And Miss Jane and Miss Pilar are my friends. Miss Jane might could be my teacher. I'm cleaning up my plate."

Sure. . .that should do it.

His mother turned to him. "Oh Mak. Jane is the one."

"Mother, please," Mak protested. "My one is gone."

"Oh, I don't mean for you." Her laugh sounded like a scoff. "She's the one for Leia. She teaches. . ."

He missed whatever she said next, but he was aware what she had said was a switch. At every ship docking, particularly the tourist ones, she would tell him of beautiful women, and because she was a generous woman, she invited most of them to their home. So now that one appeared who did get his attention by being green and obnoxious, she'd changed her mind about finding him a woman?

"Why is this one not for me?"

His mother smiled. "Oh, Miss Jane was modest about it, but Matilda blurted out the whole thing. Jane has been engaged to marry an oil tycoon's son since the day she was born."

Mak found that puzzling. "I didn't know arranged marriages went on in America."

"Oh, she doesn't have to do it. It's just that her daddy is a wealthy cattle rancher and has been friends with the oil tycoon family forever." She waved her hand in the air and smiled broadly. "So you don't have to worry about me trying to fix you up with this one, or about her being out to get you. She's spoken for."

"Good," he said and kept eating.

She wasn't finished. "And you don't have to worry about her being after your money. Her daddy and her fiancé are filthy rich." She looked at Leia. "Not filthy-dirty. That's just an expression."

Leia nodded and said seriously, "I need to go to school and learn things like that."

"Yes, you do," his mother said and looked triumphantly at him. "Did you see that girl's ring?"

"What girl?"

"Miss Jane."

"I think she was wearing gloves, and I think she might have thrown up on them."

"Well, she didn't hurt the ring. That diamond is big as. . . as. . ."

Leia stuck her hand out over her plate. "As big as a whoooole finger."

His mother's eyebrows lifted. "Close," she conceded.

This was a welcome change. As his mother said, he wouldn't have to worry about her being after his money, and she was engaged to be married. He needn't give her a moment's thought. He wouldn't need to make a point of keeping his distance.

Perhaps her fiancé would arrive. He understood his mother's excitement over having some new women to talk with, to find out about America. Just as Mak's mother enjoyed the friendship of women who visited Hawaii from other countries, he enjoyed interaction with men.

Mak was beginning to feel good about the situation when Leia said, "Daddy, I'm going to ask the Little People to make Miss Jane be my teacher."

Chapter 10

"How are you feeling, dear?" Matilda asked when she and Jane walked out of Reverend Russell's two-story white clapboard house after having a light supper in Uncle Russell's kitchen. They stood on the porch.

"Ashamed," Jane said, taking hold of the banister.

Matilda scoffed. "What in the name of wild horses do you have to be ashamed of?"

Jane groaned. "Oh Matilda. After seeing Aunt Pansy so frail, I realize all my fuss about getting sick was wrong. I have nothing to complain about."

Matilda scoffed. "Oh yes, you do. We're puny little human beings who have enough of the divine in us to want everything to be perfect. I think God put that in us so we'd keep trying to be better people."

Looking at the warmth in Matilda's smile reminded Jane of just how precious that woman was. On the outside she was all fire and energy, but inside she was a million times more valuable than those gold pieces she carried around in the purse against her bosom.

"Pansy cared about how you were feeling," Matilda said softly.

"I know, and that makes me feel bad. The attention should not have been focused on me."

"Oh honey. We all told our seasick stories. Even Pansy joked about never being able to leave Russ because she'd be too seasick going back to Boston. We were all trying to make you feel better."

"I know. And the laughing brought on Pansy's awful coughing spell, and we had to get out of there so the nurse could take care of her."

"But that was good for her. The coughing helps clear her lungs so she can breathe better."

"Maybe you're right."

"Maybe?"

Seeing Matilda take a step away and plant her hands on her hips, Jane laughed. "Okay, you are right."

"I really am in this, Jane." Matilda stepped up next to her and placed her hands on the banister, displaying her jewels and causing Jane to be aware of the single ring she wore, the diamond that sealed her commitment to Austin.

Matilda must have noticed she was looking at the ring. "That is a beautiful diamond, Jane."

"Yes, I know."

"Are you missing Austin?"

Missing him? Austin had always been in her life, and she'd accepted the fact he always would be. She didn't really take anyone for granted after her mother died, but she accepted that both her dad and Austin were there for her.

She supposed people missed those who were absent when they'd been used to their presence. She'd missed Austin when he went away to college. Then she'd missed him when she went to college. She missed him after he joined his dad in the oil business.

So she looked at Matilda's waiting face and said, "Sure. Now that you mention it. I miss Austin and Daddy and Texas. Even Inez."

Matilda smiled and patted her hand, the one with the ring on its finger.

Jane looked at the rose blue sky that was fast turning to magenta. "Like you always told me, Matilda. Life is full of wonderful adventures, and that's where we need to focus our attention—never brooding about what we don't have."

"That's right, Jane. Russ has told us of Pansy's rapid spiral downward, yet she has stayed alive to see us. She so enjoyed this evening. But she's ready for her adventure into eternity."

"So we'll just make her as happy as we can." Jane tapped the banister for emphasis. "Later we can focus on. . .adventure."

"Exactly."

Jane sighed. Well then, she never should have taken that unexpected adventure of a horseback ride on the beach with that sullen cowboy. But that was different. He hadn't wanted her on that horse, and if she hadn't been queasy, she wouldn't have ridden with him. But. . .no more adventures. She would be right here for Pansy and Uncle Russell.

❧

For the next few days, the women unpacked and settled into their individual upstairs rooms. A wide porch formed a balcony over the one below.

"I'm surprised, Uncle Russell," Jane said during the lunch that Pilar had prepared for them from food the church members brought in. "You have such a big house. Not that you shouldn't, but I mean. . .I expected it to be more. . ."

"Modest, I think you mean," Matilda interjected.

"I suppose so."

His eyes lit up with a smile. "Pansy and I are blessed. But you see, a preacher and a teacher have a community full of children—and adults, too—who often need a place to stay. But," he explained, "this was a missionary house when it was first built. Four couples lived in it. As time went by, they left, went to other islands, or built their own new homes."

"So you're really living more modestly than those who built new homes, aren't you, Russ?" Matilda said.

"To be honest, sister," he said. "It's not modesty that kept us here. We happen to like it, and it works to our advantage when there's a visiting pastor. Also, we can invite people who come here for a short visit and even have room for Pansy's Bible studies. We don't have to leave and go somewhere else."

Jane had the feeling that was not a lack of modesty or convenience on his or Pansy's part. They wanted to share their faith and whatever they had with others.

"Thanks for sharing your home with us," Jane said.

"My pleasure. Each of you is a great blessing, especially to Pansy." His smile at Matilda was affectionate. "Matilda has the best bedside manner of anyone in the world. Many a time, Pansy and I have talked about the poor and downtrodden—"

"Oh Russ," Matilda scoffed. "Let's talk about something uplifting."

Yes, Jane was thinking. Matilda was always the spark of life in any setting. Her telling about her many travels and adventures was better than seeing a stage play. Jane had wanted to be like her for as long as she could remember—at least like the exciting, adventurous side of her.

During the days that followed, Matilda relieved Uncle Russell of his almost constant attention to Pansy by taking turns with him reading to Pansy while she rested. Matilda spent as much time with her sister-in-law as the nurse would allow.

Jane took over the job of accepting the food church members and friends brought in, glad she didn't have to cook it. She took over the dishwashing, something she had rarely done, so she could organize and get the proper dishes back to the right people.

After only a couple of days, Pilar started to the school, resuming her senior year studies.

"What do you like best about it?" Jane asked her.

Her dark eyes lit up with pleasure. "I've made a friend named Susanne. She wants to know all about America, and I want to know about Hawaii."

Rose MacCauley visited one morning. She and Matilda took a walk together. Jane could tell the two were friends already.

That evening, Jane and Matilda sat in the swing on the porch watching the sun set while Uncle Russell sat by Pansy's bed as he did each night before she took the medication that would make her sleep.

Matilda lightly pushed the swing with the toe of her shoe. "I asked Rose about the MacCauley tragedy."

"What was it?" Jane said. "Or is that confidential?"

"Rose says the whole island knows. Mak's wife was thrown from one of his racehorses. His workers had to keep him from shooting that great horse. If they'd sold it to anyone except the king, Mak probably would have shot the horse and the new owner."

Jane gasped. "He's that violent?" She knew he was about as happy as a cow on its way to the slaughter house.

"No Jane, he's not violent. It's been three years since Mak's wife was killed. And their unborn baby. Rose said he just can't get over it, and if a woman comes near him, he runs in the opposite direction." She sighed. "He's such a good-looking specimen of a man. What a waste." She shook her head. "Apparently, his letting you ride with him on that horse was nothing short of a miracle."

"Well, he didn't have a lot of choice with his mother and Uncle Russell telling him to in front of everybody. I guess I've started off on the wrong foot with him."

Matilda nodded. "Rose said my mentioning your being a horsewoman, it just seemed the thing to do, and Mak was standing aside so she wanted to include him."

"He was quiet on the ride. Cordial, but I got the distinct feeling he'd rather have been elsewhere."

"According to his mother, he would. She says he's trying to pay more attention to Leia, who is becoming quite an observant and outspoken young lady. He came to the dock because they asked him to. She thinks you would be perfect to teach Leia how to ride."

"I would love to teach her." She shrugged. "But I guess he won't be giving me any more rides. Or the time of day, since he might think I'm out to get him."

"Now, there's the irony of this situation. That ring right there." Matilda reached over and tapped the set with her finger. "That is why he will give you the time of day. You're no threat. You can't get any wrong ideas about him." She leaned back and smiled smugly. "You're already spoken for."

Jane huffed. "So without even knowing me, he thinks I would be out to get him. But my wearing this ring means I'm about as significant as a. . .as a. . . doormat."

"Exactly."

Jane stared at Matilda, who lifted both shoulders and blinked her eyes innocently before focusing on the scenery ahead of them. Jane looked at the magenta sky, wondering if it were really that color or if she might just be seeing red.

Chapter 11

Pansy insisted they all go to church on Sunday and leave her at home. Her voice was barely audible because if she spoke in a normal tone, she went into coughing fits. While the nurse said coughing helped clear her lungs, the fits left Pansy visibly weaker.

"If you're needed," the nurse reassured them, "I can run up to the church. After all, that's where the doctor will be."

When she arrived at church, Jane found it interesting to see Japanese, Chinese, Koreans, and members of many other nationalities as well as American and Europeans. Sometimes, walking down the streets in the town of Hilo she felt like a minority. The stares she and Matilda received made her feel like one. She had not, however, met one person who was unfriendly. Well, unless she counted the flower-hatted horseman.

She almost laughed at that. He hadn't been that unfriendly. And he could have ridden off on his horse without her. Come to think of it, why would he even want to come near a woman who threw up in his bandana and threatened to do so in his pocket?

She wondered if he'd be at church, but when Rose and Leia came in and sat behind them, Mak wasn't with them.

Jane preferred to sit in the back where she could see everyone, but Uncle Russell wanted them to sit up front so they could easily be seen when he introduced them.

Uncle Russell had already told them about the construction of the church's walls. They were made of lava rock, three feet thick, bonded together by sand, crushed coral, and oil from kukui nuts. It was more than one hundred feet long, forty-six feet wide, and had a white steeple one hundred feet high.

Although Jane wasn't surprised by the elaborate way the women and men dressed, she was as surprised by the church as she had been by Uncle Russell's house.

"It's a beautiful church. I've never seen anything like it," she said, after turning in her seat to talk with Rose MacCauley.

Matilda agreed. "Well, we don't use lava rock much in American building because the few active volcanoes we have don't erupt very often and are in remote locations. But this is so elaborate."

Rose nodded and smiled, looking very beautiful in her European-style clothes and big hat, under which her dark brown hair was perfectly groomed. "The king donated the land, so the construction had to be the best," she explained. "Soon after the first missionaries came in the early 1800s, the queen became a Christian. She ordered all the sacred images destroyed. That's when the people began to get rid of their false gods and accept Christianity. The places of worship had to be fit for a queen." She smiled. "Or a king."

Before they could say any more, an organist began to play. A well-dressed man led a choir of men and women, and the congregation joined in singing, "O Worship the King."

Rose leaned forward, her face next to Jane and Matilda. "They're not singing about Hawaii's king."

Jane and Matilda smiled at her and at each other. Jane's eyes wandered around the beautiful wooden walls, the middle aisle separating high-backed pews, the tall columns holding up a balcony on each side of the sanctuary.

Soon however, her thoughts focused on Uncle Russell's sermon. She appreciated his straightforward approach, which reminded her of Matilda's way of not skirting the truth. Not that her preacher in Texas did that, but this sermon seemed more personal, something you could take home with you and think about. He talked about a servant's heart, which is what his congregation had been showing in such special ways for many months after Pansy's illness was diagnosed.

"Even a cup of cold water to a thirsty person," he said, "is very significant to our Lord."

His sermon made Jane uncomfortable. She'd always assumed she was useful to God, but she hadn't thought of it in such specific terms before. She supposed these days of watching Matilda and Uncle Russell put Pansy's needs ahead of everything else gave her a different perspective, too. She'd always said she wanted to be just like Matilda, but she'd concentrated on the adventurous side of her aunt.

The next morning, determined to be more useful, she asked if she could read to Pansy for a while. Both Uncle Russell and Matilda later acted as if she'd done a tremendous good and said they had enjoyed having a cup of coffee together and discussing old times when he and Pansy and Matilda and her husband had cooked and fed the needy in the church fellowship hall after a big flood.

Jane knew Matilda was good and generous, but she hadn't realized the extent of her service to the poor and needy until Uncle Russell began bringing it up and Matilda kept trying to change the subject.

Jane decided to take a walk while the doctor was with Pansy. School would be in recess for lunch soon, so she walked to the more secluded spot where the church, surrounded by lush foliage, was located.

She was in the midst of asking God how she might be of more help to Pansy or Uncle Russell when the unexpected sound of horse's hooves approaching her at the corner of the church startled her. She squealed and recoiled. Should she wait to be run over or dive into the bushes and hope for the best?

"Aloha, Miz Buckley," said a masculine voice she recognized with what she thought was a tinge of British accent and something else. She'd heard only three male voices, and this one did not belong to Uncle Russell nor the doctor, who was now with Pansy. Turning her head to the side, she saw a brown boot beneath a breeches-covered leg against a big brown stallion. Before she could lift her gaze higher, Mak MacCauley swung the other leg over the saddle and stood beside her.

He held the reins in one hand and removed his hat. The wind blew his wavy hair toward his face. His eyes held an expression of curiosity. "Is someone behind the bushes?"

He sounded serious. What kind of animals hid in these bushes? Was a fear of that why he and the big stallion had crept up silently until they were almost upon her? Without moving anything but her eyes she looked at the bushes and back at him. She whispered. "I don't think so. Did you see. . .something?"

"No. But you seemed to be talking to the bushes."

Okay, the first time they met, she threw up. Now he saw her talking, apparently, to a bush. "I was talking to God."

"God's behind the bush?" He didn't smile. "Do you think we should step back in case it bursts into flame?"

Chapter 12

Against her will, Jane's mouth dropped open. The man who had been so aloof was cracking a joke? Or was he being sarcastic? Maybe they just didn't speak the same language, but she'd give him the benefit of the doubt.

"If it bursts into flame we could run and jump into the ocean. I suppose God could part the Pacific Ocean as well as part the Red Sea. But. . .that would be an awful long walk to the other side. It took five months in a ship."

He laughed, and she joined in. Maybe his aloofness the day she arrived had simply been concern about her illness.

His smile vanished as if he had laughed in spite of himself. She gestured toward the bushes. "The bushes just happened to be here. Actually, I was thanking God that we arrived while Pansy is still alive and asking how I could be helpful to her."

With a slight nod he said, "That's commendable."

She shook her head. "Not really. I think that's what God tells us to be like." She gave a small self-conscious laugh. "I'm afraid I've been quite pampered and spoiled."

He didn't look surprised. Maybe she'd better change the subject. She turned again to face the bushes. "This is very beautiful." She touched a leaf of the huge plant. She'd never seen leaves quite so large or glossy on what must be a bush since it grew on what appeared to be stalks instead of trunks. The leaves were about four inches wide and ranged from one to two feet long. Her gaze moved up to where some of the stalks were twice her height. "What is it?"

"This variety is *Cordyline fruticosa*, a member of the lily family. There are several varieties. But this one," he said, as she felt him watching while she touched one leaf after another, "this is a Ti plant."

"Tea? Oh, you make tea from this?"

"No, no." Mak laughed. "It's spelled *t-i*, and some westerners call it 'Ti' with a long *i*. However, the correct pronunciation sounds like tea. Many of the native Hawaiians call it 'Ki.'"

"I've never seen a plant like this."

"It has many uses," he said. "The Hawaiians used to use the leaves for roof thatching, weaving it into sandals, hula skirts, and even rain capes." He touched a large leaf. "In the past and today, the roots can be baked and eaten as a dessert. Food is sometime wrapped in the leaves and cooked. There are many other uses, including medicinal. And," he added, "they're used to ward off evil spirits."

As her face swung around to look at him, she swiped away wisps of hair that the breeze had teased from her roll and blown into her face. "But that wouldn't be why they're planted around a church."

"Are you sure of that?" he teased.

"Well, Pastor Russell said two-thirds of this island is Christian. And he certainly wouldn't use plants to ward off evil." She gave him a doubtful look. "He uses God's Spirit."

"True," Mak said. "But it all depends on who you want to come to church—those who already believe the Christian religion or those who believe the myths and ancient gods. The unbelievers wouldn't come to hear the pastor because they believe in evil spirits. Even some of the Christians hang on to their superstitions."

"How can they be Christians and still be superstitious?"

He gave her a look. "Ever hear of walking under a ladder, or a black cat running in front of you?"

"I take your point," she said. "Or breaking a mirror will give you seven years of bad luck." He was a handsome man. "Is wearing flowers on your hat a superstition?"

"No, it just means we have a lot of them here. They represent this island." He shrugged. "Like that one star you have in Texas."

"One star?" Was he crazy?

"Isn't Texas called the Lone Star State?"

"Yes, but that's in the flag. And it's bigger than any star you'll find in the sky." She emphasized that with a slight bob of her head. "Texas certainly has more than one star in the night sky," she said proudly.

He shrugged as if he didn't care. "Most people say there are more stars here than anywhere in the world. And that comes from good sources since Hawaii is made up of peoples from all over the world."

"I'm not sure what a native Hawaiian is," she said. "But you're not, are you?"

"Well, yes and no," he said. "I was born here and raised here for most of my life. But my parents and grandparents on both sides are Scottish. I traveled with my dad to America when I was fourteen, then was sent to Scotland for my university years."

"I'm surprised there are so many nationalities here," she said.

"Many are like the Scots," he said. "If you know our history, we've been without a country and traveled to other places, such as America. My ancestors came here. In fact, a young Scot became friends with the king, married a Hawaiian woman, and their granddaughter became the wife of a king."

"I had no idea," Jane said.

He nodded. "In past years, all the overseers of the sugar plantations were hired from the University of Aberdeen, Scotland's college of agriculture."

Well, he seemed about as proud of Hawaii as she was of Texas. She could see he would be a good teacher, one who liked to explain things.

"And our current princess, Victoria Kaiulani, named after Queen Victoria," he continued, "is the daughter of Archibald Cleghorn, a Scotsman. She is half Scot and half Hawaiian."

Surprised, Jane said, "I've never been taught anything about Hawaii. All I know are a few stories from Pansy's letters to Matilda."

He nodded. "Hawaiian history wasn't written down until long after the missionaries came in the early 1800s and taught the people to read and write. Their history was handed down by them telling their stories throughout the generations."

She would like to learn more but wasn't even sure what to ask him. She started to ask if he missed Scotland, but instead commented, "Apparently you prefer Hawaii."

"It's my home," he said. "The best parts of my life have been spent here."

Looking at his face, she saw the misery appear. As if to shake it off, he seemed to paste a smile on his face, then looked at her hand. "That looks like an engagement ring."

"Yes." She held up her hand.

"Your fiancé must be very understanding to allow you to come on such a lengthy journey without him."

Allow her? Those words took a little thinking. She would need to clear that up. "It was really my dad who I had to ask. He's the one who pays the bills."

"Oh, no," he said, flustered. "I wasn't implying—"

"Oh, I know that. I was just trying to say in a nice way that I did not ask my fiancé if I could come. I simply informed him." He was looking at her strangely. "I think it's after people are married that those conventions are followed."

"Well yes, of course. But I was thinking about the long trip. Do you plan to be here very long? I mean," he said when she gave him a quick glance, "if I'm not being too personal."

"It's not too personal. But I really don't know. We'll be here as long as Pansy is alive. And as long as Uncle Russell needs us."

"Mmm." He was now nodding at the ground.

"But," she said, lifting her chin, "it wouldn't surprise me if Austin and my dad popped up at any time. They've never let me out of their sight for very long."

"I should think not," he said, and she saw a little color come into his tanned cheeks.

She wondered why he'd stopped. Just to talk to her? In that case. . . "I don't suppose I could take a wee little ride on that horse?" She stood and patted its neck. "I miss mine so much."

The good mood between them vanished. Mak looked like she'd asked him to pull down a star from the sky and give it to her. "I. . .I'm sorry. I must go. My horses need tending. And there's my daughter."

"Sorry," she said. "I didn't throw up on your horse the day I arrived. And I'm fine today. Maybe a tad dizzy upon occasion."

He seemed at a loss for a moment then gave a short laugh and reached up and patted his pocket. "One can never be sure."

She thought he was attempting to jest, but he seemed so uncomfortable that she simply said, "Say hello to your mother and daughter for me."

"Oh, that reminds me," he said. "My mother is eager to have you, Miz Matilda, the young lady, and Reverend Russell come to dinner when it's convenient, considering the circumstances with Miz Pansy."

"Thank you," she said.

He plopped the hat on his head and mounted the stallion, which proceeded to kick up the dust along the stretch of path bordered by tall coconut palms.

When Jane returned to the house, Matilda said, "I saw you and Mak talking."

"Yes," she said and smiled. "He mentioned my ring, and we talked about Austin. So Mak MacCauley has nothing to worry about." She flashed a glance at Matilda. "To his way of thinking, where I'm concerned, he's perfectly safe."

Matilda draped her arm around Jane's shoulder and said simply, "Yes, dear."

Chapter 13

Mak wished he hadn't stopped to talk with Jane. He'd simply made a fool of himself. She must take him for a complete idiot. But what could he have done? After she asked to ride the horse, he couldn't very well tell her to climb up and they'd ride together like they had the day she had a problem with her land legs. There had been a reason for it that day. Rather than further embarrass his mom and the reverend and cause more talk than when he'd tried to kill his horse, he'd consented.

But this was another day. She was an engaged woman. He was an avowed single man, and Jane's fiancé likely wouldn't take such an offer from him very kindly. Mak would not have liked for Maylea to climb on a horse with a man she'd just met and trot off. Maybe things were different in Texas.

And he could not let this young woman get on his horse alone. She still did not know the area. He felt confident he could control Big Brown even under the worst circumstances—that horrible thunderstorm they'd been caught in one time was proof of that, as was the time a wild pig spooked the stallion and Big Brown had reared up unexpectedly.

But no way could Mak chance any woman getting on his stallion alone and riding off. So, his mother said Jane was an equestrienne. But that was under controlled conditions in a confined area with a trained horse, and one she would be accustomed to. That was the kind of riding a lady would do. . .not hightail it off on a horse weighing more than a thousand pounds.

She'd been easy to talk to, fun to talk with. He'd had too many women try and attract his attention. This one did not. She just wanted to ride his horse.

And he could not, would not, allow that.

Perhaps he could show a better side of his character, if there was one, when she came to dinner—if she accepted the invitation.

The following morning, however, when he was less than a mile away from the school, he heard the church bells. That meant one of three things: church would soon begin, but this wasn't Sunday; something wonderful had happened, such as a ship coming in; or something sad had occurred. For death, the bells rang three times and stopped. Then they would ring three more times, and the process would be repeated over and over.

The last time the bells had rung for a dreaded occasion was back in April when Father Damien had died. That remarkable priest had given his life to help the lepers in Molokai. Then he died of leprosy. Word was spread later that he had said the Lord wanted him to spend Easter in heaven.

Father Damien was a remarkable man, willingly sacrificing his young life and health to make seemingly hopeless, outcast human beings a little more comfortable, giving them a glimpse of love and faith.

Now, Mak saw children being led from the school by an adult. When he rode by the church, the elder said, "It's Miss Pansy. She's gone to be with the Lord."

Her role in life was nothing like Father Damien's with the lepers, but it was just as remarkable. Pansy Russell had given her life for the children and adults alike on this Big Island. She'd been known not just as the preacher's wife or as a teacher, but as a servant of the Lord in her own right.

As much as he dreaded it, Mak knew he'd have to see Reverend Russell. Jane let him in and said Matilda and the nurse were putting Pansy's best clothes on her, fixing her hair and face.

Mak extended his hand to Russell. "I'm sorry," was all he could say.

"I know," the reverend said. His sad eyes nevertheless were filled with determination. "Now I know how you feel, Mak." He kept nodding and opened the screen door wider. "Of course there will be no school for the rest of the day."

"No," Mak said, taking a step back. He could not be in the house where a dead woman lay. "I need to let my mother know. She would want that, you know."

"Oh yes. I know. Thanks for stopping by. That means a lot." The reverend's smile held a mixture of sadness and strength.

&

Mak hadn't been inside a church in three years, not since Maylea's funeral. He only went then because her beautiful body was there in the coffin.

Yes, he believed the words being spoken. Those believing in Jesus were in heaven, were having a better life. He believed that for Maylea, for his dad, for Father Damien, for Pansy Russell.

The reverend spoke comforting words to others, even as the tears streaked his face. But he'd had Pansy by his side for more than thirty years as they worked together for the Lord. Mak had had Maylea only six short years. He'd been without her for half that time now.

No, on second thought, he was never without her.

And it grieved his heart.

Feeling a light pressure on his hand, he looked down. Leia's small hand lay on his. Her big brown eyes looked up at him. They filled with tears, and her lip trembled. His little girl didn't remember her mother. But she had known Pansy and had loved her. Mak put his arm around her and drew her near.

After the funeral, church members had a meal set out in the fellowship hall. His mother and Leia stayed.

Mak didn't.

He thought of the church that used to mean so much to him. It was where he had given his heart to Jesus as a young lad, where he had later given his heart to Maylea and married her, where he laid her to her final rest.

As foolish as he knew it was, there was no rest for him. He walked out to the graveyard behind the church and down to the stone inscribed MAYLEA MACCAULEY AND KEIKI, where his wife and child were buried.

Kneeling in the grass, he stared at the stone and the name. He spoke quietly. "Four more months, Maylea. I'll do it for you. It will help. It has to help."

He felt something touch his shoulder. With a slight turn of his head, he saw a hand with a diamond ring on its fourth finger.

"I'm sorry," a soft voice said.

He could only nod.

After a long moment, the hand was gone. He didn't turn. A man couldn't let a woman see him cry.

Chapter 14

Pansy was buried on Wednesday, and school resumed the following Monday. After Mak's class, Rev. Russell asked if he could speak with him. They went into the reverend's office. Mak sat across from him at the desk. "If I could, Mak, I'd like to meet with you and Matilda and Jane to discuss what we might do at the school."

Mak removed his foot from where he'd crossed it over his other knee. He leaned forward. "Maybe we could do that at my home. Mom has wanted to have all of you to dinner. She thought she should. . .wait."

Reverend Russell was already nodding, indicating he understood. "I've been waiting, too, Mak. I've thought about the school and what to do but didn't want to discuss it until after Pansy had gone to be with the Lord. I didn't want to stand in the way in case God wanted to provide a miracle for her." He made a soft sound almost like an ironic laugh. "Or for us, I suppose. She is in her miracle now."

Mak stared at him a moment, having the distinct feeling the reverend was trying to tell him something. But there was really nothing new he could say. Mak knew the facts of life. And the facts of afterlife.

The reverend slapped the arms of his leather chair. "Well Mak, you just tell Rose that we'll be glad to accept that dinner invitation. Any time."

On Friday evening, Mak saw their guests like a silhouette on the horizon. The prancing horse pulled the black surrey against a setting of green grass and clear blue sky.

What would the Buckleys think of his ranch? How would it compare with a wealthy Texan's ranch? Or an oil man's property? He scoffed inwardly, aware that kind of thinking was what turned so many Hawaiians into imitators of western lifestyle many years ago, resulting in their losing much of their own culture.

He walked away from the huge window in the living room, stepped into the foyer, and saw his mother and Leia coming down the curved staircase along the wall. They had probably been watching from an upstairs window.

His mother was dressed elegantly in western-style clothes that could compete with the finest—clothes that she didn't get to wear too often. Leia was trying to keep her lips still instead of smiling, as if she knew how beautiful she looked in her yellow dress trimmed with ruffles and a huge green sash. Her black hair curled naturally but now lay in ringlets and was adorned on one side with a pink, yellow-centered flower.

"My two beautiful girls," he said. His mother smiled broadly. She knew she was a handsome woman. Leia laughed delightedly. She made a small curtsy. "Thank you, Daddy."

All right. She was already practicing her manners.

"I'll go out and greet them, Mother," he said.

"Good," she said. She usually greeted their guests. Depending upon who they were, sometimes the housekeeper invited guests in. Feeling quite well-attired himself, in his western-style suit, Mak wished to give the impression he was not always a grump nor a crybaby. He was the man of this. . .this. . .ranch and this house.

He went out and stood on the porch as the reverend's surrey meandered up the long, stone driveway.

"Aloha, Reverend." They shook hands.

Mak held out his hand to the woman who looked as fiery as an evening sunset that lit up the world in bright red. She wore a red satin dress with the cut of the bodice like something the missionaries would have banned a few decades back. Decorating her chest was a strand of rubies set in silver. Her hair was a deeper red and in a high updo of curls and rolls and jeweled combs. She could pass for a Hawaiian landscape at sunset.

"Aloha and komo mai."

"Thank you," she said, setting her pointy-toed shoes on the ground and moving aside.

"Miz Buckley," he said to the next pair of pointy shoes. He lifted his hands and his gaze and was astounded by the contrast between the woman he'd just helped from the surrey and this one.

"Aloha and komo mai."

She lay her gloved hand in his and stepped down. "Aloha and komo mai to you, too."

Leia giggled and put her hand over her mouth.

Jane huffed. "What did I do wrong this time?"

"I'm sure you know *aloha* by now," Mak said. "*Komo mai* means welcome."

She and the others laughed lightly. "Thanks for the lesson. I do want to learn Hawaiian."

"I can teach you some words," Leia said. "And you can teach me some words. I want to learn about that filthy. . ." She looked up at his mother. "What was that?"

"Never mind, dear."

The way the two Miz Buckleys shared a quick glance, Mak thought they probably guessed what kind of conversation Leia might have been privy to.

"We've known each other long enough not to be so formal," Jane said. He realized he had been thinking of her as Jane all along. "I'm just plain Jane." She smiled. "By the way, you're looking mighty fine this evening."

He wondered if that should have been his line, but he hadn't wanted to be overly complimentary to any of them. He felt, along with Shakespeare, that discretion was the better part of valor. And he didn't have to mistake her remark as flirting, because she was an engaged woman.

He nodded, smiled, and observed that she was anything but plain. She was as refreshingly beautiful as her aunt was fiery beautiful. The high neck trimmed in a soft ruffle was light blue, and her eyes had turned that same color. Yes, they must be hazel. They'd been gray that first day when she'd thrown up, then green at the Ti leaves, now blue. Little swirls of golden brown hair lay across her forehead and along the sides of her face. The rest of her hair was arranged in a thick roll.

Until the fiery Buckley woman said, "Just a moment, Pilar. Mr. MacCauley will help you down," he'd forgotten there was a third person to exit the surrey.

He quickly held out his hand to the young girl, who looked about ready to jump out and could have done so easily. This, however, was the polite way. She looked pretty in an elegant dress, and her hair was pulled back from her face. As she stepped down, he saw a white bow fastened at the back of her hair.

He nodded at the stable boy who waited at the side of the house, then heard the women greeting each other and passing around compliments on their clothes and looks. Reverend Russell caught his arm, leaned close, and said, "These beautiful women are our dinner partners. How lucky can a man get?"

"Indeed," Mak said and laughed lightly. He walked ahead, held the screen door open, and bowed slightly as he gestured for them to enter.

In the foyer, they stopped as Matilda commented on the beauty of the white, two-story frame house and the elegance of the foyer and staircase.

"Thank you," his mother said. "I'm sure it doesn't compare with your plantation home in Texas." She gave Jane a knowing look. "I've seen some of that kind."

"Maybe not as big as. . .my daddy's," Jane said, placing the emphasis on *my daddy's*, implying it wasn't hers. "But it's just as beautiful. In Texas, they just have to make everything bigger."

She cast a teasing glance at Mak when she said, "Even the stars are bigger." He could feel his cheeks color slightly, but he smiled. "Before we go in," she said, "I have something for Leia."

Leia stepped up to her, her dark eyes shining and looked expectantly while Jane opened a shiny blue bag and took out a smaller white satin bag drawn closed with a drawstring. "Just put your fingers in the top and pull it apart."

While Leia did that, Jane said, "This is my own special lei that I'd like to give you."

"Ohhh." Leia's little mouth made an *O*, and Mak knew she was truly pleased with the strand of small pearls.

"I know it's not as big or as colorful as the lei you gave me, but this is a lei from Texas. They're pearls."

"Can I wear it?"

"Here, let me," Rose said and fastened the string of pearls around Leia's neck. Leia touched them, looked down, and then held out her arms as she rushed to Jane and threw her arms around her waist.

"I looove this," she said, after stepping back. "I never had any pearls before."

"I'm glad you like it," Jane said, and then his mother offered to show them through the house.

Mak tried not to let his thoughts show on his face, but everything reminded him of his loss. Leia's loss. Leia should have a mother who gave her pearls, who fastened them around her neck. He should have a wife to show guests the house.

He was beginning to think it was a mistake to have a woman around, even if she did belong to someone else.

Nevermore pecked at his brain like Edgar Allan Poe's raven. And although he had his land legs, he felt a stir of accustomed nausea.

Chapter 15

Jane loved the house. She learned that the ranch and house had been left to Mak by his father, wanting to make sure Rose would be taken care of. It was about half the size of her daddy's plantation house, and Rose's comment confirmed that when she said, "There are four bedrooms upstairs and a sitting room that doubles as a playroom and a schoolroom for Leia."

"Could Miss Jane see it?" Leia said. "I want her to know how much I've learned since she might be my teacher."

Jane didn't intend to be a schoolteacher and wasn't sure what to say, so she remained silent, but she smiled at Leia. Her uncle Russell came to her rescue. "Leia, we don't know yet who will be teaching the classes. Your dad is doing a wonderful job."

Mak lifted his hands as if to ward off such a thought. He emitted a short laugh. "I'm a rancher, Russ, not a teacher. Anytime one of these ladies wants the job, I'm fine with it."

"I do want to discuss that." He put his arm around Matilda. "Even if she is my sister, I can truthfully say this fine lady would work her fingers to the bone to help somebody else."

Matilda's scoff of distress made him lean away from her, but the affectionate look in his eyes was evident. "But I know, too, she'd like to explore this island from the white sands to the black sands as soon as I can assure her I'm all right without her telling me what to do."

Matilda scoffed. "I took a five-month-long trip for this? That's a brother for you. Wait till I tell you how he used to treat me."

"Now Tildy," he said. "You were the more spirited of us children. You don't want me telling stories on you, do you?"

She gave him a warning stare. "Let's change the subject right now."

Rose spoke up. "Russell, you didn't mention the green sand beaches."

"Green sand?" Matilda's mouth remained open until she found words again. "Are you serious?"

Before Rose could answer, Leia was nodding. "It's really green sand. Grandmother and her friend took me there."

Mak said, "If we're ever going to have our dinner, maybe we'd better get this tour over with."

"I believe our next room is the dining room," Rose said. They followed her down the hallway, past the kitchen on the right, and entered the spacious dining room. Over the table hung a crystal chandelier, holding many candles.

When Jane glanced down she noticed Mak looking at her. Did he suspect, or know, that Texas had electricity already?

Along two walls, the sunlight shone through wide windows that offered a view of green lawn and lush foliage, a lovely contrast to the elegant dining room.

Mak had her uncle Russell sit at one end of the long table while he sat at the other.

"Sit across from me," Rose said to Matilda, and they took their places at each side of Mak. Jane sat beside Matilda and Pilar next to Jane. Leia sat across from them, beside Rose.

After her uncle asked the blessing on the food, a heavyset, gray-haired, woman who looked to be maybe in her sixties, entered the room with a huge silver platter. "This is Coco," Rose said. "She and her husband had a restaurant in Hilo for many years. Now, we're fortunate to have her with us. She's the best cook in all of Hawaii."

Coco seemed stiff and unfriendly. "Aloha," she said in a monotone voice. "I've prepared a special dish for you. Broiled crocodile eyes on a bed of Ki leaves, smothered in coconut juice."

Jane didn't know what the others were doing, but she opted to look at Leia, hoping a child's expression might tell her this could not be dinner. Leia's lips were pressed together, and her little eyebrows lifted slightly and her widened eyes simply moved from one side to the other as if this were an everyday dinner item. But Jane thought the little girl seemed to be trying a little too hard to act like everything was normal.

In complete silence, Coco walked over to the table, set down the silver platter, and lifted the lid, revealing the most delectable piece of what looked and smelled like beef with something else beside it.

Coco's face relaxed, and Jane felt sure they all breathed easier. "I serve the beef in case anyone doesn't like fish. This is a prize Hawaiian fish called *opak-apuka*." She asked them to take their forks and sample the fish.

Jane wasn't sure about the *puka* sound of the fish, and gingerly placed a bite in her mouth. "Wonderful," she said, not caring if much of it still lay on her tongue. "I've never tasted fish so good." She looked around at the others, and they were nodding. Mak was smiling.

"I'll be back," Coco said.

"May I help?" Pilar said.

Nobody seemed to know what to say for a long moment. "Oh," Matilda said. "Pilar is a cook, too. I know she'd love to see the kitchen."

"That would be very nice," Rose said.

"Me, too?" Leia asked.

Rose nodded. "That would be nice, too."

At that moment, the dinner became very informal. Coco was even more congenial as she explained that taro was a kind of yam. Pilar brought in dishes of fresh vegetables of every conceivable kind, and Leia brought the cold food.

Coco dished out a small, stuffed green leaf and laid it on each plate. "This is rice in taro leaves," she said proudly. "You can put those around at each place," she said to Leia, who brought in two dessert dishes, then went back for more.

"This is Hawaii's famous *haupia* pudding made from coconuts. And be sure to try the mountain apple jam on your bread."

"This is fabulous," Matilda said. "I've traveled many places in the world, and your Coco has outdone them all." She looked at Pilar. "Most all of them, anyway."

Pilar smiled. "Probably all."

Jane knew Pilar had just eliminated her mother as the world's best cook.

Uncle Russell was nodding and chewing, plowing into the food.

"You really are eating some of the best food Hawaii has to offer," Rose said. "There are many restaurants here, a lot of Japanese, Chinese, and Portuguese in particular, and their food is good. But this is a collection favored by most people."

"You did give me a scare, Coco," Matilda said. "I don't think I'm ready for crocodile eyes."

Coco stood with her hands folded in front of her while they sampled the various kinds of food.

"She does something like that every time we have guests," Rose said. "That's why they say they aren't going to accept a dinner invitation unless Coco is the cook."

The older woman had transformed from a person of sternness into someone who seemed much like a member of the family. Her laughter, smile, and shining brown eyes made her look ten years younger than when she'd come into the dining room.

"She was like that in the restaurant," Mak said. "That's one reason it was the most popular place to eat in the area."

The woman's body seemed to laugh with her. "When people come from other countries to the island, they should sample good, real Hawaiian food. I'll be back." She walked to the doorway and looked over her shoulder. "And I do hide in the hallway and listen to conversations."

"I like that woman," Matilda said.

"Oh we love her," Rose said. "She's so dear to us. Our guests always say they'd love for her to join us at dinners, but she won't. Says she has her place."

"That reminds me of my mother," Pilar said. "She's a cook for the Buckleys. Oh," she added quickly, "my mother doesn't joke like that. She just cooks."

Jane felt the others now realized that's why Pilar wanted to help. Matilda spoke up. "Your mother has a particularly difficult time, Pilar."

She nodded. "If she were here, she wouldn't let me sit at this table. She's afraid I'll get big ideas."

"Well, like I've said before," Matilda said, "we're in Hawaii now. Let your ideas be. . ." She lifted her hands in the air and wiggled her fingers. "Let them be. . .flowers and sunshine and palm trees."

Soon the conversation was dominated by Matilda and Rose exchanging stories about their travels.

Jane halfway listened but was delighting in the delicious food served by a cook who had pretended to be stern. Was some of Mak's aloofness a pretense, too? Or did he really think no woman could break through his carefully guarded defenses?

Chapter 16

It seemed nobody wanted to move. "I am completely stuffed," Jane said.

"Me, too," Leia said, as Coco came in with a silver pot. "But I have room for coffee."

"Sure," Mak said. "In about ten years."

She grinned and picked up her milk glass.

"This is Kona coffee," Coco said, pouring them each a cup. "The world's best."

Uncle Russell had already introduced Kona coffee to Jane and Matilda, who were nodding as Mak affirmed Coco's statement. "That's no exaggeration," he said. "It's in great demand throughout the rest of the world. It's one of Hawaii's greatest exports."

"I will bring cream," Coco said.

Jane sipped the black coffee. "Delicious," she said. "But I do take cream."

While waiting, she glanced at Mak. "You call the ranch *Bele Chere*?" They'd ridden under the sign at the top of a wrought iron entry. "That sounds French."

"You know French, then?"

"I studied it in college."

"So, what does it mean in French?"

"Let her guess, Daddy." Leia had such expectation in her eyes that Jane figured she was waiting for her to say something funny again. She probably would.

"Mmm. *Bele* is close to *belle*, meaning beautiful. *Chere*. I don't know. Sounds like it would be close to *cherie*, meaning friend. So *Bele Chere* means *good friend*, or *beautiful friend*."

After she tried to guess, Leia said, "*Bele Chere* means *beautiful loving*."

"*Living*," Mak corrected, as they all laughed lightly. "*Beautiful living*. In the olden days, it meant something like that, could be *good life*, *beautiful life*. My dad named the ranch. It's Scottish."

"What does Leia mean?" Jane asked.

"*Meadow*," Mak said, the look in his eyes as soft as his voice.

"Grandmother says I'm like a meadow full of pretty flowers."

Jane smiled. "I think she's right."

Leia nodded. "I do, too."

They all laughed. Ah, the beauty of innocent youth.

When Coco returned with cream, Jane stirred it into her coffee. She smiled and looked across at Leia. "Leia, your beautiful skin is the color of Kona coffee with a touch of cream in it. Very beautiful."

"*Mahalo*. That means *thank you*." She looked at Jane for a moment. "Yours has little speckles on it. On your nose across here."

"Yes, it does," Jane said.

Leia squinted as she stared. "It's a little like ants crawling on the white sand."

Matilda was the only one who dared to laugh, and she did it vigorously.

"Did you put them on there, or did they just grow that way?" She was very serious.

"They just grew."

Leia looked wistful. "I wish I had some. I like them."

Jane nodded. "Mahalo. I do, too." She smiled at the little girl, giving her so much attention. "But I didn't always like them. They've faded through the years, but I took a lot of teasing when I was young."

"Me, too," Leia said, her expression sympathetic.

Mak spoke up. "What do you mean, Leia? Who's teasing you?"

Her lips formed an *O* and her eyes closed. "Sorry. Grandmother told me to forget it. I guess I forgot to forget it."

Rose appeared uncomfortable under Mak's stare. She waved a hand as if dismissing it. "Oh you know, Mak. That was last year when a man came to get the horse you'd trained, and his little boy said unkind things to her."

Leia was nodding. "He said I was crippled and ugly."

Jane joined Matilda and Pilar, who made protesting noises, and Jane said, "You're beautiful, Leia."

Leia nodded. "Now I am, but not when my leg gets tired."

Pilar was young enough to ask the question that Jane had on her mind and figured Matilda did, too. "Why does your leg get tired?"

Leia's face made movements like she was trying to think. "I forgot." But she smiled then. "But my limp is fading," she said, "like Miss Jane's freckles."

The tension was thick as that chunk of beef, Jane thought.

"What I want to know," Matilda said, setting down her coffee cup. "Is about the hula. I hear it mentioned often, but it's said like a Baptist talking about whiskey. Makes the upper lip curl up. Is this not polite dinner conversation?" She looked toward Leia. "Or not to be discussed in mixed company?"

"No, it's fine," Rose assured her, seeming relieved that the subject of Leia's leg had changed to something else, but Mak's face still looked cloudy. "The hula is a kind of dance the early Hawaiians did. After missionaries came, it was forbidden. The people were taught that God would not accept them unless they wore clothes and stopped doing the hula."

"The missionaries were mistaken," Uncle Russell said. "They thought the hula was connected with nudity. In the last few years, we've come to understand that the hula was the Hawaiians' way of communicating about their culture. Before the missionaries came, they had no written language, so they acted out their stories."

"That's right," Mak added. "The gentle swaying of their bodies and hand movements are like sign language. It's a natural artistic form of the spoken word. We point, we clap, hit, strike our fist against the palm of the other hand, slap the table, shake hands, move the hand as a warning." As if proving his point he looked at the position of his upraised hands. "We gesture."

"And this," Leia said, smacking her left hand with her right one.

"Now Leia," Rose said, "How many times have I spanked your hand?"

Mak spoke up. "Mother, if I remember correctly, once was enough." He slapped the side of his thigh. "And that was back here."

Leia's dark eyes were filled with love as she looked at her dad, smiling and nodding. "But she won't spank me there because it might hurt my leg."

"But speaking of the hula," Rose said as if in a hurry to change the subject again. "The king had a birthday party. My husband and I attended. I believe that was about fifteen years ago. Anyway, that party lasted for two weeks. Two thousand people were invited, and he brought back the hula. That helped make it more acceptable."

"And you danced the hula?" Matilda asked.

"Well. . ." The lovely woman touched the side of her coiffure and spoke in a rather sultry voice. "The party lasted for two weeks. He was the king. What's one to do?"

They all laughed.

Rose seemingly changed the subject when she said, "I'm sure you have electricity in Texas."

"Recently," Jane said. "In the big cities."

"We don't yet," Rose said, then returned to the subject of the king. "But a couple of years ago, the king installed a fantastic electric system at the palace. That cost more than it did to build the palace."

"Does the king—" Jane and Matilda both started to ask the question at the same time. Jane motioned to Matilda, who finished the question. "Does he still have his parties?" Jane knew the two of them would love an invitation to the palace.

"He does occasionally," Rose said. "He always throws a party before the island's most important horse race."

Jane would have liked to hear more about that, but Leia spoke up. "Come to my party."

"Oh, you're having a party?"

She nodded. "I have one every year of my life for my birthday."

Jane smiled at her. "How old will you be?"

She held up six fingers.

"Six. That's a good age."

Leia smiled and nodded, causing her dark curls to bounce against her face and shoulders. Such a pretty little girl. Her mother must have been beautiful. Well, her dad wasn't exactly a hobgoblin, but they'd said Leia looked like her mother.

Seeing that they had finished their coffee, Rose made a suggestion. "Mak, Jane might enjoy seeing the horses, since she's an expert horsewoman."

"I'm not expert," Jane rebutted, feeling the twinge of being second best.

"Oh, Matilda says you are."

"Matilda embellishes."

They all laughed, including Matilda, as if they agreed.

The idea of seeing the horses excited Jane. "I would love to see them. And I need to find out if there's a place where I could rent a horse for my own transportation. Matilda, would you like to see the horses?"

Matilda waved a hand. "Oh honey, I've seen enough back ends of horses to last me a lifetime. Rose has offered to show me the upstairs and some of those comfortable-looking dresses so many women wear for everyday."

Rose smiled at her. "Yes, and I want to hear more about your travels. And Texas."

"Jane and Pilar heard my stories over and over on the voyage. I think they'd get seasick hearing them again."

"Miss Jane," Mak said, seeming sincere instead of sullen, "I'd be happy to show you the horses. Some of them, anyway."

"Well, this being a ranch, I wouldn't expect to see them all. So I accept, if you don't mind leaving your company."

"You are my company. And there's something I'd like to ask you." He congenially looked at her uncle. "Russ, I know you've seen them before, but would you like to join us at the stables?"

"What I'd like to do," her uncle said, "is talk Coco out of another piece of bread smeared with mountain apple jam and a cup of coffee, sit on the front porch in that rocking chair, and just eat, drink, and. . .sit." He chuckled. "Maybe prepare a sermon on gluttony."

"Leia," Rose said, "why don't you show Pilar your rooms and collections? She might like to see your schoolroom. If Miss Jane doesn't teach, Reverend Russell has said Miss Matilda has some good things she could teach us all."

"Oh," Leia said, "I would like Miss Jane to be my teacher." She pointed to Matilda. "And you, if you can sit still long enough."

Matilda smiled. "I'll keep that in mind."

Leia reached for Pilar's hand. "Do you have Little People and Night Marchers in Texas?"

Pilar shrugged a shoulder. "No."

Leia led Pilar away. "I can tell you about them. You need to know, to be safe."

Just as Jane was about to ask, Rose sighed. "Children and their imaginations. Okay you two, go on," she said to Jane and Mak. "Matilda and I have fashion and travel to discuss."

If she didn't know better, and if they all didn't know she was engaged to be married, Jane might think somebody was trying to set her up with Mak MacCauley.

Chapter 17

"Mak," Jane said as they walked across the velvety green lawn. "What, or who, are the Little People Leia mentioned?"

He looked down at her and exclaimed, "Amazing." Then he laughed. "I mean your eyes. They've become as green as a Ti leaf."

Her chin lifted. "You mean like cooked and stuffed with rice?"

"Hardly."

She liked his laugh. She thought it was amazing how cordial he could be as long as she wasn't asking to ride his horse. "My eyes do that," she said. "They'll turn dull again in another setting."

He seemed about to say something but closed his mouth. He opened it again and said, "Mine are always a dull brown."

She might have said she thought his eyes quite dark and mysterious and she'd like to know what he seemed to carefully conceal behind them, but he quickly said, "This way."

They'd come to the lush foliage at the end of the lawn, and he led her down a shaded path bordered by Ti and other bushes and trees she didn't know the names of.

"About the Little People," he said. "I think most cultures have their fairy tales. Or tall tales. Like most legends, stories are based on fact. It's believed the Menehunes were a race of people living here long ago. People of other places came in and conquered them. The conquered people were considered inferior, and the word *Menehune* came to mean *commoner*."

"Like the Romans and Jews," Jane said. "The conquerors always think the conquered are inferior." At his quick glance, her thoughts came closer to the present. "Or like Indians, Mexicans, and. . .slavery." She drew in a breath. "Are the natural Hawaiians looked upon that way?"

"There's a parallel," he said. "As you mentioned, it's in all cultures. Sometimes it's called class distinction, society, caste system. But before we get too morbid, let me add that through the centuries, the Menehunes have become legend as Little People, no more than three feet high. They do good deeds. If sharks are about to attack you, the Little People can come in their little tiny canoes and beat them away with their paddles. You never see them. They do their good deeds at night and are responsible for many blessings."

"I can see that children might enjoy the stories," Jane said. "But Christians wouldn't believe the stories, would they?"

"I don't know," he said as they walked from the foliage into what seemed to be an entirely different world. Stretched out before her was an elaborate stable bordered by a corral.

As they neared the stables, Jane stopped in her tracks, forgetting anything but what came into view ahead of her.

"How magnificent." She hurried to the fence, heading for the huge black stallion glistening like velvet in the soft evening sun. A rider dismounted and held the reins.

"Careful," Mak said. "That's Panai, my racehorse."

Jane saw the big black eyes sizing her up. He snorted, as if trying to scare her away. Jane laughed but kept her distance. "Why, you big pretender. You don't scare me at all. You're all huffs and snorts."

Like your owner, crossed her mind.

"Don't be too sure," Mak said. "Miss Jane, meet my jockey, Chico Garcia."

Chico was a small, middle-aged man who looked as dark as some of the Mexicans in Texas. His intelligent eyes were as black as Panai's.

Chico held the reins. "Stay there," Chico said to Panai and stood between Jane and the horse.

"Aloha Miss," Chico said. Creases formed in his weathered face when he smiled.

Jane kept pretending she was paying no attention to Panai, but she knew he was watching. A proud horse, waiting for her praise of him.

"This is Panai. Panai, Miss Jane."

Jane started to take a step, but Mak said, "No, don't approach him. Chico, take him inside."

"See you later, Panai," Jane said.

She smelled the welcome aroma of horseflesh and hay. The horse had a large stall, more like an apartment.

In the stall, Panai turned and stood at the half door. Jane saw other horses with their heads sticking over their half-doors, turned their way. "I think the other horses are in awe of Panai," she said, noting that Panai looked at her when she said his name.

"No," Mak said. "They've seen him for many years. They must be in awe of you."

"I—" She started to deny that but became still. Panai moved forward and stood as if not seeing her.

Jane stepped closer.

"Careful," Mak warned. "He has teeth."

Jane studied that huge, magnificent, black velvet head with the white mark of a champion blatantly displayed down the front of his face.

She brought her hand up to stroke his head. His big black eyes held what? Curiosity? She spoke softly to him and patted his neck. His head moved up and down.

"You have a way, Miss," Chico said. "He never lets anybody do that but me and Mister Mak."

"He knows I love him," Jane said, "not just appreciate his beauty and strength. I love him because he's. . .a horse. A wonderful animal."

Chico stayed near and held the reins. "He tolerates males but shies away from females."

"Well," she said. "Maybe he's decided it's time for a little female companionship, a female friend."

Jane dared not look at Mak. She sensed the silence. The horse and his owner were somewhat alike. No females—threatening ones, that is.

As if in answer, Mak said, "We don't want him going soft. He has a goal. The three of us have a goal."

Jane looked at him. "To stay away from females?"

Even Mak laughed good-naturedly along with Chico. "Seems I've been talked about behind my back. I mean, our goal is to win a race. And Chico needs to take care of the horse."

Chico said, "He likes you."

For a moment their eyes met. For an instant she thought, *Who? Panai or Mak?* Then Chico said, "Almost as much as he likes an apple or carrot treat."

Well, that settled that—she hoped.

After a final pat to Panai's neck, Jane walked down the passageways to the other stalls, adequate but smaller than Panai's.

"These are for the carriages and daily riding," Mak explained. She spoke to a couple of stable boys grooming the horses, probably having recently been brought in from the range. Each of the horses was eager for a pat or a rub.

"Which do you like best?" Mak asked.

"I like them all, but—"

"Other than Panai," Mak said. "He's not in the same category."

Jane nodded. Panai was special, set apart. Like some people seemed to be born for a special purpose or with extraordinary abilities.

"Okay, let me see. Oh, this one I know. Hey, I think I've ridden on you." She rubbed his face.

Mak patted his neck. "Big Brown," he said.

"Sure is. What's his name?"

"Big Brown."

Jane laughed lightly. "Oh, he likes me very much. See, he's trying to nuzzle me." Mak allowed it. "Something Panai would never do."

Jane swept her gaze down to Panai, thinking, *You heard that, didn't you, Panai? But we'll see. We'll see.*

"These two," Mak said, walking farther past the stalls, "are ready to be ridden by others. Which would you choose for yourself?"

Jane looked them over. One was solid brown and looked to have a good nature. The white one was a wee bit smaller but shook its head, and she suspected it had a frisky nature and thought they'd love to ride over the range together. They seemed equally receptive to her. She felt their necks, their shoulders, gently rubbed their faces.

"I can't decide," she said. "Which would you choose for me?"

"I'll think on it," he said.

They walked back up the passageway. Chico was brushing Panai's hips.

"Nice meeting you, Chico. Panai." She winked.

She could have sworn the horse winked back. At least she knew he blinked, which upon first encounter he had not done. A horse could learn very difficult tricks. Winking was probably the least difficult.

Upon entering the stables, she hadn't noticed much of anything except the big horse as they turned left. Now on the right, she saw the carriages, the surreys, a good supply of vehicles.

"These are mighty fine," she said, touching first one, then another of the handsome vehicles, including a hansom, a landau, and a surrey, in which several people could ride in style.

"Now, what I wanted to ask you."

Jane faced him with an expectant feeling. Since he considered her no personal threat, would he offer to let her ride with him over the range?

Chapter 18

I was wondering," Mak said, "Do you think you and Matilda and Pilar would like a ride over the ranch?"

"Oh my, yes."

"In this?" He tapped the wooden side of a wagon with his forefinger.

He watched her touch the wooden sides that were about two feet high, then look into the wagon in which eight people could be seated comfortably.

"Is this a farm wagon?"

"Yes." He wondered what kind of vehicles seven people would take for an outing in Texas. Of course, that would depend upon how they were dressed. Jane and their other guests were dressed for a semiformal dinner. "Or we could take a couple of surreys."

"No, the wagon's perfect," she said, and he believed she meant it, until she added, "If it's not clean, we could sit on a bandana." A trace of mischief was in her eyes.

At that, a stable boy appeared from the passageway. "I cleaned it, Mr. Mak."

"I was kidding about the bandana," she said. "Do I need to return it to you?"

He reared back and stuck out his hands. "Oh please don't. I never want to see that again."

"I can hook up the fillies, Mr. Mak."

Mak nodded, aware that the stable boy—and Chico, too—probably strained to hear every word they spoke. Other than his mother, Jane was the only woman who had been in this carriage house and stable since Maylea. But they would see her ring, or he could tell them before anyone started rumors about anything possibly being personal.

"I think they'd love riding in this and seeing the ranch. I know I will."

"It's not too. . .rustic?"

"It's perfect."

Mak smiled and nodded to the stable boy, who struck off down the passageway toward the horses.

Mak asked the reverend to sit up front with him and have the ladies ride in the seats behind them.

Listening to the women talk and his mother describe certain sections, Mak felt he was really seeing his own ranch for the first time in a long time.

He allowed the two dapple grays to trot-walk along acres and acres of green rolling fields, past grazing sheep and cattle. At one point, they stopped to watch a herd of wild mustangs disappear along the slope of a distant mountain.

He heard his mother explaining about the bunkhouses, the many corrals, the small houses where some of the paniolos lived.

Beyond that was endless acres of green merging with white wavy lines of tide rushing in and out from a royal blue sea that melted into a lighter blue sky dotted with a few wispy clouds.

"My property ends here," Mak explained, pointing to a fence. "That's the beginning of a sugar plantation. All that is sugar cane. Belongs to friends of mine, the Honeycutts."

"Honeycutts?" Pilar said. "That must be where Susanne Honeycutt invited me to go on Sunday."

"I'm going, too," Leia said.

Mak heard his mother explain, "Leia's grandparents on her mother's side live at the plantation. But, Pilar, you must know Susanne from school."

"Yes, we're both seniors."

"Well, Rose," Matilda said. "Since our young girls will be away, why don't you visit with me on Sunday?"

"That would be perfect," Rose said. "I'll be at church."

They'd been gone for about thirty minutes. "I'll take you back around a different way," Mak told them.

"I could go on forever," Jane said. "This is the most beautiful countryside I've ever seen."

"We do still have a ride back to town, you know," Russell reminded them.

"Okay," Jane said. "But if we're going to head back, there's something I have to do." Mak stopped the horses when she began climbing over the seats.

"Uncle Russell, change places with me, will you?"

They managed to make the exchange, but Mak wasn't about to sit anywhere but right beside her. He should have expected it when she reached over and clutched the reins. "It's either this, or you walk home."

He handed over the reins.

After a while, he quit watching her every move and even enjoyed the ride when she had the horses canter. When she had them come close to a gallop, he murmured, "Ump uh," and she slowed them.

He could not remember when someone else had given him a ride. He was always at the reins. All he needed to do was occasionally tell her the way to go until, in the far distance, his home rose like a man's castle atop the gentle slope.

Seeing it as he thought his visitors would, he wondered how long it had been since he appreciated what he had.

When they returned to the house, Jane let her passengers out at the house. She drove him down to the stables. Chico smiled broadly, as did the stable boy, who came to take the wagon inside and unhitch the grays.

"Not bad," Mak said, "for a lady."

She gave him a reprimanding glance but again thanked him profusely.

She walked down to Panai, and again the horse let her touch him. Chico was right: She had a way with horses, Mak realized. They took to her, trusted her, and she wasn't afraid. She'd handled the grays expertly. "You asked about rentals," he said.

"Yes," she said, keeping her eyes on Panai, apparently sensing he was sizing her up, too. "I want to have my own transportation."

There were rental places in town, but one couldn't always be sure what one might get. He leaned against the stall near Panai. "It looks like our families have plans for Sunday. If you're available after church, I could bring a horse for you."

Her eyes, now duller than vivid green or blue but filled with anticipation, stared into his own. "You've decided which one?"

He smiled. "I'll surprise you."

ớ

He'd already surprised her by being so cordial. Was it only because she was a guest at his home? Or because she wore an engagement ring? Maybe some woman should teach him a lesson, that he was just as susceptible to a woman's charms as any other man.

Not more than ten minutes later, Jane thought she should be horse-whipped. The big question in her mind should not be what kind of man was Mak MacCauley, but what kind of woman was Jane Buckley.

Chapter 19

Almost as soon as they were settled in the surrey, they waved good-bye again, and Uncle Russell drove them down the stone drive, Matilda spoke up in a concerned way. "What a bad time that child has had in such a short while. Losing her mother and having surgery on her leg."

Pilar was sympathetic. "I asked Leia, and she said she doesn't remember her leg getting hurt. She just knows she fell and twisted her knee and the doctors had to operate."

"Rose told me," Matilda said, "that Leia was on the horse with Maylea. As Maylea fell, she held onto Leia, protecting her the best she could, but Leia's leg was twisted under her. Children's bones are hard to break," she said. "It's the twisting that was harder to deal with than if there had been a clean break."

Uncle Russell looked over his shoulder at them. "That was such a bad, bad time for Mak and Rose, but hardest for Mak. Rose had been through enough to know to turn to the Lord and others for comfort. Mak turned against God and became aloof from most others. For a while, they didn't know if Leia's leg would continue to grow the way it should."

"Jane, did Mak talk to you about it?" Matilda said, her expression troubled.

"No," Jane said.

"Like I said," Russell tossed back, "he doesn't open up to anyone about it."

Jane felt like the dirt along the road they traveled and thought she deserved to be run over by the wheels of the surrey. She hadn't had enough decency to remember to ask Mak about Leia's leg.

She felt Matilda's light pat on her hand, looked at it, and then smiled faintly at her aunt. Matilda must have thought the moisture in Jane's eyes was about Leia's plight. In a way, it was. But in another way, it was about her own plight. In the stables, she'd been thinking about horses and even entertained the idea of being able to appeal to Mak MacCauley.

What kind of hopeless creature was she?

Her other hand covered Matilda's for a moment. Matilda loved her. But Matilda didn't know how thoughtless she could be.

Did she?

If Uncle Russell preached about sins of omission, she'd probably shrivel up and sink into a hole somewhere.

❧

Sunday morning at church, Rose said Mak had taken Leia to her grandparents earlier. Pilar left with the Honeycutts. Rose, Matilda, and Uncle Russ rode into town to have lunch at a restaurant.

Jane ate a banana, changed into her riding clothes, and waited outside for Mak. "Why this one?" she said when he showed up with Cinnamon.

"After considering the pros and cons," he said with a trace of humor, "it came down to color. Since you have chameleon eyes, I didn't want to chance them turning white."

He did have a quirky sense of humor. "So you want to see my eyes turn rusty-colored?"

"Look." He rubbed his hand along the horse's side. "She's the color of your hair in the sun. A golden brown." He gestured. "Shall we?"

She exhaled heavily. "I'm more than ready."

"Fine. Since your first experience of riding on the beach a few weeks ago left a lot to be desired, I thought we might trot along a stretch of beach that's about three miles long. How's that?"

Sitting astride the horse she huffed. "Trot?"

"Yes." His determined tone left no doubt he meant it. "You and the horse need to get to know each other. Isn't that what you would tell a child you were teaching to ride?"

This was a test she surmised. If she didn't behave, he wouldn't allow her to teach Leia. And every little girl should learn to ride properly. Her expression must have been one of acquiescence because he pulled on the reins to turn Big Brown, and they trotted off together.

As they rode through town, Jane looked at the restaurant windows. "Rose and Matilda are probably in one of those places having lunch."

He looked over. "Mother really enjoys Matilda's company." He laughed. "But who doesn't?"

Jane smiled at that. Matilda had a way of making everyone feel comfortable. As they rode out of town, she said what she'd planned to say for the past two days. "I wanted to ask about Leia's leg. Does that have something to do with her not having learned to ride?"

"Partly," he said, a furrow appearing between his brows. "Of course, she couldn't for a long time after the surgery, and she didn't want to be near a horse. Later, she seemed to have forgotten what happened, but she still has a fear. She wants to ride, begs me, but when I start to put her on a horse, that fear sets in. Then my apprehension surfaces, and horses sense that. She's determined, in spite of the fear." He took a deep breath and looked out over Big Brown's head. "But so was Maylea."

Jane closed her eyes against what he must be feeling.

"The doctors say the leg is healed, but the right one is weaker than the left. As she grows, she will probably experience pain. Exercise should help the leg grow stronger. Horseback riding probably would."

Jane knew horses picked up on a rider's emotions. Maybe she could help Leia overcome her fear. Mak's was a fear of a different kind. Could anyone help him overcome his?

"In Texas, do you train your horses in the ocean?" he asked when they reached the beach.

"The horses I have for my classes have already been trained. I just need to train the child and horse to accept each other and teach the child how to get the horse to know and obey commands or movements."

"Here," he said, "a wild mustang or a belligerent horse receives a lot of his training in the ocean."

She wouldn't mind getting into the ocean in a bathing outfit, but in her riding clothes? "Is that what we're going to do?"

"Yes. Let's trot on down."

If he hadn't hesitated before saying that, she might have believed him. She shook her head, and he smiled.

"Okay Mak. So I asked a stupid question. This might be another one. Why do you train them in the ocean?"

"Not stupid at all. We take them into the ocean because they can't buck or kick while getting used to a rider and commands. That tames them. And too, it's not a bad idea for a horse to learn how to swim."

"Makes sense," she said. She soon found herself enjoying the Sunday afternoon trot along a white sand beach with a clear blue sky overhead. A deep blue ocean stretched alongside the beach, its waves caressing the shore, reminiscent of the breeze causing the palm leaves to sway. She could understand how the early Hawaiians, who had no written language, would express themselves with swaying bodies and moving hands.

This was a perfect day. Come to think of it, she couldn't think of a day in Hawaii that hadn't been perfect. And Uncle Russell said he did not want anyone catering to him but for them to enjoy Hawaii. He was delighted when she told him that Mak was bringing a horse for her.

She hadn't expected that he would ride with her. But again, she knew he valued his horses. He probably wanted to make sure she was right for Cinnamon instead of the other way around.

After a while, she laughed, and Mak glanced at her. "I just realized," she said. "I'm not quiet very often. But not talking makes me think the island is speaking to me. There seems to be a voice in the light wind and the sound of water gently caressing the sand. And it smells so good. What is that scent?"

"Jasmine," he said, and as they reached a rockier portion of the beach, he pointed out various foliage and called them by name. Some long stalks reminded her of the sugar cane fields they'd seen on Friday.

"Leia's grandparents are the Honeycutts who own the sugar plantation?" she asked.

"No. Her grandparents are Ari and Eeva Tane. They work at the plantation. My wife worked in the office primarily as bookkeeper. Coming from a Hawaiian and Tahitian background, she knew the language as well as English. I saw her and thought her very beautiful." He paused. "Her parents warned her not to like me."

Mak glanced at her and apparently knew she was about to question that.

"The difference was class," he said. "They are workers. We are owners. They were afraid my friends would not accept Maylea."

"But they did, I'm sure," Jane said.

"If they had not, they would not be my friends."

She liked his adamant attitude. Of course, she knew about class distinction. No matter how much you valued another person, color or money stood in the way of relationships many times. Dread struck her. "Do you think the Honeycutts might not be so accepting of Pilar when they discover her mother has fallen from her social standing?"

He shook his head. "No. She is American. She will be highly favored by them. And she is a friend of Brother Russell's relatives. Here," he said and grinned, "that is high society."

That being settled, Jane stated the obvious. "But you married Maylea despite the objections."

She watched his face. It seemed to relax with a memory that did not seem so painful this time. "At a king's party, she and other young women performed the hula. Her brother is a well-known ukulele player. That was the night I knew I was in love with her. But at first she was very self-conscious, shy around me. You see, a lot of Hawaiians have been clothed with material and stripped of confidence in their culture and beliefs. The effects of that remains for generations. I wanted to know her beyond the shyness. I knew she was intelligent and educated. There's the class status, but that doesn't matter to me. An employer should be shown respect from their workers and vice versa. But one is not more worthy than another."

He looked over at her. "You apparently treat Pilar like family."

Jane still found that difficult to explain. "She and her mother worked for us, and there's a difference in roles. But here, we're responsible for her and certainly treat her as family. Oh, did you know that the school is talking about teaching the hula?"

He nodded. "It's language. The Hawaiians are starting to want some of their culture back, and the white man is starting to see it's not some forbidden, sensuous dance."

"But that's what attracted you to your wife."

"No," he said. "It wasn't just the hula. Other beautiful women were performing it, but I did not feel the same about them as I did about. . .Maylea." He paused. "I don't speak of her often. When I do, I usually refer to her as 'my wife.' "

"I can understand that a little," she said. "After Mama died, Dad didn't talk to me about her until Matilda noticed and made him do it. Matilda and I could talk about her and cry together." She shook her head. "But not Dad."

Mak nodded, and she thought that must be something men had in common.

"Something you said at the stable," he said, "remained in my mind. You said Panai might need a female friend. I took that rather personally."

"I didn't mean—"

"I hope you did." He paused as if uncertain about what to say. "I could use a woman friend. One I can talk to about. . .Maylea as I just did. I can't to Mother or Leia. . .to anyone. Everyone thinks I should be over it. But enough about me, Jane. Tell me about your fiancé. Quite rich, I assume," he said with a smile, "being in oil."

Chapter 20

Oh yes," Jane said truthfully. "The oil keeps gushing out like there's no end to it. It's exciting."

"Sounds as if you have a substantial future ahead," Mak said.

"Yes. I've been. . .very blessed." She gave him a quick look. That was nothing to be ashamed of. "My father has worked very hard to make the cattle ranch successful. His father started with almost nothing."

"What's your fiancé. . .what's his name?"

"Austin Price."

"What's he like?"

"Slippery when wet. . .with oil."

He laughed with her.

She looked out ahead, having a warm feeling talking about Austin. "He's very handsome. Has dark hair, warm gray eyes, tall, nice physique. About perfect in looks. And he's the nicest, kindest, finest man anywhere. We could talk about anything and everything. And most important, he's a committed Christian. Very generous with those less fortunate." She smiled over at Mak. "And a lot of fun."

"He sounds perfect," Mak said, and she noticed the lift of his eyebrows as if that were unbelievable. But he asked, "What does he do for fun?" He chuckled. "Other than debate with you."

She wasn't sure how to take that. "Oh, we have our card games and board games and charades. He's just good at conversation and making other people feel good. Never a negative word about anyone or anything. And the best thing, we would race each other on horseback."

"Who won?"

"Usually me."

"Did he let you win?"

She scoffed. "You are the most chauvinistic man. No, he didn't let me win." She leaned forward in a jockey stance. "I challenge you to a race."

"That horse doesn't stand a chance against Big Brown. She can hardly gallop."

"I thought as much," she said. "On foot, I could race this horse *on foot* and win."

She loved making him laugh. "Let me race you on Panai."

"Never."

The way he said that made her think she'd better change the subject, but he did first. "This thing bothers me," he said. "You were promised to Austin? I don't understand that."

"Oh, it was a pact between our parents. Or a hope, I guess would be more accurate. No one would hold us to that. I mean, neither of us ever found anyone who suited us better. Austin and I are different, but we complement each other."

"Is he your age?"

"Four years older. I'm twenty-three, twenty-four in March."

"Isn't that a long engagement?"

She looked out over the ocean, seeing surfers riding the waves far out. "Yes. I think it's about twenty-three-and-a-half years."

"Apparently you're in no hurry, if I'm not being too personal."

"Don't worry about being personal. I could lie at any time," she jested.

He punctuated his concurrence with a nod.

"But I did accept his ring on my eighteenth birthday. My friends were oohing and aahing. I became very excited about a big wedding. Then Aunt Matilda gave me a long talk. What I remember most was that she said it was fine to be excited about a big wedding. But just be sure I was planning a marriage, not simply a wedding." She glanced at Mak. "She wanted me to be sure I was in love with Austin and not just the idea of being in love and that I was ready to settle down."

"Sounds like a wise woman," he said.

"Very. I tried to visualize myself settled down." She shook her head. "I wasn't ready. I decided I wanted to be independent, travel like Matilda without asking my daddy or a husband for money and knowing he might refuse. So I began to teach horseback riding and equestrian classes. In case you haven't noticed, I'm a free spirit. I wasn't ready to be. . .tamed."

"Perhaps you shouldn't be. Like a racehorse. They need to be disciplined and trained, but not have their spirit broken."

"Oh," she said saucily, "and how do you train a girl like me?"

"That part is up to you, not someone else. One should not force another into some kind of mold but encourage them to recognize their strengths and weaknesses."

"That's how Austin feels. It's why he doesn't pressure me."

A hard look came over Mak's face. "That's something Maylea didn't understand. I wanted her to be herself. I loved who she was. But she wanted to be what she thought I would want, although I denied that. That's why she rode the spirited horse that day against my advice, trying to prove she was brave enough. I was always busy training my horses and taking care of the ranch, so she decided to teach Leia." He shook his head. "Of course the horse sensed her lack of confidence. Leia might have been fearful, too."

Jane realized she had said this before. "I'm so sorry."

He nodded. After a long silence, she asked, "What happened to the horse?"

She wondered if he'd ever reply. After a heavy sigh, he said, "The horse is Panai's mother. After the funeral and while Leia was still in the hospital, my foreman and paniolos had to hold me down to keep me from killing that animal. I threatened to fire them all, but they wouldn't let me go. Somebody took the horse away, and later, I found out the king bought her. He's raced her and won for the past three years. It's like having the horse laugh in my face."

Jane didn't know if she should say anything. They reached the end of the beach, and she turned Cinnamon back around when Mak turned Big Brown.

Bitterness was in his voice when he spoke again. "The horse didn't care that my wife and unborn baby were killed. That Leia was hurt and lost her mother. That her parents are without their daughter. The world is without a beautiful, kind woman. The horse doesn't care. That's why Panai has to win that race. It's my revenge on the horse."

Jane asked tentatively, "You think the horse will know?"

He glanced at her. "I will know."

Jane wanted to reach over and touch his hand, make some physical gesture to show she cared. But he might resent that touch. He did not look receptive to any overture. What could she say, do? She uttered a silent prayer for guidance. But an answer did not form in her heart and mind.

"You've probably heard all kinds of explanations of why you shouldn't feel that way."

"Oh yes. Every possible reason—life, Satan, choices, one's time to go, accident, a better life in heaven." His voice was bitter. "You name it, I've heard it. But it doesn't make the pain go away. So you see, I have nothing of value to offer a woman. I only have. . .needs."

"Okay," she said. "Let's make a deal. I'll try and fulfill your need for a woman friend."

He sighed heavily. "I can't even be a friend in return. I've turned into a grouch who I hardly recognize."

"Yes, you can be a friend. You have already, Mak. You've shared your home, your family, your *gentle* horse." She challenged him with a glance. "We could continue with you showing me the island."

Maybe he didn't want to show her the island. After a long moment, however, he said, "You've already made me realize I should talk to my daughter about her mother."

"Have you told her why she's afraid?"

"No, I wouldn't want Leia to blame her mother for putting her in danger."

"Mak, I heard that Maylea saved Leia's life."

It took a while before he acknowledged that with a nod. "Perhaps you could fill me in on how you would go about teaching Leia to ride. Was it your dad who taught you?"

"Oh yes. I was riding before I was walking, so I've been told. My mom tried to teach me to be a lady." She wrinkled her nose, and Mak grinned. "My dad wanted a boy, so that may be why he taught me to care for animals and ride like a man. I needed those equestrian lessons to teach me how to ride like a lady."

He laughed when she said *lady* as if it were unsavory.

Then he surprised her by saying, "How do you go about teaching that to a child?"

"Easy," she said. "Sit erect and wear a stylish riding habit."

At the skeptical look he gave her, she laughed. "That's the lady part. The first thing I do is lead the children to the stall, have them take a rake, and go apple-picking in the straw."

"Apple-picking? Why would apples be in the stall? The horses would eat them."

"That's the word my daddy used for cleaning out the stall. The horse's apples would be chucked into a pail."

He grimaced. "You'd have a child do that?"

She looked him in the face. "Of course. A rider needs to know how to keep his horse's stall clean, even if they have their own stable boys. That's the first lesson. If parents aren't willing to have the child learn complete care of a horse, then I won't take the child on as a student."

He looked away, and she figured that was the end of that. "You see, after a child does the dirtiest, smelliest job, then keeping the animal clean is not at all a dirty job, but a pleasure."

The lift of his eyebrows and a brief nod indicated he agreed.

"Next," she said, "I have the child learn to feel the horse, get used to him, and allow the horse to get used to the child's touch and voice." Remembering that his wife was thrown, she said, "I also teach a child how to fall, to be prepared to hold onto the reins or grab the saddle horn, anticipate that even the most gentle horse can be frightened, perhaps by a snake in the road."

His quick laugh made her think he didn't care for her methods. The grin stayed on his face when he said, "There are no snakes in Hawaii."

Shocked, her jaw dropped. "No snakes? Not one?"

"Nope. The only things here are what people from other countries have brought in. None have brought any snakes."

While she was trying to recover from that disclosure, he said, "If you could get my little lady to. . .pick apples, you could get her to do anything."

Chapter 21

Pilar squealed, "No!"

Uncle Russell said, "Well, well."

Matilda nodded while she stared at Jane.

They'd each gotten mail. Jane hadn't read her second letter yet.

"Bet I know what this is about," Matilda had said when Uncle Russell brought the letters home. Letters didn't usually come for all of them at the same time. They'd settled at the kitchen table, each looking at the envelopes until Matilda had said, "We have to open them sometime."

"They're coming?" Pilar said. "Is that what your letters say?"

"They're already on their way. They should be here in February."

Pilar began to wail. "I don't want to go back. I don't ever want to leave here. I mean. . ." She stood and held onto the edge of the table while they all stared at her. "I can't go back to being my mother's helper, anymore. Jane, you'll be married. Matilda won't be there. I have plans. I have friends here. It's not like in Texas."

She threw her letter on the table and ran from the room.

"I'll talk to her later," Matilda said.

"I understand her wanting to stay here," Jane said. "But I can't see Inez allowing it. Where would she stay, anyway?"

"She's welcome here," Uncle Russell said. "But although I'm a preacher, her mother doesn't know me and might not agree."

At suppertime, Pilar brought the subject up again. "I'll have to do what my mother says, won't I? After I graduate from school, I could get a job. Maybe in the sugar fields." She shook her head. "That wouldn't work. Susanne wouldn't be my friend if I worked for her parents." She looked quickly at Jane. "I don't mean that you're not because I worked for your dad."

"I know that, Pilar. There's six years difference in your age and mine, so the situation isn't the same. Maybe your mother will fall in love with Hawaii, too, and want to stay."

Pilar exhaled heavily. "My mother doesn't fall in love with anything. She just wants to stay a cook and a housekeeper."

Matilda reached over and laid her hand on Pilar's. "Your mother takes pride in her work, Pilar. That's about all she has." She patted the girl's hand. "I'll reason with her."

"But she doesn't. . .I mean. . ."

"I know what you mean," Matilda said. "Your mother feels stuck in a kitchen while I gallivant all over the world. It's not really me she dislikes. I mean, if my husband hadn't left me a pile of money, I'd be spitting on his grave

80

twenty-five times a day."

A hopeful look came into Pilar's eyes. "You can make her understand about me. You can do anything."

"Pretty much," Matilda agreed. "Now stop your worrying."

After supper, as Jane and Matilda walked toward the church, Jane remembered what Matilda had implied before they left Texas. "You don't think Inez. . . and my dad. . . ?"

"Oh yes, I do. I have a feeling they're going to make an announcement, and Pilar's plight will be secondary. Oh, I don't mean they won't care, but if there's some reasonable way they feel Pilar has a better future in Hawaii than in Texas, they'll likely consent. I'm sure I can help in some way. There's no place I have to be in a hurry."

Jane threw her arms around Matilda. "I love you, Matilda. It's amazing how you can be so independent and yet care enough to be right there to help when someone needs it."

Matilda smiled. "Did you ever stop to think, Jane dear, I need it, too? I need your love. I need the feeling of being wanted and needed. I think that's why the good Lord admonished us to help each other."

"I've always known that," Jane said. "But I've mostly been on the receiving end. I don't want to be selfish, and I like the feeling of having been some help to Pansy and to Uncle Russell."

"You were always just fine, Jane. But you have matured in many ways since we've been here. We aren't born wise; we grow into it."

"I hope so. And you know, I think I can be a real help to Mak. He's opened up to me a little. And after things I've heard from you and Rose and Uncle Russell, he hasn't done that since his wife died." She stopped and caught hold of Matilda's hands. "I'm going Saturday morning to talk to him about how I would teach Leia. I know he'll be testing me, but I think this is a big hurdle for him to overcome. I so want to be helpful."

"That's good, Jane," she said, giving her hands a squeeze, then letting go. "But in the meantime, don't you think you need to give your dad and Austin some thought? In about three months they'll be here."

"Three months," Jane mused. "That's enough time to get Leia riding like a girl her age should. Time to get Mak to realize he needs to accept his wife's death and move on with his life. You know, he's stuck in the day she died. He just can't let it go. Maybe we can even get him back in church."

"Jane."

Jane turned her head to stare at Matilda.

"In three months, your dad and Austin will be here."

"Oh my," Jane said. "I feel like I'm just getting a good grasp of my land legs. Now I have to start thinking about my sea legs?" Of course, her attention would need to revert from Mak's needs to Austin.

As if reading her mind, Matilda said, "Now dear. Do we plan a Hawaiian wedding. . .or what?"

Chapter 22

Dressed in her least stylish riding pants, Jane eagerly awaited Friday when Mak would finish his classes and they'd ride together to his ranch.

"Let's stop in town and pick up something to eat," he said after the school let out for lunch. At the colorful farmer's market, Jane again felt much like a minority, seeing the food and wares of Japanese, Portuguese, Polynesian, Korean, and Chinese people. She and Mak each settled for a cinnamon-raisin-macadamia-nut shortbread cookie, and divided one for each horse. She learned of fruits that were foreign to her—lychee, lilikoi, star fruit, guava.

"I know banana," she teased.

"Probably not this kind," he said. "There are about fourteen varieties in Hawaii."

After munching on the delicious cookies, they mounted the horses and headed for a trot-walk to the ranch. Mak confided, "I did tell Leia that her fear stems from her knowing her mother was thrown from a horse. But I didn't feel the time was right for going into further detail."

Jane felt that was progress. When she and Mak rode up, she wasn't surprised to see Rose and Leia waiting outside the carriage house. As she followed Mak into the corral where they left Big Brown and Cinnamon, he murmured, "I've never before seen my daughter in pants." He took a deep breath. "Nor my mother looking quite so triumphant."

"Where did you get that outfit?" Mak said, walking up to them.

"Aloha, Jane," Rose said with a big smile before answering Mak, while Leia pulled the sides of her pants like a girl curtsying in a skirt. "Chico borrowed the pants from one of the paniolos' sons who's about Leia's size."

Mak was seeing his little lady in old-looking shoes and the clothes of the son of a cowboy who worked for him. Jane however, could visualize Leia in a real riding outfit and boots.

Rose leaned toward Jane and spoke softly. "The boy has worn these pants many times for the same purpose." Then she addressed them all. "I'll leave this to you. Later, I'll serve some refreshments."

Jane looked at her and mumbled, "No apples," and they both laughed.

Rose walked toward the house, still chuckling.

Jane knew the next few minutes were critical. With one knee bent and a booted foot braced against the wall, Mak leaned back with his arms folded while Jane explained the process to Leia.

Leia crinkled her nose. "But Daddy, you don't like for me to get dirty."

He scoffed. "Has that ever stopped you?"

Jane knew this could end the session before it even started. But she couldn't, wouldn't back down on that point. Of course, stable boys could clean the stalls. But this was an important part of discipline and the care of an animal. Long before now, Leia should have been accustomed to all parts of animal behavior. Jane had certainly learned the hard way about cow patties. She continued holding onto the rake.

Mak could change his mind in a moment, too. His next words indicated that. "No, you don't have to, Leia. Miss Jane said that many young girls in Texas have drivers who take them where they need to go. Or they can wait until their dad or family member feels like taking them into town or on excursions."

Her lip poked out. "I want to do it myself."

He said, "There's only one way."

Her eyes challenged her dad and Jane, but neither spoke. Her lips tightened, but she came over to Jane and took the pitchfork. Jane reached for another one.

Leia gasped. "You're going to do it, too?"

"Certainly. It's just part of being in your horse's life."

"Okay," she said, as if beginning to play a game. "Let's see who picks the most apples."

"Okay," Jane said back. "Just don't toss any the wrong way."

Mak watched, astounded. His little girl was helping clean out Big Brown's stall. Early that morning, he had told the bewildered stable boy to leave some of the apples in the stall.

Even so, he never would have thought such a thing could happen, or that it should. But Leia, to his surprise, stuck with the job. She and Jane would make sounds like "P-uewee" and turn their heads, then laugh.

How good to hear a woman laugh with his child. Of course, his mother often did, but he was used to that. This was different. Reminded him again of Maylea and what he and Leia both missed.

Strange, he thought more highly of Jane picking apples than when she stood around looking like a beautiful lady. She wasn't above getting downright smelly and messy. She was teaching his daughter, a young girl of privilege, what it meant to work. And his daughter seemed happier with that than when his mother was teaching her to crochet.

Well, Miss Jane could often look like a dainty, well-bred creature, but she sure knew how to clean out a stall, like a man. . .or rather, like a stable boy.

When they finished, Jane walked over to him. "You don't have any airs about you, Miss Jane," he said and watched her smile disappear and a warning look come into her eyes when he added, "except what might linger after a stall cleaning."

"Well, for your information, I love the smell of horses and stables."

Leia's smile looked more like a grimace, but she didn't dispute that.

"Now," Jane said. "For the next step."

He planted both feet on the floor. "A horse?"

"Exactly."

His little girl, or rather *stable girl*, put her hands together like she might applaud.

"Miss Jane," he said, "Do you think Cinnamon would do?"

"You mean that nice, sweet, gentle, trot-walking horse?"

"Exactly."

Jane nodded. "Bring her in."

Mak listened to what Jane was saying to Leia, who had wanted to ride for a long time. Now in the presence of such a big horse, she seemed shy, and he knew that moment of imbedded fear would surface.

"He's your pet, Leia," Jane said, "but not just a pet. He's also your transportation, and you must always be in control of him. You must learn to train him to do what you want. Don't let him do whatever he wants."

Leia was nodding. "That sounds like what Daddy and Grandmother tell me. They make me do what they want. Dry the dishes. Clean my room. Wash my hands." She lifted her hands. "On and on."

"That's so you will grow up to be a properly trained, obedient, fine young lady."

Leia looked at the apple pail in the corner. "Ladies pick that kind of apples?"

"Oh yes. I'm a lady, and I just did it."

"Does Miss Tilda?"

"She has when she took care of her own horses. She would again if she needed to. Young ladies do many things. Some sit in drawing rooms and knit or crochet."

Seeing Leia's nose begin to crinkle, Mak thought she wasn't too fond of that.

"Others enjoy outdoor activities," Jane was saying. "But you need to know how to do all things."

"I want to be a lady." His daughter looked very serious. "Like you."

"Okay," Jane said. "Now introduce yourself to Cinnamon. After that, I'll show you how to touch her. It's fine to touch her gently, but at other times you should touch her firmly. Like your daddy would hold your hand firmly to cross a street if a horse and carriage was coming toward you real fast."

Her eyebrows lifted. "He would pick me up and run."

"Okay, let's see you try to pick up Cinnamon."

Even Mak laughed at that.

He was seeing how excited Leia was about all this. Even at her young age, Leia was not content staying indoors, doing what he considered *safe* things. But how could she be? Her mother came from hardworking laborers on a sugar plantation whose ancestors had taken an uncertain ocean voyage. His parents were adventurers who had left their country to make Hawaii their home.

He was beginning to see some of the things his mother had tried to tell him about his own daughter. But he'd been helpless about what to do. Soon she came to say refreshments were ready any time they were.

"I think you need to get cleaned up first," his mother said to Leia. They walked ahead, with Leia telling his mother what she did and what she learned.

Jane looked up at Mak. "I would never have thought a horse like Big Brown could leave a stall so clean overnight."

She had a way of observing the minutest of things. "And I would never have thought a child could win an apple-picking game over an accomplished horsewoman."

"Okay," she said, "I guess that means we're both devious."

"Or," he said, "both trying to do what's best for a child."

"So the lesson went well?"

He nodded. "Better than I expected."

"You mean you didn't expect much from me?" She placed her hands on her hips.

He stopped in front of her, looking at his mother and daughter to see if they were out of hearing range. "I didn't expect my daughter to clean out a stall. I admit I don't know her as well as I thought I did." He inhaled and looked over her head for a moment. "Leia is a strong-willed, adventurous little girl."

"That isn't bad, Mak."

He'd heard Jane describe herself that way. He reached up and brushed aside a stray lock of hair the wind blew against her cheek. "No. Not bad at all."

Her expression showed surprise. Was that because he'd touched her or was it his admitting that adventurous wasn't bad? She slapped the leg of her pants. "I just realized something," she said. "I don't have a horse. Cinnamon needs to be here for Leia to talk to and feed oats and apples."

"She learned a lot today. Thank you."

"You're welcome. But I learned something, too. Your bringing Cinnamon to me had nothing whatsoever do with the color of my eyes or my hair. You wanted to find out if I thought the horse would be right for Leia."

He shrugged. What could he say?

"Mak, you could have told me that."

They'd neared the house, so he stopped again and stood in front of her. "I wasn't trying to be deceptive. I wasn't sure about allowing Leia to learn. It's like this is all happening, unfolding, when I didn't really plan it."

Would she understand that? After a moment she said, "Could this be one of those times Uncle Russell talked about when he said the Lord works in mysterious ways?"

She stared into his eyes. After a long moment, he turned and walked on. "I don't know," he said seriously. "Most of God's ways are a mystery to me." He opened the screen door. "But I'll get you another horse."

Her eyes widened, and her voice sounded incredulous. "One that can really gallop?"

She could make him laugh more in a few minutes than anyone else had done. . .in a long time.

Chapter 23

Jane thought he might choose the white horse for her, but when he didn't, she figured he thought it might be a mite too frisky. After they returned to the stables he asked a stable boy to bring Anise to the corral.

She loved the horse the moment she saw her. Mak had chosen a beautiful brown mare with a black mane and tail, not as large as Big Brown or as old, but a fine, strong animal. Maybe he did respect her ability as a horsewoman.

"Shall we gallop out and see how Panai is doing with his workout?" he asked.

"I'd love that."

"Just remember," he said as they mounted the horses. "Don't try to ride like the wind before you and the horse relate well. Like you told Leia, you need to know each other first."

Jane felt so good in the saddle, like the two of them were made for each other. "I promise," she said. "I will not ride like the wind." She gave him a sly look. "Like a Texas tornado wind, that is."

He gave her a warning look. "Just try to hold it down to a gentle Hawaiian breeze for now."

As they cantered across the velvety green range, Jane mentioned that her dad, Austin, and Inez were coming to the island. "They will probably arrive in February."

After a moment, he said, "Oh, in wintertime."

"What's winter like here?"

He sighed as if that were a problem. "About two degrees cooler and a few more inches of rain."

She laughed as he smiled at her.

"I'm sure that seems like a long way off for you."

"Long enough for me to help Leia get over her fear and learn how to properly care for horses, get them to trust and obey."

He scoffed. "That sounds rather religious."

Jane smiled. "Well, aren't we humans sometimes rather like wild horses? The Lord has to rein us in."

His head turned toward her, and his eyes held a curious look. "You don't strike me as a wild horse."

"Well I shouldn't tell you this, but Billy and I went out behind the barn to smoke one of my daddy's cigars. But first, I grabbed Billy and I kissed him right on the lips."

"No," Mak said, feigning shock. "How old were you?"

"Fourteen."

He laughed heartily.

"That's funny?"

"I was remembering the description Reverend gave me of you at fourteen."

"And that's funny?"

"He did describe you as. . .a child. I can't imagine that kiss being anything like a wild horse."

"Well, we experimented with a few more kisses. That's before we sat with our backs against the barn and began taking turns with the cigar."

"Ahhh." His eyebrows lifted. "Now you're beginning to get sinful."

She laughed at the teasing. "Oh, we paid the consequences for that. You see, that's when I learned the meaning of a sick stomach."

She liked his laugh. "And when I got off that ship here in Hawaii, the reminder returned. I so wanted to make a good impression."

"You did make an indelible one," he said. "Unforgettable." He chuckled. "Now I know how sinful you are."

"Oh," she boasted. "That was only the beginning. I determined to kiss at least two boys at every church social, every party, or whenever I got the chance." She lowered her head. "But of course, I had to pretend it was their idea so I wouldn't get a bad reputation."

"Why two?" he asked.

"I have always been promised to Austin. Aunt Matilda taught me that I had to consider other possibilities, and I thought a kiss would be the best way."

"And Austin always won?"

"He wasn't always the best kisser, but he was always the best man."

She figured turnabout was fair play, so she asked, "How old were you when you had your first kiss?"

He gazed out across the land. "Twelve? No, eleven. Yes. Eleven."

"Eleven kisses, or eleven years old?"

He shrugged and glanced at her. "Both. She was a cutie. Brown as a Kona coffee bean. Big brown eyes. Almost all eyes and lips. You know?" He made finger motions at his own lips as if trying to draw heart-shaped ones.

Jane nodded.

"But she wouldn't let me kiss her lips. Only her cheeks. She said her mother told her not to let a boy kiss her lips." He sighed. "Just being near them was heaven. On about the twelfth kiss, I made a mistake and kissed her lips. I think I was twelve by then."

"Mistake?"

He nodded. "She ran away. Never let me kiss her again."

Jane moaned, and when he glanced at her she frowned, trying to appear sad. "Oh, the consequences of being wild horses."

"Maybe we weren't so bad. Just children."

Jane realized his mood had gone from playfulness to serious. What had he been thinking? Three years without a kiss from his wife? Of course he missed that. Her closeness, her love.

"You were just a child when you lost your mother, weren't you?" he asked.

"My mother was killed in a tornado. She was a schoolteacher. The school collapsed. She had herded the children into the storm cellar beneath the school. I was one of those children. But she didn't make it."

"You know loss. Yet you seem so happy. Is it time that does it?"

"Matilda made me cry and grieve. She's known many losses. But through the years, she has taught me that people are different. Some are uptight, and some are. . ." She turned her face toward him until he looked. "Some are free spirits."

He smiled. "I think there's more to it."

"Sure there is. But I can't teach you everything about life in only one day."

He laughed. "We'll just have to have classes together, teacher." He paused. "Speaking of teaching, my mother thinks I should have Leia in the mission school. I've thought she was better off being tutored by my mother. But I'm beginning to think she may be right. Leia begs me to let her go there. You've been a girl and without a mother. What do you think?"

"I think, Mak, that you're having as much trouble letting go of Leia as you are with letting go of. . .your wife."

At his surprised expression, Jane apologized. "I'm sorry. I shouldn't have said that."

He gave her a long look. "Why did you?"

"Because," she said, afraid she had just alienated him. "Sometimes my tongue is as uncontrollable as tumbleweed in a windstorm."

He looked at her quickly. "I have no idea what you're saying. Tumbleweed?"

"Tumbleweed is a plant. The wind breaks it off from the roots and rolls it along wherever it will. So what I mean is I talk a lot and sometimes say the wrong thing."

They trotted along for quite a while. She feared he'd tell her to turn around and go back to town. He finally said, "Jane, I've said we could be friends and that we can talk about what's important to us. I've had so many people tell me how I should feel and not feel, that I'm afraid I have a short temper where that's concerned. I'm sorry."

"Okay. Do you still want my opinion?"

He grinned. "Go ahead. I'll hang on tight in case a tumbleweed heads my way."

She began. "We both know I can't tell you what to do. But it would be nice, I think, if Rose could be more like a grandmother. She can fill a mother's role but can never replace her. Matilda was my wonderful, wonderful aunt, and we both have benefited from that. And the school seems to be a really fine school. The children are happy, the teachers are caring. . .ahem."

His puzzled look changed to understanding. "Thank you, Miss Buckley," he said with mock formality. "But this teacher is temporary. I don't intend to return after Christmas holidays and may leave sooner if Russell gets a replacement.

Besides, it's a long way for Leia to go to school."

"She could stay home and be taught by you or your mother in bad weather."

His expression was amused. "We don't have bad weather."

"Oh yes. I forgot. This is paradise."

"Right," he said. "We only have tidal waves, earthquakes, and volcanic eruptions."

Chapter 24

B y the way," Jane said, realizing they were headed in a different direction than town. "Where are we going?"

Mak brought Big Brown to a halt. "Sorry. I'm assuming instead of asking. Would you like to see more of the ranch?"

She gave him a big smile. "I was afraid you were escorting me home. Tell you what. Let's just be really honest, and if one of us starts to take advantage of the other's time or anything, just say so. How's that?"

He took off his hat and held it against his heart, causing the breeze to stir the waves of his hair. "It's a deal. Would you like to see Panai's workout?"

"Look at it this way, Mak MacCauley. If you came to Texas and knew my daddy had a ranch, would you want to go see an oil well?"

With a grin, he returned the hat to his head. The next thing she knew, Big Brown had responded to his leg and hand motion and they were galloping across the green grass.

"One of these days," he said, "we might stroll through a field of lava and walk along the black sand beaches."

"Ach." She pulled the horse to a halt.

Mak stopped. "What's wrong?"

"You just said the strangest thing I ever heard in my life."

"What? What did I say?"

"You said we'd walk through lava."

He shrugged. "So?"

"That's worse than if I would say, 'Let's stroll along the lawn, amidst the cow patties, and listen to the mooing.' "

When he could stop laughing, he said with irony. "Ah, our different worlds. Yes, I suppose you're right. But I bet you my lava setting is more appealing than your cow-patty one."

"Prove it," she teased.

"I can." Then he surprised her by taking Big Brown into a fast gallop.

"I'll catch up," she called, bringing Anise to a trot while she took the pins from her hair and loosened it with her fingers.

Mak slowed and looked over his shoulder. She fast-galloped up to him, and they rode side by side. He kept looking over, and his eyes seemed to linger on her long hair blowing out from her head like the tail of a horse.

"Ahhh," she said.

He pushed his hat back so it lay between his shoulders, ran the fingers of one hand through his dark hair, then grimaced. "Not the same," he said.

She laughed. Was that some kind of offhand compliment?

The stables, corral, and bunkhouse came into view first. Several men were tending the horses. Cattle and horses grazed in the open fields beyond, but with a wave of their hands, she and Mak kept riding.

Jane was speechless. Lying ahead was a fenced racetrack so huge she couldn't see the end of it. Chico was leading Panai in a slow trot over to the fence. Jane was off Anise before Mak could dismount.

"Careful," Mak warned as Panai stuck his head over the top of the white wooden fence.

"He's inviting me to come over," she said as Chico dismounted.

"You're right," Chico said, climbing over the fence with a broad smile that creased his browned face.

Two other men walked up, and Mak introduced them. She learned that Tomas was one of Mak's trainers and Clint was the ranch's foreman. The men seemed to already have heard about her, mentioned her uncle Russell, took off their hats at the mention of Pansy, and asked a couple questions about her daddy's Texas ranch.

After a moment, Clint said he needed to get back to work. "The boss might catch me loafing." The next moment, he was galloping off on his horse.

Chico made a strange sound like a grunt, and his hand moved to his stomach as he bent over a few inches.

"Chico?" Mak said. "Something wrong?"

Chico's hand dropped to his side, and he straightened. His face took on an innocent look, but it seemed to have lost its healthy glow. "No. Why?"

Jane saw Mak look at Tomas, who gazed off across the racetrack like he wasn't even listening.

"Don't lie to me," Mak said, giving Chico a hard look.

Chico shrugged. "It's only an upset stomach. The cook made pancakes this morning, and it's just too heavy in my stomach to eat that and come ride. I'll change my way of living."

Chico laughed as if it were nothing.

Mak didn't. "I've never known you to have a sick day in your life, Chico. But I don't want you on Panai if you're ill. Tomas here can ride Panai and get somebody to keep the time. If you need to see a doctor, see a doctor."

"I will, Mr. Mak. Now, I need to take Panai around one more time."

When Mak looked at him skeptically, Jane stuck her arm over the fence rails and rubbed the horse's neck. "Let me ride him."

Mak didn't bother to laugh. "No woman has ever been on that horse."

She was looking in Panai's eyes. "He would let me ride him."

"He's not just a horse. He's a trained racer."

Drawing in a deep breath she lifted her chin. "So am I."

At his withering stare, she corrected that. "Well, not the kind you and Chico are. But I've raced my dad. And as an equestrienne, I've not only ridden with speed but had the horse jump"—she measured with her hand—"This high."

She added, "I've even won awards."

There it was again. That sinking feeling that she'd never come in first.

He stuck one booted foot on a rail, swung the other up, and over the fence he went. She did the same. "Let me ride with you."

He mounted the horse, and by that time, Tomas had climbed over and helped Mak lift her onto the horse.

"I don't believe this," Mak murmured.

Jane looked at the two silent men, both bug-eyed like they didn't believe it, either.

"No timing," Mak said to Tomas. "Just call it a. . .workout."

"Oh you beautiful, beautiful, wonderful horse," Jane told Panai, leaning over his magnificent mane. "You like me here, don't you?"

Mak started him off slowly, knowing it was a test for them all. Jane wasn't concerned about herself or Panai but wondered what emotion the horse might sense from Mak. But he knew Mak as his master. She knew Panai didn't want to trot, then canter, then gallop. He wanted to fly.

As Mak allowed the horse more free rein, she felt the power, the warmth, the strength, the determination. And that's what she felt sitting in front of Mak with his arms around her. She knew his total focus was on the horse.

She tried to make it hers, but her silly brain kept feeling the warmth of his body leaning against hers, the strength of his arms around her, the sound of his voice touching the top of her head as if it were entering through her hair, and it affected her mind as he talked to Panai, saying, "Let's hold back. Save the best for the race, Panai. Good boy."

She was flying. Faster than she'd ever flown in her life. Lifted higher than she'd ever been. The wind was in her face. The scenery sped by like a green ribbon. Nothing existed but the wish that this feeling of being completely unfettered might last forever.

It ended too soon.

"How was it?" Mak said, dismounting and lifting his arms to her.

Her chest heaved with excitement. "Exhilarating." As her feet touched the ground with his hands at her waist, she instinctively wrapped her arms around him, her head against his chest. His heart was thundering, too. "Thank you. Thank you."

"Do you have your land legs?" he said, taking hold of her arms.

She shouldn't have done that. But so much was going through her mind. She'd just had the ride of her life. She felt tears of joy smart her eyes, and she climbed over the fence to reality.

Later, after riding back to town—without Mak feeling he had to escort her—she could hardly wait to tell Matilda all about it. After gushing like an oil well about the ride, she said, "I felt so free, Matilda. Sometimes, looking at this ring and thinking about marriage, I think I may not be ready. And this is such a breakthrough that Mak allows a woman—a single woman—to be near him."

Matilda shook her head. "Don't forget, dear. The reason you're allowed to ride that horse, to be near Mak, is because you're wearing that ring."

Chapter 25

"Oh, I'll never get the syllables right," Jane wailed. "I keep saying *Kalimikika* or *Keli ki ka ma* instead of *Kali. . .Kali. . .*" She threw up her hands. "What's the use?"

"What's the use?" Matilda gave her a studied look. "We may need to say it to the queen. Or more important, to children. Now, Rose taught me how to say it, and you girls can learn, too. Let's try word association." She took a deep breath. "Think of this sentence: My cart is leaky from spilled milk while I'm riding in my cart."

Jane's eyes swung to Pilar, who was shaking her head and covering her mouth to hold back the laughter. Matilda ignored it. "Now think 'cart leaky, my cart,' but instead of 'my' say 'ma' and instead of cart say 'ca.' "

"Okay." Jane could hardly get the words out while holding her stomach from the laughter that filled her body. "My horse is leaking while pulling Ma's cart."

Pilar cleared her throat. "My ma doesn't have a cart, and I don't think she leaks."

Matilda slapped her hands down on the kitchen table. "Oh, you girls are impossible. Now try this. *Kart-liki ma-cart.*"

Jane and Pilar spoke in unison. "*Cart-leaky, ma-cart. Cart-leaky ma-cart.*"

Matilda moved her hand like waving a baton. "Not bad. Leave out the *r* and *t*. *Kalikimaka.*"

"*Ca-leaky ma-ca.*"

"Perfect. Now add the *Mele* in front of it and you have *Merry Christmas.*"

Uncle Russell walked into the kitchen, laughing. "You could just say *Merry Christmas.* Everybody understands that."

"Oh Russ," Matilda chided. "We're in Hawaii. The Bible says when in Rome do as the Romans do."

"It does?" He pulled out a chair. "This isn't an exact translation," he said, sitting. "But a phonetic translation. When Christmas first came to the islands, the Hawaiians had difficulty pronouncing *Merry Christmas.* Think about the pronunciation here. It sounds a lot like *Merry Christmas.*"

"Now why didn't you say that, Matilda?" Jane jested. "That makes it so much easier. She jumped up and hurried to the door. "I think I hear their wagon."

The rest of them followed. Mak had some of his men take the farm wagon up in the mountains and bring down Christmas trees and cypress boughs to decorate the school and church. Sure enough, there was Mak driving the farm wagon.

Before they got Uncle Russell's tree unloaded and the boards nailed onto the trunk, Rose and Leia drove up in a horse-drawn cart loaded with greenery and boxes.

A couple other wagons pulled up. This was the day to decorate Uncle Russell's house, the church, and the school.

When Rose and Mak came in with cardboard boxes, Jane tried out her new words. "Mele. . ." She thought, *My cart is leaking*. "Maca leaky."

Mak smiled broadly. "Merry Mas-Christ to you, too. And a *Hau'oli Makahiki Hou*."

She stomped her foot. "I'm going to forget Christmas altogether." Then she gasped with pleasure as Leia opened a box lid and exposed bright red, silk flowers they would use to make leis. "Oh, I just got an extra dose of Christmas spirit."

They left some of the greenery at the house, went to the church, and unloaded more. Uncle Russell directed them to a closet where last year's decorations had been stored.

"Pansy packed them away," he said. "She labeled all the boxes."

Leia piped up. "She will have Christmas with the baby Jesus." She looked at Jane. "Is that right?"

Jane had begun going to the ranch three mornings a week for Leia's lessons. She was also telling her about the difference between the myths about Little People and the truth about Jesus.

"Yes, she will celebrate Jesus' birthday in heaven, and we will celebrate it here. By the way, do you know about. . ." She was reluctant to say it. "Santa?"

"Oooh." Leia clapped her hands. "Yes, I saw Santa another Christmas. He brings presents." Her eyes grew big and excited. Then a worry line formed above her nose. "Is he a Jesus story or a Little People story?"

Jane looked to the men who had nailed the wooden pieces to the bottom of the tree trunk and set it on the stage. Mak glanced over his shoulder at her, as if wondering what she'd say. Rose and Matilda were hanging garland. They didn't offer to answer. Okay, she'd try.

"It's a story, like the stories of the Little People." She looked around, hoping to signal the others to step in at any moment because she wasn't even sure what she would say. "Santa is a symbol, like Little People are a symbol. Do you know what a symbol is?"

Leia shook her head.

"It's like the lei is a symbol of Hawaii. You greeted me with one. It's welcoming me to Hawaii. Santa is a symbol of someone giving gifts because God gave us the gift of His Son, Jesus, to the world."

Leia smiled. "Okay."

That seemed a little too easy. Looking around, Jane saw that others smiled. They seemed to think it was okay.

Good. She'd take it further. "In America, Santa comes down the chimney."

"The chimney?"

Mak tossed out, "We don't have chimneys here."

"What's a chimney?" Leia wanted to know.

"Well," she said to the eager little girl. "There's a fireplace where we burn logs and the smoke goes up the chimney."

"Won't he get burned up?"

"He doesn't really do that. It's just part of the story."

"Oh," Leia said. "Santa could come down our stovepipe. If he was"—she brought her hands close together—"about this big, like the Little People."

When nobody disagreed, Leia added, "He would be a little symbol."

"Okay," Jane said. Maybe Leia wasn't ready for theology.

When Leia delivered an ornament to Rose, Mak stepped up to Jane. "Not bad," he said, "for a woman."

She jested, "Maybe you should dress up like Santa and make the message clearer."

"Not a bad idea. Maybe next year."

Jane felt good about him. He was making an effort to become more involved with people and his own family. Yes, maybe next year. . .a lot of changes would have taken place.

The thought hit her like a thunderbolt.

Next year.

What would she be doing next year?

Jane looked down, and her gaze landed on her ring. Next year, would she be in the U.S.A., celebrating Christmas as Mrs. Austin Price?

Chapter 26

Although Hawaii had its mountain topped with snow and a volcano spewing fire, the town and Mak's ranch were situated in the green valley where temperatures remained pleasant. The sun kept shining even when a light misty rain fell.

"It's not going to be a cold Christmas," Jane said somewhat wistfully as she sat around Uncle Russell's kitchen table with Matilda, Pilar, Rose, and Leia making silk leis.

"That doesn't slow down the celebration," Rose assured her. "Everybody comes out to celebrate on Christmas Eve."

"It wasn't always that way," Uncle Russell said, pouring himself a cup of coffee. "The Hawaiians worshiped false gods."

"I guess the early missionaries brought Christmas to the islands," Matilda said. "Come sit down." She gestured to the chair near the table. "We can scoot."

"Wouldn't want to chance spilling this coffee on those leis," he said. "I'm fine." He moved the chair back farther and sat in it. "The early missionaries brought the message of Jesus and salvation. But the Puritans had left England for religious purposes. They were against some of the customs and revelry that flourished in Europe. Since the Bible didn't teach anything about Christmas, they didn't even talk or preach about it. They brought Christianity to the islands, but not Christmas."

"So how did it come about?" Jane asked.

"Inevitably some whalers, business people, and travelers from other countries would be here at Christmastime. They would celebrate and give gifts, and the word got around that was another way the white man worshiped his God."

"But you say it's a big thing now?" Matilda said.

"Yes, the king can be credited with that. About thirty-five years ago, long before Pansy and I came here, the king had spent Christmas in Europe. When he came back, he declared Thanksgiving as a national day to be celebrated on December 25. But since most people on the island are now Christians, they consider December 25 as a celebration of the birth of Jesus Christ."

Rose commented, "And it's grown bigger every year. It's really spectacular."

"Yes," Leia said. "I'm bigger, and I'm going to sing in the choir."

"So are we all," Matilda said. "Not in the children's choir."

"So am I," said Pilar with a big smile. "And Susanne."

Despite the beautiful weather and the mist that the others called rain, Jane got caught up in the spirit of Christmas. The house looked festive, and they made plans for food and parties, including one for Leia on Christmas Day.

"What we ladies need to do," Matilda said, "is go downtown for lunch and go shopping. I'll treat."

"Yes, yes!" Leia was about to come off her seat.

"Sounds like a great idea," Uncle Russell said. "I'll just take myself a nap and later on get to work on my Christmas Eve sermon."

Unable to decide where to have lunch, Rose made a suggestion. "Why don't we order a couple of plates and sample various foods?"

They entered the first in a line of Hilo restaurants and soon dipped into a bowl of Hawaiian Portuguese bean soup and fresh fish caught right at the shore and flavored with ginger, soy, and garlic. "I must try breadfruit," Jane said. "Are people looking at us funny?"

"No, no," Rose assured them. "This is what all visitors or newcomers to Hawaii do. They just think you're Americans or Europeans."

"Oh," Matilda scoffed. "I thought I would be inconspicuous in this *muumuu*."

They all laughed. Matilda stood out in any crowd. They had all decided to wear muumuus, a casual style of island dress that was lighter and looser than western dress. Rose lent Matilda one. Jane purchased one from a store. Her preference however was pants, since she was riding not only to the ranch several times a week but also along the beach and along trails bordered by lush foliage.

After lunch, they walked down the street and saw a couple of boys staring in the candy store window and singing. "Oh, they're singing a song we made up at school," Pilar said. "Do you know it, Leia?"

"Some of it," she said.

The two girls walked up to the boys, and with all four putting forth their best efforts, they were finally satisfied with their chant:

Candies red as a sunset sky
Cakes that please the tongue and eye
Sugared flowers not for a lei
But for children on Christmas Day.

As they walked on, Matilda said, "I thought of giving them a penny or so, but children need to wait for goodies at Christmas. Makes it more special."

"What do you want for Christmas, Leia?" Pilar asked.

"I want a new saddle and to ride Cinnamon all by myself."

Jane exchanged glances with Rose and Matilda. They already knew the surprise awaiting Leia. It would be both her birthday and special Christmas gift.

They spent the afternoon visiting one shop after another.

"Look at all those pastries," Rose said, pointing to the bakery window. "And the confectioners will have candy like you don't see any other time of the year."

Jane marveled at all the toys, dolls, fabric, jewelry, books, Bibles, and Christmas decorations representing many countries. Everyone was friendly and would even stop to introduce themselves instead of bustling around in a rush.

After the wonderful, fun-filled outing, Rose took Jane aside and held her hands. "Jane, I want to thank you for what you're doing for my son and my granddaughter."

Jane started to protest, but Rose shook her head. "Don't be modest. You're exactly what Mak needed. No one else had been able to get through to him. The rest of us were just nagging. But you have made him think. Made him feel again. I think he's in the process of healing. Just. . .thank you."

She wrapped her arms around Jane, and they embraced. When Jane stood back, she could honestly say, "It's my pleasure."

The expression on Rose's face was warm. She smiled before walking away to the cart. Jane thought about what she'd just said. She'd never had the opportunity to give of herself like this before. Of course, she helped out, visiting the sick and taking food when there was a need. But this was different. Teaching Leia to ride and the difference between Little People and Jesus was a highlight of her life. That was such a wonderful opportunity God had given her. Also, being a friend to Mak. Yet she received so much from him. She could not imagine enjoying the island so much without him.

As she watched the cart disappear down the road, her aunt observed, "You're going to twist that finger right off one of these days."

Jane gave her a look. Maybe the finger, but the ring had to stay on it. Without it, as Matilda had emphasized, she would not be teaching a little girl to ride, or riding across the range and associating with that challenging man, her friend. . .Mak MacCauley.

Chapter 27

Mak stood on the crowded beach with the other islanders. Last year, he'd done his duty and brought his mother and Leia. He'd swooped Leia up onto his shoulders so she could see everything and get an early glimpse of Santa. His heart had not been in it.

Now, he stood without a member of his family, was not an active participant, but felt a part of it. He spoke to those near him and they commented on the festivities. He applauded with the others when the candles on the huge Christmas tree were lighted. The tree was adorned with garlands of colorful flowers.

A band of men began strumming their bragas. Schoolchildren were wearing white blouses with red and white skirts reminiscent of hula skirts. Red leis hung across their chests and down their backs, and red bands of leis circled their heads. They sang and signed the language with their graceful hands. Marching down the beach in front of the islanders, they sang Christmas songs. Pilar and Susanne walked side by side, singing.

Susanne's parents, his friends the Honeycutts, would be around somewhere. He hadn't kept up that friendship very well. Only now did he stop and think they had lost Maylea, too—as a friend.

Thinking of a friend, he felt a smile when the church adult choir, singing their hymns, came onto the beach. Pansy was conspicuously missing, but Jane, Matilda, and his mother were there. His mother had volunteered to sing with them this year, and she had been happier lately than he'd seen her in years.

They were followed by the children's choir, all wearing white dresses with the red leis and headbands that had been assembled in Rev. Russell's kitchen.

The choir director led everyone on the beach in singing "O Little Town of Bethlehem" and "Noel." After the sky turned from orange-red to gray, fireworks exploded like myriad multicolored stars over ships displaying flags in the harbor and the boats along the shore.

He wondered what Jane thought of all that. That the stars and everything else in Texas were bigger and better? Texas couldn't be bigger than the ocean.

A canoe came into sight. Children began to yell and wave and crowd the shoreline. Santa arrived in his canoe, dressed in red. His flowing white hair and beard moved in the gentle night breeze as men wearing red leis rowed him to the shore. He stepped out with a big canvas bag from which he drew a gift for every child.

After Santa returned to the canoe, men bearing torches led the way to the church. Mak hesitated. He hadn't attended a service in so long—except for two funerals.

It was like he was seeing the church for the first time, although he'd grown up in it. His eyes wandered to the attendees, who crowded into the high-backed wooden pews and meshed together around the walls. A few stood at the doors and open windows, still able to see the church adorned with cypress branches, a Christmas tree with flowers and gifts, and candles of red and green. Rev. Russell delivered his message of Christmas, the birth of the world's Savior.

That was his pastor. Many of these people were his friends. His students sang. His mother and child sang their praises to God and the Savior. This was a world he hadn't allowed into his heart in more than three years.

After the final prayer, the torchbearers distributed red and green candles. The first one was lighted by a whale-oil lamp and then used to light another. The procedure was repeated throughout the congregation, representing their fellowship one with another.

He thought of the money the king had spent to illuminate his palace. His little girl, holding one little candle, was as important to God as the king.

He lit his own candle from another and passed the flame to the wick of another. One could go through the motions of living without really being alive.

Then the reverend was asking everyone to stand, and he began singing "Blest Be the Tie That Binds."

Mak needed to let Jane know just how much her friendship meant to him. Maybe he'd get the opportunity tomorrow when his new friends came for Christmas dinner.

&

Mak had not been so excited about Christmas since he was a child. No matter how festive a Christmas Eve, there was a church full of islanders for the Christmas Day service. Mak sat with his mother and Leia on the pew with Matilda and Jane. Leia sat very straight and kept smoothing her pretty new red dress his mother had given her that morning.

They would all go to his home after the service and have a feast Coco and his mother had been preparing for days. Maybe next year, he'd have a luau for all his workers, like his dad used to do. But for now this would do. Getting back into life was almost overwhelming for him.

The fabulous dinner and nice gifts were a treat for them all. Leia was completely happy with the new saddle she got for Cinnamon, and more than once, Mak saw her look at it and feel it, her eyes shining with the hope that she might finally be able to ride Cinnamon all by herself. She kept saying she wasn't afraid anymore.

"I think it's time for my present to you," Jane said.

Leia loved the stylish little riding suit to go with the boots Mac had bought for her, with Jane's help. She ran from the room and returned, turning and posing.

Jane described her perfectly. "You look like the world's greatest equestrienne, Leia."

Everyone applauded.

Mak picked up the saddle. "It's time."

He had her wait in the corral while he brought out Cinnamon. He helped her up. Jane held the reins and walked them around the corral. "Now you do it," she said, "like I taught you."

Mak didn't expect what happened. He was not a crying man. But seeing Leia—his and Maylea's child, yet a person within herself—was overwhelming. He left the corral, and after composing himself, he came out with her surprise.

Fortunately, Jane had already taken Leia off Cinnamon, otherwise the child might have jumped off and broken her neck. She stood frozen, her hands on her face, her little lips forming a big *O*, and her eyes wide.

Mak led the snow-white pony into the corral and handed the reins to Leia. "Happy birthday," he said.

Her eyes roamed over the beautiful pony. "The pony is for me?" She pointed to her chest.

"Yes, she's yours."

"Ohhh." She dropped the reins and ran.

He thought she would run and maybe try to get on the pony, but she ran to him, threw her arms around him, and said, "Oh thank you, Daddy. Thank you. I love you so much. You must love me"—she spread her arms—"a whole bunch."

Had she doubted it?

"Okay, your pony's getting lonesome."

She stepped away and asked, "Can her name be Hoku?"

"Whatever you like," he said, "but why Star?"

"Because," she said as if he should know, "this is not a Little People story. Miss Jane said it's real. Jesus was a little baby. And a star was moving in the sky. A biiig one. And kings brought gold like Miss Tilda gives to everybody. He was important, and the kings kept looking at the star, and it helped them find the baby." She smiled broadly. "I'm important to you, and if I ever ride off like the wind like Miss Jane does and if I get lost, this Star will bring me back." She punctuated that with a nod.

"Sounds like a deal to me," he said. "But you know you have to get to know Hoku before you can ride her. You and she can grow up together."

"But I can ride Cinnamon." She pursed her lips. "I mean, when you and Miss Jane tell me."

"You're one smart little girl."

Smiling, she turned to pat the neck of Hoku firmly and speak softly to her.

❧

Jane couldn't have asked for a better Christmas. She felt like she celebrated it in a way that Jesus would be pleased. She silently wished Him a happy birthday and thanked Him for the people she cared about and with whom she had spent Christmas Day.

When the others went out to the surrey, Mak said to Jane, "Just a moment."

With happy voices sounding outside, Mak looked down at her. "You've given so much to me and my family. How can I ever repay you?"

She didn't think he really expected an answer. It was simply a way to express his gratitude. Indirectly, she had a part in bringing father and daughter closer together. Seeing that was payment enough.

She could get all serious and tell him to stop trying to get revenge on a horse, to let go of his obsessive grief over Maylea. But that wouldn't be answering what he could do for her.

What could Mak give her?

Rather than get all serious after such a lovely day, she lifted her chin, gave him a challenging look, and said, "Show me something in Hawaii that I can never forget, something to take my breath away."

Immediately, he said, "A green sunset."

She laughed. "I've seen the unbelievably brilliant red and orange and golden sky at sunset. Is this green thing one of those Little People stories?"

"It's for real. It's right as the sun dips into the ocean or vanishes into the horizon. There's a blue-green flash." Grinning, he said. "I would like to see the color of your eyes when that happens."

"Have you seen the green sunset?"

"Once," he said. "I was riding across the range on Big Brown, looking for a horse that had escaped from the corral. And it happened."

"Were you alone?"

His eyes looked puzzled. "Other men were nearby, also looking for the horse. But yes, I think you could say I was alone."

"You never saw the green sunset with. . .Maylea."

He seemed to study her for a moment before he answered. "No. She had seen it a few times in her life, but we didn't try to see it together."

She would really like to do something or see something that was his and hers alone, that he hadn't done with Maylea. "I think," she said, "that's what would take my breath away."

Chapter 28

Mak liked to give his paniolos and all the workers he could time off around Christmas and New Year, which meant more work for him. He didn't want Jane to spend her holiday teaching at the ranch. He thought it a good time for him to spend time with his little girl, and they even trotted along, he on Big Brown and she on Cinnamon outside the corral and on the range.

He and his daughter were bonding in a new and delightful way. They could talk about horses and ranches, and he realized she loved the ranch. He even talked to her about Maylea, and she smiled at his stories.

A week after Christmas, the invitation came from the king. The Royal Prerace Party would be held the third week in January. He and his mother were invited.

"Mak," his mother said, excitement coloring her voice, "even if you don't want to go, Matilda and I could."

Guilt washed over him like a tidal wave. He'd believed his mother over the past few years when she'd said she felt fine about not going, that she didn't want to leave Leia alone. And there had been the matter of the king purchasing that horse.

"Yes, Mother. Let's invite Matilda and Jane to accompany us."

"Oh." She rushed over, held his shoulders, and kissed his cheek. He had pleased his mother. He seemed to be doing a lot of that lately.

After that, it was like living in a different world. Jane continued to teach Leia horseback riding and how to take care of her pony. The women got together and talked about fashion and hairstyles.

As Mak shrugged into his dark waistcoat, trousers, and tailcoat, he wondered if the party would take Jane's breath away. Mak had seen the palace since the electricity had been installed, and it was still the talk of the island, but this party would be on the king's yacht. The king had many friends on Hawaii, but many of them found it too far to make a trip to Oahu. The king enjoyed having yacht parties, anyway.

Mac's mother stuck her head in the doorway of his bedroom as he tied the white bow tie at the neck of his winged-collar shirt. She called him handsome, but she was biased.

"You look beautiful, Mother," he said when she walked into the room.

"Thank you. But I wonder how the queen will be dressed. Matilda said the latest style coming in Europe is dresses without bustles, if you can imagine that." She pointed her finger at him. "But I will not give up my corset."

"Well, I should think the bustles could go," he said. "Maybe they should put some of that material on the neckline."

"Oh, Mak," she chided. "This is the style. I don't want to look old-fashioned."

"Now haven't you women been trying on dresses for the past two weeks? And I'll bet Matilda knows more about the latest style than the princess. Regardless, you don't want to outdress the princess."

"I don't?" She patted her hair in an elaborate upsweep, decorated with jeweled combs. He had not seen her in formal dress since his dad had died. She had missed a lot, having lost her husband and taking care of Mak and Leia. He'd taken her for granted.

The clatter of horses' hooves and wheels outside sent his mother hurrying into the hallway. The next thing he knew, Leia, Coco, Pilar, and Susanne were gushing over each other's attire. Mak had contacted Susanne's parents, and when he discovered they were going to the party, he had invited Susanne and Pilar to stay the night at his house.

Matilda was elaborately dressed in purple satin and wore jewels like a queen. "You're particularly stunning this afternoon," he said.

She thanked him graciously.

Jane came up to him. "And who is this handsome gentleman?" She straightened his white bow tie.

"I don't know anymore," he said. "This friend came along and—" He didn't need to get morbid, or gushy. "Your eyes are so blue." He liked the way she dressed. The look was elegant but less elaborate than the other ladies. Her hair was in an updo with little tendrils framing her forehead and the sides of her face. "I like your dress," he said.

"Thank you," she said, and soon they were in the surrey headed for the dock where they'd board the yacht that was waiting to take them away from civilization.

As they drew near, Matilda exclaimed, gazing at the gleaming white yacht larger than most ships, "My, that's a far cry from the ship we came over on."

"The king and princess try to copy Europe in every way they can," Rose said. "They do not want to be thought backward."

"This yacht," Mak explained, "was built in the United States. It was sold to the king for eighty thousand dollars' worth of sandalwood."

Rose nodded. "Our island is now almost bereft of sandalwood. It was in such demand in other places, and logging it provided a livelihood for islanders."

Matilda put her hand to her ear. "I hear music."

"The royal family are avid musicians," Rose explained. "They write songs, and the king has his own Royal Hawaiian Band."

"As soon as guests are aboard," Mak added, "the band will play, and we will sing 'Hawaii Ponoi,' written by the king. It's the Hawaiian national anthem. The royal family particularly likes the instrument called a braga or cavaquinho."

The dock was inundated with guests arriving by surreys and carriages. Some came in canoes and boats.

Royal horsemen were on hand to park the vehicles. Mak could feel the excitement. One didn't arrive late for the king's party.

Soon, guests were gathered on the deck, talking and greeting newcomers and others they'd known for many years. A nearby band strummed the bragas.

"We're moving out into the ocean," Jane said, leaning toward Mak to whisper. Her eyes shone with excitement.

"You don't have a yacht in Texas?" he teased.

She shook her head. "Not even a king."

"Ah," he said. "We finally have something bigger and better than Texas."

"No, no," she corrected him quickly. "We have oil, remember."

"I do," he said. "But our whales used to provide the world's oil supply before oil was discovered in Pennsylvania."

"Oh." She looked around. "Hawaii has disappeared."

"Yes," Mak said, "and about time for—"

The glass doors opened. A royal servant, looking stiff in his formal European clothes, announced, "King David Kalakaua and Queen Kapiolani."

The guests applauded.

The queen looked like a European monarch and wore her tiara. The king was dressed in his royal regalia, including his crown. They stood at attention as a band inside began to play the national anthem and the guests sang.

Jane looked up at Mak questioningly, but he just smiled. She'd find out what was going on soon enough.

The king and queen turned and reentered the room. The servant announced each guest as they followed. The guests found places at tables while the king and queen stood somberly on a stage.

"Well," Matilda said. "Their clothing and way of announcing guests is how they do it in Europe."

Mak figured that meant she had visited such royalty.

"The king is quite handsome the way his beard seems like long sideburns fluffed out," Jane added.

"And that's a massive mustache, too," Matilda said. "How old is he?"

"Fifty-three," Rose said in a low tone. "He's been ill. But he looks fine tonight."

"The queen is beautiful," Jane added.

Mak agreed, but she did not outshine these ladies at his table.

As soon as the guests were inside, the king's face became all smiles, and his eyes danced. He removed his royal coat. His shirt was exquisite, but he could pass as simply a well-dressed man. "Now," he said, "we dispense with this formality. Let the fun begin."

Other men took off their formal coats. Some, like Mak, rolled up their sleeves and removed their ties.

"There's food," the king said.

At that, sliding-glass doors opened.

"My," Matilda exclaimed. "That aroma is enough to tempt the whales."

"I don't think there are any," Jane said. "They've all been used up to make oil for the lamps here in Hawaii."

Mak shook his head.

"And we drink," the king said, "including Hawaii's famous Kona coffee." Servants in black pants, flowered shirts, and red vests lined up inside the doors, waiting to ensure the guests were properly served their dinner.

"And be merry," he shouted.

"He is known as the merry king," Mak said as the lively music began, and the king grabbed his queen, and they began to dance.

Others joined them, while some went into the side room for food and drink.

After that dance, young men and women ran in from a side room and onto the stage.

"They may try to copy the Europeans," Matilda said, "but that is not ballroom dancing."

On stage, the hula dancers were swaying and moving their graceful hands while a man crooned a song. When they finished, the hula dancers came to the guests, taking several on stage. His three ladies were selected. Matilda was a riot. His mother had talents he'd been unaware of, and Jane was adorable.

When the guests returned, the dancers kept Matilda on stage to demonstrate dances from Europe and some Texas square-dance steps. Mak looked beyond the glass doors. "Looks like the sun is getting ready to set. Shall we?"

Chapter 29

This is a wonderful party," Jane said as Mak led her outdoors and around to the back of the deck where the music and voices sounded faintly in the background. The sky had turned Jane into gold, and he smiled, remembering Leia saying, "Gold like Miss Matilda gives everybody."

Miss Matilda couldn't give this strong-willed young woman to anybody.

He leaned over, his arms against the railing. Jane stood holding on with her hands. She looked over at him. "You seemed to be having a good time. During the hula, were you thinking of Maylea?"

He straightened. "Yes and no," he said honestly. "Of course she was in my memory. But thanks to you, I was thinking of. . .you. . .the fun. . .your having a good time. Sometimes with you, my friend, I am in the moment. Thank you for that."

She turned toward him about to say something, but he caught hold of her arm. "The sky is magenta, without any clouds. Everything is right for the green flash."

Jane shifted her gaze to the sun.

"No, don't stare at the sun. That's not good for the eyes. Look away until only the very top of the sun is about to disappear into the ocean."

"Okay."

He saw her shoulders and chest rise with her accelerated breathing, anticipating as she stared at him, glanced at the sun, and at him. She whispered. "It's almost there."

"Now," he said. "Look at it and don't blink."

She squealed. "Ah! I did. I saw it." She grabbed his arms, looked up into his face and back at the horizon. "I really did. It was only a moment. All the greens of Hawaii are different from any I have ever seen. This was even greener. And even more beautiful. I don't know how to explain it."

"Nobody does," he said, looking into her delighted, lovely face.

Then her lips parted. An ethereal expression bathed her face. "There's a rainbow. Am I crazy, or is that a rainbow?"

"Of course it's a rainbow. It always happens after the green flash. You see, a rainbow is created when a raindrop—"

"No," she said, "Don't explain it. Just let me bask in it."

As she basked, their faces were so close. Neither was looking at the rainbow. He felt her warm breath tantalizing his lips. She seemed to lean forward. It must have been him. But her face lifted to his.

As if they had a mind of their own, his lips met her soft warm ones, and he felt lost in the moment until finally it was as if he were saying to himself what he had to say to Panai so often: Hold on, hold back, you mustn't give it your all, be controlled.

Where the will came from he didn't know, but somehow he stepped back and grasped the railing, feeling as panicked as if a tsunami was upon him.

What could he do? Run? Jump in the ocean? What was she doing? He was afraid to look. "I'm sorry. Forgive me."

"No, it's all right."

"I have no right. I've ruined everything. I don't know why—"

"Mak, it's because we're a man and a woman."

He exhaled heavily and managed to look at her. She was facing him. "But you're engaged," he protested, "and I'm as together as a shipwreck."

She gave a weak smile. "But you're not engaged, Mak. So I'm more to blame if we're going to place blame. After I saw the green flash and the rainbow, I just had to do something. So I closed my eyes and—"

"You closed your eyes?"

"Well I had to blink, didn't I?"

"Of course." He took a deep breath. "Jane, I know you're trying to make light of this—"

Before he could finish, her fingers touched his lips. They were soft as her voice. "Friends can kiss." She kissed his cheek.

She was trying to make it sound so innocent. "Your fiancé might not think so."

"Austin would understand. It was. . .a moment. Not something bad or evil."

"No," he said. "It was—" He shrugged.

"Human?"

He nodded. "Very human." He paced. "I'm supposed to be the more mature, older, been married—"

"I know, Mak, that you feel guilty. Your whole life is wrapped up in guilt and anger. This was only. . ." She smiled. "A lovely moment."

He looked down. Was that all?

"We are both single, you know."

Yes, he was making too much of it. But single? Was he? No. He was married to his guilt and grief.

"Did you see the green sunset?" she asked.

Staring at her, his hand touched her arm. "I saw the blue green flash in your eyes."

"Oh, so here you are," came Matilda's voice as the sky darkened to a dull gray. "I just finished dancing with the king. Wheee! They'd have me dancing all night if I would. It's social time now, but I thought I needed a little reprieve."

"Excuse me," Mak said. "I want to speak to some friends I haven't seen in a while."

❧

Jane turned and leaned against the railing. "You saw?"

"Yes dear. I was fascinated by the idea I might see a green sunset. Too bad

I didn't bring a gentleman friend with me."

"Matilda!"

"Sorry dear. I'm just doing what you did. Trying to make light of it."

"Shocked?"

"Me? Oh honey. Not even surprised. He has become your goal, your purpose. He needs you, and you responded to that. Austin never needed you that way. Mak has touched your heart in a different way. You're growing up."

"Austin would never hurt me," Jane said. "Mak. . .could."

Matilda stood so close their shoulders touched. "You say you love Austin." Jane nodded. "And that you and Mak are just friends. Do I have that right?"

"Yes, I claim that."

"Pray about what is right, Jane."

"Okay. But I'm not sure Mak prays anymore. Maybe what's right for me isn't right for him."

"Everything here is new and different. You've been rather sheltered in Texas. You're trying your wings. When the time is right, all those befuddled questions will. . ." She gestured out over the ocean. "They'll float away. Shall we join the others?"

Jane nodded. "I'll be right there."

She stood looking out over the deep blue water. Austin was out there, heading her way. The stars in the sky winked like they were playing some kind of trick on her.

Lifting her chin, she straightened her shoulders and turned to walk back to the royal party.

She'd seen her green sunset.

But that wasn't what took her breath away.

Chapter 30

In mid-January, everything changed. Leia was allowed to start attending school, in part because Rose took Mak's teaching spot. Matilda offered to assist. The two women loved the arrangement.

Two afternoons after school each week, Jane continued her lessons with Leia. Mak spent most of his time making sure Panai was ready for the big race. On the days she didn't see him at the stables, she rode out to the racetrack.

Sometimes he was there. He didn't seem to mind her presence, but his mind obviously was on the horse. One day when Mak wasn't there, Chico brought Panai over to the fence and dismounted.

He barely spoke to Jane and looked distressed. "Be back in a minute, Tomas."

"Your stomach again?" Tomas said.

Chico ran into the stable. Tomas looked worried. "He's been getting that lately," he confided to Jane. "Seems to be getting worse."

Chico soon returned. "I feel better now," he said, but his brown skin looked pasty.

"You're in no condition—" Tomas began.

"I have no choice, Tomas. You know that."

There was only one thing a well-meaning girl could do. Not that she wanted Chico to be sick, but her heartbeat accelerated at what she was thinking. "Let me ride him," Jane said.

The two men looked at her like she was *loco*.

"No way," Chico said at the same time Tomas said, "Never happen."

"Why not?"

Chico looked like a little color had returned to his face. "Nobody rides Panai but me and the boss."

"I rode Panai with the boss, remember?"

"But that was a pleasure ride. He didn't take the horse for all he was worth."

"Let me be your substitute. I'll give Panai a good workout."

As if Panai understood, he stepped up and nuzzled the side of Jane's face with his soft nose. She turned, laughed, and patted the lucky white spot on his face. "See, he loves me."

Chico seemed to hold his breath.

Tomas glared at him. "You'll have to fight me to get on that horse, Chico."

"Tomas, my health means nothing if I don't win this race for Mr. Mak. You know that's what will bring back to us the man he used to be."

"And what was that?" Jane said.

Tomas looked away as Chico said, "Not depressed, I guess. He's not been right for three years. Just as I can tell when a horse likes a person, I can tell when a man likes a woman. Mr. Mak likes you, Miss Jane. If you were not wearing that ring, you maybe could help him get back his sanity."

"Thank you, Chico." But if she wasn't wearing that ring, she wouldn't be there.

Chico grabbed his stomach, then let out a ragged breath. "Just one time around. Slow." He paused, looking doubtful. "He may not even let you get on him."

"Of course he will," she said to Panai, who seemed to nod in agreement. "We understand each other."

He nodded. "I've heard you teaching Miss Leia. You know horses."

Jane thought that was a pretty good compliment coming from a jockey who would race a horse against the king's horse.

"Please let me help," Jane said. "Mak trusts me with his daughter. Surely a horse isn't more important than his daughter."

Both men stared at her as if they weren't sure about that. Neither was she.

"Chico, give me a few pointers on how a jockey sits and leans into the horse."

He did, and when he said, "You have to control him, hold him back," she knew he was consenting and began climbing the fence.

"You can't let him go at top speed. He wants to, but he has to save that for the race. He'll understand when he gets on that racetrack. But for now, he has to hold back."

Jane remembered Mak leaning into her and telling Panai that exact thing. She could do it.

Like Mak had guided Panai the day she rode with them, she started him at a trot, then picked up speed. She could tell he wanted to go, but he yielded to her control. If she gave the signal, or he decided to, he could jump that fence and they'd fly away like a bird.

Now there was no Mak to distract her. As much as she wanted to give full rein, she held Panai—and herself—back. Nevertheless, although she thought she'd ridden like the wind before, now she knew she had not. Panai took her for the ride of her life, as if she had wings.

As they neared Tomas and Chico, she didn't want to stop. But she had to obey the rules.

Tomas and Chico complimented her profusely. There was only one thing she could say. "That was almost as exhilarating as a green sunset. . .almost."

111

Chapter 31

Mid-February arrived. So did Austin, Buck Buckley, and Inez Ashcroft. The bells rang, and the islanders turned out to watch the liner come in. Mak knew he had to be there. These American visitors were relatives and friends of. . .his new friends. To stay away would be the height of impropriety.

So he stood back as he had done when Jane, Matilda, and Pilar had arrived. He held his hat in his hand and observed as his mother and Leia, along with his new friends and Reverend Russell gave leis and hugs and kisses.

Jane and Austin's kiss was brief. But they were in public.

He mustn't stand aside as if not a part of the group, so he stepped up and held out his hand to be introduced. Miz Ashcroft was a fine-looking woman. The men would be tremendously impressive to the islanders, who never got their fill of what, or who, a ship might bring in. They would not be disappointed by these men, fine specimens of what cultured westerners should look like.

Mak felt rather like a rugged paniolo in comparison. On second thought, he supposed that's what he was.

Then Jane was telling her father that Mak's ranch was even bigger than his.

Her daddy almost roared. "I didn't know they made ranches any bigger than what's in Texas." He pointed at Mak. "This I gotta see to believe, son."

"Will be my pleasure." Despite his dignified appearance, Mr. Buckley, who said to call him "Buck," smiled broadly, and Mak liked what he believed was genuine friendliness.

"And this," Jane said, "is my. . .Austin."

Was she going to say my fiancé? Or was she saying "my Austin" for emphasis? It didn't really matter. Mak shook the hand of the well-dressed, nice-looking, tall, friendly man. Like looking at a horse, you could tell when it was well-bred.

Mak said what he needed to say to friends of his friends. "Jane, I know you'll want to show Austin the island. I'll handle Leia's lessons. Next week if it's convenient, come out to the ranch for dinner, and I'll show everyone the ranch."

"Yes," his mother said. "Buck and you, Inez. And of course"—she gestured around—"all of you."

❧

A week later when Mak's mother and daughter returned from school, his mother said Jane wanted to come the following afternoon for Leia's lesson. Austin would come with her, and Mak might want to show him the ranch.

Just as Mak was thinking they probably weren't interested in accepting his polite dinner invitation, his mother added, "They are looking forward to having dinner with us, Mak. And Buck is anxious to see the ranch. Right now, they're getting Inez settled in Pilar's bedroom. Buck and Austin are staying in a hotel in town."

"They could have stayed here."

Her eyebrows lifted. "You didn't ask them to."

When Austin and Jane rode up, Mak realized he hadn't asked Austin if he would like to take one of his horses while on the island. But one couldn't think of everything upon first meeting. Austin wore a smart-looking riding outfit and rode on a fine-looking horse he must have rented in town.

He and Jane looked. . .good together.

Leia came out in her riding outfit, ready for her lesson. Austin said he'd heard she was a very good rider and had a pony named Star. "Texas is called the Lone Star State," he said.

Mak remembered he and Jane had talked about that and laughed together.

Leia looked up at him. "I don't ever want Miss Jane to leave. Are you going to take her away?"

After a quick glance at Jane, he knelt in front of Leia, getting down to her size. "Well, from what I've seen of Hawaii this week and from what I've heard, it seems that many people who come here never want to leave."

Leia seemed to take that as fact. She smiled and took Jane's hand in hers. They headed for the corral.

As the two men rode out on the range, Mak noted that Austin sat in the saddle like one accustomed to good riding habits. He wondered if Austin was really interested in seeing a ranch. But what else did he have to show him? Then it occurred to him. He could show friendship.

Before he could ask Austin about the oil business, however, Austin said, "Mak, Jane told me about your wife. I'm sorry about that."

That was nice of him, and Mak acknowledged it with a nod. "Have you ever lost anyone close?" he asked.

"Not immediate family," he said. "I've been blessed."

Mak wondered how Austin would feel if he lost a wife. . .or a loved one. He wouldn't wish that on anyone.

"From what Jane's said about you, Austin, I get the impression you've never loved anyone but her." He was surprised when Austin hesitated.

Austin looked out over the range and the corral as they approached it. Finally, he said, "To be honest with you, Mak, I've had my years of indiscretion, sorry to say. During college, but they were passing fancies."

Mak said what was on his mind. "I'm surprised you waited so long to marry her."

"So am I, in a way," Austin said. "After my college years, I was ready to make that lifetime commitment. She wasn't. She was smarter than I in knowing she wasn't ready. I was willing to wait and threw myself into the business."

Mak thought Austin had a good outlook on things. He was surprised that he talked so openly about his and Jane's relationship. But then Austin was talking about someone he had a future with. Mak didn't have a future with Maylea.

"I've given this a lot of thought in the past few months," Austin went on, "being thousands of miles from Jane, with her completely out of reach. I knew when she said she would come to Hawaii it would be a milestone. She'd told me she would be ready to settle down after this trip." Austin was nodding. "I was right. She's different."

That surprised Mak. "Different?"

Austin nodded. "Different than when she was in Texas. She's matured. She's found purpose in teaching your daughter and in being your friend along with relating to her uncle Russell."

"She's changed my life." Mak felt warm under Austin's scrutiny.

"Mak, I don't think Jane knows she's changed your life."

"Well I haven't changed a lot of my actions or my attitudes, so it doesn't show."

"The changes in Jane show. I now know that at eighteen, she couldn't be the mature woman I wanted." He smiled over at Mak. "She's matured a lot since being here. Her goal is no longer winning the top spot in equestrienne events."

"What?"

Austin laughed lightly. "She's always been second. Absolutely couldn't stand it to think anyone would beat her in any competition."

"I figured she was first," Mak said.

Austin shook his head. "Second."

Mak was trying to absorb why the conversation was going this way. Was Austin warning him not to take Jane's relating to him personally because she found purpose in it? Was he saying don't bother letting Jane know she changed your life because she'd never accept being second place, or rather second wife, in a man's life? Had Jane told Austin about the green-sunset *friendly* kiss?

Mak drew a deep breath. He started to say maybe they shouldn't be talking about her. But Austin said he and Jane had talked about him. Austin and Jane had talked about Mak. What should a man in love talk about—coconut palms?

They rode up to the racetrack and dismounted to watch Chico give Panai his workout. He could tell Austin appreciated the horse, but not in the way he and Jane did. Then again, Austin wasn't a horseman; he was an oil man.

Mak mentioned they might go back to the house, but Austin expressed the desire to ride farther. "Jane mentioned the sugar fields."

"Yes, we'll ride out that way," he said, glad Austin wasn't bored.

"Mak," Austin said, as they rode across the velvety green range. "You asked if I lost anyone. I've heard about your situation. So I'm going to be honest with you."

Which situation? came instantly to Mak's mind. Then he reminded himself there was only one situation, and that was the loss of his wife and his getting revenge on that horse because of it.

"I haven't lost a person," Austin said, "but when I was abroad studying in England, away from authority, from prying eyes, I lost my way for a while. I lost my relationship with God through philandering. I didn't even think of it that way at the time. My letters home were the same. My feelings for Jane and family were the same. But the—I guess you call it the baser side—surfaced. At the time I called it fun, just young people having fun."

Mak nodded. "I suppose many of us can identify with that, Austin."

Austin agreed. "But after graduation, I realized how foolish I'd been, how I'd disappointed God. I felt like a worm. By the way," he said, looking over at Mak. "I didn't tell Jane about that. I had to find myself, to identify with God. There comes a defining moment when. . ."

Mak's mind wandered. A moment. . .a kiss. . .a green sunset. But what was Austin saying? A moment when a person as an adult decided to live for the Lord, no matter what. No longer straddle the fence.

"I felt Jane would find that in this trip, and she has."

Mak realized Austin was describing a spiritually defining moment. He'd never thought of things in quite that way. If he tried to identify a defining moment, it would be when he decided to marry Maylea, be a husband, a dad, a man.

But was that a commitment to a woman, to a lifestyle. . .and not to God? To love and serve Him, regardless? No, he had not had a spiritually defining moment as an adult.

Maybe after Panai won the race, he would think on these things. Everything would have changed then. He would have had his revenge. Jane, Austin, and the others would leave Hawaii. Leia would again be without a mother figure except the one who should only be a grandmother.

"Thank you, Austin, for your honest words." A short ironic laugh came from his throat. "I wouldn't be able to talk with you or even listen to anything personal, anything spiritual, had Jane not laid the groundwork."

"Maybe that's because we're visitors to the island, Mak. We won't be around to remind you of your having spoken your heart."

They came to the fence and stopped the horses. "That's sugar cane," he said, and they gazed out on the acres of slender green leaves swaying in the gentle breeze.

Mak knew Jane was the one who had encouraged him to speak his heart. "Austin, I don't think I spoke personally because you're a visitor who will leave. I wouldn't mind if you were a permanent resident. I think we could be friends."

Austin nodded. "I think we are. Who knows? Jane might decide she doesn't want to leave. This is a special place. I can understand why it's called paradise."

Mak liked having a friend, speaking his heart to a man. Most men didn't do that. Austin was, as Jane had implied, a special kind of man. Like Rev. Russell in some ways. Yes, it would be nice to have a male friend. But things with Jane would be different. They should not have kissed; she should not have seen the green sunset.

His heart was troubled. Without being obvious, he turned his head far enough to see Austin's expression.

The man looked at peace. There was a warmth in his eyes, a strength in his being. Probably that came from loving and being loved by a wonderful woman with whom he planned to spend his life. Yet Austin had attributed his confidence to a relationship with God.

Chapter 32

"Daddy," Jane said, "is there something between you and Inez that I need to know about?"

"Nothing I can talk about until after I have my beautiful daughter married off and settled. Now, how long you gonna keep me waitin', girl?"

"You don't have to wait for me, Daddy."

"But I will. I'm not about to have some old maid spinster around tying me down." He laughed and drew her into his arms.

Later, Uncle Russell was showing the school, church, and town to the others. Jane and Matilda sat at the table, drinking Kona coffee and talked about how Inez had taken on the airs of a demure southern lady, widow of the once-prominent Mr. Ashcroft, and worthy of the likes of Mr. John Buckley.

Jane thought she was.

"Do you think she would consider letting Pilar stay in Hawaii?"

"Pilar is making a good argument for it. She has plans to attend that nursing school along with Susanne. Inez was impressed by that."

Jane sighed. "I know how Pilar feels. I would love to stay in Hawaii for a long time. Austin mentioned having a second home here."

Matilda gave her a long look. "Isn't that supposed to make you happy?"

"Well, it would really be three homes. One of them would be the long voyages from Hawaii to America and back again. And those ships are not yachts."

"My dear Jane," Matilda said resolutely. "When you're in love, you don't care if it's Texas, Hawaii, the middle of the ocean, or the swamps in Florida. You just want to be with the one you love."

Jane brought her hand down on the table. "Of course it makes a difference."

Matilda wasn't rattled by her reaction. "Certainly you can prefer some places over another. But you wouldn't choose a place over the one you love."

Jane took a deep breath. "I think you're trying to tell me something."

"I don't think I have to tell you. You've known since you were eighteen years old and began to postpone marriage plans."

"I've always had reasons."

"I know," Matilda agreed. "No one ever marries if there's a death, an accident, a tornado, college." Matilda smiled—one of those caring, I-know-what-you-feel smiles that made Jane want to cry.

Jane knew she might as well say it. They both knew it anyway. "You said a place doesn't matter that much. I think the opposite can be true, too. No matter how much you love a place, it can lose its allure if you're not with the one you love."

Matilda nodded. "I've returned to some of the places my husband and I visited together. And you're right. It's not the same. It reminds me of that verse in the Bible. It must be in Proverbs. I can't imagine anyone else saying it, unless it's Solomon in Ecclesiastes. Anyway, it's something like it being better to live in a corner of a housetop than with a brawling woman in a wide house."

Jane gasped. "Matilda. I'm trying to get some advice from you, and you're changing this all around. Sounds to me like you're saying that's what Austin's life would be like if I married him."

"Well, it could very well be. My motherly advice is you must think of him, too. What kind of favor would you be doing him if you don't love him?"

"But I do love him. Of course I love him."

"I know, dear. But there are many kinds and degrees of love. You need to have a few butterflies in your tummy and hear the bells ring."

☙

The bells had been ringing all day, every hour on the hour, reminding everyone of the race tomorrow, Hawaii's biggest event of the year. Mak felt sick. For him it wasn't just a race. It was his life. He'd been preparing himself and Panai for three years.

That night, unable to sleep, he walked out into the night several times, feeling like the edge of darkness was within.

He wouldn't go to the stables and check on Panai, lest he awaken Chico. His jockey needed to sleep. He kept telling himself that Panai was in perfect condition to win. He couldn't even pray about it. How could he ask God to help him get revenge on a horse?

He had arranged for Inez, Jane, and Austin to ride in Mak's surrey driven by Mr. Buckley. Rev. Russell would take his mother, Leia, Pilar, and Matilda.

Mak needed to go alone. He would need that regardless of the outcome, but particularly if his horse lost. But when he arrived and went to the holding area, they were all there—his friends and well-wishers.

"I'd like to quote a verse and pray," Rev. Russell said. "It's from Philippians. It goes something like this. 'This one thing I do, forgetting those things which are behind, and reaching forth unto those things which are before. I press toward the mark for the prize.' "

Then he prayed. Not for Mak's horse to win, but that it might be a good race for all concerned. Good clean entertainment. And for the Lord's will to be done in everything. He prayed for Chico.

Chico?

Mak didn't know if the reverend said *Amen* or not, but he almost shouted, "Where's Chico?" The loudspeaker was saying they should take their places. The others looked around.

"He'll probably be here any minute," Rev. Russell said.

"He should be here now." Mak took off running toward the stables.

Chapter 33

Tomas was standing over Chico, who lay on the straw, curled up in a corner. His breath was ragged, his eyes squinted, and his face drenched with sweat.

"What's going on?" Mak demanded.

"He needs a doctor."

Mak motioned for a stable boy. "Son, run get a doctor."

"No," Chico got to his feet. "I'll be all right." His jaw was clenched, and Mak knew he was fighting pain. . .and losing.

A doctor rushed in from one of the ambulances always on hand at a race. He ordered them to move back. Tomas mentioned previous attacks. The doctor said, "It may be appendicitis."

"Take his clothes off."

Recognizing the voice, Mak turned and stared hard at Jane. The others stood around her, staring, too, as if she'd lost her mind.

"I'll ride Panai."

His laugh was short. "That doesn't even deserve an answer."

"Please. I can do it."

"Mak," Austin said, and for an instant, Mak thought he might have an ally. Instead, Austin affirmed, "If she says she can ride him, she can."

Chico grunted as the doctor poked around his stomach. Between his gasps, he said, "Somebody has to, Mak. You know that. She may not be able to win, but she can ride him."

Tomas confirmed that with a nod. "He's right."

And how would they know? He didn't need to ask. Their sheepish looks told him they'd gone behind his back and let her ride alone. Realizing his hands were now fists, he unclasped them.

Why should he be so concerned about keeping Jane safe, when neither she nor those who claimed to love her, including her fiancé, didn't? With a lift of his hands and a snort like a disgruntled horse, he stomped out.

He'd probably have ridden off if Leia hadn't run after him and taken his hand. She looked up at him with pleading eyes. Her little lips trembled. "Daddy, Jesus will take care of Miss Jane. And Chico."

Mak didn't think he could stand it if God didn't take care of them. And what would that do to his little girl, to a faith that had begun in her? Not long ago, she would have credited the Little People.

He led Leia to the seats reserved for racehorse owners. The others filed in behind him. Leia sat on one side of him and Austin on the other. A glance around revealed a full stadium and spectators crowded around the edges.

Mak felt like he had sea legs when he stood with the others for the singing of the national anthem. He didn't attempt to join in.

After they were seated, the announcements began, followed by cheering. When he announced the black stallion Panai, son of the king's horse Akim, ridden by a substitute jockey, Miss Jane Marie Buckley, Mak was shocked. Amid the applause and shouting, both Austin and Matilda stood and whistled through their teeth.

Leia looked and stuck her fingers in her mouth, but the sound came out as "*Fffff ffffff.*"

He couldn't begin to cheer at a time like this. It could be dangerous for the best of jockeys. His gaze scanned the riders. They looked like what they were—winning jockeys. Jane sat erect in Chico's jockey suit, looking like an equestrienne who might have her horse jump over a two-foot hurdle.

As soon as the race started, he leaned over and held his face in his hands.

"Maybe I can catch a sunbeam and get this to shine in the eyes of the other horses," Austin said.

Mak looked as Austin brought the ring out of his pocket. That was a good idea. Take off the rock. It would certainly decrease the weight. "Aren't you afraid of what could happen?"

"Mak, I can't control what happens." Then he shoved the ring into his pocket. "I'll be praying and cheering."

Mak shook his head. "I don't care about winning. I only care about her safety." He gazed at the racetrack. It was no surprise that Akim was ahead from the beginning. Panai was midway. He stayed midway even when some horses passed him. He then passed another and eased to the outside.

Panai was easing on up. Mak knew his horse. A horse like Panai made racing look easy, and so could a jockey like Chico. Jane was doing well, even holding Panai back the way he'd done the day he let her ride with him.

Those around Mak were standing and cheering and yelling. "Come on, Jane! Come on, Jane!"

It dawned on him that nobody cheered for a jockey. They cheered for a horse, and usually one they'd bet on.

Austin said, "Look, she's inching up."

Mak got to his feet. He couldn't yell. He heard his own pitiful whisper, "Jane."

They were nose and nose, and the finish line was right ahead. Mother and son. Would one give in to the other? No, they were champions. The one who killed his wife. And the one who would have the revenge.

The crowd went wild.

He couldn't tell which horse crossed the finish line first.

The announcer declared Panai the winner.

Mak sat down, put his hands over his face, and closed his eyes. This was the race that was to take away his grief and misery. Then why did he feel the way he did?

Austin sat down. "Hey, Mak. Did you see the finish?"

"Are they all right?"

"Look."

Mak looked. Jane and Panai were in the winner's circle. The announcement was still coming over the speaker. The princess was presenting her with the award. The king came from across the aisle, shook Mak's hand, and congratulated him.

"Shouldn't we go down?" Austin asked.

"You go congratulate her," Mak said.

"Not without you. It's your horse and your jockey. And your Big Island Cup."

Yes, Mak thought. *And your fiancée.*

Chapter 34

Jane watched Mak come into the winner's circle, heard his name announced and the applause that followed. He came over to Panai while photos were being taken. Lifting his head slightly, he nodded toward Jane, as if in thanks. He stared at the camera but made no attempt to smile.

After the photos, he accepted congratulations with handshakes. He thanked everyone, then said he would go to the hospital and see about Chico. He would see them all later.

Maybe he wasn't angry with her for riding, but he didn't appear pleased about the win. Perhaps he was just concerned about Chico. Her displeasure with him turned to guilt when she realized she had not thought of Chico from the time she dressed in that jockey suit and began the ride of her life. . .again.

"Did I do wrong?" she asked her companions as they left the racetrack.

In unison, they answered no.

"You and Panai won the most important race of the island. And you did it against the king's horse," Rose said. "That's what Mak has wanted for more than three years."

Regardless of whether Mak was angry with her for riding Panai, he wasn't thinking only of himself—he was concerned about Chico.

Much later, after returning home, bathing, and getting into comfortable clothes, Jane asked Austin if they could walk outside. They ambled out into the cool evening and went to the schoolyard, where Jane sat in a swing.

"Aren't you exhausted, Jane?"

"I think I'm still excited," she said. "But my emotions are so mixed. I'm elated, yet worried about Chico. I'm happy for Mak, but I'm not sure he is."

"Jane," Austin said, standing in front of her. "Let's talk about. . .us."

He took the diamond ring from his vest pocket. Jane looked down at her lap, where her right hand was folded over the left. She didn't raise it. Neither did he.

The night breeze whispered in the coconut palms. The rope swing was still, but her heart was doing an unfamiliar dance. When she looked up at Austin's disturbed expression, he said, "I have a confession to make."

Jane waited.

"You know Rebecca," he said.

"Rebecca?" Jane said. Rebecca. The one who got first place in equestrienne events. The twenty-four-year-old blond daughter of the president of Austin's company. The girl who could never return to her carriage without Austin accompanying her. The one whose blue eyes seemed to turn green with envy when she saw Jane and Austin together. The one Jane didn't want to get Austin—the top prize.

A sense of possessiveness rose in Jane, but if Austin confessed something, should she? This inner sense of honesty was getting to be a nuisance. "You wouldn't be talking about the person you and I have discussed for the past few years, would you?"

Austin shook his head as he had other times when they simply let the subject of Rebecca go by the wayside. He stared into her eyes. "She said you don't want to marry me; you just don't want to let me go. That I deserved better than being strung along for years."

It flashed through Jane's mind that Matilda had said something similar. More than once. "Do you feel strung along, Austin?"

"Maybe. . .kept waiting. But I wanted you to be sure. I'd never thought of it quite the way Rebecca said it." He paused, then blurted out, "She kissed me."

It looked like the two of them might be in the same boat. She couldn't help the ironic laugh that escaped her throat. "You kissed her back. I mean her lips?"

He scoffed. "Jane, how can you sit there and act like this is some child's prank? This amounts to disrespect for you. I've struggled with this. And about telling you." He paused. "Don't you care?"

"Well, yes. Describe it."

"Describe what?"

"The kiss."

His poor Adam's apple seemed to be getting a lot of exercise. "She is. . .was. . . very passionate."

"Were you?"

He took a step away and gazed at the ground. "I. . .surprised myself."

She could hardly believe it. "You were passionate?"

"Well, I was. . .tempted. Although I never told you details, I was honest about not living the way the Lord intended during my college years. But I've tried to since recommitting myself to the Lord. That's why I have to tell you this. I—I did return the kiss, but then I broke away and I turned and marched right out of the office."

"You left her standing there?"

"Yes, but she ran after me and made me talk. Or rather, listen."

"What did she say?"

"She said that she and I were made for each other. That she'd been in love with me for years. She thought I should know it. She said that your leaving for Hawaii made her decide to speak up. She thinks you don't love me the way she does."

Jane stood from the swing, still holding onto the rope. She wasn't really surprised, yet she felt jealous. She and Rebecca had been rivals since school days. She supposed that challenged them both to be their best. But this was not a game. Where was this leading?

Austin looked at the diamond ring he still held. He looked at Jane with a troubled expression. "Well," he said. "Do you? Love me that way? You've never. . .kissed me."

"What? Austin! I've kissed you all my life."

"I mean not like that. With your heart in it."

"Oh. You mean. . .that passionately."

His face tilted slightly, and the lift of his eyebrows indicated that was it.

"Well, we weren't supposed to."

"Rebecca and I weren't supposed to, either."

She nodded.

"Jane. I don't want some momentary indiscretion of mine to get in the way of what you and I mean to each other. But are you sure that you and I belong together. . .forever?"

She took a deep breath. All this needed to be faced, to be talked about, because what she had thought, she now said. "Austin, all of my life, I've believed that you and I were part of each other. Our families, even after my mother died, were like one family. I've always believed we were best friends, were going to be married, and live happily ever after."

"It's a beautiful dream," he said. "But I think you may have a different one now."

She grasped the rope tightly.

"Today, you risked your life for that man. You love his child. They're in your heart."

"So are you, Austin. You've always been there. You always will be. You've been my dearest friend."

"Yes," Austin said. "I made this trip because I knew we had to get this settled once and for all. Seeing that race, you on that horse, it was like seeing you as you really are for the first time. Riding toward another goal, away from me." He looked at the ring. "Mak is your equal, not I."

"He doesn't want me."

A wan smile touched Austin's lips. "That's for him to say." He returned the ring to his pocket, and Jane didn't know if she could stand it. "Oh Austin. You're wonderful. I've loved you as long as I can remember." She rushed to him.

He lifted a hand to still her words. "I didn't say he's better than I. Just your equal in many ways."

"You and I could have made a good life together."

"Yes, I think we could have."

Could have. Those words changed the thinking of a lifetime. With eyes that blurred, she fell against his chest. He held her tight. The sound coming from him sounded like the kind of sobs she felt in her own throat.

"I do love you, Jane," he said, when they could let go.

She took the handkerchief he offered. "I've always loved you. Always will." Strange. This felt like. . .salt in a wound. It hurt. But it would heal.

Like the night, a calm seemed to settle over them.

"Jane, on the voyage over, I had a lot of time to think. I wonder. Maybe we've been more like a very close brother and sister."

She was shaking her head. "No. More like cousins."

He laughed, tears again forming in his eyes. "Kissing cousins."

She nodded. "But not. . .passionately enough."

He took his handkerchief from her and wiped her tears away, then swiped at his own. "You don't have to tell me, but I wonder. Do you know what it means to kiss someone passionately?"

She thought of the teenage kiss she had given the boy behind the barn. That was as passionate as she could get at the time. She thought of the nearness of Mak, his face, his lips, just his nearness that sped up her heartbeat and made her long to be in his arms. "In my dreams and in my weak moments, yes, Austin. I do. I haven't experienced it like you and Rebecca, but yes. I know."

He took a deep breath. "I thought so."

Chapter 35

After Mak walked away from his family and friends, he went to the area where the king and others stood with Akim. The king shook his hand. "Congratulations, Mak. I can imagine what this means to you. And if Akim had to be beaten, I'm glad it was by Panai."

The king held his hand a moment longer than necessary, with a strong grip as his gaze held Mak's. Yes, the king knew the story. All the island knew about the tragedy that had become front-page news. It had been repeated when the king bought Akim, and again during the following years when Akim had won the cup.

"Who would have thought that lovely lady I met at the party was a fine jockey?" He chuckled and let go of Mak's hand.

Mak turned his lips into a polite smile. He didn't need to respond to that rhetorical question. But he knew the answer. Jane's fiancé knew.

As Akim was being led away, Mak walked over. "Just a moment, please." He stared at Akim while examining his own mind and heart. The horse had his eyes on Mak, who laid his hand on Akim's warm, moist neck and whispered, "I forgive you."

એ

Mak was kneeling at the front of the church the following morning when he felt a hand on his shoulder. Looking back, he saw Rev. Russell. Mak stood.

"For a long time," Mak said, "coming in here and getting things right between me and God has been in the back of my mind, and even more so since Jane has spoken her mind to me—more than once."

The reverend's face relaxed into a knowing expression, but he made no comment, apparently sensing that Mak had to make his peace.

"I've been coming to the conclusion that I needed to forgive God for letting Maylea and my baby die." He shook his head. "I don't think that anymore. I think I needed to ask God to forgive me."

"He understands, Mak. God still loves you, and He's still as close as you let Him be."

Mak nodded. "I know that. But it's easier to accept when things are going well."

"Is it?" the reverend said. "Or do we tend to take God for granted when things are going well?"

Mak stood and looked at the wooden cross on the wall behind the pulpit. The reverend had a point. He'd taken a lot of his blessings for granted. "In the past three years, I've talked about, thought about, questioned, and tried to reason things about life that didn't suit me more than in the rest of my life combined."

"It's a maturing process, Mak."

A defining moment, Mak thought.

"Do you remember the verse I quoted to you before the race?"

"I can't quote it," Mak said, shifting his weight from one foot to the other. "Something about winning the race."

"That was about winning the physical race, Mak. Here, look at the ending of that sentence." He turned the pages of his Bible and read: " 'I press toward the mark for the prize. . . .' " He paused, then read the rest. " 'The prize of the high calling of God in Christ Jesus.' " He closed the Bible. "We have our human races, Mak. But the one that makes the biggest difference is the one we race daily. The spiritual one."

∼

"Well Jane," Matilda scolded a few days after the race. "You had enough courage to ride the most powerful horse on the island, and you can't face the likes of Mak MacCauley? Is this my niece talking?"

Jane tried to explain it to herself. Finally, it hit her. "It's like I told you before. Austin would never hurt me. But Mak can."

"Then maybe you should book the next ship back to Texas."

Jane stared into Matilda's challenging eyes. Then she promptly went into her bedroom, changed into her riding clothes, marched out the door, and rode Anise to the ranch.

Big Brown stood in the corral. Mak was brushing Panai. Across from Panai in a niche she hadn't noticed before was the Big Island Cup. Mak had what he wanted. His revenge, his big win. He wasn't talking to Panai, and his face did not have the look of someone who had lost his grief and misery.

Panai gave a low whinny. Jane walked over to the horse and rubbed his face. The horse wasn't angry with her. She heard Mak's quick intake of breath when he saw her.

"How is Chico?"

Mak looked behind her as if expecting someone else. He again focused on the horse. "It's not appendicitis." If he wasn't careful, he might brush a hole in that horse.

"Chico's wife remembered that his dad had a bad reaction to taking salicin. Chico had been taking it for a while for a headache he had after pulling a muscle in his neck."

He laid the brush aside, and she stepped back so he could swing the door open and come out. Again he looked toward the doorway. "The last I heard, they were planning to test further, but they suspect he has an ulcerated stomach from the salicin." He added, with relief in his voice, "That is treatable."

She gestured at the cup. "I see you've given the cup to the one who deserves it—Panai."

"You deserve it, too." He began walking toward the doorway, and she followed.

"I'm not sorry. Chico said I might not win, but I could ride him." While Mak washed his hands at the water pump, she felt her words coming out like a tumbleweed. "He was right. I couldn't win. But Panai could. He did the work. I was just along for the ride. It was the ride of my life, and I won't apologize for it. I just wish you hadn't been so angry about it." She gave him a hard look. "After all, I didn't throw up on him."

He shook the water from his hands and wiped them on the sides of his shirt. She thought he grinned. "Why do you think I was angry?"

She took a deep breath. But it didn't stop the tumbleweed. "Because you didn't really want Panai to win. You wouldn't have anything to hold onto without your grief and misery."

"Jane," he said. "That might be true if you hadn't come into my life. You've changed me. I didn't know just how much until you determined to get on that horse. I knew then you were more important to me than the horse, than the race."

Jane knew that was saying a lot. But did he mean the value of a human being in general. . .or. . . ?

"During the race, I didn't care if Panai came in last or didn't come in at all." He reached out and took hold of her hands. "I wanted you to be safe. For your sake and. . .I did not want Austin to feel the pain of losing someone he loves. Since I'm being honest, I kept thinking that you made me realize that I could love again. God might bring into my life a lovely young woman whom I could come to love, yet. . .I worried that she might not be available—"

His words stopped, and he focused on her left hand, the ring finger. His glance moved to her face and back again, questioning.

"Austin felt that my riding that horse was my racing away from him. He didn't return the ring."

Mak looked pained. "I'm sorry if I caused that. Ruined that for you."

"You are. . .sorry?"

"Yes. No. I mean—"

"Mak, I couldn't accept that ring again. Austin and I both realized we're the best friends in the world. We love each other. But we're not in love. My being your friend has saved me from the prospect of a friendly, boring, good life."

"No. You would make each day exciting just by being in it."

"Well, as I said, I feel like you saved my life."

He stepped closer, and his hand came around her waist. "There's a Chinese saying—"

"Finally," she interrupted. "Why do you think I kept repeating that you saved my life? But go ahead and finish the proverb."

A loving look came into his eyes. "There's a Chinese saying that if you save someone's life, you're responsible for them for the rest of your life."

"Do you mean. . . ?"

"I mean I love you, Jane. I would like nothing better than for you to become my wife. Is there a chance?"

"There is. And I want you to know this, Mak. I want to plan a marriage with you every day of my life. That's where I want to focus. I want to be a wife you can respect and cherish and love."

He put his fingers against her lips. "Let me ask you this. Can you ever forget Austin?"

"No." Her heart began to hammer, anticipating what he was about to say.

"I can't forget Maylea, either. And you're the one who has made me realize I don't have to. But the amazing thing about these hearts of ours is there's room for more love than we can ever realize. I love you completely. You, as you are. There's no competing. I may think of her at times, like when Leia graduates from a class, is baptized. And when she marries, I may think that her mother is watching. But here, you are her mother."

"I know," Jane said. "And I will probably always remember Austin's wealth and think he could probably buy the entire island of Hawaii, and I'll remember his sweet kisses."

"Aarrgh," Mak growled.

"But yours," she teased, "if we ever get that far, could probably make me forget everything else in the world."

"I can live with that," he said. "There's something I've wanted to do for a long time, without feeling guilty. . .or miserable."

He brought his hand up from her waist and gently touched her lips. Hers parted to take in a breath. "Don't say any more," she said. "Show me."

So he did.

His lips were only a breath away. She closed her eyes to experience her own personal, passionate adventure in paradise.

Chapter 36

Jane insisted she wanted a simple ceremony, but as plans evolved, Mak began to understand the meaning of everything in Texas being big. These people didn't know the meaning of simple.

"I'm not going to recognize this house when you women get through," Mak grumbled to Matilda and his mom, who were changing everything around.

"You're not supposed to," his mom said.

"Jane can rearrange, or we can build a new house after we're married."

"But that takes time." Matilda's hand shooed him away. "This is a woman thing, trust me," and they insisted upon giving new master bedroom furniture to him and Jane instead of using what had been his mother's.

He didn't even know how to argue with those women.

After receiving a wedding invitation, the king sent his regrets but offered a guest cottage on the palace grounds for their honeymoon. Since it was such a long boat trip to Oahu, his mother, Matilda, and Leia were taking the king up on the offer instead. Mak and Jane agreed they'd rather stay at his—their—house.

When they'd all had dinner at Russ's house one evening, Jane told Mak they'd have a lifetime for making adventurous trips. And he didn't need a wedding rehearsal; he should just do as he was told.

"You have my condolences," Austin said. He'd also said he wanted to make sure Jane was happily married before he left the island. Mak had gone with him to look over some property Austin might buy, and Mak thought that had a lot to do with Austin prolonging his stay. Austin told him he planned to go back and marry Rebecca. He'd already sent a letter so Rebecca could be making her plans.

The day finally arrived.

Doing as he was told, Mak holed up in Austin's hotel room. He did not see Jane all day and was told he wasn't supposed to.

When evening came, Austin drove him to the beach.

The public was invited, and it looked to Mak like more people lined the three-mile stretch of beach than at Christmastime. But then, Jane was now more of a celebrity than Santa. She'd become an island hero, and all the little girls wanted to be jockeys. Jane said they'd probably settle for being equestriennes.

Austin drove Mak right up to where chairs had been set out for personally invited guests. Mr. Buckley stood with his hands folded in front of his black formal suit and top hat.

Mak walked down the aisle, looking from side to side, greeting the guests. But where was Jane?

Reverend Russell stood smiling, in a light green robe beneath a white arbor elaborately decorated with every color and type of flower imaginable. "Stand here," the reverend told him, and Mak stood at one side of the arbor and faced his guests.

Music began. Mak looked to the side where a band of men he knew, some of his own paniolos, strummed love songs on their bragas. One began to sing. Pilar and Susanne, in light green dresses, passed out leis like the ones the two girls were wearing to the guests in chairs.

But where was Jane?

Seeing a movement up the beach, he thought his heart might beat right out of his chest. Riding up on her little white pony was his little girl. Mr. Buckley aided her in dismounting and handed her a basket.

In a white dress with a green sash and wearing a colorful lei, she paraded down the aisle, carefully dropping orchid petals. Seeing that she had some remaining when she reached the arbor, she looked concerned, then turned the basket up and let the rest of the petals float to where Jane should be standing. With a big smile, she turned, sat in a chair beside his mom, and smoothed her skirt, looking like a little lady.

Hearing a cry go up and applause begin, he looked. Big Brown was galloping along the beach with Jane astride him, a long white cover over her lap and thighs and streaming out behind her like a wave on an ocean.

Several persons helped her get rid of the cover, groomed her long, brown, sun-brushed hair that took on the golden glow of the sun. While love songs were being sung, Jane's father escorted her down the aisle.

Happiness flooded Mak's soul, yes, his soul as well as his heart, as he thanked God for this gift that, not long ago, he could never have imagined could be his. White flowers and green leaves encircled Jane's head. She carried a bouquet of white orchids and green leaves, with long green ribbons flowing from it.

As the color of the sky changed to deep gold with a touch of crimson, Pilar and Susanne handed both the bride and groom a white and green lei.

"You may exchange the leis as a symbol of your love for each other," the reverend said, and Mak slipped the lei over Jane's head and lifted her long, soft, fragrant hair, taking a moment to revel in the feel of it as he had never dared do before.

She placed her lei over his head.

Mak could not take his eyes from her. The reverend said many things, and one that registered was, "What God has joined together, let no man put asunder."

At the appropriate time, Mak slipped on her vacant finger a band set with small emeralds that matched the larger set of the engagement ring they'd picked out together.

She said it had to be green, in memory of the night of the sunset when he'd taken her breath away.

"I now pronounce you man and wife. You may kiss the bride."

And he did.

After a moment, Jane leaned away. "Remember your instructions to a race-horse. Don't give it your all until you come into the home stretch."

He exhaled heavily. "Good advice."

The reverend had the guests stand and led them in singing "Blest Be the Tie That Binds."

Mak and Jane hurried up the aisle. He mounted Big Brown and lifted Jane in front of him. As they rode across the beach in the golden, crimson evening toward the ranch, Jane turned her face toward him. "I've practiced this," she said. "Aloha au la oe."

Thanking God for his being the most blessed man in the world, Mak said, "I love you, too."

PICTURE BRIDE

Dedication

To Carmen Leal for her suggestion of a picture-bride story, and to DiAnn Mills for her invaluable comments.

Author's Note

The term *picture bride* refers to the practice in the early twentieth century in which tens of thousands of immigrant workers (chiefly Japanese and Korean) in Hawaii and on the West Coast of the United States selected brides—sight unseen—from their native countries. A matchmaker (also called a *marriage handler* or *go-between*) paired bride and groom using only photographs and family recommendations of the possible candidates. This is a practice akin to traditional arranged marriages, the securing of brides from Europe by the early settlers of the American continent, and the concept of mail-order brides.

Chapter 1

Spring 1910, San Francisco

This is so unfair."

Mary Ellen Colson smiled at her sister's outburst. She looked up from the papers on her desk and at Breanna, who mumbled, "Europe." After filing the papers in the metal cabinet, Breanna picked up another folder. "Japan."

She walked to another cabinet, and a ray of late afternoon sun shone against the tendrils of her golden blond hair falling gracefully along the sides of her pretty face.

Having filed that stack, Breanna came over for others. Her eyes, usually as blue as a peaceful sky, seemed filled with emotion reminiscent of a cloudy day.

"What now?" Mary Ellen said, although she'd heard every reason for her sister's dissatisfaction. Breanna called it boredom. Mary Ellen called it teenage wanderlust.

Breanna sighed. "I spend my days in school, afternoons in this stuffy old office, and nights in the dingy boardinghouse, studying. I mean, that's my life. And old Mr. Crank won't give me a penny of my own money." Making circles with her thumbs and index fingers, she put them up to her eyes.

"That's not funny," Mary Ellen chided.

Breanna struck a pert pose. "Then why did you laugh?"

"Because of the face you made. Not because you called Mr. Frank a crank."

"That's how he looks with his mouth turned down and his eyes squinted behind those dark-rimmed glasses."

Mary Ellen picked up the letter opener and sliced the edge of another envelope. "What would you do if Mr. Frank gave you money?"

Without hesitation, Breanna picked up the sides of her dress, exposing her ankles above the flats she wore to school. She curtsied to a make-believe partner and danced a graceful imitation of a reel. "I'd see the world."

After a few more dainty steps, her expression turned serious. She grasped the sides of the desk. "Oh Mary Ellen. People pass through this office, mainly only in letters and folders. But they represent people traveling to and from all parts of the world. Outside these windows are the real people coming and going. I want to be one of those persons who does something. Who goes somewhere."

"You're still in school, Breanna."

"I'll graduate in a couple of months. But I won't have any money until I'm twenty."

"That's only a little over two years."

"But I don't want to get stuck. Like you. You've never been anywhere. You don't meet any. . .men." She groaned. "I mean, I know you're more like Uncle Harv. But I'm not." She stomped a foot and nodded. "I'm different."

"You're going to be penniless if you don't finish that filing."

With a moan and slump of her shoulders, Breanna picked up the stack, laid it on Uncle Harv's desk, and resumed her filing.

Mary Ellen took the folded paper from the envelope she held, but her thoughts delved into the past when the 1906 earthquake and fire had taken their parents. Any fanciful dreams of hers had been swallowed up by the quake and burned up in the fire. Being five years older than Breanna, she'd tried be like a mother to her. So many times, she felt she'd failed.

And being like Uncle Harv? Mary Ellen knew Breanna was referring to his being a confirmed bachelor. That's how he liked his life. Mary Ellen didn't like the idea of being a spinster. But she had never allowed herself to consider taking a man seriously as long as Breanna needed her. And she did need her, whether or not she knew it.

Mary Ellen understood the job was boring to Breanna—although she worked only a couple of hours after school.

Much of the office work was routine, checking arrival and departure passenger lists. Accuracy of names, surnames, age, gender, ethnicity, nationality of the last country of permanent residence, and arrival date or departure dates needed to be noted. If the individual was going to join with a friend or relative, that had to be checked out.

With a sigh, Mary Ellen unfolded the form in her hands, expecting it to be like thousands she'd dealt with over the past few years.

But her fingers brushed against a square of photo-quality paper as it fell to the desk. She read the writing on the back:

> *American citizen, seeking a young American*
> *blond woman for a bride.*
> *Occupation: sugar plantation in Hawaii*
> *I am a moral person.*
> *If you can help, please reply to:*
> *C. Honeycutt*
> *General Delivery, Post Office*
> *Hilo, Hawaii*

This was highly unusual. Mary Ellen turned the photo over and gazed at something even more unusual. Staring at her was a man with a perfect face. One couldn't be sure of color in a black-and-white photo, but the wavy hair and eyes were definitely dark. Instead of a posed expression, he had a rather roguish look with a slight tilt of his head, a hint of a grin on his lips. His eyes seemed to tease.

She estimated his age anywhere from twenty-five to thirty. Hearing her breath, caused by an increase in heart rate, she placed her hand on her chest and felt the fast beating.

That was unusual, too, her having a reaction over a photo of an appealing man as if she were a teenager like Breanna seeing an acclaimed stage actor. Oh, but Breanna could have a conniption just seeing a boy on the street.

Well, she could look at the form. This man could be seeking an American he'd lost touch with.

No. The information on the form was from a Japanese male, aged forty-two.

The photo should not have been with the Japanese man's form. Maybe she should contact C. Honeycutt and inform him the office did not handle requests like this.

The return address revealed it came from the immigration office. But Mr. C. wanted a reply to general delivery at a post office. This was by no means official.

Maybe. . .she shouldn't bother Uncle Harv with it. Perhaps the man got caught up in the thousands of picture brides arriving in Hawaii and impulsively did this to see what might happen. What kind of man would do such a thing?

Well, a man looking for an American wife? But why blond?

Despite what Breanna thought, Mary Ellen was not completely devoid of appreciating a little joke. And this did give her a moment's respite from the usual business of the day. This Mr. C.'s occupation was working at a sugarcane plantation.

Uncle Harv, who had been to Hawaii to inspect their office, had spoken of green sugarcane fields flowing across the land like waves across the ocean.

"What are you doing, Mary Ellen?"

"Huh?"

Mary Ellen left the green cane fields and focused on Breanna, sitting in Uncle Harv's chair. "You've been staring at your desk forever, and you're about to twist the button off your blouse."

"Oh." Mary Ellen stopped twisting. "I was daydreaming."

Breanna giggled. "I didn't think you did that."

Neither did I. She eased the form over the photo. Breanna noticed and came over. "What do you have there?"

"Just the usual form and—"

Before Mary Ellen could stop her, Breanna picked up the photo. "Oh, he's gorgeous. If I had a button on my blouse, I'd twist it off, too." She sighed. "Now see, if I could travel—"

Her words stopped in midair when she turned the photo over and read the message. Then she looked at the form. "These came in the same envelope?"

"They did. But this photo should not be in here."

Breanna gasped like she'd received an early Christmas present. "Oh, I think it should."

"No." Mary Ellen reached for the photo. "We have to show this to Uncle Harv."

"My foot!" Breanna held it away. "I have to think about this."

You?

Mary Ellen should answer that, for once in her life, maybe she would like to think about something different, however illusive. But that was foolish, and she couldn't blame it on teenage immaturity. She was twenty-three years old and had made a commitment to be there for Breanna as long as her sister needed her.

Breanna returned to Uncle Harv's desk and moistened her red, heart-shaped smiling lips with her tongue, as if the man in the photo were good enough to eat.

"Dream on if you want," Mary Ellen said. "Then come back to reality."

The door opened, and Uncle Harv walked in, looking his usual dapper, middle-aged self. "Good afternoon, ladies. How is everything?"

Mary Ellen opened her mouth to speak, but Breanna beat her to it. "Same as usual. Nothing out of the ordinary. Forms for your approval are right here." She laid her hands on the pile as if she had been the one who had reviewed them. "And I've filed folder after folder all afternoon."

"Good." He smiled at her, nodded at Mary Ellen, stuck his cane in the ceramic urn by the door, and hung his top hat on a coatrack peg.

Mary Ellen shot a warning glance at Breanna, who simply stood and motioned for her uncle to sit at his desk. He sat, straightened his tie, and focused on the forms he needed to review, then approve or disapprove.

Breanna continued filing and slid a glance at Mary Ellen. Her face was the epitome of innocence. There was no photo in sight, but she did have a large skirt pocket.

Mary Ellen knew what she would say if she were as young as Breanna, or as pretty, or as impulsive, or as lacking in sense.

Even if the photo and message were a mistake or a prank, she would have said something like, *I saw him first. . . .*

This is so unfair.

❧

Green fields of long, slender sugarcane leaves rippled in the wind like ocean waves. The breeze tugged at her hair, her dress, and her heart. An emotional breathless feeling was overwhelming as a tall, dark-haired man with eyes full of mischief strode toward her. His smile meant she was the joy of his life and she—

She began to cough and struggled to sit up, trying to get her breath.

"Mary Ellen, are you all right?"

After several deep breaths and attempts at clearing her throat, Mary Ellen managed to speak. "I got. . .choked."

"Ugh! Maybe you swallowed a bug."

It was Mary Ellen's turn to say, "Ugh." She pictured a roach like the occasional ones showing up in the kitchen, causing the cook and landlady to go on a cleaning frenzy and sprinkle powdered poison in pantries and corners. Swallowing a bug wasn't what happened. "It was my own saliva."

Breanna laughed, getting up to pull the string for the overhead light bulb, dispelling the faint morning sunrays seeping through the curtains. "Let that be a lesson. Don't spit in your sleep."

"I'll remember." Mary Ellen slipped to the side of the bed and stepped into her slippers. What she intended to remember was to dispense with foolish dreams. She had not gone to sleep thinking about Mr. C., except she'd prayed Breanna would forget the photo and any notion of going to Hawaii to meet a stranger.

"Did you—" No, she wouldn't ask if Breanna had dreamed. "Did you sleep well?"

"Like a newborn baby." A playful look settled in her eyes. "Until somebody started choking herself."

Maybe Breanna hadn't taken the photo episode seriously. Neither of them mentioned it or going anywhere except school and work while they dressed for the day. Soon they descended the stairs to go into the dining room for breakfast.

After Mary Ellen took the cable car to the office, she poured hot tea into a cup. "Uncle Harv." She set the cup and saucer in front of him. "On your trip to Hawaii, did you see the Honeycutt sugarcane plantation?"

"Of course, my dear. It's the largest on the big island. After the United States annexed the islands, I was sent there to ensure all those foreign workers and picture brides were needed."

"Did you meet any Honeycutts?"

After taking a sip of tea, he shook his head. "Don't believe I did. My contacts were government officials." He laughed lightly. "Although government officials are made up of businessmen and landowners. Why do you ask? Is there some discrepancy?"

His shoulders straightened, and he focused on her. Uncle Harv was meticulous about his work.

"I come across the name of Honeycutt quite often."

"Well, like I said, men and women are coming and going from those plantations all the time, and I'm sure you've seen the name on bags of sugar."

Honeycutt Sugar. Yes, she had. She'd never had occasion to buy any. She and Breanna ate most of their meals at Mrs. Bonemark's Boarding House and occasionally went to a restaurant.

"The Honeycutts are well respected, I'm sure."

He nodded. "The landowners are descendants of the early missionaries. Many are American, European, Scottish. Most of the workers are Asians, primarily from Japan."

Mary Ellen knew of the overpopulation of males in America and in Hawaii. Men had immigrated from Europe and Asia, looking for better jobs. The American citizens, however, could advertise for a mail-order bride through a catalog or correspond with Europeans and meet women through families, or photos, or in person. So why had Mr. C. sent that photo?

She'd been intrigued with the picture-bride process after coming to work for the immigration office. Some requests came to the United States, but hundreds of Japanese women left their countries and voyaged to Hawaii each month to marry men they'd never met.

"Amazing, isn't it, Uncle? Men and women are willing to marry each other sight unseen."

He sniffed. "More amazing is that they marry at all."

At her gasp, he looked at her, and a rare spark touched his eyes. "I'm joking with you."

If he hadn't told her, she would not have known. Uncle Harv didn't joke.

He touched the bridge of his eyeglasses. "I'm not against marriage. It's just not for me."

She thought a hint of sadness touched his eyes, but they were immediately covered by his eyelids as he frowned at the papers in front of him. He picked up his cup, and if she hadn't known better, she'd have thought his hand shook a little. Was Uncle Harv getting old? But he was only in his mid-forties. Or did he have some kind of emotional tremor? She never thought of him as emotional.

A thought stabbed her. Breanna had described her as being like Uncle Harv. Did he pretend as much as she did? Pretend all was well and relationships didn't matter?

How did Breanna really see her? Was it not as a mother figure who put Breanna first, but as a domineering older sister who lacked human feelings? But she'd never wanted her sister feeling guilty that she'd sacrificed anything for her. She hadn't really. Breanna was her family. She loved her. They belonged together.

But now, Breanna wanted to break the bonds. That was part of growing up, she knew. Maybe, it was time for Mary Ellen to reveal she had some personality, had some impossible. . .dreams.

"Mary Ellen," she heard, and for an instant felt like she had when awakening from a dream, choking. "Are you all right?"

To be honest, no, she was not all right.

She was not content with her life being spent in this office. She was not content to try to keep Breanna from having fanciful dreams. She could not allow herself the luxury of dreaming.

Always. . .reality.

But suppose her imagination ran wild? Just for a moment?

"I was thinking, Uncle. You've traveled all over the world and say the United States is more prosperous than any other nation. Then why are so many also traveling to Hawaii?"

"Ah, my dear. Since America annexed Hawaii, it is not a foreign country. Hawaii is a paradise. A jewel in the sea. The new land of opportunity. It's like a conglomeration of all nations. On the island of Hawaii, you have the ocean and valleys at sea level; then you have the mountains, the tropical jungle, everything in one place—and a beauty unimaginable."

Mary Ellen caught her breath.

"There's always a soft breeze, and the sugarcane fields flow like gentle waves of an ocean as far as the eye can see." A trace of a smile touched his lips. "I've about had my fill of travel. But one place I wouldn't mind seeing again is Hawaii."

Could he possibly be a romantic at heart?

"Well," she said without putting a stop to her imagination now taking flight, "wouldn't the immigration office in Hawaii take you on as an inspector?"

"Surely. An American would be an asset to their office. Particularly one who has traveled the world. But I—" He shook his head. "I would not disrupt my life. It's planned. Settled."

"Would they hire an American woman who has worked in an immigration office in America? Even if she speaks only English and a little classroom French?"

He had become cardboard again. Blank eyes looked at papers in front of him. Just as she turned to pull up the chair to her desk, he said, "With the proper recommendation, that is likely."

For the rest of the morning, before Uncle Harv had to go to the port of entry to oversee the work of immigration inspectors, Mary Ellen opened envelopes, put forms or letters into their appropriate folders or piles, and deposited the needed ones on his desk.

Their conversation appeared to be forgotten.

Perhaps Breanna had forgotten Mr. C.'s photo and had gone on to another dream. The man was too. . .too what?

Too mature for her sister—that's what.

In two months, Breanna would be eighteen, out of school, and moving on to college or finding a position if she didn't work with Uncle Harv. She could do as she wished.

That meant Mary Ellen could have the luxury of making her own dreams.

What would they be?

Perhaps she could take a job at the immigration office in Hawaii. Of course, she wouldn't leave her sister behind. And Mary Ellen had her inheritance, small but enough for her needs until she could get proper wages. She would check out that Mr. C. Maybe he would prefer a more mature blond woman than Breanna.

"You seem in particular good spirits today," her uncle said. "Different somehow."

She smiled and shrugged as if she didn't know what he meant. But after he left the office, she positioned her chin on her clasped hands and pictured fields of green waving gently in the breeze, and she dared to believe. . .in dreams.

Could it be that in Mary Ellen Colson's future there was paradise?

Chapter 2

I nstead of taking the letters directly to the Hilo Post Office, he went in the opposite direction. He ducked into the Matti-Rose Inn.

Matilda caught him creeping down the hallway "What are you up to?" Her green eyes, set off by her thick red hair the color of Kilauea's volcanic fire on a dark night, must have guessed he was up to mischief.

"Emergency."

"The grandson of a missionary should be studying for the ministry, not sneaking around like he doesn't want anybody to see him."

"I just want to visit an inside bathroom. Maybe you shouldn't have installed those modern contraptions."

"Shouldn't you be working instead of being a *pupule kolohe*."

He laughed at her calling him a *crazy rascal* in the Hawaiian language. Shaking his head, he put his arm against his waist, hoping the envelopes wouldn't slip down his pants leg.

"Oh, I smell my pie." She headed to the kitchen.

Getting no response when he tapped on the bathroom door, he entered, closed the door, and slid the lock.

He rescued the envelopes and sat on the commode beneath the water tank. The box labeled SCOTT PAPER COMPANY that would be filled with small squares of tissue made a good table. He ignored the stirring of uncertainty in his stomach. He'd planned this and would see it through.

There was nothing unusual about his being at the immigration office since much of his duties required that. But for a while, he'd made a habit of stopping by when Mr. Hammeur was at lunch. Many times, it was his job to take the Japanese men to the office to help them fill out the forms for acquiring a wife. Too many men had lied about their age and the amount of money they had to lure some pretty little Japanese girl over here to marry them.

Well, now he understood better how a deceptive Japanese man might feel—guilty yet hopeful.

He'd offered to lick a few envelopes for Akemi when he saw the ones addressed to the office in San Francisco. He'd only pretended to moisten one of the flaps.

He slipped the photo into the envelope and licked the flap before he could change his mind. He left the bathroom and hurried out the front door before anyone could call to him and headed for the post office.

"We might be getting some special kind of mail from the mainland," he said to the clerk recently hired. Not that it mattered. Honeycutt mail was sent out and picked up at any time most days. "It will be addressed to C. Honeycutt for general delivery. Keep it separate from the other mail. I'll ask for it."

"No problem." The clerk took the letters. "All you have to do is ask for it."

Would it be that easy to get a beautiful blond from the American mainland? Just ask?

~

San Francisco

Mary Ellen kept glancing at the wall clock. Breanna always came straight to the office and rarely had after-school activities. At twenty minutes past the hour, her sister rushed in, breathless and with flushed cheeks.

"I was worried. Where've you been?"

"I stopped by the boardinghouse." She deposited her books onto Mary Ellen's desk and slipped out a photo that was tucked between the pages. "I had to find this."

She laid two photos in front of Mary Ellen. "Now, Miss Matchmaker. What do you think?"

Mary Ellen was not a matchmaker. She only matched up official forms and gave them to Uncle Harv, who approved or disapproved anyone requesting entry into the United States.

Mary Ellen would have to admit they appeared to be a perfect match—if Mr. C.'s request had been an official one.

The photo had been taken at Christmas when Breanna's light-colored hair hung in loose waves around her shoulders. She'd worn a stylish dress that Mary Ellen had made for Christmas. If Mr. C. saw that photo, he surely would be captivated by beautiful Breanna.

"Well, tell me." Breanna gripped the edge of the desk. "Is this the right picture to send?"

Mary Ellen needed to put aside her own foolish thoughts about Mr. C. The whole idea was preposterous. She looked up at her sister, who leaned over the desk. "If this were the right thing to do, this picture is the perfect one to send."

A delightful sound escaped Breanna's throat.

"This, however, is not the way to do things."

Breanna gazed at Mary Ellen. "We've talked about the hundreds and thousands who do this. Parents arrange marriages. Men order brides through catalogs. We work for an office that encourages the Asians to do that in Hawaii. So why is this so wrong?"

"It's wrong for you. It's just not right for us."

"Us?" Sadness settled in Breanna's eyes. "I'm a poor girl, without parents, without a dowry. What kind of man is going to be interested in the likes of me?"

"You're beautiful, Breanna. Everybody says that."

"A pretty face without money means nothing. I know I seem like a scatterbrain, but I don't want a man who would buy me because I'd look good on his arm."

Mary Ellen was glad to hear that.

"This is the best possibility I've had. Oh, the waiter at the restaurant, the half-dozen middle-aged friends of Uncle Harv, the gawking fishermen, even the Asians who aren't supposed to look at me, the boys I go to school with, and the bachelor teachers. And yes, I've been introduced to some of the more acceptable men at church. They're not acceptable to me." Breanna lifted her chin saucily. "Nor to you, so I've been told."

Mary Ellen had said she didn't know a man who appealed to her enough to get serious about. There had been a connection with William Barr, an assistant in the boys' dorm when she'd worked at the orphanage as a seamstress. They'd taken long walks and had ridden over pastureland together. But when he became too serious, she'd reminded herself she'd taken the job to be near Breanna.

"Oh, please, Mary Ellen. Loan me the money for passage. All yours does anyway is sit in the bank drawing interest. This is like—" She placed one hand over another where her heart was likely pounding furiously with anticipation. "Like my big chance in life."

"You're impatient. In a couple of years, you'll have the money that's in your trust fund. You'll think this photograph is ridiculous."

"Really? Look again."

Mary Ellen dared not lower her gaze, but focused on the wall clock. She was not surprised when Breanna declared, "I'm going to Hawaii even if I have to swim."

Her sister had a stubborn streak that could be difficult to reason with. But she had to try. "Look, Breanna. Uncle Harv is your legal guardian. But I'm your sister and have tried to look after you."

Breanna had the consideration to nod and look down at her hands clasped in front of her skirt. "I know that, Mellie. You won't believe this, but I have listened to you. And I pray every night that I'll do what's right."

Mary Ellen had to squeeze away the moisture forming in her eyes. Her sister could get to her, especially by calling her by the name Breanna had used when just a toddler.

"Mellie, I can't be content here, and I'm not a child anymore."

But either she or Breanna had to be sensible, and which one was clear as day. "This is not the legal process."

"Oh pooh on legal process. This is personal. Now, what do I do? Do I just send my photo and wait to hear from Mr. C.?"

"If I'm the matchmaker, then let me handle it."

"Oh, you'll scare him away."

"This is a lifetime decision. What the Asians are doing is different. Their culture is different. They're accustomed to having a relative or matchmaker pair them up with someone. And it has worked for them. Sometimes I wonder if that's not better than. . .than. . .butterflies in the stomach and bells in the brain."

Breanna put her hands on her hips. "How would you know about that?"

Mary Ellen looked down at her desk, and her gaze fell on Mr. C.'s photo. Her heart could go pitter-patter as quickly as any other girl's. She sighed. "Hawaii is over twenty-six hundred miles away, and you don't know anyone there."

"But Uncle Harv does. He told us about those nice people from the tourism department and the two women he dearly loved, who ran an inn where he stayed. I even have a pamphlet here somewhere." She opened her notebook and pulled it out. "This was written by Mark Twain. You know him?"

"Who doesn't know the most popular columnist for the *Sacramento Union!*"

Breanna wasn't much for reading the daily news. At least she was reading that entertaining column by Twain.

" 'No alien land in all the world has any deep strong charm for me but that one,' " Breanna read. " 'No other land could so longingly and beseechingly haunt me, sleeping and waking. . .' "

"Okay, Breanna. I'm the one who encouraged you to read his columns. And thousands of people are visiting there. I understand anyone could fall in love with that place. But. . ."

Mary Ellen closed her eyes rather than finish. Could she honestly say she didn't see how anyone could fall in love with a photo? Of course she could say it. Instead, she shook her head.

"Mellie, will you help me write the letter?"

If she said no, Breanna would write it herself and not ask the appropriate questions. "Yes, I'll help you."

What would she write if Breanna had not snatched the photo from her and if she had been imprudent enough to contact Mr. C. for herself?

Mary Ellen picked up a blank sheet of paper and rolled it into the typewriter. "Study." She pointed to the schoolbooks.

"Yes, ma'am." Breanna hurried over to sit in Uncle Harv's chair and opened a book. She looked at Mary Ellen, who gave her a warning glance. Then she seemed to read her book in earnest.

Mary Ellen almost giggled as she readied her fingers to type.

She thought of writing *Dear Sweetheart.*

But of course she wouldn't type that.

She cleared her throat as if she had done such a silly thing. She could see his face in her mind, those dark teasing eyes. She could imagine he would laugh if she typed those words. The room, however, was soon filled with the *click-clack* of the typewriter keys striking the roller:

Dear Mr. C.:
> *Your photo with the contact information on the back arrived at the immigration office. Perhaps this was sent by mistake, or perhaps it is a practical joke from someone else since there was no official form attached.*
> *If your intention is to find someone you've known, please inform us.*

If you are looking for an American bride at random, I would like to know that, too. If this is serious, please send more information.

Yours truly,
Miss Colson

She had not made any mistakes—unless the entire letter was a mistake. When she pulled the paper from the typewriter, Breanna made a beeline to her. She read it.

"No, Mary Ellen. If I send that, he will think I'm some stiff old prude like. . . like Uncle Harv."

Mary Ellen thought she was about to say *like you*. After all, Breanna had already accused her of being like Uncle Harv.

"What would you say?"

"Dear Sweetheart." Breanna giggled.

Mary Ellen closed her eyes and shook her head.

"Okay." Breanna conceded, seeming to think Mary Ellen would never be so bold or so flighty. "Now, type what I dictate."

Mary Ellen typed as her sister dictated.

"Not bad," she said when Breanna finished. That's what Mary Ellen would liked to have written. "Let's add the words *the Lord willing*."

Breanna's face screwed up. "The Lord willing?"

"He said he was a moral person. How can you be moral if you're not a Christian? That will let him know you're no heathen."

"I want to do this, Mary Ellen. And I prayed about it. See, I'm not completely a lost cause."

Mary Ellen felt a twinge of guilt. No, Breanna was a good girl. She studied hard and did the work assigned to her. So she fancied a more romantic life. Wasn't that better than deciding she may never have one?

The time had come for her sister to spread her wings. She had to reach out for life. Maybe what she dreamed of didn't exist in Hawaii.

But maybe it didn't exist in San Francisco either.

Mary Ellen felt as if she'd just lost a sweetheart. Nevertheless she said, "You won't be able to do this without Uncle Harv's approval. Let's make this legitimate, and see if he can get you a job at the immigration office in Hawaii. If you're still determined after you've finished the school year and turn eighteen, I'll give you the money for the trip."

Breanna threw her arms around Mary Ellen's shoulders. "I love you, Mellie. And when I get to Hawaii, I can turn down the marriage proposal if I don't like the man. But I do want your blessing."

"If this works out for you," Mary Ellen said, letting Breanna know she wanted her to be happy, "I'll make your wedding dress for you."

Chapter 3

Mary Ellen approached Uncle Harv the morning after the letter had been typed to Mr. C. She hadn't mailed it, wanting to make sure Breanna would not be alone in Hawaii with only a photo as her means of self-preservation.

"Uncle Harv." She set his cup of tea in front of him. "Could I talk with you. . . personally?"

"Of course, my dear." But he seemed quite surprised when she rolled her chair over to his desk. He moved his cup and saucer aside, took off his glasses, folded his hands in front of him, and gazed at her.

His face looked younger and even handsome without his glasses. Had he removed them to see her better or not to see her at all? But he was making an effort to listen.

She reminded him that he'd said the immigration office in Hawaii would be glad to hire someone from the United States.

"Yes, and I thought you might be considering such a change." He unclasped his hands and laid the palms flat on his desk. "You have every right."

Surprised at his discernment, Mary Ellen stared at his hands toying with his glasses. He focused again on her. "I know Hawaii is appealing, and I'm afraid my descriptions have made it so."

She realized for the first time that his blue eyes resembled her mother's eyes, which many people said were like hers and Breanna's.

The similarity gave her a warm feeling for him. He began saying how much he had appreciated her work. "Although it's been over four years since the earthquake and fires that destroyed so many records, there is still work to be done in that area. You've been invaluable to this office."

That touched her. "Uncle Harv, it's Breanna who wants to make the trip to Hawaii."

He looked dumbfounded. "I thought you—"

"Breanna is intent upon this."

The look of relief on his face prompted her to speak further of Breanna's determination to leave when she reached the age of eighteen.

He nodded as she spoke, then gave his opinion. "Her work experience is limited. But she does speak English, and she can file." Putting his hand to his mouth, he cleared his throat. "I could recommend her for the Hawaii office. If they accept her, then the office will pay her passage."

Oh no. If it were discovered there had been a deception and Breanna's reason for going to Hawaii was Mr. C.'s photo, there could be trouble for Uncle

Harv, Breanna, even Mr. C., and herself. The authorities might take control.

"No, Uncle Harv. Please let me pay Breanna's passage. I have been against her leaving. If I do this, it will show her I'm not angry. Things will be right with us again."

"Oh, she's not the kind of girl to be angry with anyone."

"Not angry, no. But hurt."

"Maybe I should pay—"

"Oh Uncle," she interrupted, not really knowing what he was about to say. "Her passage could be your going-away gift to her. And her birthday present."

"Yes," he said. "I like seeing her here. She is a breath of fresh air, although sometimes it seems she is more like a storm brewing. I've never paid her much"—he drew in a deep breath—"money or attention. I just—"

"Oh, we know you love us, Uncle Harv. We agreed the best place for Breanna was at the orphanage instead of with you, since you had no wife."

"You were good to work at the orphanage so you could be near her."

"You visited." He had made monthly visits to ensure they were cared for properly. "But she would be so grateful for you to pay her passage and give your blessing."

"You think so?"

"Yes. And so would I."

He lifted a hand. "Done. I'll book her passage on the best liner and find someone to watch over her."

She would like to hug him, mainly for this personal talk. However, he slipped the glasses over his eyes and slid his cup in front of him.

"Thank you, Uncle Harv. Let me get you some hot tea." She reached for his cup.

"Thank *you*." He stared at the papers on his desk. For some strange reason she thought he was thanking her for something other than a cup of hot tea.

&

Hilo, Hawaii, one week later

"Any general delivery for Mr. C.?" He'd asked that for the past three days, although a carrier pigeon couldn't get a letter there so soon.

Now a week had passed from when the letter would have arrived in San Francisco. The clerk searched a stack and pulled out an envelope. That was it. A letter with the San Francisco postmark. He put that on top of Honeycutt mail he'd take to the office later.

He walked up the street to a restaurant and ordered a knife and a cup of coffee. His instinct was to rip it open, yet another part of him was concerned about what he'd find inside.

The waitress's stare questioned him. But he supposed not many people ordered a knife along with their coffee—and he'd asked that the knife be brought right away.

She brought it, laid it on the table, and took a step back.

He'd seen Akemi and other workers slice open envelopes with one quick movement. It didn't work that way for him, and he didn't like the little jagged edges he was making.

"Want me to do that for you?" The waitress was more amiable now that she saw his purpose for the knife.

"Please." His palms were sweaty.

She opened the envelope effortlessly and returned it, but took the knife away.

He felt the envelope. There seemed to be something like a photo in it, but maybe that was wishful thinking. He peeked inside. Okay. But the letter first. He laid the photo face down and read the letter:

> Dear Mr. C.,
>
> Your photo arrived at the immigration office. If you're serious, I'm interested. I am planning a trip to Hawaii within a few weeks, to the immigration office to be exact, where I expect to be offered a job.
>
> I shall be glad to speak with you, the Lord willing.
>
> I look forward to your reply.
>
> Yours truly,
> Miss B. Colson
> Immigration Office
> San Francisco, California USA

His thoughts trembled. His elation turned to suspicion. Miss B. probably worked at the San Francisco office since she now had a job in Hawaii. The immigration office wouldn't normally hire someone sight-unseen and without references.

The waitress brought his coffee, and his mind conjured up new possibilities. Maybe she was a middle-aged spinster. If she was part of that office, she might have a way of making him marry her even if he wasn't pleased or if she was too old. Until now, he hadn't thought about the negative aspects. She didn't mention being blond. If this was legitimate, she was fat and ugly.

Why would any decent-looking America woman travel this far to meet him? Was she desperate? Was this God's will, or was she some kind of prudish religious fanatic by saying *if the Lord was willing*?

Why?

Why? He emitted a short laugh.

The photo.

That's why.

With that, his mind eased, and he slowly turned over the photo. It took his breath away.

No, he mustn't touch that coffee cup. He would surely spill it. His hand might never stop shaking. There was the most beautiful girl in the world. More beautiful than the widely acclaimed Akemi.

Miss B.

I am in love.

And I must do everything in my power to keep you from going to the immigration office before we talk.

A few weeks. Yes! He would reply immediately.

His mind came alive with plans.

Just as quickly, a new fear arose.

What if she misrepresented herself as some Japanese men had done in seeking a picture bride?

What if she turned out to be nothing like the beauty in the photo?

What if she was thinking the same thing about him?

Chapter 4

San Francisco, a week later

Mary Ellen held out the letter addressed to Miss B. Her sister squealed like a greased pig at the county fair caught by its hind legs.

Breanna had known at least a week would pass before a letter reached Hawaii, and another week for a reply to reach San Francisco. Nevertheless, she moaned that it was the longest two weeks of her life. She lived and breathed for a letter from Hawaii.

The thought occurred to Mary Ellen that Mr. C. might reply that Breanna looked much too young for him and ask if she had an older sister. But she knew that wouldn't happen.

Breanna's words confirmed that as soon as she began to read the letter. "He thinks I'm the most beautiful woman in the whole world."

Mary Ellen hoped her reply would not be perceived as jealousy. "There's no doubt about your looks, Breanna. Or his, judging by that photo. But building a life with someone takes more than having an appealing outer appearance."

Breanna spoke seriously. "But without something to excite you about another person, wouldn't marriage be like. . .just another job?"

Mary Ellen supposed she had a point. Breanna slumped into a chair as if the words in that letter weakened her knees. A few ahs and oohs escaped her throat while she held what appeared to be another photo. Finally, she clutched the letter and photo to her chest. "You can stop worrying. This is much deeper than how he looks. His words are touching my heart."

What did a man like Mr. C. say to touch a woman's heart? She waited. But Breanna did not share what the man of her dreams had written. Looking at the contemplative, secretive smile on her sister's face, Mary Ellen suspected her sister had, seemingly overnight, become a young woman.

Mary Ellen walked to the window, feeling quite alone now that Breanna had pulled out a sheet of stationery and concentrated on what she was writing, likely a response to Mr. C.

Breanna considered Mary Ellen as having lived in the dark ages. And in a way, she had. Candles and oil lamps were becoming a thing of the past. One could now walk at night without a lantern. In the city, gaslights bordered the streets, and electric lights shone from the windows of many homes.

Life was moving at a fast pace. When Mary Ellen was Breanna's age, horses were the main mode of transportation. Now cable cars were full of passengers. Buses and automobiles were fast replacing horses. Her own life seemed to be at a standstill. But she should be thankful. She had prayed that Breanna would enjoy her young life. It seemed that her prayer was being answered.

The Hilo immigration office sent a letter from Mr. Hammeur, assuring Uncle Harv that the recommendation from him was well received and a position would be made available for his niece.

"That's nice," Breanna said when Mary Ellen told her, as if she were speaking of a typical sunny day and not what might keep her in the necessities of life.

Uncle Harv began to spend more time in the office, and he talked more. He spoke of the time, not too many years ago, when the passage to Hawaii from San Francisco took at least five months. Now, the voyage could be made in five days, or a week at the most.

The days seemed to be passing as quickly as those steamboats he talked about plowing across the ocean. Breanna's time was taken up with school, planning what she would pack for the trip, and writing letters to Mr. C., who sent one or two letters a week. She said he was describing Hawaii and telling all about himself. But she did not share those details with Mary Ellen.

Uncle Harv booked passage for the day after Breanna's eighteenth birthday and contacted a middle-aged couple who had booked passage at the same time. They expressed delight at functioning as Breanna's guardians on the voyage.

Single young men at church expressed disappointment that lovely Breanna would be leaving to work in Hawaii, which sounded so permanent. The young women wanted to accompany her. Mary Ellen didn't say so, but so did she.

Mr. Frank disapproved when Mary Ellen told him of her need to make a withdrawal. Being her financial adviser, he had every right to express his opinion. "It's your money, of course," Mr. Frank said. "But this is a large amount."

She told him about Breanna's new job in Hawaii. He wasn't pleased. "She has badgered me for her money for at least two years. I hope you aren't going to let her waste yours. You planned to buy a home together, and you've been faithful to add to your account monthly." He scoffed. "She has never added one penny."

"She works only a few hours a week," Mary Ellen said in defense of her sister. "She contributes to our well-being."

"Yes." His eyes rolled like he didn't believe a word of it.

"She's just a child, Mr. Frank."

"Yes. And that child is off to Hawaii alone?"

Mary Ellen could have asked who could stop her. Instead, she said, "Breanna is almost eighteen."

His yes sounded like a moan. "I've been eighteen, believe it or not, and had two boys who were in that dastardly state of being." He mumbled, "Still are, if you ask me." But he wrote her check. "Here you are. It's your money."

Their gazes held. He seemed to be saying it had just become Breanna's money. But a sister had an obligation to make sure her younger sister had enough money to live on until she could earn a wage in Hawaii.

Mary Ellen needed to give Breanna both a birthday and going-away present.

And as an expression of her blessing, she would make the most beautiful wedding dress in the world for the world's most attractive couple.

Finally, the day arrived when Mary Ellen and Uncle Harv stood on the dock and waved good-bye to Breanna. All too soon, the steamship disappeared into the horizon.

The days passed slowly, and Mary Ellen knew firsthand how Breanna had felt while waiting for a letter from the island.

Two weeks after Breanna's departure, Mary Ellen could share with Uncle Harv that a postcard had arrived:

Dear Mary Ellen,
    Arrived today. All is better than I expected. Not working at the immigration office.
    Don't worry if I don't write for a while. Getting settled. And I won't marry without you here.
    My best to Uncle Harv.
    Thank you both again.

        I love you, Breanna

Mary Ellen felt like she'd been holding her breath until a message came. Uncle Harv was pleased, too, but concerned. "Does that mean she is not working at the office yet? Or not planning to?"

A shrug was all she could offer him. If all was well with Mr. C., he might not want his wife to work. Maybe tomorrow a long letter with details would arrive.

It didn't.

But getting settled would take time. Breanna might be looking for a job somewhere other than at the immigration office since she had enough money to live on for a while.

But she'd written that she would not marry without her sister there. Mary Ellen went shopping. The first stop was for the latest Parisian fashion magazine for the designs of the newly acclaimed Coco Chanel. At the cloth shop, she acquired materials and patterns she could modify, if necessary, to be exactly like a Parisian gown. She envisioned thousands of seed pearls on her beautiful sister's wedding gown.

The following day, Uncle Harv frowned when he read the letter from the Hawaiian immigration office. "It's been three weeks since she arrived in Hilo," he said. "But she still has not reported to the office."

"Then her remark on the postcard meant she did not intend to work at the immigration office. Or being adventurous like she is, she will want to see the sights of Hawaii you've talked about."

"I suppose."

A week later, no further word had come from Hawaii. Something didn't feel right. What was Breanna doing?

There was one way to find out.

Mary Ellen decided Breanna needed her more than Uncle Harv did. She dreaded having to tell him.

"Uncle Harv. I must go to Hawaii."

He shocked her by saying, "I'm not surprised."

❧

On the second day of the voyage, the long, elegant steamship seemed like no more than a flyspeck on a vast ocean that could be swallowed up in hungry, chomping waves. Storm clouds rolled in, and lightning split the sky. While the ocean slammed the portholes and the ship rocked, Mary Ellen prayed and tried to believe the captain and crew when they assured the passengers all was well. They would be out of the storm soon, and the ship had been through much worse. They knew the routes.

Mary Ellen shuddered to think what passengers had gone through when the trip had taken five months. Riding the waves for even one day during a storm was scary enough.

The passengers sat at tables in the dining room at mealtimes, talked and laughed perhaps a little too much to cover any anxiety. The musicians played much louder than when the sea had been calm.

Mary Ellen thought of it as analogous to her feelings over the past weeks. She'd lectured herself, prayed, and tried to accept what Breanna planned to do, but her emotions had been in turmoil.

She'd met many of the passengers during the ship's welcome party the first night. Most were Americans. Although some were travelers and tourists from Europe, many were businessmen, and some were honeymooners.

Several passengers were government officials whom Uncle Harv knew personally. Mary Ellen accepted the invitation to sit at a table for meals with a family going to Honolulu on vacation. They were from England and had visited a daughter in San Francisco. The parents had two young boys and a seventeen-year-old girl named Enid.

Mary Ellen glanced questioningly at Enid, who kept moving her hand to the side of her skirt.

Finally, the girl sighed. "I have a tear in my gown. It caught on a deck chair when the wind started blowing."

"I can mend it for you." Mary Ellen had brought along her sewing equipment since there had not been time for her to finish making Breanna's dress.

By the time she'd mended the dress, they had become friends. Mary Ellen arranged the girl's hair in a becoming style, as she had done for Breanna many times.

"Your hair is such a pretty color," Enid said.

"Thank you." Mary Ellen glanced at her hair in the mirror. She'd become accustomed to wearing it in a roll above her ears and around to the back of her head. She wore jeweled combs on special occasions, which had been few.

She focused on Enid's brown hair. The girl was plain, but with a little fixing up, she presented a comely appearance. She and her parents were quite pleased with the attractive young woman Enid had become.

Sometime during the night, either the storm abated or the ship navigated out of it. The sunshine greeted them on a calm ocean, and Mary Ellen started a morning Bible study on deck.

Parents were glad to have their children involved in scripture study, and a few mothers attended. She patterned it after the Bible studies she'd helped with at the orphanage. After she and Breanna moved to the boardinghouse, Mary Ellen had kept up the practice. At the orphanage, the girls weren't allowed to question the scripture. But with Mary Ellen, Breanna had questioned almost everything, and often Mary Ellen felt she couldn't answer sufficiently.

She would soon see her darling Breanna. She'd been lonely without her. She anticipated the exuberant hugs they would exchange and the exciting Hawaiian adventures her sister would relate.

Perhaps Mr. C. would be standing there, hat in hand, his face aglow with his appreciation of Breanna. Mary Ellen would not allow her heart to beat fast as it had done when she looked at his photo. As the sea calmed, so would she. She would be the spinster sister-in-law to Mr. C. Not because she couldn't have gotten a man, but because she had put Breanna first.

"*Kala mai ia'u.*"

Mary Ellen stood with Enid at the railing, looking out over the ocean for any sight of land when the words sounded over the loudspeaker.

"This is your captain speaking. I have just wished you a good evening. My Hawaiian is limited, and my pronunciation is atrocious, but I want to say your voyaging with us has been a pleasure. Farewell, until we meet again. Aloha, *a hui hou.*"

Enid shrugged. "I only see water."

"Maybe he climbed up there." Mary Ellen pointed to the sail high above them. "And has binoculars."

In a matter of moments, the deep blue of the water and sky began to turn red. Far on the horizon, a jagged dark edge emerged.

Enid gasped. "You don't think that's another volcano eruption, do you?"

"No. It's the sunset. My uncle described the sunsets as scarlet or crimson. He says the color is more brilliant and different than anywhere he's ever traveled. And he's been all over Europe. Even went to Japan when he was a boy. His parents were in the shipping business."

"Oh, people can go anywhere nowadays," Enid said. "I mean with steamship travel. And automobiles. We have one."

"Uncle Harv has one for business and one of his own."

"I guess America had telephones before we did. And electricity. That's why everybody wants to come to America." Enid sighed. "You get everything first."

"Oh no. We still don't have the English accent."

Enid laughed.

The horizon continued to rise out of the ocean as the world turned to scarlet. By the time they docked, the red sun had dipped into the ocean, and the sky deepened to magenta. Tall trees appeared like gigantic umbrellas, protecting the island from hot sun or rain, although she'd heard rain rarely fell on most of Hawaii.

"Look." Enid pointed.

Passengers had gathered around the ship's railing, looking and waving. Mary Ellen had been told that men in canoes would meet the ship. Even in the fading sun, this was an impressive scene. Using their strong arms, bronzed men with garlands of flowers draped around their necks and down their chests rowed the canoes.

In San Francisco she might have been embarrassed to see so many men without shirts. But they looked natural—as if they fit right in with this exotic island.

"Are they wearing skirts?" Enid asked.

"Looks like it." Mary Ellen observed the red, orange, yellow, and green material wrapped around them. "But they are handsome and colorful."

"Pretty as a parrot." Enid giggled. Her eyes widened. "You think they're going to kidnap us?"

Mary Ellen glanced from the men to Enid. "We should be so lucky."

The rhythm of the oars made music with the water, and the canoes formed paths of white-tipped furrows on the ocean. When they neared the ship, they lifted their oars and shouted, "Aloha. *Komo mai.*" They turned in unison and led the ship into dock.

Ahead on the beach stood men, women, and children dressed in colorful clothes and flowered necklaces.

When Enid and her family bade her good-bye, Mary Ellen assured them that her sister would meet her. As she walked down the gangplank, she tried to take in the scene around her while remaining on the lookout for Breanna. Greetings and welcomes began from the moment passengers' feet touched the white sandy beach.

She felt bombarded with music, greetings, and conversations. Some women carrying colorful leis and wearing white blouses and flowered skirts were telling others they were from the tourism company. She didn't see Breanna. But the beach was crowded with welcomers, passengers, crew members taking baggage off the ship, and men at the dock coming forward to help.

Maybe she should have contacted someone, perhaps the tourism company. She had felt it useless to send a letter to the immigration office since Breanna had written she was not working there. Mary Ellen sent her letters to C. Honeycutt at general delivery, that being her one way of contacting her sister.

She scanned the crowd. Breanna should be rushing toward her. She should have gotten the message.

Trying to dispel her growing anxiety, she focused on the music, flowers, laughter, anything that spoke of her having landed in a magical place.

The crowd, however, was dwindling. Palms swayed in the chilly breeze. Shadows were moving in.

But her sister was nowhere in sight.

Chapter 5

Aloha, my dear. Welcome to Hawaii," said a pleasant female voice. Oh my, the sun had set, but it seemed to have risen in this woman. The coppery-red hair was akin to that sunset, and her eyes even in this creeping twilight were as green as the pictures of Hawaii's famous grasses.

Mary Ellen looked into the face of a lovely, exuberant woman, maybe around sixty years old, dressed like a stylish San Francisco woman. The lovely, elegant woman with her smiled, said aloha, and draped a flowered lei over Mary Ellen's head.

"I'm Matilda," the colorful woman said, "and this is Rose. We help with the tourism office, but we are not official greeters. We're just your friendly, everyday persons who want you to feel at home and make sure things go as you expect here."

If she represented an everyday woman, then Hawaii's advertisements didn't do it justice. "Thank you." Mary Ellen felt like she was among friends.

"Are you expecting someone to meet you?" Rose said. "We know everyone and everything around here."

"My sister, Breanna Colson. I haven't received a letter from her in a while, but I wrote to say I was coming. Maybe she was delayed."

"Breanna Colson." Matilda glanced at Rose, who didn't offer any information. Their lack of knowledge about her sister seemed to indicate there were some things they didn't know.

"She's younger than I. She's eighteen. We resemble each other—coloring and everything—but she's prettier."

Matilda scoffed. "I can't imagine any girl prettier than you."

Rose nodded agreement.

That confirmed it. They hadn't seen Breanna.

"Do you have an address," Rose said, "or some way to contact her?"

Mary Ellen hesitated, not wanting to say the name of the man in the photo. He might not take kindly to her revealing he advertised for a bride. "I sent my letters to general delivery at Hilo Post Office."

Matilda waved. "This may be as simple as her not picking up her mail."

"My uncle sent a letter to the Hilo immigration office, and they offered her a job. She helped out in the San Francisco office. Uncle Harv is an official. He—"

"Harv?" Matilda squealed. "Not Harv Skidmore."

Mary Ellen nodded but wondered if Matilda thought that was good or bad.

Rose punched Matilda's arm. "The same Harv Skidmore we did the town with? Yes. He was from San Fran."

"Exactly," Matilda said. "Oh, we had some grand nights."

Mary Ellen was dumbfounded. Uncle Harv struck her as being rather stodgy. She couldn't imagine him doing the town. On the other hand, she could imagine these women doing it—whatever it entailed.

"You said she's working at the immigration office?"

"She wrote that she didn't take the job. I haven't heard from her in several weeks." Oh, how could this have happened?

As if she didn't know. It happened because of a photo of a handsome man with daring eyes.

"I don't know where to go, what to do—"

"Fluff and feathers," Matilda said. "You know us. Now, how long has your sister been here?"

"A little more than six weeks."

Despite the many sounds around them, a silence seemed to settle. Then Matilda, in her positive tone of voice, reasoned aloud. "You said she didn't take the job at the immigration office. She might have gone to another of our islands. She could be on a boat that's running late. Don't worry. If she doesn't show up in a little while, you can come with us. We'll leave word around here that she's expected, and they can tell her to come to our place."

"Your place?"

"The Matti-Rose Inn."

She breathed easier, hearing the name of the inn Uncle Harv had spoken about. Maybe he *had* done the town with these two.

"We live in a house near the inn," Matilda said. "We like to be near town so we can know everything that goes on."

Mary Ellen was reluctant to say it, but she must. "But you don't know anything about my sister?"

"That means," Rose said quickly, "if anything troubling had happened, we would know about it. This is just some misunderstanding."

"Come home with us." Matilda smiled and touched her arm. "Tomorrow, we can decide what to do. But first, let's ask around the docks." She called, "Billy! Jack!" A young man and a muscular middle-aged man looked around. She motioned, and they hurried to them. Matilda asked if they'd seen a pretty young blond woman in the past couple of months or so. "She would look something like this one."

Mary Ellen thought, judging from their broad smiles, they maybe looked at her a little too long.

While they appraised her, Matilda explained. "Blonds always attract attention because so many Asians with dark hair are arriving constantly."

"You mean the picture brides?"

Both women nodded.

The men said they didn't remember anyone that fit Breanna's description.

"If you see a blond, tell her to come to the reverend's house or the Matti-Rose."

"Yes, ma'am," the older man said. "You want us to get her baggage?"

At Matilda's questioning glance, Mary Ellen nodded and pointed out which were her bags and trunk.

The men apparently knew the nearby wagon belonged to these women. They thrust her bags into it, and both hefted her trunk up beside them.

Matilda drew out a change purse from which she took a couple of gold coins. Their eyes grew as wide as their smiles. "I can take these to the Matti-Rose, if you want me to," the younger one said.

"Take us all to the reverend's house, Billy."

The young man jumped up onto the wagon seat and grabbed the reins. Mary Ellen followed Matilda and Rose as they stepped up into the wagon, and the three of them sat behind Billy. He flicked the reins, gave a command, and off the horse trotted away from the dock and along the street of a small town.

Mary Ellen saw no cars, but many people walked along the sidewalks. Matilda and Rose pointed out businesses and restaurants.

After they'd traveled not more than a half mile, the huge moon hung low in the sky, giving a soft yellow glow to the muted green grass, thick foliage, and tall palm trees.

"One of you is married to a reverend?" Mary Ellen said.

"No, dear. Rose and I have too much to do and too many places in the world to visit instead of taking on a man to tie us down."

"I was married for many years," Rose said. "I value those times, but now Matilda and I do as we please."

"The reverend was my brother," Matilda said. "He died a few years ago. Rose and I decided to stay here, renovate a little, get some electricity and a refrigerator. You could stay at the inn, but I think you'll enjoy being with us instead of where you have to traipse down the hall for a hot bath."

"That settles it. A hot bath would be heaven. But I've heard so many different stories. I wasn't sure what kind of facilities might be here. Even in San Francisco, many people have had electricity and phones and modern conveniences for only a few years."

"Oh, we know, dear," Matilda said. "Rose and I have traveled throughout Europe and the U.S. You see, I'm from Texas, and Rose is from Scotland."

Soon Billy drove up to a charming, two-story, white clapboard house surrounded by thick foliage. He jumped down and slid the trunk down a board he took from the back of the wagon. Matilda took the leather handle on one side of the trunk, and the two of them carried it up the steps, across the porch, and into the house.

"Let's just take these upstairs," Matilda said to Billy.

Mary Ellen and Rose followed with the other bags into a bedroom.

"Here you are." Matilda withdrew another gold coin and flipped it to Billy. He caught it as if he were accustomed to the game. He and Rose went downstairs.

"Freshen up if you need to," Matilda told her. "Then we'll trot over to the inn."

In the bathroom, Mary Ellen looked longingly at the claw-foot bathtub, but settled for washing her hands, splashing cold water on her face, and drying with the hand towel.

Returning to the bedroom, her attention was drawn to the trunk. She unfastened the leather straps and took a key from her purse and unlocked it. She removed the large bundle wrapped in tissue paper and laid it on the bed.

She carefully unrolled it, held it up to her, and walked to the mirror. She imagined the man in the photo standing next to the dress. He was in a black tux, standing tall and having the darkest hair and most brilliant eyes she'd ever seen. His straight nose and full lips made a perfect picture.

How much more appealing would he be in person? Breanna would be breathtakingly beautiful in the white dress. She could almost see the two of them together in front of the preacher, saying their vows.

"Mary Ellen?"

Her mouth opened and her eyes widened to see not Mr. C. standing beside her in the mirror, but Matilda.

"Oh."

> ~

"I didn't mean to startle you." Matilda touched the dress. "This is beautiful. Are you to be married?"

"It's for Breanna. For when she marries. I haven't finished it yet."

Matilda looked astounded. "You made this?"

"Yes. I took sewing in school and worked as the orphanage seamstress while Breanna was there. I thought we should be together, since we lost our parents."

"You've given up your life for her, haven't you, dear?"

"I didn't really have anything to give up. We lost everything in the earthquake and fire." She drew in a shaky breath. "Breanna and I are. . .family."

"What about your uncle?"

"It was comforting to know we had an uncle. But the relationship was really just a working one. He's a bachelor, set in his ways, and didn't want any females disrupting his life." She was quick to add. "But he always tried to do right by us. He just didn't know how to relate." She smiled. "Breanna came close to drawing him out of his shell. She's so appealing."

After a moment of thoughtfulness, Matilda smiled. "Consider me and Rose your family. We're here for you."

Mary Ellen had trouble keeping back the moisture that threatened her eyes when Matilda reached out and gently touched her cheek. She wished Breanna had met Matilda and Rose on her arrival.

As they trotted across the street and down the sidewalk, Matilda said, "Did your sister come to meet a man?"

Mary Ellen couldn't fathom why she would ask that, but she spoke truthfully. "Yes. She did."

When both women smiled, she said, "What?"

"Oh," Matilda said. "I'm just thinking about when I was eighteen. If a particular man were involved, I, too, might be delayed in meeting my sister. In fact, there was a span of ten years when I didn't see my brother. I loved him. But I was. . .occupied."

Mary Ellen thought of Mr. C.'s photo.

Before that, she would not have understood.

"This used to be the mission school," Matilda said when they stood in front of a two-story, white clapboard building. The upper and lower porches were surrounded by banisters. Light blue shutters flanked each side of the windows. A lava stone walkway was bordered by flowers and bushes that appeared to grow wild and natural.

Before they went inside, Matilda told her about Akemi, a girl who had traveled from Japan three years ago to become a picture bride when she was sixteen years old. "The man lied to her, so we could not let the marriage take place. She helps at the inn."

"She also works at the immigration office part-time," Rose said. "She might know if your sister went there."

They found Akemi in the kitchen. Mary Ellen was struck by the girl's beautiful fair face surrounded by straight black hair. Her dark eyes reflected the same friendliness as her smile.

Akemi bowed.

"Please. You don't need to bow to me."

"Oh, Miss Matilda and Miss Rose tell me that all the time. But I forget. I just naturally do it. Like you shake hands."

"Then it's okay."

Akemi made them each a cup of tea.

Mary Ellen took a picture from her pocket and handed it to Akemi. "My sister might have gone to the immigration office."

Akemi smiled. "She pretty like you." Then her face saddened. "Mr. Hammeur say American woman come work with us. But I no see her. If she come to the office, I remember." She shook her head. "Sorry my English not good."

"You speak fine. I understood."

"She's very smart," Matilda said. "Working part-time at the immigration office, helping at the inn, and taking a few classes at school."

Akemi smiled shyly. "I try. Maybe your sister come when I away from office."

Mary Ellen didn't like seeing the sadness on Akemi's face. "Maybe she didn't go to the office. She decided not to work there. She's. . .headstrong."

"Oh, we identify with that, don't we, Rose?" Matilda said.

Rose laughed. "Even more so after I became acquainted with Matilda. But don't you worry. If your sister comes tonight after you're asleep, we will wake you."

Mary Ellen tried to dismiss the word *if* from her mind.

"We will check at the office in the morning, just in case. But your young, headstrong sister is probably"—Matilda waved her hand—"having a fling."

Mary Ellen grimaced, and Matilda patted her hand. "A nice fling."

That could be.

Or not.

"You said, *we* will check in the morning?"

"Oh yes. We can't let you traipse around alone. Besides, this is too juicy to pass up. I'm dying of curiosity. You see, I've been young."

Mary Ellen had a feeling Matilda still was, except chronologically, and with her, it didn't seem to matter.

"When I came here, twenty-something years ago, my adventurous niece and her companion came, too."

Rose smiled. "Her niece, Jane, married my son, Mak, who owns the cattle ranch a few miles from here."

"Oh, the good times we had," Matilda said. "Racing horses, visiting royalty. Those were the days. Now," she said. "We've become a part of the United States."

The way she said that made Mary Ellen wonder if she thought that was good or bad. Finding out might be interesting.

Being adventurous, headstrong, and impulsive began to have an appeal to Mary Ellen. For someone like Matilda, Rose, Jane, and. . .Breanna.

❧

Early the next morning after a good night's sleep at the house, Mary Ellen dressed in the clothes she'd taken from her trunk the night before. She had followed instructions on how to pack and had rolled her outerwear around her underclothes which prevented excessive wrinkling.

She wore light lipstick and her usual practical hairstyle, a tailored dark skirt, and a white blouse, wanting to give every impression she meant business when she asked about her sister.

Matilda and Rose also dressed in skirts and blouses, but entirely different from hers. Matilda's was a brightly flowered skirt against a green background and a grass green blouse. Rose wore a slim burgundy skirt with a burgundy-trimmed pink blouse.

Those women would certainly stand out in any crowd, especially the exuberant Matilda with her copper-colored hair and green eyes.

"We'll take the automobile, since we have time before the office opens. If we were late, we'd take the horse and carriage. We'd get there quicker."

"Those autos can be more stubborn than a mule—just refuse to move," Rose said. "And a flick of a whip makes no difference at all."

Mary Ellen climbed into the backseat of the car. On the street were a few men on horses, a couple of carriages, and several wagons. "Are there many autos here?"

"Last I heard," Rose said, "there were three. But there are seventy or more in Oahu."

Matilda drove across the way to the Matti-Rose. Akemi came out as soon as the car stopped, but Matilda tooted the *chaoooga*-sounding horn anyway.

"That's a beautiful kimono," Mary Ellen said as Akemi climbed into the back beside her.

"Thank you. Most days I wear Japanese dress."

As soon as Matilda swerved out into the road, she tooted her horn loudly at a man on a horse in the road. She shouted out the window. "An auto can't move sideways. Get that animal out of the road before I run over it."

"Now 'Tilda, settle down," the man said. "You're gonna cause this mare to sprint and run away, and you'll be responsible for my death."

"Well, you won't be around to complain about it. Now move it."

He laughed, tipped his hat, and galloped on.

"That's ol' Scooter. Works down at the docks. He thinks I'm joking when I say things like that."

Mary Ellen didn't. Even in this short period of time, she figured Matilda would barrel down the road and anyone in the way had better move or else. Rose just smiled pleasantly, as if everything was normal.

Chapter 6

"Mmmhmm," Lalani hummed. She set a cup of Kona coffee on the table without his having to order it.

The middle-aged waitress had told him time and again, "Claybourne Honeycutt, you have the perfect name for a man like you. You're a honey if ever I saw one. Mmmhmm." She'd shake her head and grin, then hold out her hand. "If it wasn't for this ring, and my husband having killer instincts, and my being twenty years too late, I'd do the town with you, honey."

Lalani had said that since before he'd turned sixteen and had finally condensed it to "Mmmhmm" and a grin.

He took a big gulp of the steamy coffee and hoped it would give him the lift he needed before breakfast and the questionable conversation he'd enter into soon—one that would not be with Lalani.

"I heard your kind of woman arrived last night," she said. "Some of the dockworkers were saying there was another one for Clay." She raised her eyebrows. "They wouldn't dare call you *honey*." She laughed.

Clay didn't. "They weren't disrespectful about her, were they?"

"They know better after those fights you've had. We don't allow that kind of talk in here any more than you do."

Lalani looked around, as if someone might be listening. She leaned forward. "They were talking about a beautiful blond and said you'd want to know. Now, doesn't that whet your appetite?"

His appetite wasn't whetted as much as it had been when the game had started a few years ago. "This morning, I have an appetite for breakfast. But I'll settle for coffee until Jacob shows up."

"Oh, you gonna get yourself converted by that Bible-thumping preacher-boy?"

Clay forced a small laugh before taking another drink of coffee. Apparently, she couldn't tell his conversion had happened when he was a lad of nine years old. Was baptized in the ocean. Pastor Russell had said his sins were taken away farther than the eye could see on those waves. At that time, he hardly knew what sin was.

Lalani apparently took his laugh to mean *not a chance*. He set his cup down, and she refilled it.

"Jacob's not a preacher yet, Lalani. At least, not officially."

"Well, look who just walked in."

Lalani greeted the tall, lean man. "Aloha *kakahiaka*, Jacob."

Jacob answered with the same respectful, "Good morning, Lalani." He asked how she was and about her family, something Clay hadn't gotten around to. "Coffee, please," he said at last.

For the first time since he'd begun to play the game, Clay wondered if what he'd done had been perceived as fun or as a tainting of his reputation.

Jacob touched his shoulder. "Been a while, Clay." He took the seat across from him.

Clay acknowledged him with a nod. They'd grown up together—in church, in school. Had been baptized together that Sunday afternoon in the ocean. Later in high school, they'd noticed the girls, surfed, raced on the MacCauley ranch, run through the sugarcane fields, enjoyed being young. Then came a time of growing up. After getting higher education in Europe, Clay went into the sugar business with his family. Jacob became a teacher, specializing in Bible studies.

There was still a bond between them. But they now had their different interests and ways of life. Just as whaling had once been, and then cattle ranching, sugar was now Hawaii's biggest product, sent all over the world, and Clay took seriously his responsibilities in the Honeycutt Sugar Company.

But that's not what separated him and Jacob. Several years before, Jacob had fallen in love, but his girlfriend had gone to Europe to study. While there, she married a Scotsman. Jacob tried to absolve his grief by denying it. Clay had been sorry about his loss, but glad to have a friend who also enjoyed taking girls out on dates and showing them the sights of Hawaii.

The last time he and Jacob had had a serious talk, Jacob had said he himself needed to accept that his former girlfriend was not the one God had chosen for him and that he felt it was time he and Clay settled down and took life more seriously.

Clay had scoffed. "You have no right to tell me how to live my life."

"Sure I do," Jacob said, "because we're friends, and I love you."

There had been nothing more to say. After a long silence, Jacob had stood, clasped Clay's shoulder, and walked away.

After that, Jacob's younger brother had taken his place in joining Clay in this game of life.

Now Jacob had walked into the restaurant, again laid his hand on Clay's shoulder for a moment, and taken a seat across from him.

Maybe Jacob wanted them to be close again. Or perhaps he needed Clay's help in some way. A donation to some charitable event. Clay would like that. It's not like he was a heathen. He simply chose the single life, which included beautiful women.

Lalani brought Jacob's coffee. "You ready to order?"

Clay liked the Portuguese sausage. He ordered it, along with two fried eggs, white rice, and guava juice.

"Sounds good to me," Jacob said, giving Clay the impression his friend had something specific on his mind.

Jacob opened the conversation by talking about what each of them had been doing. After Lalani brought their meal and Jacob asked the blessing, Jacob continued along the same line.

"Looks like the sugar business is booming, judging by the new mills and the workers that keep swarming in from Japan."

"Honeycutt Sugar has become Hawaii's biggest export," Clay responded. "I guess we're known throughout the world. We export the sugar and import the workers."

"You did a good thing, Clay, making those strict rules about the Japanese workers being honest with the brides they're having come over to marry them."

"I can't take a lot of credit for that. Matilda and Rose brought it to my attention after Akemi was so upset and felt she had no recourse but to marry the dishonest man." He shrugged. "They made me realize a lot of other picture brides could have been in similar situations but were afraid to speak out about it. I do care what happens on the plantation."

"Your taking a personal interest will keep a lot of those young girls from thinking their only recourse from marrying a man they don't want is going into those houses of ill repute."

"I don't like that anymore than you, Jacob."

"I know that. I know you."

Clay wasn't sure where this might be leading. Could be negative or positive. He was grateful Lalani chose that moment to refill their cups.

Jacob poured milk into his coffee and stirred slowly.

Clay watched him over the rim of his glass of guava juice. Waiting.

"I have a favor to ask."

"Sure, Jacob. If I can help with anything."

Jacob's intense gaze held Clay's. "I want you to look after Geoffrey."

Clay feared the piece of Portuguese sausage he'd popped in his mouth might just cause a problem. For a moment, he wasn't able to chew. Jacob focused on his plate and cut several pieces of sausage. After a long moment of trying to figure out if Jacob was being serious or had lost his mind, he chewed slowly, then swallowed.

"Jacob, Geoffrey is twenty-five years old."

Jacob glanced across at him. "But you're twenty-nine and have a huge influence on him."

Was Jacob saying Clay was a bad influence? "You're his brother."

"You're implying," Jacob said, "I'm the one who should be a good influence on Geoffrey."

Clay shrugged one shoulder, indicating that's exactly what he meant.

"Who listens to his brother?" Jacob shook his head. "But I'm saying this because I am his brother."

Clay shrugged both shoulders. "He got his college degree. He's a good worker, Jacob. He's just trying to figure out where he belongs and what he wants—"

Jacob held up his fork. "I know all that, Clay. No need to get defensive. I haven't said a thing to condemn you or Geoffrey. You make your own choices like I make mine, and they haven't always been right."

"Okay, what do you want me to do with Geoffrey?"

"Continue to befriend him. See that he's okay." He paused. "I'm not going to be around."

"What do you mean? Are you ill?"

"No. God is leading me into the ministry. I've applied to a seminary on the mainland to get my doctorate."

That didn't surprise Clay. "When do you go?"

"The semester starts in September. Less than two months. I'd like to spend some time with my parents before I go. And with Geoffrey, if he will."

Lalani appeared with the coffeepot. Jacob said, "No thanks," but Clay accepted another refill.

"Clay, I'd like for you to come to church Sunday and bring Geoffrey. He hasn't attended in a long time."

"Sure." Clay figured he could do that. His conscience could bother him away from church as much as inside it. "If he's back on the island. Thomas needed him to train his new shipment of Japanese men."

After they finished eating, Jacob reached into his pants pocket and brought out money to pay for the breakfast. "My treat."

Clay thanked him and picked up his cup.

Jacob spoke in a low tone. "Something else I want you to do. Let's go outside for what I have to say."

Lalani was on her way over again. Everybody knew she liked to overhear conversations and didn't mind repeating them. Jacob stood.

"I'll be in church Sunday," Lalani said. Jacob nodded and smiled.

Clay downed the rest of his coffee, and the two of them walked outside.

The morning peace was shattered with *chaoooooga-chaoooooga*.

"Sounds like Matilda." Clay laughed. He and Jacob stood on the sidewalk. "Looks like she's pulling over at the restaurant up the street. Let's find out what she's up to."

They started up the street. Matilda and Rose got out of the front seat. A blond climbed from the back. Akemi, unmistakable in her flattering kimono, exited from the other side and walked around to the sidewalk.

That must be the blond Lalani had mentioned. Clay started to pick up his pace, but Jacob turned and rushed to Clay's car. He opened the door and leaped inside.

Clay would have liked to speak to the women, particularly the blond. But they were disappearing into the restaurant. Only Matilda looked his way and lifted her hand. He did the same, then hurried to the car, wondering about Jacob's strange behavior.

Jacob's face had paled, and his gaze focused on his clenched hands.

Clay had no idea what was going on. He knew Jacob loved Matilda and Rose. What bothered him wasn't those two, although they were dynamic, hard-headed women.

Was it the blond? Did she remind him of his blond girlfriend who'd left him? Had she brought back those haunting memories of so long ago?

≈

After they were seated in the restaurant, the waitress came to the table and was introduced to Mary Ellen as Phyllis. "She was one of our school girls," Rose said, and they all smiled like that had been a pleasant experience.

"Kona for all?" Matilda asked, and they each nodded, although Mary Ellen had no idea what a *Kona* was.

"We've taught just about everybody on the island," Matilda said, as Phyllis walked away. "That is, the ones who are making good decisions. The others we don't know."

Rose laughed with her, and Akemi smiled, looking at them as if she dearly loved them.

Phyllis returned soon. "Here you are." She set four cups of brown aromatic liquid in front of each.

"Smells wonderful," Mary Ellen said. "Almost as good as the scent of flowers that seems to be everywhere."

"We are an island of flowers." Matilda smiled. "You just can't imagine the variety. But this is the world's best coffee." She added cream to hers. "It's only grown in Hawaii."

Mary Ellen took a sip. She nodded. She'd never tasted coffee so rich and good. She could drink it without the cream. But she decided the cream was probably the best in the world, too, so she picked up the little white cream pitcher.

Before long, Matilda was suggesting what Mary Ellen might like to eat. "Their specialty is macadamia nut pancakes."

"The banana are good, too," Rose said.

"Yes. And the chocolate."

"Don't forget the strawberry."

"Or blueberry."

"They're all delicious," Matilda said. "And so light and fluffy you have to set your cup on them to keep them from sprouting wings and flying away like a honeycreeper."

Phyllis giggled. "Most people keep them on the plate with a lot of our dairy-fresh whipped butter and a little powdered sugar."

"Or syrup. Oh my gracious," Matilda said. "They have a special, fresh-fruit syrup the cooks make every day."

Phyllis was nodding. "We have maple, guava, coconut, and boysenberry today."

"Mercy." Mary Ellen laid her hand over her stomach. "I feel stuffed just hearing that."

"But of course," Phyllis said, "we have the usual breakfast foods. Eggs, meat, juices."

Mary Ellen decided. "Since I've never had macadamia pancakes, I'll have that. Oh, and bring me a honeycreeper."

She was glad to see Matilda appreciated her humor as much as she appreciated Matilda's. But she knew she was far from ever being as delightful as that colorful woman.

"All right," Matilda said. "What we normally do with a new person is order something different and then we sample everybody's. It's expected here."

The *someone new* remark turned Mary Ellen's thoughts to her sister. After Matilda said the blessing and their food was brought, they sampled each other's, but remaining in the back of Mary Ellen's mind was what might be revealed at the immigration office, where they would go after breakfast. Surely someone there had at least seen Breanna and knew how that photo had gotten into the envelope with the Japanese man's official form.

Matilda suggested they walk to the office about a half mile away. "With all the horses crowding the road, we'd have a time making our way through in that car. Besides, I just have it as a conversation piece, mainly."

As they walked, the aromas from the bakery mingled with the fresh, morning breeze, rife with the fragrance of flowers. Each restaurant emitted a new and different intriguing scent.

Before long, the unmistakable moist salty air meant they were near the dock. Soon, Mary Ellen viewed the white sand beach that spread peacefully along the ocean, fringed with green swaying palm leaves high on tall, slender tree trunks.

They walked past an impressive, four-story building that Matilda said was the Hilo Hotel. The only building in town larger than the Matti-Rose.

"I wonder if she's staying there," Mary Ellen said. "Or if she did."

Rose offered to have them check their records. "You can go on to the office. I know Akemi doesn't want to be late."

Mary Ellen, Matilda, and Akemi walked on down the sidewalk to the immigration office. Matilda opened the door, and they entered. The office in San Francisco had been in a several-story, brick building. This was one level. Light and airy. The docking area was visible from side windows. A man sat behind a waist-high partition.

"That's Mr. Hammeur," Akemi whispered.

Mr. Hammeur was a slight man with a thin nose and quick eyes. He said aloha, nodded at Akemi, and greeted Matilda warmly. When Matilda introduced her as Harvey Skidmore's niece, he took on a guarded look. "Yes, I remember Mr. Harv. Because he is a fine businessman and I respect him, I agreed to take you on, but—"

"No, that was my sister, Breanna. Did she come here about the job?"

"She did not." A furrow dented the space between his eyebrows. "I stayed late. But she did not come into the office. I did not feel it my place to inquire."

"I don't agree," Mary Ellen said. "A young woman was to take a job here, but you didn't inquire about her whereabouts?"

"I offered to hire her, sight unseen, because of the recommendation of Mr. Harv. That, already, was beyond my usual practices."

"I'm sorry," Mary Ellen said.

Mr. Hammeur exhaled a deep breath. "Your uncle did send a letter, apologizing that his niece did not take the job."

Mary Ellen could imagine that if C. Honeycutt met Breanna when she disembarked, she would have been more intrigued with him than with going to the immigration office about a job.

But so much time had passed. And these people hadn't seen her. At least, this man *said* he hadn't. She hated being suspicious, but she needed to find her sister. "She might have been ill, or hurt."

"Now, now." Matilda touched her arm. "If anything like that had happened with an American young lady, the news would have spread. Why, it would be in the newspapers. But we will check with the hospital later."

Rose came in. "Your sister hasn't been registered at the hotel."

"Thanks for checking." She addressed Mr. Hammeur. "There is another matter."

"Yes?" He raised his eyebrows.

"Our office received correspondence from a C. Honeycutt."

"That would be Claybourne Honeycutt. The picture brides are for the Japanese men working on the Honeycutt plantation."

"I mean," she said, trying to be careful, "I got the impression from some correspondence that he was looking for an American wife."

"Looking?" He scoffed, and they all gazed at her.

"I mean someone sent his photo to our office."

"No." He shook his head vigorously. "That would not go through this office. Men like him do not advertise for a bride."

Matilda agreed. "He wouldn't need to. Women from sixteen to six—"

Rose elbowed her. Matilda grinned. "As I was saying, women from sixteen to 105 would go for Claybourne Honeycutt. Believe me, he does not need to advertise. There's some mistake, or someone is playing a practical joke."

Not too practical, Mary Ellen was thinking. *A joke was supposed to be funny. This was not.*

Mr. Hammeur repeated his earlier words, adamantly. "Such an indiscretion could not happen through this office."

Mary Ellen nodded. "I do know that isn't the way things are done." They all knew this Claybourne Honeycutt. If Breanna was safe with Mr. C., Mary Ellen didn't want to cause trouble for them.

"Is the job opening still available?" she asked as calmly as she could.

Mr. Hammeur was shaking his head before she finished her sentence. "After she did not arrive for two weeks, I filled the job with a young man who serves the multiple purposes of working in the office and on the dock, which had been my thought from the beginning."

"That was Billy," Matilda said. "The boy who drove us to the house last night."

Mary Ellen remembered the friendly young man who said he had not seen Breanna. But he now had the job that had been promised to her.

She was trying to force herself to believe that Breanna had not gotten her mail or was simply delayed. But the uneasiness she felt grew worse by the moment.

Chapter 7

Did your sister come to meet Claybourne Honeycutt?"

Mary Ellen wasn't surprised that the discerning Matilda asked that question as soon as they exited the office.

"I'm afraid so."

"Now tell me exactly what was in the letter you received."

"It wasn't a letter. The photo was in the envelope with an official form from a Japanese man. The two apparently had no connection. The only information was on the back of the photo: C. Honeycutt. General delivery. Post office. Hilo, Hawaii. I'm not sure of the exact words, but he said he wanted an American wife."

She paused. "Oh yes, he wrote *occupation* and beside it he wrote *sugar plantation*."

Matilda looked perplexed. "That young man's problem is keeping the women away from him."

"You don't think he sent the photo?"

"Well," Matilda said, "I can image he might do that, but openly. He might even go to the U.S. or anywhere and make it known he's eligible."

Mary Ellen fell in step with them as they started up the sidewalk.

Rose asked, "Was the form you received from a Japanese man who worked at the sugar plantation?"

"I think so. But I'm not sure I'd recognize the name if I saw it. Do you think a Japanese man did that to lure an American girl here?"

"No. They're well supervised. And for a Japanese man to approach a *haole* would be worse than committing the unforgivable sin."

"Hay. . . ?"

"Haole," Matilda said again. "That's a Caucasian or white person."

Someone sent the photo. Whether it was Mr. C. or a Japanese man, Mary Ellen didn't have a good feeling about this. She hated to say it, but she must. "Suppose Mr. Hammeur lured her here and met her."

They stared at her like she'd lost her mind. She didn't care. She had to find her sister.

"His wife would kill him," Rose said.

Matilda huffed. "She nearly does that without a reason."

"Mr. Hammeur isn't happily married?"

"Oh yes. And has five children."

"But you said—"

Matilda waved away her speculation. "She swats him with this and that, but

171

it's all playful. He likes it."

"How well do you know Mr. Honeycutt?"

"We know the family intimately," Rose said. "Clay's grandfather and my husband were dear friends. Clay's dad and my son, Mak, were best friends. Clay's dad owned the most productive sugar plantation on this island and in Oahu." Sadness crossed her face. "Clay's parents were killed in a shipwreck." Her voice softened as she added, "Mak has been like a dad to Clay."

"And," Matilda added, "Mak owns a cattle and horse ranch. My niece Jane married him. We came here together back in 1889." She looked beyond them, as if seeing her memories. "Jane was from Texas. She won the biggest horse race Hawaii has ever seen. That's how she scared Mak to death and made him realize how much he loved her."

Rose laughed softly. "It's a great story. Jane became a hero in these parts. Those were the days of royal races."

"There's so much to tell you," Matilda said. "I know your mind is on your sister right now. But part of the reason I say everyone would know and be talking about any American woman who landed here is because Jane made American women even more famous here by winning that race. Over the king's horse, mind you. The respect for American women rose to 100 percent."

Mary Ellen let out a weighty breath. "Maybe. If Mr. C. didn't send the photo, and the sender told her Mr. C. sent him to pick her up, she might go with him."

They reached the car, and Matilda started the engine. "This is confusing. Surely no one would write for an American girl in order to do her harm. That's. . ."

She didn't finish her sentence. Had she been about to say that was insane? Such a thought was more frightening than if the person was sane.

Matilda said. "I saw Clay's automobile when we went into the restaurant this morning, but I didn't notice if anyone was in it."

"Think about this," Rose said. "If Clay sent the photo and met her, then she is probably at his plantation. Or he's showing her the islands."

"Right," Matilda added. "I can imagine you and Clay together. So if your sister is like you've described her, he wouldn't let her out of his sight."

"But this morning. . ."

"This morning," Matilda said pointedly, "he was with Jacob. Jacob assists our pastor. Maybe Clay was talking to him about the wedding you're making that dress for."

"But would Mr. C. be that impulsive? To marry so soon after meeting—"

Before she could finish the sentence, Matilda patted Mary Ellen's hand. "Love can happen instantly. Isn't that what happened when your sister saw the photo?"

Mary Ellen whispered, "Yes." Even an ordinarily sensible person could have such a moment of weakness.

"I'll find Clay," Rose said, "and catch up with you two later."

"All right," Matilda said. "We'll go back to the house. In the meantime,

Mary Ellen, would you like to see the perfect place where you can work on your sister's wedding dress?"

Mary Ellen couldn't refuse that offer. But her thoughts were a jumble. One minute, she feared something dreadful had happened to Breanna. The next, she could imagine her sister at Mr. C.'s plantation. What else could she do but let these women lead her around?

❧

Less than thirty minutes later, Mary Ellen could hardly believe her eyes. On the small-town street of Hilo was a shop that stood out from all the rest other than the Hilo Hotel across the street. The sign across the window read: MATTI-ROSE HAWAIIAN & WESTERN WEAR.

"The display window is beautiful. As fine as any exclusive shop I've seen in San Francisco."

"Or Europe." Matilda spoke proudly. "Rose and I love to travel and decided to make a business of it, too. Newcomers and visitors to Hawaii delight in the Hawaiian attire that's much cooler than Western wear. Native Hawaiians want everything Westerners have."

"Those are beautiful mannequins."

"The newest. These are made of papier-mâché. Only in recent years have we women shed those corsets and crinolines, so we don't need the heavy mannequins now. We carry only the more fluid lines of clothing. Oh my"—she fanned her face with her hand—"we had to have men to haul around and dress those old-fashioned wax mannequins. Their faces were ugly, too." She laughed. "I'm referring to the mannequins, not the men."

Mary Ellen laughed with her, and they entered the shop, accompanied by the tinkle of a little bell.

She met Pilar Scott, an attractive brunette who looked to be in her late thirties. "When Pilar was only seventeen, she came over with me and Jane." Matilda and Pilar smiled at each other. "I'm hoping you two will have a lot of time for conversation, but for now, let Pilar see the dress you made."

Mary Ellen took it from her bag. "I still need to add the seed pearls."

"Oh, it's gorgeous," Pilar said. "And the work is expert. Matilda, have you found the new employee you've wanted?"

"Rose and I talked about that last night." She turned to Mary Ellen. "We thought you might consider helping us out here."

Mary Ellen needed time to process the offer. She had no idea how long she would be in Hawaii. How long before she found Breanna?

"That is, if you're wanting a job. While you're thinking it over, you can work on your sister's dress here. Incidentally, Pilar, have you seen Clay lately?"

Pilar shrugged. "Who can keep track of Clay?"

Matilda explained. "Clay is the younger brother of Pilar's best friend, Susanne."

Pilar shook her head. "What that *nohea haole* needs is to settle down."

Was she cursing him?

"Nohea haole," Matilda explained, "means *handsome Caucasian*."

Mary Ellen already knew if he looked anything like his photo, he was handsome. The more comments she heard about him, the more she suspected Breanna had met him and forgotten everything else. "I'll be glad to help out here. I have no way of knowing for how long."

"Let's call it temporary and part-time, if you like," Matilda said. "When would you like to start?"

This was not a time for saying she'd like to see the island. "Now?"

Matilda smiled kindly. "I thought you'd say that. Pilar can tell you all about the shop and introduce you to the workers in the back. I will return later this afternoon. And Rose will be in as soon as she learns anything. You may want to talk with Pilar about your situation. I'm sure Clay will respond to this matter right away."

Matilda laid her hand on Mary Ellen's shoulder, and her green eyes held sympathy. Mary Ellen needed to meet Mr. C., but fear of doing so must have been written all over her face.

⇨

Clay looked up from the ledger when Mak knocked on the office door and walked in. "I'd like to talk with you, Clay. Could we step outside?"

"Sure thing." Clay asked his accountant to excuse him and walked away from the thundering machines inside the sugar mill.

They walked out to one of the wooden benches beneath a row of banyan trees where mill hands often ate their lunches.

"What's on your mind?" Judging by the serious look on Mak's face he must have come on business. With the tremendous influx of workers and their requested brides, Clay could barely keep up with their need for beef. His herd couldn't produce as fast as the workers and their families could consume beef, and Mak's ranch was his biggest producer. "From the expression on your face, you must either be raising your price on beef or have decided to keep that horse I want."

Mak gave him a sidelong glance. "More serious than a cow or a horse, according to Mom."

"Is she ill?" Rose was one of the most active, energetic women he knew.

"No. She asked me to talk with you about a disturbing matter. Maybe there's a simple explanation."

"A matter?" Clay couldn't think what action he'd taken that would disturb Rose.

"It's about a woman. Or I should say, a girl."

"A girl? Come on. What is this?"

Mak related the story Rose had told him, rendering Clay momentarily speechless. If it wasn't for knowing Mak MacCauley as a fine, Christian man, he'd punch him in the mouth for telling such lies.

Mak drew a deep breath. "Miss Colson thinks her sister might be with you."

Clay jumped up, and his right fist pounded his left palm. Pacing in front of

Mak, he tried to absorb what his friend had said. Finally, words spouted from his lips. "That's ridiculous. You think I'd do a thing like that?"

"I only know what Mom said the woman told her and Matilda."

Clay had him run through it again, then he scoffed. "I don't have some girl stowed away. If I wanted a wife or a companion, I could have one."

"That's not the point, Clay. She claims your photo was sent to the immigration office in San Francisco, along with your name and the request for an American bride written on the back of it."

"My name?"

"Mom said she refers to you as Mr. C. Apparently you—I mean someone—wrote the name C. Honeycutt."

"I'm far from being the only Honeycutt in the world or in Hawaii, for that matter. And I didn't advertise for a wife."

"Glad to hear it. Now all you have to do is convince that woman whose sister is missing."

"Why should I bother with this nonsense?"

"Because it's not just a matter of your reputation. The woman could accuse illegal activity. . .or worse."

Clay plopped down on the bench. "Why would anyone make up such a story?"

"She said a photo of you was sent."

"But you said the photo was in an envelope with a Japanese man's official form from the Hilo immigration office." Clay scoffed. "That proves this person is lying. No Japanese man can just walk into that office and fill out a form. Any worker from my plantation would have to be accompanied by one of us in authority."

"She claims her sister came to Hawaii because of the photo, to marry you. The sister is missing."

"Missing." Clay looked at the clear blue sky over his head, then at Mak again. "You said her sister was supposed to meet her last night. This is only a half-day later. Anybody could be delayed for any reason. If the sister story is true, her horse could have gotten sick. She broke a leg. Got hit in the head with a surfboard. She could have a headache. Anything. And you said that sister is eighteen?"

"That's what Mom said."

"Frankly, I'd rather a woman be ten years older than me, not ten years younger. What in the world would I want with an eighteen-year-old?"

Mak stared at him, and Clay looked away. Finally, he shook his head. "I don't have time for this."

"You need to listen to her in case there's something to it."

"Oh, I think there's something to it. She's seen the sugar unloading at the docks in San Francisco, seen the papers where Japanese men are employed with Honeycutt Sugar, and she's looking to sweeten her life with a part of the profit."

Mak scoffed at that. "Then how did she get a photo?"

Clay sighed, thinking. "A girlfriend. Or maybe she's not telling the truth about that either. Sounds like a made-up story if I ever heard one."

"You're guessing, Clay. You don't know the facts."

"But I will. Just as soon as I tell my accountant we'll have to go over the ledgers another day. You say she's with Rose and Matilda?"

"Matilda was taking her to their dress shop."

Clay stared at Mak. "What are you grinning about?"

"Mom said she's a pretty blond. That may cool your temper."

"I've made an issue of liking blonds. But I've never lost my head or my heart to one. And don't intend to. Not some conniving one anyway."

Mak laughed.

"Now what?"

"After my first wife died, I vowed there would never be another woman in my life."

Clay watched a warmth come into his friend's eyes.

"Jane and I have been married for. . .let's see. . .about twenty years now."

Clay chuckled. "You'd better make sure. You may have an anniversary coming up. But seriously, if I found a woman like Jane, I might change my mind, too. I don't think they make many like her."

Mak smiled. "None. None at all."

Clay saw the softness come onto that tough rancher's face. He rather envied that his friend could feel that way about a woman.

Since he'd calmed down some, Clay began to think more clearly. "I appreciate your coming and talking to me." He stood and smiled at his fatherly friend. "I'll check this matter out and get it settled. I'll just bet it's not my photo at all that found its way to San Francisco. And the woman, if she's not a schemer, will know it when she sees me."

Mak nodded.

Clay watched him get on his horse and lift his hand to tip the brim of his paniolo hat in a farewell gesture and ride away.

Mak hadn't said he didn't believe the woman's story. Did he think Clay would have sent a photo and request for a woman? And why did he feel a sense of guilt when he hadn't done what he was being accused of?

Accompanied by a sense of chagrin, Clay knew if there was any truth to the story, he'd be better off to have the girl with him instead of her being missing.

Chapter 8

Mary Ellen heard the tinkling of the tiny bell and turned from the dress form to face the door. Whatever smile and greeting she'd planned stopped short. The tiny seed pearl slipped from her left hand and fell to the wooden floor. Such a small bead couldn't possibly make a sound, but it seemed to cause a roaring in her head like she'd heard when holding a seashell to her ear.

She could not think what to say. Jumbled in her mind was that Pilar had gone for sandwiches, leaving Mary Ellen to greet any customers. She'd practiced saying *aloha* and *welcome* but now she couldn't remember the word for *welcome*. It would not be appropriate, anyway.

This was not a dream like she'd had after seeing his photo and awakening the next morning trying to get her breath.

In front of her stood the man whose photo had made its way to San Francisco. The photo that had changed her routine existence, like an hourglass being turned upside down, and started life anew.

Now, however, the sand in the hourglass seemed to have filtered down to her feet.

He was not a black-and-white photo. Thick hair, slightly mussed, perhaps by the trade winds, looked black. But not his eyes. They were deep blue and seemed to be staring as though questioning her heart and mind and soul. He would find nothing there, for she felt depleted. His handsome, bronzed face held a more rugged appearance than in the photo. His full, creamy brown lips reminded her of the coffee she'd had at the restaurant, and she could almost taste the delicious flavor. She moistened her dry lips with the tip of her tongue.

This was her Mr. C.

No. Not hers.

An arch of one dark eyebrow appeared to be a command for her to speak.

"Breanna." Her voice was shaky. "Is she. . .with you?"

His nostrils flared, and a firmness settled on his lips. "I do not know a Breanna." He folded his muscular arms across his broad chest that was covered by a multi-colored, short-sleeved shirt, open at the neck. His stance widened with the movement of his right foot, and he shifted his weight. "Tell me your story about this. . .Breanna. The tale you apparently told Rose. And others, it seems."

His jaw tightened. She sensed he was holding back anger.

"Breanna is my sister," she said, surprised that her voice had strengthened. But the matter of Breanna took precedence over anything else. While he stared at her intently, she told him about the photo and the exchange of letters.

"You read the letters?"

She had to admit that she had only seen the envelopes. "But through the letters, it was arranged that she would come here and meet you. A Mr. C. Honeycutt."

Instead of denying or admitting anything, he gave a short laugh. "I suspect you have a vivid imagination about all this."

"Are you C. Honeycutt?"

Moving one arm to his waist, he made a gallant bow. "Claybourne Honeycutt, at your service, ma'am." He straightened and raised an eyebrow again. "And who might you be?"

"Mar—" She stopped and closed her eyes. He seemed to think this was some kind of joke. "I am the sister of Breanna Colson, who came here to meet you." Mary Ellen lifted her chin and gazed at him. Good looks could certainly mask a scoundrel, and she suspected that's exactly what he was.

His lowering those long dark lashes over his eyes for a moment infuriated her. She pointed to the white dress on the dress form. "I have been making this for Breanna's marriage to you. Now, you can tell me what you know about this, or I can contact the authorities."

His focus seemed to be on the wedding dress, and he appeared thoughtful for a moment. Then his deep blue gaze fell upon her again. "What about this scenario?" His head lowered just a bit, and his eyes seemed to dance. "Maybe you don't have a sister. Maybe you made this up, having seen my name on papers passing through the office on the mainland."

Her jaw developed a mind of its own, and she didn't seem able to close her mouth. His audacity rendered her speechless.

"Maybe you have been influenced by this picture-bride activity and decided to become one yourself." He gestured toward the wedding dress. "You say you were reluctant for your sister to come to Hawaii. But you're making a wedding dress for her?" He scoffed. "Your stories don't add up. Hold it. Don't move."

Moving had not been an option since he walked through the door. But that sounded like a threat, and she was now about to bolt. Just then, the spark that had been in his photo appeared in his eyes. What was it? Daring? Skepticism? Challenge? He grinned. "I can picture you in that dress. Looks like it's just your size. I propose that the dress is yours, and it is you, not some"—he spread his hands for emphasis—"some illusive sister, who wishes to marry."

"Why. . .why would I want to marry you?" she managed to say above the thundering of her heart.

He shrugged. "I wouldn't know. I certainly wouldn't want to marry someone like me."

Mary Ellen had never experienced anything like she was feeling. The world seemed to have stopped turning—or at least in her mind. Time was suspended. She could not look away from the eyes that challenged her. It was as if she was feeling what she had felt before Breanna snatched his photo and that ridiculous possibility from her. Here that photo-man stood in front of her, saying the dress was for her, that she wanted to marry, and he even used the word *propose*.

Where had her senses gone? Mentally, emotionally, and maybe even physically, she was still at sea. Her world had been shaken when her parents died. But she had known what to do. She'd had to be strong for Breanna. She had to have an emotionally controlled life to set the right example. But now, she felt like an earthquake had happened inside her, and she knew not where to turn.

Along with the wreckage, however, was a tiny flame. Somewhere deep inside, she was able to think. "I saw your photo. I saw the name *C. Honeycutt*, the note saying your occupation was with a sugar plantation and you wanted an American wife. The address was on the photo."

Feeling like she might topple over, she put one foot in front of another and made her way to the counter. She sat on the high stool in front of the cash register.

That didn't help much. He turned to face her. "You say you look like your sister?"

How many times must she continue to remind herself and everyone else that she was plain compared to Breanna? "She is five years younger, more outgoing, prettier." She glared at him. "And much more trusting."

He kept staring. She refused to look away no matter how piercing, dark, and probing his eyes. Finally, he spoke in a low, serious tone. "I can imagine many young women being more trusting." He shook his head briefly. "But I'm trying to imagine a young woman being prettier than you."

That remark stung because she felt he was making fun of her. Something inside her seemed to burst. Maybe like things exploding during the earthquake that caused the fires back in San Francisco.

She closed her eyes against the pictures that flooded her mind, like a group of photos laid out on a tabletop for others to view. The first was when she was seven and Breanna was two. Mary Ellen had been so proud of having lost her two front teeth, knowing big-girl teeth would come in. But a friend of her mother talked about Breanna's getting her teeth while Mary Ellen lost hers. Before that, everyone commented on how beautiful the baby was. Mary Ellen had thought so, too, and it was fine with her. But when the comment was made about teeth, Mary Ellen felt ugly, no longer proud of growing up, and learned to smile with her mouth closed.

Then Mary Ellen had to look and act like a proper young lady, while Breanna was always the baby, the last child their mother could have, and Mary Ellen was supposed to set the right example.

She couldn't say these things to Mr. C. And she could not comment on the pretty remark as if she believed a word of it. But maybe he didn't mean Mary Ellen was pretty. Maybe he really was trying to imagine how Breanna could be pretty while he looked at Mary Ellen.

While the presence and words of Mr. C. had so knocked Mary Ellen off her equilibrium, she could imagine that Breanna would have been completely swept off her feet. Not that she thought he had any charm. Yet she could imagine that he might. But then, she was still influenced by the photo. This. . .this Mr. C. could very well be a vile scoundrel, and he was definitely arrogant.

"Have I rendered you speechless, Mar. . . ?"

Mar? Then she realized she hadn't told him her name. "Miss Colson," she said formally. "And no. I have plenty of speech. I'm just trying to figure out where to start. Until I have proof you did not send that photo, I cannot trust you. That would be the ultimate foolishness."

"I see." He gazed at the ceiling. "I suppose I must prove my innocence to you." He exhaled heavily. "You said there was an address on the photo."

"General delivery. Hilo Post Office."

"Let's go."

She stammered, looking around. "I have. . .we have customers that could—" He interrupted. "This shop operated before you came here. I think it can continue. Now, if you're telling the truth, let's go to the post office."

Those challenging eyes. What did he have in mind? Abduct her for illegal reasons? But if so, then maybe she would end up with her sister. "Just a moment." She went in back to tell the women at the sewing machines she had to leave.

"Aila, will you tell Pilar I'll be back soon? I need to go somewhere with Mr. Honeycutt."

"Oooh." Aila's response sounded like a song, and her eyes twinkled. "Anybody would go with Mr. Clay. You go on. He could charm the coffee bean off the Kona bush."

Mary Ellen wasn't sure she should risk her reputation by being seen with him. But for the possibility of finding out something about Breanna, she had no choice. "This is strictly business," she said staunchly.

The woman's eyebrows traveled up. "His business is making sugar." Aila giggled. Mary Ellen stared at her, and the woman ducked her head and returned to her table and the sewing machine.

Mary Ellen stood until the machine began to whirr. She reached over to a table and picked up small scissors, which she slipped into her skirt pocket.

"I'm ready," she said, returning to the front room. Her quick step halted when she felt something beneath her shoe and heard the faint crunch of a little seed pearl being crushed.

෨

"Shall we walk or ride?" Claybourne Honeycutt asked.

Matilda had mentioned seeing his car and had said there were only three in Hilo, other than rentals. The white vehicle parked down the street a couple of buildings away must be his. Why had he not parked in front of the dress shop? Had he walked up there and stood outside, observing her?

Her glance at him revealed that daring look in his eyes and slight upward turn of his lips. "How far is it?"

"Within looking distance. See the ocean down there?"

180

She gazed toward the wharf and saw a steamer anchored in Hilo Bay. Tall palm trees swayed gracefully against a clear blue sky. "The post office is in the ocean?"

"I deserved that," he said. "Actually, the post office is located on the corner of Kamehameha and Waianuenue."

Those syllables rolled off his tongue as smoothly as the gentle waves caressing the seashore.

"Incidentally," he said, "across from the post office is the depot of the Hawaii Consolidated Railway. Our sugarcane is transported by rail from the fields to the mill and on down here for shipping."

Mary Ellen thought she would like to know more about this sugar business but pretended disinterest in case he still thought she had traveled over two thousand miles just to meet him.

She wouldn't have.

Would she?

But. . .Breanna had.

She felt her skirt brush against her legs, caused by her brisk pace and the warm breeze.

Many people were on the sidewalks, some coming out of shops and others going in. A couple of young women in Western dress stood across the street. "Aloha, Clay."

He returned the greeting. They seemed to smile at her before entering the restaurant. A man on a horse rode up the street. He was wearing a cowboy hat with flowers around the band. He tipped the brim with his fingers. "Aloha, Mr. Clay. Miss."

Clay laughed lightly when she turned to look after the man as he rode past. "The flowers?" he said. "People who are not from Hawaii question that. It's a common practice for paniolos to wear a band of flowers on their hats."

"Paniolos?"

"Cowboys. Matilda, whom I understand you met, is from Texas, and she still calls the paniolos cowboys."

"Do they mind?"

He shook his head. "There's a mixture of peoples and languages and cultures here. We tend to accept the differences and don't get upset about them."

"So I've noticed. Not even about a young girl who—"

He stopped and faced her. "Of course I care if you have a missing sister. And I also care about being falsely accused. The sooner we get this cleared up, the better." He strode faster down the sidewalk.

She kept pace with him. She would run if necessary.

He reached the door of the building before she did and held it open for her to enter. A postal clerk stepped up to the opening. "Aloha."

"Jennings," Clay said, "do you have any general delivery mail for me?"

"You picked up your mail this morning, Clay."

"I'm aware of that." Clay laughed lightly. "This would be addressed only to

C. Honeycutt in general delivery."

"I'll check."

Clay's smug glance seemed to say that was proof he hadn't received general delivery mail.

The man returned holding several letters. "Here you are. C. Honeycutt. I didn't know about the box. Sorry." He spread his hands and chuckled. "But what do I know? I'm only the postmaster." He handed the letters over. "Looks like you haven't picked them up in a while."

Mr. C. Honeycutt's bronzed coloring seemed to fade. Mary Ellen tried to give him a smug look, but he kept staring at the letters. Finally, he thanked Jennings and hastened to the door.

As soon as they stepped outside, she reached to jerk the letters from his hand.

He held them away, looking at them.

"This is proof that you received mail through general delivery."

He handed her the envelopes. "This is proof, all right. But not about me."

Mary Ellen shuffled through them. There were three. All addressed to Breanna Colson, c/o Mr. C. Honeycutt. The return address was Mary Ellen Colson, San Francisco, California.

"She. . .she didn't get my letters. She didn't know I was coming."

"That explains why she didn't meet you or send word." Clay smiled broadly, and his dark eyes danced with a gleam in them.

"I realize that. But. . ." Mary Ellen felt the fear that sounded in her voice. "Where is my sister? Why did she not write to me? Why do you say you know nothing about this? Something isn't right. I have to go to the police."

&

When she jerked away from his outstretched hand, Clay dropped it to his side. She did not trust him. And the fear in her eyes and voice was real.

He hated seeing the pain on her face. This young woman was beginning to believe the worst. She had paled considerably.

"Look. This involves me and the name of Honeycutt, too. I know this may sound selfish to you, but I know what the newspapers can do to a business if there's a scandal. And with your story, the implication is against me. I have a right to clear my name. Can you agree?"

She drew in a deep breath and weighed her words carefully. "Your name was on your photo, and someone had a box at the post office in your name."

"No," he said quickly. "Anyone could send mail to anyone's name. Now, do you have the photo?"

"My sister has it."

"But you saw it?"

"Yes, Breanna and I saw it at the same time. She was intrigued immediately."

She *was intrigued*? He could return to that thought later. Now, he needed to concentrate on her sister and the consequences of a police investigation. "Okay. Let's look at this realistically."

Despite the skepticism in her eyes, he continued. "The name Honeycutt means something around here." She shook her head and frowned. "That's not pride. It's fact. The police would have a hard time believing I had anything to do with this. And all the evidence you have against me is letters you sent to a post office box."

"I have a missing sister. And I can prove it."

Now that was a problem.

"Let's go back inside." She didn't pull away when he took her arm and led her in. He went again to the postmaster. "Jennings, I think somebody took a box in my name and got mail in my name. Maybe someone from my office. Can you check around and see if anyone remembers my making those arrangements?"

Clay stood silently beside Mary Ellen while the man checked.

Jennings returned. "Nobody remembers it. We get a lot of mail for you, but not through general delivery. Sorry if something went wrong. But you know we have hundreds of visitors who get their mail general delivery. We put the person's name on a card that says HOLD TILL ASKED FOR and put them in those alphabetical boxes. It's not something we try to remember."

"Okay. Tell me this. Who picks up my mail?"

The man looked as though he had lost his mind. "Um, you. Your employees. Your secretary, someone from your office. Are you looking for something in particular?"

"No. It's fine. Thanks, Jennings. But ask your workers to give more thought about who asked for a general delivery box in my name."

Mary Ellen headed for the door before him this time. She paused on the sidewalk, her eyes brimming with determination as if they were screaming for the police. Maybe he could reassure her. "The police would do more than I've done. They would question if anyone in the post office noticed anything unusual."

"So you want me to trust you instead of the police? Is that what any intelligent, sensible person would do?"

"Yes, because I have a better chance of getting to the bottom of this than the police."

"How?"

"I can ask questions without anyone being afraid they're going to be arrested. You heard Jennings say that only about six people can get my mail. I'll get the truth out of them."

"But you told me anyone can get a post office box in your name."

"But not just anyone could have had my photo."

He thought he had her there. But she came back with, "You're the suspect."

"But I'm not the person guilty of anything. Just give me a chance."

Her blue eyes flashed. "So, begin the investigation, and I'll let you know how well you're doing."

He had to think fast. "Let's go to the immigration office."

"Matilda, Rose, and I have done that."

"But I haven't." He turned and strode down the sidewalk. She couldn't very well physically detain him. He tried to hide the grin he felt forming on his lips when he heard the fast tapping of those pointed-toe shoes as she hurried to catch up with him.

Miss Colson was giving him a chance to prove himself and help find her sister. A chance. But she had seen his photo along with her sister. The sister had been interested—but this Miss Colson had not been.

He'd never had to work at gaining a woman's interest.

Herein was a challenge.

Different. Even intriguing.

After they would get through this sister problem, perhaps he'd work on the one who had not been interested in him. After all, she was quite an attractive blond. Had spirit, too.

He slowed when she reached him. "Tell me again exactly what was on the back of that photo."

She repeated what he'd already heard several times. "I've told you everything. No. Something else. You said you were a moral person. That seemed like a good thing at the time. Now, I wonder if you. . .someone was trying to convince us of that because he had ulterior motives."

Clay's mind stuck on the word *moral.*

"I'd never say that." When she gave him a quick look, he amended the statement. "I mean, of course I am. But one doesn't go around saying it."

She looked doubtful.

Who would say that?

He knew. The game.

The question he had asked Mak returned to his mind. *What would a man want with an eighteen-year-old girl?* Mak's glance had meant, plain as day, it depends on the man. Clay shuddered inwardly at the myriad of answers.

Maybe he should let the police handle this. Otherwise, she might discover that Mr. C. Honeycutt is—although indirectly—involved.

☙

Mr. C. had said one thing that made sense. If Mary Ellen went to the police, he might be jailed and then not be in any position to help her.

And, too, Breanna did not get Mary Ellen's letters. She didn't know her sister was coming to Hawaii. But why did no one know about Breanna? Or was everyone simply claiming not to know?

"She expected to meet you, Mr. C. If no one showed up to meet her, she would have tried to get in touch with you. Someone met her."

"We'll check it all out."

When they arrived at the immigration office, Akemi greeted them with her beautiful, sweet smile, her black eyes filled with warmth and welcome. "You found your Mr. C. Aloha, Mr. Clay." She made her little bow, and Mary Ellen thought her adorable.

Akemi summoned Mr. Hammeur. He entered the room, smiling, but one glance at Mary Ellen, and he exhibited the same aloofness she'd detected earlier.

Clay asked Mr. Hammeur if he'd checked the passenger list and if Miss Breanna Colson had disembarked.

"Yes, of course. The captain presented his passenger list to me. He assured me that all passengers for this island had disembarked."

"Do you remember the night she was to arrive?"

Mr. Hammeur's responses were what they had been earlier.

Clay thanked Mr. Hammeur, who then left the front room. Mary Ellen watched as Mr. C. walked over to Akemi, who was folding letters and putting them into envelopes. She did not look up.

"Akemi," Mr. C. said softly. "You know my photo had to go out from here. The Japanese man's official form was sent to the mainland. How could that have happened?"

"I do not know."

"Did some Japanese man come in? Did you do him a favor? Or perhaps the wife of a Japanese man?"

"No Japanese man could come in without a boss, like you. It is not allowed. I would be deported for that."

"A restaurant owner might. Someone who doesn't work on the plantation."

"No. If anyone needed me to help with a letter or a form, I wouldn't do it from here."

Mary Ellen believed her. She felt that Mr. C., although asking kindly, was torturing the poor girl.

"Is there any way my photo could have gone out from this office? Has anyone ever helped you with the mail?"

Akemi's lower lip trembled. "Please, Mr. Clay. Don't ask me any more."

He lifted a hand, as if to say *wait*. He left the room. Soon he returned. "I told Mr. Hammeur that you're not feeling well and need some air. Please, Akemi. Come outside with us."

She did.

They walked down the sidewalk to a bench. Mary Ellen sat beside Akemi.

Mr. C. stood in front of her. "Who has helped you?"

"Only Geoffrey. He's not like his brother, but he's good. He wouldn't hurt anyone. I know he would not."

Mary Ellen watched Clay look at the sky and call on the Almighty and then glance at her. "That, Miss Colson, was a prayer."

"He would come and talk to me when Mr. Hammeur went to lunch. It was during a time when a big shipment of men were to come in. I was busy. He took mail to the post office a few times. He sealed some envelopes for me. I saw no harm in it."

"It's all right. He takes my mail to the post office all the time. And we don't know if he tampered with your mail. You didn't do anything wrong, Akemi."

"Mr. Hammeur will think so."

"Maybe we can get this straightened out without Mr. Hammeur."

Mr. C. obviously knew more than he was saying. Before Mary Ellen could ask who Geoffrey was, they were assaulted with the *chahoooga, chahoooga*!

Matilda parked in front of them, jumped out of her car, and waved an envelope. "You have a letter from San Francisco, Mary Ellen. It was just delivered to the Matti-Rose."

Mary Ellen reached into her skirt pocket and took out the scissors. She opened them and used an edge to slice open the envelope. A quick glance around revealed curious looks from Akemi and Matilda. Clay's mouth opened slightly, and his eyes turned toward heaven. If he thought she'd put those scissors in her pocket as a weapon to use against him if necessary, he was right.

Another envelope was inside the one she opened, addressed to Mary Ellen Colson, c/o Uncle Harv. "It's Breanna's handwriting," she said. "See how she curls her letters?"

She read Breanna's first:

Dearest Mary Ellen,
    Everything is going so well for me. I'm on the island of Oahu. Will write more when I have time. I have so much to tell you.
    Don't worry about me, but write and let me know how things are with you and how that wedding dress is coming along. You must come here.

Love,
Breanna

"What's the address?" Clay asked.

Mary Ellen let out a sharp breath. "Breanna Colson. General delivery. Post office, Oahu, Hawaii."

"Oh, we can find her then," Matilda said. "She's all right."

"I'll find her." Clay said. "Someone used my photo and my name. I will find out who."

"Her safety is the most important thing at the moment, Mr. C. Whoever is behind this is secondary."

His bronzed skin deepened in color. "That goes without saying."

"Is that another letter there, dear?" Matilda said.

"Oh." Mary Ellen unfolded the sheet of San Francisco immigration office stationery. "This is from Uncle Harv":

My dear Mary Ellen,
    This letter came to you from Breanna. She obviously sent this after you left for Hawaii. I'm sure you two are having a wonderful time. I hope you are well and find time to write to me.

Affectionately,
Your Uncle Harv

Akemi's voice was full of hope. "Your sister is okay now. She say she okay."

"Yes, but why is she in Oahu? She came here to meet Mr. C." Mary Ellen had thought of him so long as Mr. C., she couldn't easily think of him as Clay. "I don't understand this. She didn't mention Mr. C. in her letter, but she was so looking forward to meeting him." She glanced from Akemi to Matilda. "She must be devastated that she wasn't met." She took a deep breath. "If that's the case."

"I will telegraph Oahu," Clay said.

"Telegraph the post office?" Mary Ellen saw that Matilda and Akemi were looking at him with the same kind of questioning she felt.

"I have business friends and relatives in Oahu. I will telegraph them, and you will get your information." He paused. "Now. I will go now."

"Do that." Mary Ellen knew her voice sounded short instead of grateful. But this Mr. C. Honeycutt was one strange bird. She could only pray that Breanna was safe. For now, she would pretend she trusted him.

What choice did she have?

Choice?

Of course she had a choice. She deposited the scissors into her pocket, lifted her chin, and said, "Let's go."

"And I will chaperone," Matilda said with a lilt in her voice. Her green eyes sparkled.

"Protect me might be a better word," Clay said, "since Miss Colson carries a weapon in her pocket."

"Oh, Pilar had gone to get us sandwiches when I left. I asked Aila to tell her I would be back soon."

"Did you tell her you were leaving with Clay?"

Mary Ellen felt uneasy, remembering how the worker had acted. "Yes, I did."

"Then Pilar will understand if you don't hurry back. Nevertheless, Akemi," Matilda said, "would you run across the street and let someone know Mary Ellen won't be back for a while?"

"Sure thing, okay." Akemi lifted her graceful hand as she turned to go.

"I'll use the telegraph system at my dock office," Clay said.

Mary Ellen was grateful to Matilda for her thoughtfulness or curiosity, whichever it was, in accompanying them. She was not comfortable being alone with the enigmatic Mr. C., who aroused a myriad of fluctuating emotions in her.

Chapter 9

Mary Ellen watched Clay handle the telegraph system. Matilda explained, "They get orders from all over the world, since the U.S. annexation. Sugar is Hawaii's biggest business, you know."

She'd heard that, but it wasn't what mattered at the moment. She was torn between thinking Mr. C. might find Breanna and the question of how he knew where and whom to call.

He said the words as he punched out the code. "Seeking whereabouts of Breanna Colson. Eighteen years old. Blond. Blue eyes." He glanced at Mary Ellen and back at the machine. "Pretty. Contact sugar mill at the dock on Hawaii. Have Geoffrey contact me ASAP."

"Do you think he's wiring the Oahu Post Office?"

Matilda shook her head. "No. That would be his brother, Thomas. The Honeycutts own plantations and sugar mills in Oahu, too. Clay has access to many contacts." She smiled. "Don't you think, Mary Ellen, this is just miscommunication between you and your sister?"

"Not entirely. Our letters not getting to each other is one thing. But her not mentioning the man she came to meet tells me something is not right."

"But her letter did not sound as if she were in trouble, did it?"

Mary Ellen took the letter from her pocket and read it again. "No. She sounds like she's looking forward to a wedding. But right here is the Mr. C. in the photo. Is there someone who looks like him?"

Matilda sighed. "Ahh. Nobody looks like your Mr. C. He is like the racehorse my Jane rode that beat the king's horse in the royal race. Some animals are simply one of a kind."

At Mary Ellen's quick glance, Matilda added, "And some people."

"Well," Mary Ellen said, "there are two sides to people. The outside and the inside."

"So true. I think you should get to know your Mr. C.'s insides."

She suspected that would be much too complicated.

He came over to them. "The word is out. The communication system isn't always efficient, but the sugar office in Oahu will get the message and pass along the information. All Oahu will be looking for Miss Breanna. I will be contacted as soon as a reply comes in."

"I keep hearing the name Geoffrey."

Clay nodded. "He's one of my and my brother's employees who may be able to help us."

188

૭

Clay knew he wouldn't be able to keep his mind on the account ledgers, so he needn't go to the sugar mill, or to the other five appointments that had been on his agenda for the day.

Everything pointed to Geoffrey. If he was involved in this, Breanna would likely be safe. If not, there were questions Clay himself couldn't answer. And he didn't want to accuse Geoffrey before he had some facts.

Clay felt useless until later in the day when one of his employees called to him. "Wire for you from the Oahu office."

He read the message hurriedly: "BREANNA WITH ME. ALL FINE. GEOFFREY."

As fast as the system would work, Clay punched out the code that Breanna's sister was in Hawaii and worried. He demanded that Geoffrey have the girl wire her sister within thirty minutes.

Geoffrey opted for an hour.

Clay agreed, feeling both anger and relief. But the anger wasn't directed only at Geoffrey. The scripture he'd learned when a child at the mission school circled around in his brain—*"Be sure your sin will find you out."* On second thought, it was beginning to look like neither he nor Geoffrey had a brain, maybe just empty space.

A short while later, Clay stood outside the Matti-Rose Hawaiian and Western Wear Shop, watching Miss Colson, as he had done that morning. Amazing, what a few hours could do to a person's thinking.

Earlier, he had seen her as a lovely blond, but also as one who had invented an elaborate ruse to get to him. She had even been getting her wedding dress ready. Thinking about that, he realized how uncouth and arrogant he'd been that morning. His dad would not have been proud of him.

Now, he stood looking, not at someone with whom he might play games, but a young woman who had traveled many miles to find her younger sister. And she was making a wedding dress for that same sister.

As if sensing him there, Miss Colson's head slowly turned. She looked over her shoulder, and their gazes held. After a moment of showing no emotion, she again turned her attention to the dress. He felt that indicated she didn't expect anything from him—not anything good anyway.

He looked around, as if seeing the main street of Hilo in a new way. Maybe he was seeing himself. And that, too, was based on selfishness. For as long as he could remember, he'd been occupied with how he saw women. Right now, he was concerned with how this woman saw him.

૭

When Mary Ellen looked around at Mr. C., she thought of what Mrs. Dampers had said many times. Whenever an orphan claimed she would do something like study harder, scrub better, or clean her plate, Mrs. Dampers would thrust her big fists into her ample sides, scowl, and say, "Missie, that's only lip service. The proof of the pudding is in the eating."

Mary Ellen took her words to mean a person's word meant little without the action. Come to think of it, the Bible had something to say about that: *"Faith without works is dead."* That wasn't exactly the same thing, but she felt it also meant lip service without action didn't mean much.

Since she didn't know what to think of the enigmatic Mr. C., she had to rely on proverbs and sayings and clichés. Right now, a dominant one was *handsome is as handsome does.* So far, he was lacking in the *does.* Although he appeared to be helping, he also seemed to be holding back information.

She did not turn when the bell tinkled.

Mr. C. and Pilar spoke to each other like familiar friends. "I told Mary Ellen," Pilar said, "that you know everyone in Oahu and you will find her sister."

"I do have some news. Mar—"

She felt her shoulders rise. He must have noticed, for he quickly said, "Miss Colson, a friend and employee of mine knows your sister. He is to have her wire my office in less than an hour."

Mary Ellen had let him talk to her back. Now, words seemed to fail her. Those ambivalent feelings. Was Breanna really all right? Or was Mr. C. pretending to help when, in reality, he was involved in Breanna's disappearance? If Breanna wired from Oahu, would there be a request for a ransom?

Mary Ellen turned. She could only shake her head. "I don't know you, Mr. Honeycutt. I need someone to accompany us. Matilda will return soon."

Pilar laughed, and he scowled. Then she cleared her throat and appeared quite somber.

Mr. C. spread his hands. "There's a building full of people. Dockworkers are all around. People on the street. Why, all of a sudden—"

"Why? Because you've led me on too many wild goose chases, Mr. C. I am tired of that. I go to your office, and there's no telegram from my sister, and then what? And how can I know it's from her? You might have me on another wild goose chase."

His brows almost met. "You have goose chases on the mainland?"

"This is not about gooses." She closed her eyes and breathed in through her nose. "I mean, geese. And I will not be duped. Do you understand *duped*?"

Further comments were cut off by *chaooooga, chaooooga.*

Pilar's smile and the lifting of Mr. C.'s eyes toward the ceiling indicated they knew who should accompany them to the sugar office.

❧

Inside the office, Clay stood back where neither Miss Colson nor Matilda would be looking straight at him, lest his concern be reflected in his face. He turned away from his desk and looked out the window away from the dock. The white sand beach stretched out between the softly lapping ocean on one side and palm-fringed trees on the other. This should be a day for walking along that path with a beautiful woman instead of having one standing in his office, her every expression one of distrust, suspicion, and dislike.

But that was the way of it and—

"Your wire is coming from Oahu, sir," an office worker announced.

Clay read it as it came in:

MARY ELLEN. WHAT A SURPRISE. CAN'T WAIT TO SEE YOU. WILL
ARRIVE MONDAY. WILL WIRE TIME. LOVE, BREANNA.

"See," Clay said. "All that worry for nothing. Your sister is fine. It's just that you two communicate about as well as our interisland system, which is almost nil."

"Communication between me and my sister is not the problem, Mr. C. If this is on the level, then it's a problem between you and your"—she paused—"your *friend*."

How well he knew. But he wasn't going to admit it until he had to.

"Send a wire to her," she said. "Ask if she's alone and where she is."

He did. The words came back:

WITH GEOFFREY'S PARENTS. HE AND I ARE IN LOVE.

"Geoffrey?" she said, shaking her head and looking helpless. Her eyes closed as tears trickled down her cheeks.

How many times had he said he had never hurt any woman. He could no longer claim that. This one was hurting. "You want to send another message?"

"Just tell her I love her and be sure to telegram what time she will arrive."

She turned to Matilda. "Breanna says she's all right and in love with someone named Geoffrey," repeating the message as if Matilda hadn't heard it and Mary Ellen couldn't believe it.

"Then she is all right," Clay said.

"According to the telegram, yes. But I can't be sure." Her eyes threatened him. "She came to Hawaii because she was in love with you."

He scoffed and heard his voice rise at least an octave. "In love with a photo?"

Her lips trembled. Her eyes became teary again, and she turned away. Matilda put her arm around Miss Colson's shoulders.

❧

Clay dressed in his finest, taking particular care to look like a decent, respectable gentleman attending church. Before the service, he spoke to Jacob.

"Sorry I couldn't bring Geoffrey with me, Jacob. But I talked to him, and he may be here on Monday. I'll let him know you'd like to see him."

Disappointment settled on Jacob's face, but he thanked Clay and turned to shake another person's hand and speak to him.

"Good morning, Clay." That was Rose's voice. He turned to see her, Matilda, and Miss Colson. The older women, as usual, were dressed like owners of a dress shop, in latest Western fashion.

Miss Colson looked serene but lovely, as if everything about her was perfect, exactly as it should be. Any decent, respectable gentleman would be proud to win her approval.

Miss Colson did not extend her hand; she simply nodded as an acknowledgment that he existed.

He felt his pasted-on smile disappear when Matilda spoke in a reprimanding way. "Well, Claybourne Honeycutt. It's about time you got yourself back in church."

Leave it to Matilda!

"Matilda, Rose." Jeannette Hammeur, holding her skirt with one hand and her hat with the other, rushed up to them. "Oh, Miss Colson. That's right, isn't it?"

At the affirmative nod, the woman frowned. "Did you find your sister?"

When Miss Colson said yes, Jeannette lifted her hands. "Praise the Lord. I prayed you would." She turned to Matilda and Rose. "Do you have any word on that dress I wanted?"

Clay took the opportunity to try to show there was a hospitable side to him. "Miss Colson, perhaps you'd be interested in the history of this church."

Her chin lifted, as did her eyes, cornflower blue today with a touch of indignation. Her gaze held his. "Perhaps," she said.

He took her elbow, felt the exquisite material of her dress and the warmth of her flesh beneath it. With an almost indiscernible movement, she shifted her arm away but continued to walk alongside him. He pointed to the top of the church.

"That steeple is one hundred feet high."

She didn't say anything. He looked down at her upturned face. The pert little hat covered most of her blond hair. But a couple of locks that begged to be wrapped around a finger lay along the sides of her face. Her eyes were as blue as the summer sky, sparked by the silver glint of the sun. They turned to gaze into his. Her full lips, the color of coral, parted slightly.

"What's the significance of that?"

The significance? "Well, Miss Colson—" He quickly put his hand to his mouth and cleared his throat. He'd been about to tell her the significance was that she was quite lovely.

But her focus had returned to the steeple. He felt it coming from deep inside and couldn't hold it back. He laughed. "Sorry," he said. "That's as far as my history lesson goes about that steeple."

"I just wondered. Is there a bell in it?"

It began to ring. Ah, saved by the bell. "Complete with a young boy swinging on a rope. Now this might interest you. Matilda's brother, Reverend Russell, preached here for more than thirty years. He taught in the mission school and was greatly admired and respected."

Matilda and Rose caught up with them near the entrance. Miss Colson thanked him and joined the other two women, who walked down and sat in a pew on the left side of the church, a few rows from the front where Akemi sat. People near them began to turn and be introduced to Miss Colson.

Clay found a seat at the right on the second pew from the back, near the aisle. He surely failed the history lesson. He could have told Miss Colson about the ti plants that surrounded the church, planted at a time when many natives believed the plant warded off evil spirits, so they felt brave enough to enter the church. After being inside, they were presented with the gospel message.

While the choir sang, his gaze scanned the church, where he had attended most of his young life. He could have told her the church was made of lava rock, bonded together by crushed coral, sand, and oil from kukui nuts. She might like to know the king and queen had attended this church.

He should have said the current pastor was from the mainland and that the congregation liked his stories about America. Clay listened more closely when he began one of those stories.

"I came from the mountains of Colorado where there are a lot of snowy winters," the pastor said.

Hawaii didn't have snowfalls like in the United States and Europe, but Clay knew much about the snow on Mauna Kea, so he got the preacher's image in his mind. He prided himself on having been an unofficial tour guide for more than a few European and American young woman. He'd formed a few snowballs during a ski trip, and he'd experienced the enveloping of the cold snow when he'd taken a few tumbles down the slopes.

The congregation was exchanging glances and smiles as the pastor told of his personal mishaps on the slopes. Then he began to talk about thoughts being like a snowball.

He presented a vivid picture of a thought turning into contemplation, and from there into desire, and then action, and that little tiny snowball had rolled down a hill and become too big and too cold and too heavy to budge or melt. The preacher was talking about sin.

Clay became increasingly warm and uncomfortable despite the snow sermon. He'd simply wanted to go to the snowy mountain and pick up a snowball here and there. He wouldn't let them roll down the hill. Just hold them awhile.

And no, his snowballs hadn't rolled down the mountain. That was fun, exciting, a game. Yes, it had all started with a snowball of a thought.

It seemed to be slipping from his hand, threatening to roll down the hill.

Considering the uncertainty about Miss Colson's sister and Geoffrey, how long would he hold on to the snowball?

❧

After the church service ended, and Mary Ellen felt she'd been introduced to everyone, she turned to Akemi to compliment her on her beautiful kimono. By the time Akemi said, "Thank you," Clay Honeycutt was in the aisle, motioning to the man who had given the announcements and led the prayer.

When the man reached them, Clay introduced him as Jacob Grant, a teacher and assistant to the pastor. Then Clay surprised her with his invitation. "If you ladies and Jacob don't have lunch plans, perhaps—"

Matilda turned to them. "I've already made reservations at the Japanese restaurant. You young people can have those. Or join us, either one."

"I'm sorry, Clay." Jacob said. "I do have other plans. Excuse me, please."

Mary Ellen wondered about the puzzled look on Clay's face and the furrowed brow of Jacob, as if he was truly sorry he couldn't join them. But it was presumptuous of Clay Honeycutt to assume she and Akemi might want to lunch with him. He might have asked sooner, unless this was a spur-of-the-moment impulsive idea.

Her glance at Akemi revealed the girl no longer smiled and her head was bowed. She was not looking at anyone. Was Mr. C. interested in Akemi?

Rose touched his arm. "Join us, Clay."

"No, I don't want to intrude."

"Intrude." Rose scoffed. "Clay, you're family."

Mary Ellen didn't know what to make of Rose having said Clay was family. On second thought, however, Matilda and Rose seemed to treat everyone like family.

"Some other time, perhaps. Good day, ladies."

Mary Ellen tried not to be obvious watching him being greeted by friendly people. Were they greeting him like that because they liked him, or were they welcoming him more like a prodigal son, as Matilda had intimated?

～

At the restaurant after much discussion about food, Mary Ellen read from the menu. "I've never had this. So I'll try the fried calamari with saffron pepper sauce."

"Great choice," Matilda said. "And, remember, we can sample each other's food."

While they ate, Mary Ellen once again mentioned how much she admired Akemi's kimono.

"I am trying to show that I am proud to be Japanese. But since I have learned about God and Jesus, I cannot worship Buddha. Some do not understand that I can be Japanese and not worship Buddha. That is why I try to show them I care about the Japanese. Maybe even more now."

Mary Ellen saw the sadness on her face and was impressed that Akemi cared about the souls of her people. "Was it hard for you to leave your country?"

"Both sad and exciting," she said. "There is much poverty and disease in Japan. Most young men have come to Hawaii. Here they have job. Live in a beautiful place. Some bring picture bride so they have wife and children. That is better than most have in Japan."

"You must have been terribly disappointed when marriage didn't work out for you." Mary Ellen thought of Breanna. *What happened that she wasn't met by Mr. C.? Was she sad? Pretending all was well?*

"Yes, at first," Akemi said. "But now I think God had a different purpose for me. The plantation workers will not listen to haole talk about Jesus. But they listen to me. They feel sorry for me that I am not in their community and don't have a husband and children."

"We're your family, Akemi." Matilda patted the girl's arm.

Akemi smiled and nodded. "I know."

"Is that what you meant, Rose, when you told Mr. C. that he was your family?"

Rose's brow knitted. "Not exactly. His parents were killed in a shipwreck coming back from Scotland. That's when such a trip took months instead of days. There was a particularly bad storm. After that, Clay took over the business on this island, and it has thrived even more. He worked so hard. Now his brother and sister are settled in Oahu, and Clay runs this business like a shrewd business-man, in the best sense of the word."

Mary Ellen felt compassion for him, knowing the heartbreak of losing one's parents. Was she misjudging him? But she had to remember: His photo had shown up in San Francisco. Breanna had corresponded with Mr. C. and come to Hawaii.

No. She mustn't ignore the signs that all was not right. She could not trust him completely, at least not until after she saw and talked with Breanna.

Chapter 10

After the wire came in with the boat's arrival time from Oahu, Clay talked to Jacob and told him all about it.

After a long, stone-faced silence, Jacob said, "I'll have to do a lot of praying about this one."

Clay figured he'd do a lot more than pray. Increased anger rose in him as the boat approached the harbor. Anger that Geoffrey had done this to him. Anger that Miss Colson had every right to press charges against Geoffrey for tampering with U.S. mail. Would anyone believe that Clay had not been involved? He could only hope that the younger sister had not been coerced in any way. But she had been. With Clay's photo.

What had Geoffrey been thinking?

He closed his eyes against the question that Mak had asked and feared the answer. The snowball sermon came to mind. He had a feeling God was telling him something.

And Geoffrey needed to be taught a lesson.

But so did Claybourne Honeycutt. He sensed more lessons were to come. This was not over; perhaps it was just beginning.

Clay stood apart from Mary Ellen, Rose, Matilda, and Akemi. He had a few choice questions for Geoffrey, and he didn't need anyone in the way when he got his answers. He could almost see the newspaper headlines about Claybourne Honeycutt being mixed up in a scandal of illegal and immoral activity. Breanna Colson only had to say one negative word, and both he and Geoffrey could be carted off to jail.

He recalled the anger he'd felt when one of his workers had deceived Akemi. How much worse for this to happen to a member of one's family. He shuddered to think if his sister had been eighteen and lured anywhere under false pretenses.

There they were. Geoffrey holding onto the arm of a young girl who did indeed resemble Mary Ellen. This one was all smiles. She was quite well-dressed. Her hair fell loose over her shoulders, and she held onto her wide-brimmed hat.

Geoffrey and the girl were laughing and talking and thanking the greeters who placed leis around their necks. They looked like a couple of youngsters playing—

Clay's thoughts stopped. That's exactly what Geoffrey was doing. Playing a game. And Claybourne Honeycutt was the one who had taught him.

A squeal of delight came from Mary Ellen as she rushed toward her sister. Breanna threw out her arms and ran. They shared a lengthy embrace until Mary Ellen stepped back and laid her hands on Breanna's shoulders. Her hand came up, and she caressed her younger sister's face.

Clay saw the resemblance and the differences. The young sister was quite pretty and seemed to exude a lively spirit. Mary Ellen was a few inches taller than her sister, who was a few pounds heavier. Breanna had a childlike quality about her that was appealing. He could readily see why Geoffrey would be enamored of her, as exhibited by his watching her every move.

But Mary Ellen was a lovely young woman who was trying to be an authority figure for her sister. He knew the feeling of taking authority, although his efforts had been in business rather than with his older siblings.

Geoffrey ambled up to them, all smiles, and from the corner of his eye, Clay saw Akemi walking toward them.

Clay took a deep breath. He did not return Geoffrey's wide smile. "You sent my photo to the mainland?"

"Yeah, but—"

"When you pretended to help Akemi?"

He scowled and looked toward Akemi. "I did help. But yeah—"

"You lured this—"

"I didn't lure—"

"You know this is illegal?"

"No." Geoffrey grimaced. "I never thought of that."

"You know it's immoral."

Geoffrey seemed to be comprehending. He began to shake his head. Dread filled his eyes.

Clay nodded and drew back his arm.

Someone grabbed his arm before his fist could hit its intended target. He turned his head quickly to identify who. Jacob?

"He's my brother."

Clay stared at him. Jacob held on until Clay relaxed his fist. "Your brother has acted totally irresponsibly. It also involves the Honeycutt reputation and yours, too, for that matter."

"I know," Jacob said. He faced his brother. "And this could mean Akemi loses her job."

Geoffrey scoffed and spread his hands. "That won't happen." He started to smile. In a flash, he landed on his backside, his mouth open, his fingers moving to his jaw and his eyes wide, his brown curls spilling over his forehead into his eyes. Jacob's arm was outstretched, his fist still clenched. "Like I said, he's my brother." He looked at Clay again.

"But you don't hit as hard as I do."

"No, but I don't want him knocked out. I want him to feel the impact of my fist and of what he's done."

Geoffrey moved.

"You get up, and I'll do it again," Jacob threatened.

Geoffrey settled back.

"Oh. Oh. Oh." Young Breanna rushed to his side and knelt. She brushed aside his unruly curls. "Are you all right, Geoffy?"

"It hurts." He looked at her with that sick cow expression that Clay had vowed he would never have about a woman.

She leaned his head against her shoulder. She looked up at Jacob. "You awful, awful man."

"I'm his older brother." His voice held authority. "And if he doesn't have enough sense to behave properly, it's time he got some knocked into him. I do believe in being my brother's keeper."

"He hasn't done anything wrong." She looked lovingly at Geoffrey, who basked in her attempted vindication of him. "He's good, and he's wonderful."

Matilda walked up. "I was thinking back, Geoffrey. How did you manage to get the photo in the envelope without being seen?"

He admitted what she appeared to have already surmised. He had gone to the bathroom at the inn to slip the photo inside the envelope.

"Stand back, dear." Breanna wasted no time in obeying. Matilda removed the lei from around Geoffrey's neck. She slammed it back and forth across his head. He covered his face with his hands.

When she finally quit, he wailed, "That has shells in it."

Matilda huffed. "I was hoping for shark teeth."

Clay stepped back when Akemi came up to Jacob and looked at him with those dark, doelike eyes of hers. Her soft voice trembled. "It is my fault, too. I should not have let him help me."

Jacob eyed Geoffrey but spoke to Akemi. "Did you ask him to help?"

She bowed her head and looked at the ground. "No. But I didn't mind. I am sorry. Don't be angry. Please forgive me."

"Akemi."

Clay had never heard Jacob say anyone's name so softly. He watched as Akemi lifted her head and her eyes to Jacob. Her face was full of adoration.

"Helping is all right, Akemi." Jacob was looking at her. "It's his deception that's wrong." Abruptly, he turned from her, slid a glance past Clay, and focused on Geoffrey.

What was going on?

~

Mary Ellen didn't think a sock on the jaw or a lei lashing would do much for the situation where Breanna was concerned. She would, however, take the route that Jacob had taken. "I am your older sister, Breanna. Regardless of how you feel, I have a responsibility."

"You're not going to have him arrested, are you?" Breanna's face clouded.

Tears or pleading wouldn't change Mary Ellen's position. "I don't know all the facts. We need to talk."

"She can have the bedroom across from yours," Matilda said to Mary Ellen.

"Excuse me," Akemi said. "I'm expected at work. But if you need me—"

None of them seemed to think it necessary she go with them and chance losing her job.

"Just one question," Jacob said. "How did Geoffrey go about starting to help you at the office?"

Akemi looked puzzled at the question. After a moment, she met Jacob's gaze. "He was very kind. We would talk about how my Bible classes with you were going. And my English."

"Bible," Jacob repeated. Mary Ellen saw the clench of his jaw and his fist as if he might punch Geoffrey again.

Akemi seemed to have noticed and said quickly, "And you. He would talk about what a good man you are."

Jacob glared at Geoffrey again, but his words were addressed to Akemi. "I think it's fine that you go to work, Akemi. You will not lose your job. If Mr. Hammeur needs to get word of this, the blame will fall on the coercion of Geoffrey. Be assured of that."

Akemi whispered. "Forgive me."

Jacob's eyes closed for a moment, and he shook his head. "You did nothing wrong."

"I try," she said, "to be perfect."

"You are." Jacob spoke so quickly, the entire group seemed stunned. Akemi turned and hastened across the sand as swiftly as her small feet and kimono would allow. Looking at the group around her, Mary Ellen saw that Jacob stared at the sand. Jacob reached out to his brother. Geoffrey accepted Jacob's hand and stood.

As soon as Mary Ellen and her sister were away from the men and could speak alone, she asked, "Has everything really been all right with you, Breanna?" Matilda and Rose, walking behind them on the sidewalk, might hear, but that was fine. She needed the support of those two women.

"Better than you can imagine. I am sorry you've worried." Breanna's blue eyes danced with the glint of the sunlight, and her smile melted Mary Ellen's heart. "But I'm so glad you're here. We can talk now, woman to woman."

Mary Ellen was afraid to ask what that meant.

As soon as they arrived at the house, Rose began brewing tea. Matilda took cups down.

The tea was ready by the time the three men entered the house. Mary Ellen assured Rose and Matilda she did want them sitting in on the conversation.

They gathered around the kitchen table. Jacob sat directly across from Geoffrey. "Perhaps we should have a prayer before we start this discussion," Jacob said. They bowed their heads, and Jacob offered a brief prayer for guidance and restraint. After the *Amen*, he took the lead. "Tell us why you did this, Geoffrey."

"Well. You all know the men outnumber the women here two to one. I've seen all the women. Whenever any visitors or new ones come, most of them fall for Clay. I decided to get one for myself before she had a chance to see him. Women are crazy about him and I get leftovers."

Clay scoffed. "But you sent *my* picture."

"To get her attention. And it worked. Then after we began to write to each other, I sent my own picture and told her the truth. If I'd sent my picture in the beginning, she might have thrown it in the trash."

"Oh no, Geoffrey. I fell in love with you the moment I saw your photo. Nobody is more. . ." Breanna looked around and grimaced. "Nobody is more adorable than you. You are the cutest, most best-looking man I've ever seen."

His smile widened, matching hers, and their eyes seemed only for each other.

Finally, Breanna looked at Mary Ellen. "He sings. He plays the ukulele. And you should see him on a surfboard. He's wonderful."

Mary Ellen lifted a hand. "I understand. But you came here because you fell in love with the photo of Mr. C."

"Well." She shifted in her chair and pushed back a lock of hair. "Mr. C.'s photo did intrigue me. I mean, enough that I would have traveled this far just to see him. And I was going to take the immigration office job. I was going to make sure Mr. C. was as good as he looked. But then Geoffrey wrote the truth."

"You knew Geoffrey would meet you and not Mr. C.?"

"Yes. His letters told the truth right away."

"Why didn't you tell me?"

"I was afraid you would tell Uncle Harv and you both would forbid me to come." She paused. "I let Geoffrey know I was an orphan but had an older sister. I told him I was not a rich American, but was poor and worked part-time at the San Francisco immigration office."

Her quick glance at Mary Ellen seemed to mean she had not told him about the inheritance she would have.

"That was wise of you."

"Ahh!" Breanna smiled as if that were quite an accomplishment, being wise.

"I wanted her to get to know me," Geoffrey said. "I've been afraid that when she saw ol' Clay here, she'd dump me. He does favor blonds."

"Oh Geoffrey. I'm not so shallow." Breanna looked pained. "Besides. I think Mr. C. is too old for me. If he had met me at the dock, I would have told him he was more suited for my sister."

Mary Ellen choked on her tea, reminding her of how she'd choked on her saliva after dreaming of Mr. C. She emitted embarrassing croaking noises, fanned her hot face, and waved away Breanna, who kept asking, "Are you all right?" Mary Ellen finally was able to only repeatedly clear her throat.

While six sets of eyes stared at her, Mr. C. spoke. "I believe Miss Mary Ellen Colson just expressed her opinion of me."

Chapter 11

Clay had never felt so divided. After his parents had died and he'd taken over the main island business, he'd known what to do. His dad had trained him and given him responsibilities, but he'd never had to make any final decisions. So he'd called together the board members, those who knew how his dad thought and acted, and told them he depended on them.

They understood that. The business and their own well-being depended upon the business continuing to run smoothly. With the help of his dad's business associates, the business had prospered.

At stake now was his personal reputation. Seeing Jacob taking responsibility for Geoffrey, Clay wondered what his own dad would have done at a time like this. What would Mak say and do?

Mak was a great one for emphasizing morality based on the teachings of Jesus. Clay had reinforced those principles with Geoffrey. He'd told him they could play the game. As single, fun-loving young men there was nothing wrong with meeting and escorting beautiful young Western women. But he'd stressed it was never about conquest. They had a moral responsibility to treat women with respect.

But the way Geoffrey's thoughtless actions had caused Miss Colson weeks of fear for the safety of her sister raised both moral and legal questions.

"Geoffrey," Jacob said, nodding toward Mary Ellen. "Do you realize that all Miss Colson here has to do is contact the authorities about your tampering with the mail and you can be imprisoned?"

"She wouldn't do that," Breanna said just as Geoffrey scoffed and said, "I did nothing malicious. It was impulsive. But I wasn't thinking of doing anything illegal. It was a fun thing, like a—" He paused and, after a quick glance at Clay, added, "A harmless game, in a sense."

Clay tried not to show any emotion. Was this the time to admit he was part of that game?

But the current discussion was not about meeting single Western women. That in itself was not illegal or harmful or even underhanded. The women he and Geoffrey had met had been delighted to spend time with them. The fact was, Geoffrey had tampered with the U.S. mail. He had lured a woman to the island under false pretenses, at least initially, and whisked her off to another island.

When and how much is a person supposed to admit?

Mary Ellen Colson already didn't like or trust him. Should he speak up and destroy any possibility of that ever happening? He had a feeling if she knew he was involved, however indirectly, she would, without hesitation, take this to the authorities.

That was different, too. He'd never known a woman—of any age—not to like him as a friend, as a substitute son, or as someone special to her. Never! And a woman had never had the upper hand with him.

Jacob point-blank asked Mary Ellen what she intended to do. Clay wasn't about to look into her eyes. He had the feeling she'd recognize him as less than what he should be. She would see the snowball rolling down the mountainside. Perhaps already in a lump at the bottom.

Glancing at her, he saw that she focused on the table, thoughtful. Finally, she spoke. "I think Geoffrey deserves the chance to prove himself responsible. And Breanna, too. They need to get to know each other better before they jump into. . .anything more serious."

Jacob and Mary Ellen began to discuss Breanna and Geoffrey as if only the two of them were there. Clay sat back as if he were not involved. Yet Jacob knew he was. Geoffrey knew he was. Matilda and Rose knew he and Geoffrey made a practice of meeting the ships and escorting women. That hadn't been wrong. But now he and Geoffrey had cold ice on their fingers.

"We want to get married," Geoffrey said. "We're of age."

Jacob gave him a cool look. "Legally, yes. But what about maturity? Thinking with a level head? You need to think about this and the possibility of going to jail. To see the error of your ways."

"I can't see that it's an error," Geoffrey said, "except using Clay's photo instead of mine and sneaking the picture in official mail."

"Those were immoral and illegal actions," Jacob said staunchly.

"But it worked out so perfectly. I love Breanna. I don't ever want to look at another woman."

"Do you know what the Bible says about love?"

Geoffrey sighed heavily. "I was raised like you, Jacob. The same parents. In the church. In the mission school. Love is patient. Love is kind. Love is not puffed up."

"Love is action," Jacob added, and Geoffrey acknowledged his words with a nod and a lowering of his gaze.

"Breanna," Mary Ellen said to her downcast sister, "don't you want to plan a wedding instead of jumping into it?"

Clay couldn't help interjecting, "I've seen the wedding dress she's making for you. I can't imagine you'd want to pass that up."

Breanna relented. "You've always been so good to me, Mary Ellen."

Matilda gently rubbed the back of Breanna's hand, soothing her. "It doesn't mean you have to give Geoffrey up. Just get to know him. And get to know Hawaii. This should be the most romantic time of your life. Without your having to cook and clean and shop for a man."

"I wouldn't mind."

"And I'd work my fingers to the bone for her," Geoffrey said.

"I know," Matilda said. "But after a few days of that, all you'd have is bony fingers."

The two young people glanced at each other and away, as if daunted already.

Matilda brightened. "Take time to enjoy and feel the love so that it grows and can never fade, just like our beautiful flowers on this island. Breanna, be like a lovely flower. And Geoffrey, be the one who tells her about these flowers."

Breanna sighed. "Mary Ellen, I can't believe you would even consider sending my Geoffrey to jail."

Clay saw the sudden moisture that filled Mary Ellen's eyes, heard the way her breath caught before she spoke, as if it hurt to say the words: "Believe it." She rose from her chair, took her cup to the countertop, and stood for a moment. He saw the way her shoulders lifted, the way she squeezed her eyes shut for a moment and took a few breaths before pouring her tea and returning to the table as if she had not just uttered what were probably the most difficult words she'd ever spoken to her sister.

"I think it's settled then," Jacob said. "The conditions of not going to the authorities is that you two get to know each other. Mary Ellen will be the guardian of Breanna. And Clay, if you will, see that Geoffrey holds to his end of the bargain. He works for you most of the time. Would you do that?"

Clay knew what that meant. Although Geoffrey was responsible for his own choices, he and Geoffrey had both played this game with blond Western women. This was Jacob's way of saying it was time for Clay to show his own sense of responsibility. At the same time, Jacob was throwing him right in with this lovely blond Western woman—a woman who didn't care one whit for him.

Clay glanced at Geoffrey and saw a little gleam appear in the boy's eyes. He was likely thinking that with Clay in charge of him, they'd both have their fun and forget all this talk of responsibility. Clay would be easy on him. Much easier than Jacob.

Had Jacob lost his mind?

One look at Jacob, however, revealed that he knew what he was doing.

Clay pretended chagrin. "What all would this entail, Jacob?"

"That you and Mary Ellen chaperone these impulsive young people in lieu of a court case."

Clay gave Mary Ellen Colson his best charming smile and meant for his eyes to express a challenge. "I'm not sure Miss Colson is willing to be escorted around the island by the likes of me."

That was enough to make most women's cheeks color. Many would lower their eyelids and look at him through lowered lashes and say demurely, *Why, Mr. Claybourne Honeycutt, I would be delighted.*

Mary Ellen stared at him for a long moment. He thought her face might have deepened in color but not from pleasure. She turned to Jacob. "If this should be a foursome, could you not be the one to chaperone Geoffrey?"

Jacob shook his head. "I hadn't planned to broach the subject at this time, but I see I must. Before long, I'll be leaving for seminary training on the mainland."

"What?" Geoffrey was surprised.

"We'll talk about it later. Now, we need to get this settled." Jacob turned to Clay. "Will you do this for me, Clay?"

"You know I can't force Geoffrey."

"But you can influence him."

Right. That's what this was all about. Clay's bad influence that had gone too far.

"I will take responsibility for my sister."

Breanna returned her smile. "We could have fun, Mary Ellen. You've never had any always looking after me."

Mary Ellen reached over for her sister's hand, which met her halfway across the table. The two had moist eyes.

Geoffrey met Clay's gaze and nodded. Seriously.

Clay looked at Jacob and around at the other women. He could almost read their minds. Finally, a young woman who seemed to consider Claybourne Honeycutt as some kind of villain instead of sweeter than Hawaii's acres and acres of sugarcane.

❧

Long after the scarlet sun dipped into the ocean and the sky changed to sparkling stars and golden moonlight, Mary Ellen listened to Breanna talk about her exciting adventures with Geoffrey in Oahu.

Neither of them could bear for Breanna to go to her own room. They leaned on pillows against the headboard of Mary Ellen's bed.

Mary Ellen loved the closeness of hearing Breanna confide her personal feelings for Geoffrey. Her prayers for Breanna's happiness had been answered. Her sister had someone who adored her and had respected her enough to take her to his parents' home.

"They didn't mind that Geoffrey and I had just met. They understood love at first sight. Oh, Mary Ellen, I don't know if you believe in that."

"I'm beginning to." She didn't add that she also believed in many degrees and kinds of love. She'd had feelings for William but, in retrospect, thought that had simply been the natural process of growing up.

"Geoffrey and I talked about our future. He wants to buy some of the Honeycutt land and run his own sugar business." She sat straighter and faced Mary Ellen. "You'll never guess what I want to do."

"You want to be the world's greatest female surfboarder."

Breanna grabbed her pillow and threw it. Mary Ellen shielded her face with her hands. Laughing with Breanna felt good.

"No, silly. Mrs. Grant took me to the hospital and the orphanage where she volunteers. Now guess."

"You either want to be sick or an orphan."

"Grrr." Breanna rolled her eyes, then became quite serious. "I want to work with orphans. I'll go to college like you said I should. Then, depending on Geoffrey's plans, I will run an orphanage, work in one, or volunteer like Mrs.

Grant does. Oh Mary Ellen, Geoffrey's parents don't have any girls. They would like me as a daughter."

Tears sprung to Mary Ellen's eyes. "I am glad for you. And I do want you to be happy."

Breanna leaned back. "I haven't been this happy since I was little and we had Christmas with Mama and Daddy."

Mary Ellen understood. "Now tell me all about Oahu."

They settled back on the pillows. Mary Ellen closed her eyes while her sister droned on and on about her exciting life.

She awakened to the flutter of curtains moved by the soft breeze filled with the aroma of exotic flowers. Breanna looked so youthful. Her lips were parted with soft breathing, and her hands were folded on top of the coverlet.

But last night, she'd talked of love and life and goals in a mature way. As proof of her maturity, a short while after awakening, Breanna said, "I want to apologize to the immigration office official."

๛

"I am sorry, and I will volunteer to work for you without pay," Breanna said later that morning. "As I have time."

Mr. Hammeur was quite taken with her and forgave her. "Akemi could use some help with the abundance of picture-bride information that arrived this morning. But I, too, need to apologize."

That surprised Mary Ellen. He had seemed so staid before.

"I should have met you on the dock upon your arrival instead of waiting in my office." He smiled. "To show my good will, Akemi can take two hours for lunch, and she can explain how you might help her."

Mary Ellen realized he did feel guilty about not meeting Breanna and surmised that might explain why he had seemed defensive when she first inquired about her sister.

As they walked down the sidewalk, Mary Ellen looked forward to when she would visit all the shops they passed. Akemi led them into a Japanese restaurant.

In a break in Breanna's conversation while they ate, Mary Ellen asked, "What was your childhood like in Japan, Akemi?"

"My parents were schoolteachers. I was learning some English, too. They talked of the paradise that Japanese men wrote about. In the letters, the men would say, 'Lucky come Hawaii.' "

She smiled at that, but it soon faded. "My parents said we would visit Hawaii someday. I was twelve when they were killed in a village riot. I was in another village with my grandmother. She died when I was fifteen."

Mary Ellen and Breanna said, "I'm so sorry."

"I okay now. I stayed with a family as housekeeper. I learned to cook and clean and sew better. Then a matchmaker made plans for me to come to the beautiful land my parents wanted to visit."

Akemi told Breanna about the man who had sent for her.

"I'm sorry you didn't find love with him," Breanna said.

Akemi shook her head. "I find love. But not with Japanese man."

Mary Ellen and Breanna shared a glance. Akemi didn't elaborate but continued eating.

Mary Ellen ate, too, and watched the two young women becoming fast friends. She felt sure Breanna would soon be told about Akemi's secret love.

This seemed to be the time for young love. . .but not for older sisters to find love.

Chapter 12

In the middle of the week, when he could get away, Clay stopped by to see Jacob. They walked to the church and sat in a pew.

"Jacob, thanks for the suggestion of me and Geoffrey escorting those Colson sisters around the island." He gave a short laugh. "Mary Ellen is something of a challenge."

"Pretty, too."

"She didn't seem to believe that when I mentioned it."

His friend teased, "Maybe she has discernment."

But Clay agreed. "She looks beyond the surface. But I came to talk about Geoffrey."

Jacob's head turned. "What's he doing?"

"Everything he's supposed to. He's always been a good worker for me and Thomas and Mak. He has a carefree spirit. But he is responsible. And. . ." He wanted to be honest. "I think he's really in love with that girl."

"After seeing them together, I can believe that. But it's the illegal thing he did. He took things too far."

"He knows that now."

Jacob nodded. "Maybe I carried this too far, trying to make Geoffrey prove he's responsible. When I lectured him about responsibility, perhaps I was talking to myself."

"Yourself?"

When Jacob hesitated, Clay said, "Hey. There was a time when we could tell each other anything. Everything."

Clay followed Jacob's gaze to the front of the church and the cross on the distant wall. He spoke as if to someone other than Clay. "I've fallen in love with a Japanese girl. How can I have an effective ministry if I even think of pursuing a relationship with her? Or making her an outcast to her own race?"

Several things fell into place. Jacob's strange behavior had been motivated by his trying to avoid Akemi. "Is God telling you not to pursue her? Or are you concerned about prejudiced people?"

"It would harm the ministry. It would change our culture."

"Akemi is different."

"Yes. But she is Japanese. Only a few break out of the work force. You know that."

Clay gave an ironic laugh. "But she has. Everyone loves her."

"Yes. But she would be scorned by her people and by many Caucasians if we marry. How could I do such a thing to her?" He scoffed. "She is nineteen. I am twenty-nine. She respects me. How can I think she would consider me? She did not accept the man who paid her passage from Japan. She turned down the son of the Japanese restaurant owners. How can I think—"

"Why did she turn them down?"

"She said she does not love them. That she does not think like a picture bride. But I have been her schoolteacher. Her Bible teacher."

"Jacob, you'll drive yourself loco trying to figure this out. Tell God the desires of your heart, and let Him handle it. I've seen how she looks at you. She has feelings for you."

"She has feelings for everybody, Clay. Since she's asked Jesus into her heart, she shines. She can't get enough of life and faith. She wants to share that with her Japanese brothers and sisters."

"And what kind of woman would God want you to have as a minister's wife?"

Jacob didn't answer. He didn't need to. God would want a woman devoted to Him. A woman of faith excited about her Christian life and eager to share it.

Strange, how he could give advice to Jacob about life and love and God. Clay had never seriously considered a wife. But if he did, he'd want one like he'd just described.

But would that kind of woman want him?

He laid his hand on Jacob's shoulder. "I know how you feel. The thought of love can knock a person senseless, like being pushed under by a wave, getting caught in the undertow, coming up to take a breath, and getting slammed in the head by the surfboard."

Jacob drew back. "That bad, huh?"

Clay shrugged. "So I've heard."

It was good to have a laugh with Jacob. "I want to ask you something. Why is the church steeple one hundred feet high?"

"Take a brochure that's in the foyer. Figure it out."

Jacob didn't make things easy.

"And do what you want with Geoffrey," he said. "You will anyway."

Clay grinned and said aloha to his friend. Outside, he looked up at the steeple, then stuck the folded brochure into his pocket.

Riding along the streets of Hilo, lifting his hand to those walking and on horseback, he thought about Geoffrey. The decision of what to do about him wasn't really his, but Mary Ellen Colson's. She was the one who could bring charges against Geoffrey. He should talk with her.

He parked a couple of shops away from the dress shop and walked down the street. Standing at the side of the display window, he looked inside.

This wasn't the first time he'd done that. His first glimpse had been when he wondered what kind of trick that woman was playing on him. He'd watched her sewing little pearls on a wedding dress. Then he'd confronted her, and she'd stood up to him, suspicious and accusatory and without a smile.

He smiled, seeing her now. That's how she should be, instead of worrying about a sister old enough to make her own decisions. She was wearing a *holoku*.

She was laughing, and her eyes seemed filled with joy. Perhaps she had begun to get into the Hawaiian relaxed, carefree lifestyle.

But she hadn't yet let her hair down.

ᐖ

During much of the morning, Mary Ellen sewed seed pearls onto the wedding dress and listened to how Pilar talked about the clothing and related to customers. When they were alone, Pilar talked about her life in Texas, contrasting it to a new beginning in Hawaii.

"What was your life like in San Francisco?" she asked.

Talking about the shock of her parent's sudden death and the devastation to San Francisco seemed to release a burden in Mary Ellen that she hadn't known she carried.

Then Pilar confided about her own life. She had lived in Oahu. "Clay's sister and I are best friends. We went to nursing school together. Susanne became a pediatrician, married a doctor, and has a family. I married a doctor, too, but. . ." She paused. "After he died of tuberculosis—"

"Oh, I'm sorry."

Pilar smiled sadly. "I was blessed to have a good life with him. I try to focus on the good. After he died, I moved back here to be with Matilda and her niece, Jane, who are like family."

Mary Ellen felt warmth in her heart, thinking of Matilda and Rose, who were in back, unpacking a recent shipment. "They treat me and Breanna like we're their own."

Pilar nodded. "They're like that."

The bell tinkled, and while Pilar helped the woman who entered the shop, Mary Ellen thought about family. Although Breanna talked about missing Geoffrey terribly, Mary Ellen loved every moment of her time with her sister. She liked seeing her and Akemi walking up the sidewalk, talking and laughing. They would knock on the dress shop window and wave at her. Sometimes, Mary Ellen went to lunch with them.

As if her thinking made them materialize, the two girls came back from lunch and into the shop just as Matilda came out from the back with a couple of dresses and laid them on the countertop. Rose pushed in a mannequin on wheels.

Matilda held out a dress. "Try this on, Mary Ellen. Let's see how it looks."

In the dressing room, she felt like a different person wearing something brighter than the bland colors she'd worn at work. The dress fell loosely from the bodice. Cream-colored eyelet bordered the overlay falling a few inches from the shoulders and down from the scooped neckline. The overlay rounded halfway down the back, resembling a shawl.

She joined the others. "I love it. This color reminds me of last night's sunset when the sky was pinkish orange."

"It's coral." Matilda touched the trim. "This eyelet sets it off perfectly. Now, how does it feel?"

"Light. Airy. Comfortable."

"That's the point," Matilda said. "This is Hawaii's version of the European tea gown."

"The first one, similar to this, came about at the request of Queen Kalakua," Rose said. "She loved the missionary women's clothing when they came here in 1820 and asked, or demanded, the wives make her a dress like theirs out of white cambric."

"This one is more formal." Pilar held up the white one. "It's fine white cotton."

Matilda touched it. "Our queens and princesses wore these for informal occasions. For formal occasions, they wore the latest European fashions."

Rose said she was going to put the cotton dress on the mannequin for the display window.

"The Hawaiian people wanted a Western look with the loose, comfortable feel," Matilda said. "That's why this style is called holoku."

"Holoku," Mary Ellen said. "I'll need to remember that in case a customer asks."

"Western women like the explanations," Pilar said

"Will they ask what holoku means?" Mary Ellen asked.

"They will be as interested in that as you just indicated." Matilda said. "There are two versions of the story. One is that when the native seamstresses sewed their dresses they said *holo* when they turned the wheel to start the sewing machine. They said *ku* when they stopped at the end of a seam. *Holo* means *go* and *ku* means *stop*."

"That's interesting," Mary Ellen said, "I can hardly wait for the next one."

Matilda obliged them. "When the Hawaiian women wore the dresses for the first time, they said, 'We can run in it; we can stand.' They were not restricted by tight or binding clothes."

"I understand," Mary Ellen said. "I could float or dance in this." She made a fancy dance step like girls did at the orphanage when having fun. The others clapped rhythmically for her.

Just then, the bell tinkled.

She stopped abruptly.

Mr. C.'s dark eyes looked her over and gave them all a quizzical glance. "If I'd known there was to be a performance, I'd have come sooner."

Realizing she still held the sides of the dress, Mary Ellen let go and smoothed it.

"The new shipment of holokus," Matilda said. "What do you think?"

His glance slid to Mary Ellen again. "Quite attractive." He walked to the wedding dress. "But this is my idea of an eye-catching dress." He reached out.

"No," Mary Ellen said, louder than she meant. "I'm sorry. But the oil from hands will cause the seed pearls to change from their natural color."

"What a pity," he mused. "Such a beautiful creation. . .untouchable."

Chapter 13

The outing Mr. C. had suggested of seeing the plantation and sights of Hawaii with Breanna and Geoffrey had to be postponed.

On Monday morning, he stopped in to say a wire had been received that picture brides would arrive by the end of the week.

Mary Ellen was excited about that and began asking questions.

"A lot goes into this over a long period of time. We can talk about it if you'd like to help me at the immigration office."

"What about Akemi and Breanna?"

"They had the option of buying personal items for the brides or helping with files."

"I can guess their choice."

His smile was wide, and he nodded.

"I am interested in the picture brides, particularly after meeting Akemi, but. . ." She glanced at Pilar.

"Go on," Pilar said. "Your volunteer status here means you come and go as you please."

"It's payment enough to learn about fashion and to meet the customers." Mary Ellen's Hawaiian experience had not extended beyond working at the shop, exploring the town of Hilo, and taking walks on the beach. But those activities alone were like a fragrant breath of fresh air after having spent so many years in an orphanage, a boardinghouse, and an office.

Just walking from the dress shop to the immigration office with a man was more exciting than riding a cable car in San Francisco. "What happened to the Japanese man who deceived Akemi?"

"I told him he'd be deported on the next ship to Japan. But first, I took him to Akemi to apologize. She mentioned a widowed aunt who would like a man like Ke. Hoping that would ease Akemi's distress, I went along with it."

The conversation halted when a horse and carriage came alongside them and slowed as the driver greeted them. Mary Ellen had not met one unfriendly person in Hawaii. Aloha was beginning to come natural to her.

"And what happened?"

He shrugged. "Nothing unusual. He just spoke."

She gave him her best exasperated look. "With Akemi's aunt and Ke?"

He grinned down at her, and she knew he had teased her.

"Ke went through the proper procedure, and the widow arrived. They're married, and are among my best workers, along with being leaders in the village. That can happen when you give someone a second chance."

She glanced up quickly, but he seemed focused on the ocean ahead of them. Was he trying to tell her she should give Geoffrey a second chance?

Mr. Hammeur already had the records in a room where Mr. C. could review them.

"What I do," Clay explained after they went behind the desk on which folders were stacked, "is put each worker's and bride's forms together, along with their photos. Check for complete and correct information. After the brides arrive, if we find any discrepancy—as in the case of Ke—the bride should be returned to the ship and my worker deported."

Mary Ellen nodded. She'd worked with similar procedures in San Francisco.

"Also look for full payments. In the past when workers were on a payment plan, many stopped making payments after the marriage. That led to more stress and less work getting done."

The work wasn't complicated; it simply required meticulous checking of many items. Mary Ellen checked the brides' forms while Mr. C. checked his workers, and then they combined them.

"You know what you're doing," Mr. C. complimented.

She glanced at him. "It's not exactly deep-sea fishing."

He conceded that with a nod. "Mr. Hammeur will be grateful that you, instead of he, reviewed the forms. So much so that if you decide to file charges against Geoffrey, Mr. Hammeur will favor you and testify against your sister's beau."

"Then Geoffrey should be doing this to get into the good graces of Mr. Hammeur."

"I thought of that. But then I said to myself, 'Self, which do you want more—Geoffrey in the good graces of Mr. Hammeur, or yourself in the good graces of Miss Colson?' "

"This," she mocked playfully, "is supposed to put you in my good graces?"

"Whoa." He grimaced. "Guess I got that one wrong. I'll try and come up with something else. You're mighty hard to please."

Mary Ellen reached for another form and photo. No, she really wasn't. Working in the Hawaii immigration office beside Mr. C. was a sight more appealing than the lonely office in San Francisco. Strange, how a man's presence could make a menial chore seem like the most important thing at the moment.

But then, wasn't that a trademark of Mr. Claybourne Honeycutt? Making women feel that being near him was all any woman could dream of? She preferred not to dwell on such a thought.

She remembered when Breanna had laid her picture beside Mr. C.'s and Mary Ellen had thought them to be a most attractive couple who could belong to each other. Now, looking at the pictures of men and women, she could visualize them together, too.

"Something wrong?"

She realized she'd stared long at a picture. "Sorry. No, my mind wandered. I was thinking that if I didn't know better, I'd believe these couples already belonged together. But I do notice something."

"What's that?"

"The eyes. Almost all the men seem to have an uncertain look. The brides have a hopeful and excited expression in their eyes."

"The French have a saying: *Les yeux sont le miroir de l'âme.*"

Ah, classroom French. "The eyes are the mirror of the soul."

He turned to her. "I wonder, if I looked into your eyes right now, what would I learn about your soul?"

She focused on the papers, determined not to indicate she found him the slightest bit appealing. To become like a silly infatuated schoolgirl would be humiliating.

Of course, she wasn't infatuated.

What could she say about her eyes? Let him look into them? What would she see in his? She had already seen the daring, the challenge as if to ask if any woman could resist him.

Pray. *Lord, help me.* As if in answer, she thought of something. "I remember a Bible verse saying that the light of the body is in the eye."

"What does that mean?"

"Um," she hedged. "I think it means you can sometimes tell if a person has light or darkness in them."

"Hmmm. Do you suppose some of your light might seep into the darkness of my soul, Miss Colson, if you were to look deep into my eyes?"

She didn't know if he taunted or jested. But she was not about to look into his eyes or allow him to look into hers. Her soul, her heart, her mind, her good sense seemed in turmoil so much of the time. Perhaps it was due to the voyage over a churning ocean, or the swaying of palms, or the constant trade winds. In San Francisco, her life had seemed so static, so controlled. Here, it felt like sifting sand. She wasn't sure of her footing.

No, she couldn't let him see her uncertainty. "Let's finish this," she said. "I'd like to get back to the shop."

She worked with the files representing people committing to spend the rest of their lives together. The men worked so hard. The women traveled so far, in the hope of finding love.

And with few exceptions, they found it through the most unlikely of things: a photo.

⁂

"Today, you get to see the picture brides," Matilda said, while she, Rose, Breanna, and Akemi put the baskets of personal items in the wagon.

Mary Ellen felt the excitement of seeing how the couples would react when they first met. Would they be mistaken about their true love like Breanna had been about Mr. C.? Would they feel like Breanna did about Geoffrey? Would they be special to each other?

Soon, they stood on the sandy dock, their heads turning at the sound of the train coming down the rails.

Mr. C. exited, followed by Japanese men in dark suits and white shirts, wearing their hair slicked back. They looked much like they had in the photos, except one. "Why is that one wearing a hat?"

Matilda shrugged. "He may be the only one who could afford a hat."

Twenty men shifted uncomfortably on the sand until Clay had them line up. They then stood like statues with gazes fixed on the ocean.

Mary Ellen guessed the anxiety they must be feeling, remembering her anxiety about meeting Mr. C. even after she thought Breanna would be his bride. These men were committed to a lifetime with a woman they'd never met in person.

Geoffrey was last to exit the train, along with a couple of men who gave each worker the photo of his bride.

"Rose and I will take their leis," Matilda said. They struck off with the baskets of colorful, flowered necklaces.

Akemi said, "When I arrived as a bride, the men had leis, but the brides did not get baskets. We had only what we could bring. Matilda and Rose started the practice of helping picture brides feel welcome. Maybe because I felt so lost and sad. See, God makes good comes from the worst things."

Mary Ellen smiled at Akemi, impressed with the young girl's positive attitude.

Clay and Geoffrey walked up with Matilda and Rose.

"The men dress nicely," Mary Ellen said.

"They want to look their best," Matilda said. "But they have only one suit. Sometimes a suit is borrowed or rented. It's worn when they have their pictures taken so that the matchmaker in Japan can see they look nice. The same suit is worn for weddings and funerals."

Geoffrey laughed. "Clay and I used to say why not? They're one and the same." He looked at Breanna. "That's before I met the most wonderful girl in the world."

"For your information, Miss Colson," Clay said, "this is a small part of the work Geoffrey does. Most of the work is in the fields."

Geoffrey added, "I plan to start saving. Clay says I could buy one of his small fields if I show enough responsibility to manage one. I can do that."

"I know you can do anything you set your mind to, Geoffrey," Breanna said.

"For you, I can."

Mary Ellen watched them stare into each other's eyes. She glanced at Mr. C. He shook his head and looked out to sea. That seemed to confirm his opinion of love.

"The Japanese men look scared to death," Mary Ellen said.

Clay laughed. "Those men have worked for years to buy a wife. They've saved, had their photos taken, bought or rented their suits, paid the passage for the bride. Now they must be wondering what kind of woman they're going to live with for the rest of their lives and if it is all worth it."

"It's not only the men who are scared," Akemi said. "I know. I traveled across the ocean with hopes of a wonderful life with a man I would learn to love. But none of us expected to be like Breanna and Geoffrey. Our homeland is very poor. Our young men went away to make their fortunes in this place they had heard was paradise."

Mary Ellen was curious. "How did you know who to be matched with?"

"The men's photos came to the matchmaker's office or the immigration office. On the request form, the man tells his age, what part of Japan he came from, which island he is working on in Hawaii. He tells if he is very religious, how much education, and any special gifts. The matchmaker knows the bride's information. But mostly we only have the photos to go by. The matchmaker tries to see what is in the face and eyes of the man in the photo."

"Photos can be deceiving, can they not, Miss Colson?" Clay asked.

What did he expect her to say about his photo? "Apparently, Mr. C., Akemi was deceived by a man twenty years older than his photo. The one sent to the office in San Francisco was even more deceptive. It was the wrong man and sent in an illegal way."

Akemi spoke up. "Oh, but like I say, God makes good come from everything. I did not think so when I saw the man who was to be my husband. But God allowed that bad thing so good could come." She smiled at Mr. C. "And Clay has changed so many things for his workers and their brides. God has used him in such good ways."

"I don't know how good that is, Akemi." Clay's voice sounded abrupt. "They're not brought here for a romantic adventure. They're here to work and help the men be more content with their work and lives. They're brides, yes, but they're also my employees."

"They know that, Mr. Clay," she said. "But it's good to give them one good day of romance."

It sounded as if he mumbled, "Women," then gestured toward the docking area.

Mary Ellen saw Billy nod and come toward them with a rolling cart.

"Oh, we'd better get a move on," Matilda said. "The ship is docking."

❧

After boarding the ship, Mary Ellen stood outside the door where the baskets were placed. Chatter inside the room where the picture brides were ceased when Clay walked into the room. He welcomed the women as brides for his workers and as his employees who had come to work in the sugarcane.

"That's the *luna*," Akemi said of the woman translating his words. "She make many trips with brides."

He came out and nodded at Matilda. Looking as serious as his tone of voice had sounded, he left the ship. Mary Ellen could understand that the brief encounter would cause the women to think about life after a wedding. She hoped the message got through to Breanna, too.

A hush again fell over the cabin when Mary Ellen and the others entered. The middle-aged luna bowed and spoke in broken English.

One of the picture brides looked to be in her late twenties and two others in their early twenties, but the rest appeared to be no more than fifteen or sixteen years old.

"They look scared," Mary Ellen whispered to Matilda.

"They are. Without money, they can't return to Japan. The men pay their passage."

Akemi walked to the middle of the floor. "Do any speak English?"

"I Shizue," said a heavy-set girl, quite different from the thin, short ones. "I speak little. I get point across." Most of the girls giggled.

The oldest one rose from the corner, tall and serious. Her hair hung over one shoulder. She bowed. "I am Kohana. I speak Japanese, Chinese, and little English."

Shizue nodded. "She teach us on the voyage."

Several began saying words they thought were English. "Aloha, thank you, good meet you, yes, no."

Akemi asked questions in Japanese and received answers. Then she turned to Mary Ellen and the other women. "The girls have already washed and dressed in their finest, other than their wedding dresses." Akemi had them sit on the wooden storage benches around the wall.

Matilda said, "She will tell her story in English and in Japanese."

Akemi related her experience of disappointment, but also the wonder of learning about Christianity and having Jesus in her heart.

Most of the girls looked at their hands folded on their kimonos. "You will not be forced to be Christian," Akemi said. "But you will hear it."

She told them that she knew the luna had warned that they now belonged to the man who paid their passage. She told them that had changed and they could report any mistreatment. "Your boss, Mr. Honeycutt, is good and kind."

Matilda returned Mary Ellen's glance and smiled.

Now Akemi was telling the brides that with few exceptions there were no jobs for Japanese women. But Matilda and Rose had made it their project to help any who had misgivings about the man they were contracted to marry.

"What if he not look good, like his picture?" asked Shizue.

The women began to talk at once.

The luna held up her hands for silence. "Everything will be explained." She nodded to Matilda who said, "We can give the baskets now."

Mary Ellen felt their joy as they smiled and laughed. In the baskets were all sorts of items any girl would want, including lotions, soaps, hairbrushes, decorative combs, a little mirror, and other personal items.

Kohana stepped to a mirror on the wall. She made an elaborate hair arrangement on the top of her head, using decorative combs from the basket.

Shizue paced. "I will not marry a man if he no suit me."

Akemi began telling how lucky they were that things had changed. "Marriages used to be performed at the immigration office the day picture brides arrived. Miss Matilda and Miss Rose now have you meet the men. You will stay at the inn. Then you will see where the men work and meet the people in the village. After that, you will prepare for your wedding day."

They seemed fearful, and eager, to walk down the gangplank to the beach. The captain checked the names and papers of each girl as she left the ship. Each carried her basket and photo of her contracted husband.

"We will stay near them," Matilda said. "They need to know we're supportive because the luna will return to Japan after the wedding."

The men had separated into three groups. Geoffrey and the other Caucasian men stood behind the grooms. Farther down, dockworkers looked on, and Mary Ellen recognized the uniform of immigration officers.

Clay walked up. "Now," he said, "we get to observe what happens when arranged love meets reality."

Akemi said, "The day I refused the older man, he dropped the lei on the sand and bent head. He walk to train with shoulders slumped. These men look okay young."

"The one on the end could be in his thirties."

"That one for Kohana."

Mary Ellen remembered putting their files together.

The brides and workers were studying their photos, making sure who belonged to whom.

The thirty-year-old man seemed so serious. Perhaps he expected to be rejected. "This must be embarrassing," Mary Ellen said.

Akemi expressed surprise. "No. It is honor. They offer hearts and lives to each other. It is good."

All the Japanese men were thin except the one wearing a hat. He was short and had an abundant abdomen.

Shizue walked up to him. The top of his hat reached almost to the top of her head. She frowned, her head bobbing as she looked from the photo to him several times. "Fumio?"

Off came his hat as he bowed deeply, revealing a bald spot on top of his head.

Shizue began to laugh and pointed at him. "Okay, Fumio. You have hat, but you not richer than others. You balder."

"So much brains push out hair."

"Careful." She touched her hair, and he grimaced. "You don't look like much, but. . ." She looked at the form in her hand. "You better sing."

He bellowed out a song in Japanese, making others laugh. Shizue put her hands on her hips. "Fumio, my name means quiet inlet. You better know I'm more like a—"

"Tsunami?"

"Exactly."

"Yippee. Just the kind of woman I want." Before she could lean forward for it, he had the lei over her head and hanging from her neck. He plopped the hat on his head and wore a big smile.

217

Shizue reached into her basket and brought out a long thread and a folded fan.

Akemi explained. "The linen thread means gray hair of old age. The fan can spread out to show future wealth and many children. Now they are engaged."

The others were becoming engaged in the same way.

Others were exchanging names and bowing. Some smiled boldly, some timidly, but each seemed to accept the other. Except the tall ones on the end, who were talking.

"I have a goal, Kohana," the man said in English. "I save. I will someday have my own land."

"I, too, have a goal, Miyamoto," Kohana said with equal pride. "On that land I will plant a garden and write a book about Japanese gardening."

"I have many books." He lifted the lei.

Kohana bent her head for the lei. She gave him the thread and fan. He stepped back, with his hands folded in front of him. Kohana stepped back and looked off down the beach as if studying the place that was now her new home.

"The women will go to the inn now," Matilda said. "We have a big room on the second floor and cots so they can stay together to prepare for their wedding. Most bring their wedding dresses with them. Some could not afford them."

She nodded toward Clay. "Just as Clay makes sure the men all have suits, Rose and I make sure the brides have wedding dresses."

"But you need to know," Clay said, "these are laborers from another country. They're not accepted into the general population. They're not U.S. citizens. They are under contract for work."

"He's right," Matilda said. "He's gone out of his way to accommodate them. But they're here to work, and he's not even under any obligation to allow the workers to have brides."

"Then why do you?" Mary Ellen looked up at him.

"The men are better workers when married and with children, instead of being bunked with hundreds of other men."

"They all seem pleased," Rose said. Mary Ellen followed her gaze to where the luna was grouping the brides together. Geoffrey had gathered their contracts.

"The men can refuse the women, too," Matilda said, "but I don't know of that having happened, do you, Clay?"

"No," he said. "None of my men have refused the match made for them that started with nothing more than a photo. Women are harder to please, I guess."

"Or just more discerning," Mary Ellen said and regretted her words immediately. She'd never known anyone to bring out the worst in her like Mr. C. managed to.

"That's how someone described you." He grinned at Mary Ellen and walked toward the men being led to the train.

Chapter 14

Chairs had been set along one wall of the spacious dining hall in the Japanese village at the sugarcane plantation. Clay sat in the center with Matilda and Mary Ellen on each side of him.

"The wedding ceremony will take place along the wall opposite us," Matilda explained.

"Let's move our chairs in front of them," Breanna said to Akemi, "so we don't have to lean in to hear what they're saying." They did.

"I don't often come to these ceremonies," Clay said. "For the past two years, Matilda, Rose, and Akemi have. Wives of my foremen help. The owners of two Japanese restaurants bring their cooks and prepare the food."

Mary Ellen looked at the adjacent wall where Rose and two other white women and several Japanese women in colorful kimonos worked at long tables with white cloths, flowers, and dishes.

"Do the other workers come to the wedding?"

"No. If that were allowed, they'd be attending weddings all the time instead of working. But they have their good time with their own religious traditions, music, dancing, and games." He said what Akemi had earlier. "We can't force them to be Christian. We can only influence them by showing Christian love."

"Is that why you let them have this ceremony?"

"No. My brother doesn't do it this way. His workers and their brides are married soon after they dock in Oahu. I let this happen because Matilda and Rose talked me into it. It's their project, and they pay the Japanese restaurant owners in town to provide the wedding feast."

"That's good of you to allow this special day."

"I don't know," he said. "They seem to appreciate it. I try to respect their culture. You see, the early missionaries didn't respect the culture of the Hawaiians. They saw them as heathen because they wore little or no clothing. And they considered Hawaiians sinful to move their bodies in a hula dance. Much of their culture was lost."

Matilda added to that. "The businesses and politics here are run by descendants of those missionaries. They became wealthy while the native Hawaiians became poorer. Why, not too many years ago I was partying with the king. Now, Hawaii is annexed to the U.S., and royalty has been replaced by Westernized politicians."

"But we are beginning to see the value of the Hawaiian culture and appreciate their history," Clay said. "When I say *we*, I'm not referring just to me personally. Hawaiians are being appreciated again. And we're beginning to see that

219

Hawaii's uniqueness is in the many nationalities and cultures."

Akemi turned. "Jacob said most of Hawaii is Christian."

Clay agreed. "The missionaries made some mistakes, but two-thirds of Hawaii is now Christian."

Breanna spoke over her shoulder. "Are those two preachers?"

A man in a black suit had entered and stood in the middle of the platform near the front.

"Not preachers," Clay said. "The seated one is a Japanese priest from the temple in Hilo. The one standing is a civil official. This is not a Christian ceremony."

Matilda said, "This is a combination of Japanese, Western, and Hawaiian."

Twenty men entered in their black suits and lined up on in two rows, looking as stiff as they had when awaiting their brides at the dock.

Akemi looked back and spoke softly. "In Japan, if the man could afford it, or borrow it, he would wear a black silk kimono."

"Do they feel badly about not wearing a kimono?"

"No. They know they are in the United States, so this okay. The women know it, too. But wait. You see the women."

"Look," Matilda whispered.

Mary Ellen drew in her breath at the lovely parade of women entering the dining hall from the far end of the room. They wore white silk kimonos. Their faces were painted creamy white, contrasting with their dark eyes and upswept hairstyles fastened with tortoiseshell combs.

The civil official said something to the men. The luna stood aside as if ready to coach if needed. But each groom seemed to know to whom he belonged.

"The white means a beginning and an end," Matilda said.

"Just like aloha means hello and good-bye," Clay added.

Akemi nodded. "The bride wears white because she 'dies' as her father's daughter and is reborn into her husband's life."

When the men approached their brides, they bowed. The luna said something, and the women bent slightly. Each man put a white and purple lei over his bride's head.

"Those are white and purple orchids," Akemi said. "In Japan, purple is the color of love. The iris is a favored flower."

"What is our color of love?" Breanna said.

"The red rose is a symbol of love," Matilda said. "Then there's the white dress for a wedding."

Mary Ellen patted Breanna's shoulder. "Like the one I'm making for you."

Breanna touched Mary Ellen's hand, then spoke to Akemi. "Did they practice that ritual?"

Akemi answered. "They do not practice. They be very careful to hear what the official and the luna say."

"With few exceptions," Clay said, "the Japanese are very meticulous in all they do, in work and particularly in personal cleanliness."

"Now," Akemi said. "They will honor the spirits. The priest waves a branch called a *harai-gushi*. That is to bless the couples."

They moved as couples to a table, where each groom drank from a small cup, then handed it to the bride. They did that three times.

Mary Ellen touched Akemi's shoulder as a signal she wanted an explanation.

"There are three cups," Akemi said. "Each larger than the other. That is called *san san kudo*. The groom takes three sips from a cup, and then the bride takes three sips. That is nine sips each. Nine is lucky number because it cannot be divided by two. So they are now becoming one."

Next was the rosary. Akemi explained that, too. There were twenty-one beads of two different colors. Eighteen beads represented the couple, two represented each family, and one represented the Buddha. "All of the beads on one string," she said, "means the couple and their families are joined, even though their families are in Japan."

The ceremony ended, and a photographer appeared. Clay explained to Mary Ellen there would be a group picture, and one of the couple pictures would be for the official records. "I think I'll take my leave," he said.

"You know we can join them for the wedding feast," Matilda said.

"I never have," Clay said.

"Why?" Mary Ellen asked.

The first thing that crossed his mind was, "I'm the owner. They're my workers."

"Don't they know that?"

"Sure."

"Then what are you conveying by not eating with them? Is there some significance to that?"

He looked at the ceiling. That word again. She'd used it when asking about the church steeple. Did there have to be significance to everything? Some things just. . .were.

Matilda spoke up. "You're never too old to change."

Tripping over Clay's mind was the question, *Claybourne Honeycutt change?* What would it hurt to stay for the meal?

The priest stood at the head of the tables. Clay moved to the opposite head. Matilda and Rose moved to his left. "You and Breanna are special guests today," he said. "Sit here." Mary Ellen sat next to him on his right, next Breanna, then Akemi.

With amusement, he watched Mary Ellen and Breanna exchange glances over the plates of fish. The head and tail had been formed into a circle. "That is the symbol of eternity," Matilda said. She laughed at their wide eyes indicating they were unsure about the fish.

"And the clams served with two halves is symbolic of the newly married couple," Akemi said.

The brides and grooms came to the table and remained standing. The priest said an invocation and blessed them again. When he finished, all the men turned toward Clay and bowed. Seeing that, the women did, too.

Clay figured Miss Colson would not like that, but his quick glance revealed her looking around at them as if she were pleased about everything.

He gestured for them to sit. "This is your day," he said. "I will give a gift to each of you."

He hadn't thought of that before. But people do change. While his words were being translated, or those who understood were thanking him, he mumbled to Mary Ellen. "What should I give?" He leaned over for her answer.

"You said they love cleanliness. What about soap or candles or something that smells sweet for the woman. Maybe a little money for the men?"

"Excellent," he whispered. Aloud he said. "Your gifts will be delivered to you tomorrow morning." He almost added, "not too early," but realized in time that might not be well-received by Miss Colson and some of the others.

He sat. Mary Ellen looked at him and smiled. For the first time, she smiled at him. Did she, for an instant, like him?

People can change. . . .

While they ate, Mary Ellen and Breanna discussed the beauty of the wedding. He could readily see it didn't hurt a thing to show some special kindness to his workers. Then he wondered if he heard Breanna correctly.

"I've decided I want a different kind of wedding."

Mary Ellen's hand returned the forkful of food to her plate. Breanna continued about the kind of wedding she wanted. "A Hawaiian one. On the beach. In a Hawaiian kind of dress. Like Matilda and Rose said Jane and Mak had."

Breanna didn't know it, but she had just broken her sister's heart. Mary Ellen's stark face reminded him of the white-faced Japanese women. They would wash the white from their faces and tomorrow would wear hats in the fields to keep the sun from turning them brown or red. What could rid Breanna's sister of her disappointment?

He glanced at Matilda, who returned his look with a knowing smile. She knew the love and time Mary Ellen had put into that dress. Now he wondered what she would do after Breanna married Geoffrey. Remain in Hawaii? Could he and she have no differences between them and be. . .friends?

Friends with that beautiful blond Westerner who did not particularly like or trust him?

He thought not.

At least, not friends. . .only.

❧

They were having breakfast when Breanna asked, "Do you mind if I pick another wedding dress?"

Since yesterday, Mary Ellen had known this question was coming. She spoke honestly. "Every bride should have the dress she wants."

"Do you want to m—"

"Why don't you come to the dress shop?" Mary Ellen interrupted. She would not make another wedding dress for Breanna. "Matilda and Rose can help us look in the catalogs and find what you want."

"I didn't want to be at the office anyway without Akemi. Jacob is leaving this morning, and she's seeing him off. Geoffrey will be there, too." She sighed heavily, then smiled. "But I can't see him without you."

Half the morning was taken up with their poring over catalogs. The silk kimonos had influenced Breanna. "I'd like something silk and soft and flowing. Oh, like this."

They all agreed the one she had chosen was lovely. The simple lines were similar to the tea gowns. Sheer, flowing drapes fell gracefully over the shoulder and down into the moderate-length train. Mary Ellen could imagine Breanna slipping her fingers in the small ribbon loops on the drapes and making dainty dance steps while turning in sweeping motions of delight.

The drapes could be removed, revealing the narrow straps of the dress that was lined with China silk.

Breanna moaned. "Look at the price."

"That's all right," Mary Ellen said. "I told you I would provide your wedding dress."

Breanna hugged her. "You're so good to me." She stood back and glanced at the dress on the form. "You really don't mind?"

Mary Ellen tapped the catalog. "This is you."

Akemi stopped in later and asked the two sisters to lunch with her. While eating, Akemi said, "I could not let Jacob leave without saying I love him."

Breanna leaned forward. "What did he say?"

"He say I am young, should find Japanese man and have five children. He say if he had a right, he would ask me to wait, but he had no right." She shook her head. "I told him that while he is gone, I will go to college and be ready to help him when he returns."

"What did he say?" Mary Ellen and Breanna both asked.

"That I should not sacrifice my life for him." Her smile was precious. "But I say, it would be my pleasure. He say he write to me." She paused. "If he marries someone else, I will go to Japan and suffer. I could not be on the same island with him. It would be hard being in the same world with him, without him."

Mary Ellen was speechless for a long moment. Finally she said, "I will pray." Exactly what she would say in her prayer, she didn't know. But she would pray.

After lunch, she stood beside the white wedding gown. She touched the satin and lace, but not the pearls. A dress with thousands of seed pearls, hand sewn, lovingly made.

She felt a tear.

The bell tinkled. She blinked to dry her teary eyes. She turned. Clay stood in the doorway. He walked up to her. "Would you have dinner with me? At a hotel. We should talk about Breanna and Geoffrey. Say, seven o'clock?"

Matilda, who was dressing a mannequin, turned to them. Mary Ellen had no idea why Clay winked at Matilda. She laughed and waved. "Get out of here," she said.

After he left, Matilda said, "Let's find you the perfect outfit to wear."

"I didn't even say I'd go. But no thank you on the outfit. This is about Breanna and Geoffrey, not like we're"—she decided to use Matilda's words—"out on the town or anything."

Matilda scolded. "You're going out with Hawaii's sugar king, our most ineligible bachelor, and I'm sure you've noticed how heads turn just to look at him."

Mary Ellen glanced away.

"Except yours, of course," Matilda added.

She laughed. "I'm not blind."

"Then let's dress you up to match him. That doesn't mean you can't talk about business."

She agreed, not wanting to look frumpy and embarrass him.

Matilda went in back and returned with a box. "Let's go home and get you ready. If we need a tuck or two, we can manage that."

Shortly before seven, Mary Ellen picked up the deep pink dress, still as awed by its beauty as when she'd taken it from the box. It had fit perfectly. Now, Matilda helped her slip into it. The silk floated down her body and fell easily to her feet where the material was fuller for walking freedom.

"Look in the mirror," Matilda said.

Mary Ellen could hardly believe what a dress could do. She'd never worn such a low neckline, but in the V was a lovely lace insert. A wide row of glass beads and sequins adorned the neckline from the shoulders to below the lace. The beads came together in a large cluster. Two-inch delicate strands of glass hung from the cluster.

She touched the ruffle of gathered silk on the sheer sleeve that reached her elbow. The skirt had an overlay of pink net. A row of glass beads traveled down one side of the dress to a third of the way from the bottom. The net was gathered to form a graceful loop over the silk and was adorned with a cluster of beads.

"I've never worn a dress like this. It's so elegant."

Matilda agreed. "It will fit in wherever Clay takes you. It's perfect for evening or very formal."

"Now, my hair."

"Your natural wave is lovely, and long hair suits you." Matilda tapped her cheek, thinking. "But this dress requires an upswept hairdo. Let's go a little more elaborate than your everyday style and have a few tendrils fall along the sides of your face."

Mary Ellen surprised herself by beginning to feel attractive enough to go out with Hawaii's most gorgeous man.

"Wonderful," Matilda said when they finished. "Now you're perfect for going out and. . .um. . .talking business." She laughed. "Ah! Keep that blush on your cheeks, and you're absolutely beautiful."

Mary Ellen felt a moment of doubt. "You think we've overdone it?"

Chapter 15

The moment Mary Ellen stood at the top of the stairs and saw him sitting in the living room with Rose, she knew outshining Mr. C. was impossible. He looked up and stood while she held on to the railing and descended the stairs.

Although he wasn't wearing a tuxedo with long tails, his suit seemed similar in style, and he wore a bowtie. His eyes were enhanced by the dark blue fabric as his glance swept over her.

A couple of times before, he had implied she was pretty. She'd thought he was making fun of her. But tonight, for the first time in her life, she felt beautiful. Would he tell her so?

Would she thank him without stammering?

She reached the bottom of the stairs, still holding on to the railing.

His gaze lingered for a moment before it moved to Matilda and Rose. "Now there's a dress fit for the queen."

"Yes," Matilda said. "But we don't have royalty anymore."

Mary Ellen's prepared *thank-you* was lost somewhere in her throat. He hadn't complimented her. And the stupid, stupid remark she heard herself say was, "Oh, but there's a sugar king."

Mortified, she had to swallow hard lest she choke. Matilda and Rose looked amused. Mr. C. plopped his top hat on his head. "Good evening, ladies," he said and escorted her out.

At the white car, he held open the door. With a sweep of his hand, he said, "Your royal coach, mademoiselle."

She hoped her response sounded like *merci*, and not *mercy*!

To her surprise, he did not head down the street to the Hilo Hotel. Instead, he drove in the opposite direction, along a strip of road above the beach, going higher into the hills.

The evening sun shone golden on the caps of the ocean waves. The palm branches swayed gently as the car passed. The fragrance of flowers filled the air. Mr. C. pointed out various plants and flowers and places as they drove by. He passed several horses and carriages along the way. Then a magnificent mansion rose on an incline. He parked where a sole black car sat.

"The grounds cover five acres," he said. "Would you like to stroll through some of the gardens before we go in?"

"Yes, I'd love it. This is so beautiful."

They walked along the paths in the gardens, exchanging greetings with other guests. He described the native plants, the palms, fruit trees, ferns, and orchids.

225

The hotel entrance looked like some wealthy person's parlor or living room. A man in a tuxedo was playing classical music on a grand piano. Several couples sat on couches, listening or talking.

Mr. C. walked Mary Ellen around the room, showing her pictures of royalty. "This is Queen Liliuokalani, who considered this one of her favorite places to dine.

"This might interest you. Do you know the author Jack London?"

"Oh yes. He's a famous American writer. He was born in San Francisco." On a sadder note she added, "He wrote a lot of articles for *Collier's Magazine* about the earthquake and fire."

"I didn't know that." He smiled. "But I do know he stayed here for a month about three years ago."

The pianist and Clay nodded at each other as if they were acquainted. When they approached the entry into the dining room, a maître d' said, "Good evening, Mr. Honeycutt. Ma'am. Your usual table, sir?"

"Please," Mr. C. said. They were led through the dining room to a table in front of a wide window overlooking the bay below.

The waiter brought menus. After one glance, Mary Ellen had to say, "Much of this is Greek to me."

"Only the names," he said. "Mostly Hawaiian. A cow is a cow no matter how you pronounce it. But you might be interested in the *humuumunukunukuapuaa*."

"You're making that up."

He turned the menu and pointed. "Right here. And here's how it's pronounced: *whomoo-whomoo-newkoo-newkoo-ah-pu-ah-ah*. It's a fish. Repeat after me."

She did. And was about to laugh until she realized his focus was on her puckered lips. Well, if there was anything to Matilda's saying her blush made her look beautiful, she would look beautiful all evening.

She lowered the menu. "I've sampled a lot of fish already. I might like a steak. What would you suggest?"

"That's what I was thinking. Besides, we have to keep Mak in business. He has beef cattle and horse ranches."

"I'll take cattle, thank you."

He laughed lightly. "All right. Let's look at the steak entrées."

She read silently while he read aloud two of his choices. " 'Kalani's Kulana Big Island Kalbi Ribs with Nalo Farms Tatsoi Kimchi. Grass-fed, braised, boneless beef short ribs served with a sweet soy-ginger sauce, smoked sweet potato, Nalo Farms tatsoi and baby bok choy kimchi, and poblano-sweet pepper relish. Niman Ranch, Grilled, Roasted Garlic, Ribeye Steak with Hamakua Mushrooms. Beef with a soy balsamic glaze, marinated ali'i oyster mushroom, wasabi-Dijon aioli, potatoes au gratin with smoked bacon, local tomatoes, and wild onions."

"The ribeye," she said.

"Great. I didn't know which I wanted. I'll have the kalbi ribs. We can taste each other's, if you wish."

She scoffed. "In a place like this?"

He shrugged. "Guests shouldn't be looking at anyone other than the persons at their own table."

She was glad he had said that. She hadn't really looked at anyone, or anything, but him.

The waiter must have been looking. As soon as Mr. C. laid the menus aside, the waiter came. Mr. C. ordered, and soon their fruity pineapple drinks were brought in long-stemmed glasses. He lifted his glass toward her, and she let her glass touch his. *"Mahalo nui loa,"* he said. "Thank you very much. To God, and to you."

She repeated, "Mahalo nui loa," assuming that was his blessing for the food to come. Silently, she was thanking God and Mr. C., too, for an evening in paradise as Cinderella. She would try to push aside the thought that midnight would come. The sun was turning a deeper gold. She'd seen enough of the Hawaiian sunsets to know that soon the depth and brilliance of color would be almost too beautiful to bear.

"Speaking of God," she said, facing him again, "Akemi's talking about God so freely has made me wonder if I've tried to play God with Breanna and Geoffrey. Who am I to say who should marry and when? Or what is God's will for another?"

"You're her sister. And you've tried to be like a mother to her."

"Yes. But I'm not her mother. And she's making her decisions apart from me. Maybe I'm just reluctant to let her go."

The waiter brought their food. It looked wonderful. She stared at it.

He said, "Would you like to say a blessing?"

She nodded. "Dear Lord, thank You for Your abundant blessings. Guide me, us as we discuss Breanna and Geoffrey. Help us to make decisions according to Your will. Amen."

He said, "Amen."

After a silence of cutting the meat and tasting, they agreed the food was delicious.

"I was afraid," Mary Ellen said after swallowing a few bites, "that Breanna was caught up in the idea of love. That's about all she and Akemi talk about. I suppose you know Akemi loves Jacob."

He nodded. "And he loves her."

"Then there was the beautiful weddings of the picture brides. There's the great romance of Jane and Mak I hear so much about. I see couples with eyes only for each other."

"Makes one feel rather left out, doesn't it?"

She glanced at him quickly. Had he reverted to his initial belief that she was after him? "I was speaking of Breanna. We've picked out her wedding dress."

He waved his fork at her. She waited until he finished with the bite of food in his mouth.

"Keep sewing on those little pearls. I may know someone who would be perfect in that dress. It has to be the right person, because you've put your heart into it."

She nodded. Was Mr. C. getting wedding fever, too?

"And I've been thinking. If God sent Breanna here to find love, then He sent me to help her. Not hinder her." She didn't say so, but she wondered if she looked to others like a jealous spinster older sister. "I need to think of what she wants. I don't want to be their judge, to hold over them the threat of Geoffrey's imprisonment."

"What do you want?"

"I want her. . .to have a good life."

"Mary Ellen, what do you want for you?"

Mary Ellen? He called her by name without putting the *Miss* at the beginning or the *Colson* at the end. What did that mean?

It meant. . .that was her name.

Her fork played with the food on her plate. She remembered holding the wedding dress up and looking into the mirror. She had imagined Breanna in the dress with Mr. C. beside her. But the face in the mirror had been her own. Then came the reality of Matilda standing there.

&

"Even little girls have dreams, don't they? I mean, even the picture brides value the wedding day, although the next day and every day for most of their lives they will work in the fields."

"I'm not a little girl or a picture bride."

"No, but a man would be fortunate to have you as a bride. You're special, Mary Ellen. Has no one ever told you that?"

"Sure. Uncle Harv."

He stared. Until she had to laugh. Then he did.

"Then, you've never been kissed?"

She laughed lightly. "Well, I had a beau once. William."

"Oh. I am jealous."

She appreciated his trying to joke, to keep away any tension. The evening had been too good to allow that intrusion. She was more at ease with him than she had thought. Telling him about William came easily. But there wasn't much to tell, other than that they walked and rode together and shared a few kisses. "I knew I was too young to be serious. And I had Breanna to think of."

"Consider yourself told," he said in a serious tone, "by a man old enough to be your beau, and not your uncle or your young William, that you're special."

&

Clay knew the color that rose to Mary Ellen's cheeks was not a reflection of the sunset. The guarded look he'd grown to recognize invaded her eyes. "Well, I am a blond." She looked mortified. "I should have said thank you."

"No you shouldn't. My reputation has preceded me, along with Geoffrey's actions. And, too, you came to Hawaii because of me."

228

She gazed at him so long he thought he might become lost in her eyes. The sky had turned red, but her eyes were soft and as light blue as a noontime sky. "Well," she said finally, "only indirectly. I'm here because of Geoffrey. Which reminds me. You called this meeting to talk about him, and I've done most of the talking."

Was that all their evening together meant to her? Or did she say that because he had intimated it was only to talk about Geoffrey?

"What I have to say about him is much like what you said about Breanna. He's not perfect, but basically good. He has some growing up to do, which I can say for a lot of us. But primarily, I wanted to talk about me. I didn't think you'd agree to this if I told you that earlier."

Those long lashes almost touched her cheeks as she lowered her eyelids. He felt she was not receptive to that. He was accustomed to women trying to impress him and asking all about the plantations, Hawaii, the sugar business and. . .him.

"To do that, however, I need to sweeten your attitude." He lifted his hand, and the waiter came. "Marlon, how about describing my favorite chocolate cake?"

"Yes, sir, Mr. Honeycutt. It is an unforgettable chocolate experience that combines layers of rich chocolate cake and semi-sweet chocolate ganache made with heavy cream and chocolate liqueur, all topped with slivers of milk chocolate."

"We'll have that."

"And Kona coffee," Marlon said, and Clay nodded.

He leaned toward her. "Almost daily, for all of my life, I've been surrounded by dark-haired, dark-eyed people. So it's refreshing to see a blue-eyed blond. I happen to like blond hair. But I don't hold it against a woman who isn't a blond. I'm not that small-minded."

"I wouldn't think that."

"But you may not think much of what I'm about to tell you. About me and Geoffrey."

"You don't have to tell me anything."

"Yes, I do. Because I'm the reason Geoffrey sent the photo to your office in San Francisco."

She didn't look surprised, just curious.

He was grateful Marlon chose that moment to bring the desserts.

He told her about the game. It had started innocently with him and Jacob meeting single women who came to the island. After Jacob decided that wasn't for him, Geoffrey had been eager to step in. "I'm not sure how it became like a contest, or game, to see who would escort the most blonds around the island. I was winning."

He felt like a loser. Her interest was focused on the cake instead of him.

"Like Geoffrey told you, that led to his sending my photo to the mainland. I don't think it was wrong to meet single women and take them out. But to make a game of it, turn it into some kind of contest, was wrong and disrespectful. Geoffrey is old enough to make his choices regardless of me. But I was the older, more mature one."

She had dug into that cake. At least she liked something. "You have a little bit of chocolate, right there." He almost reached over to touch the corner of her mouth, but quickly touched his own instead. What was he thinking? He wasn't.

"Thank you." She wiped the corner of her mouth with her napkin. After a sip of Kona, she looked directly at him. "I'm beginning to think age doesn't always make one more mature than another."

He nodded. "Geoffrey was wrong. But if anyone is to be punished, it should be me."

She seemed to study his eyes. Was she trying to see his soul? What kind of punishment would she want to enact? For Geoffrey, the punishment was she wouldn't let him get married. . .yet.

"I'm not doing that anymore," he said. "It's time I—" He stopped and looked down at his plate. If he was going to act maturely, this might be a good time to start. "Time I ate my cake."

He saw the sky turn gray, the ocean deep blue. But the lights in the dining room made the trim on her dress dance and gleam and sparkle. She was beautiful. And he had just confessed he wasn't going to do certain things anymore. Was that mature or foolish? Or a lie?

On the way back, she said, "Mahalo."

He looked over at her, and she explained. "For a wonderful evening. I've never had one like this. And thank you for confiding in me. I do appreciate it. How long would it take to wire San Francisco?"

Was she going back? Did she have someone to see there? William? "Two days at the most."

"I want to wire Uncle Harv so he can be here for Breanna's wedding."

At the house, he walked her to the door. Her glances made him think she was wondering what he might do. He wondered what she might do if he did.

"Mary Ellen."

She turned to look up at him. Little glass beads winked and twinkled at him. He folded his hands behind his back and held them there. "I want to invite you and Breanna to my place Friday night. She and Geoffrey can talk about their plans."

She nodded. Then she stared at him like he was out of his mind when he said, "I want to show you how I treat women I take to my plantation."

Chapter 16

Mary Ellen finally gave in to Breanna's pleading, and they bought the latest style in swimwear. Not the kind with stockings and skirts, but the one-piece with the legs halfway up the thighs. She definitely would not wear hers.

"I'm not sure we should go," Mary Ellen said to Matilda.

Matilda disagreed. "This is the perfect time for you to observe Geoffrey and Breanna and see if you think they're ready for marriage. Go. And have a good time."

Mary Ellen and Breanna wore comfortable, colorful *kohalas*. Clay and Geoffrey showed up in the car. They wore casual pants and flowered, short-sleeved shirts.

Mr. C. seemed so happy and carefree that Mary Ellen wondered if his confession of his wrongdoing had given him a clear conscience about the entire situation. Just what was he going to show her at his plantation?

They stopped at Mak's ranch, and she met him and the lovely Jane she'd heard so much about. Geoffrey wanted to show Breanna where he often trained horses that were used on Clay's plantation.

After leaving there, the car traveled along the dirt road across fenced pastureland where cows and horses grazed. Soon, Mary Ellen felt as if her heart were in her throat. Ahead were the fields Uncle Harv had talked about. Sugarcane leaves as far as the eye could see, swaying gently in the breeze. She'd seen them in her day—and night—dreams.

The road ran through the fields. On each side were hundreds, perhaps thousands of men and women working, their heads covered with wide-brimmed hats. They were chopping, weeding, and cutting.

Clay and Geoffrey told the girls about the sugar-making process and that one acre produced an average crop of three tons. Clay drove through the Japanese village, where a couple of women watched young children play.

"All this sugar supplies the world," Geoffrey said.

"And harvest is almost here," Clay added. "All this cane will be burned so it can be harvested."

He drove out of the fields and up and around an incline until they came to a lovely plantation home. They got out of the car. "This is where I live," Clay said.

"It's beautiful."

"Clay has a Japanese gardener," Geoffrey said. "May I show Breanna the gardens?"

"Sure," Clay said, and the young couple, hand in hand, scurried around the corner of the house.

"My parents built this," Clay said as he and Mary Ellen walked up onto the wide porch. He opened the door. "They enjoyed many years in it. I feel their absence here." She felt a stab of pain for him. Then he smiled. "Also I feel their presence."

She nodded. "Breanna and I felt the absence. And the shock." She took a deep breath. "Nothing was saved."

She liked the lanai best. She stood at the screen and looked out at the tropical flowers, trees, and ocean beyond.

"This is my favorite place," he said.

This setting could provide memories. Two people standing side by side in a favorite place, looking at the scenery. What was he thinking? She thought he began to turn toward her. But no. That was Breanna and Geoffrey coming around the house.

They got back into the car, and Clay drove them onto a narrow dirt lane, hardly wide enough for the vehicle to pass. Heavy foliage provided a canopy, and the late afternoon sun made lace of the shadows.

They emerged into the sunlight and drove between a row of palms and parked at the side of a small house. "My brother, Thomas, lived here," Clay said, "until after our parents died. After he took over the business in Oahu, Geoffrey has stayed here. It's a relaxing, informal setting. The beach is private."

"Let's get into our bathing suits," Geoffrey said.

Mary Ellen was about to say she wasn't going to change, but as they walked around to the front she heard laughing and talking. People were getting out of a long canoe.

Her instinct was to say she thought the beach was private. But they all began to call to each other. Two females and three males were wearing much more revealing bathing suits than she and Breanna had brought. The males wore no shirts, but she'd become accustomed to that. Even in town, the men's shirts were often unbuttoned. That began to seem natural, like the men in canoes who greeted passenger ships.

In the middle of the floor, Mr. C. shucked out of his pants and shirt. Well yes, he certainly did look natural with most of his bronzed body showing, with its strong, rippling muscles, wide chest, broad shoulders, and trim waist. Geoffrey was equally well built, but something about Mr. C. made her feel. . . rather unnatural.

"I'll go on down," Clay said.

"Come on down when you're ready," Geoffrey said and ran outside.

Mary Ellen turned to Breanna, feeling her eyes were stuck open.

"I know," Breanna said. "Those are surfer bodies. But I've learned that's the natural look of Hawaii."

When they joined everyone else on the beach, Mary Ellen saw that Breanna was right. The three males had athletic builds. The females complimented each other's bathing suits, and from there nobody appeared to notice or care about bodies. They all had them.

They were all introduced, and Mary Ellen learned the strangers were friends, four of whom sang professionally and played ukuleles, along with their manager, the brother of one of the female singers. She couldn't pronounce some of their Hawaiian names. The manager laughed. "Just say aloha, and we will answer."

Any thought of tension had vanished. Everything was fun and talk and getting to know each other. They made sandwiches together and ate at a wooden table beneath palms. They sat on the sand while the group sang, then taught Mary Ellen and Breanna some Hawaiian songs. Mary Ellen had only sung in church and was surprised how free and good she felt to sing aloud with this group. Clay and Geoffrey had wonderful voices.

While the sky turned orange, gold, crimson, pink, and scarlet, they set out on the vast sea in a canoe, seeming to be the only people in the world. They returned to shore, then screamed as they raced into the water to swim and play. Breanna explained to Mary Ellen, "Geoffrey taught me to swim better. And I tried surfing. All I do is fall." She laughed and swam out.

Mary Ellen walked along the edge of the shore, letting the water wash up on her feet and feel like it was pulling the sand out from beneath her feet. She had never felt so free, nor had so much fun.

"Come on in," Clay called.

"I'm not good in water. Don't bother with me. I'm fine."

She wasn't afraid, just not natural with it. The others, except Breanna, were fish.

"I'll show you how," Clay said. "Here comes the wave. Now jump. "

They played with the waves, pushed each other into the waves to see who could push the other under. She lost every time but liked the fun. They laughed and joked and pushed each other under.

Then she didn't see the others. Night had settled. She and Clay were farther out than she felt comfortable.

"You're okay. Come on."

They swam toward shore, and soon her feet could touch the bottom. She pushed him under. When he came up, she pushed at him. "That's for taking me out too far."

"It's not far. I can swim to that horizon."

"I don't see a horizon."

"That's my point."

His face seemed to be right at hers. His hands were on her shoulders. When a wave rocked them, his arms wrapped around her. He was shining, silver in the moonlight.

The waves pushed her closer. Something inside asked, *Must I go forever without really being kissed, except by a young boy? I'm in the arms of the most handsome man in Hawaii.* And he was looking at her like she was the only person. . .in the world.

She let the waves sway her. Or was it something inside herself, the man, the moon, the swaying palms, the songs, gentle nature, aloha love?

He was searing her soul, his eyes seeing. She closed them, raised her face to his, felt the warmth of his breath on her face, his intake of breath seemed to draw her own into his. She was losing herself.

His arms tightened, drew her even closer, and she could not stand were it not for his strong hands, her body against his, longing, yearning, then she felt his lips touch hers, no thought, or time, or place except his lips on hers. She was in the arms of her beloved, her love.

But her lips were longing for what did not come. The side of her face was against his bare chest, and his hand was pressing her wet hair against her head. She felt two hearts beating as one, or was it only one, only hers? Strong arms wouldn't let her go. Suddenly, he let her go as a giant wave washed over them. Just as swiftly, he rescued her as he had been doing before they had stood so close together. He grabbed her hand and ran, almost pulling her onto the beach.

Others that she had forgotten laughed. He laughed. She had to laugh. She did not reach for a towel to wipe her face. It might get wet again from the ocean inside threatening her eyes.

Then she remembered he'd wanted to show her how he treated women. She'd been warned, but she'd played along anyway. His game. Lure a woman, charm her, prove she could not resist him.

She wasn't sure why she felt anger. Was it because he stopped the game before she experienced more than the brush of his lips across hers?

The friends began packing up their instruments and soon said their good-byes. Mary Ellen hurried into the house to change. She came out dressed in her casual clothes, with her hair towel dried.

Clay had slipped into his clothes. "Let's walk down the beach," he said.

"You. . .you're staring at me," she said.

He stopped, and so did she.

He reached out and touched her hair. Gently wound a strand around his finger. "Your hair looks silver in the moonlight." He paused. "I want to ask you something. I'd like to talk with you, Mary Ellen. Just the two of us. At my house. Geoffrey can take Breanna back. I have horses, carriages."

The sand felt like it did at the edge of the water, like it was being pulled out from under her. Was that the forerunner to asking her to spend the night? When they'd had dinner at the hotel, he'd been specific about saying he never coerced a woman.

It would be her decision.

What would she say?

She would be lost in his kiss. She'd already been lost in his arms.

Was that the kind of memory she wanted for the rest of her life?

Mary Ellen had not known she could be tempted to compromise her morals. But how did one know if she was really moral if she had never been tempted?

Yes, God must be in this, because although the thought occurred that a night with Claybourne Honeycutt would be wonderful, something inside warned that there was a tomorrow.

So far, all she'd lost was her voice.

When she said nothing, Clay gathered everyone in his car and drove past his house and through the fields of sugarcane, their leaves mocking beneath the silver moon, sounding like rain. Breanna and Geoffrey chatted happily and sang.

Once in a while, Breanna or Geoffrey asked her or Clay a question, and one responded. But they didn't say anything to each other.

After they returned to Hilo, Clay took her hand and led her to the side of the yard. "Mary Ellen, you have Breanna's wedding to plan, and I have a harvest to bring in. Will you think about giving me a chance to show you that I care about you and want to spend time with you? Will you think about it?"

Mary Ellen nodded. How could she ever not think about it?

❧

In the following days, time was taken up with planning Breanna's wedding, which would take place the day after Uncle Harv arrived. Matilda and Rose took Mary Ellen and Breanna to the house where they'd held the beach party to make sure some of the Japanese women could have it cleaned and ready for the married couple when they returned from their honeymoon.

Mary Ellen stood on the beach and looked at the ocean.

She thought about Clay's question.

On the day Uncle Harv was to arrive, Mary Ellen, Breanna, and Matilda stood on the dock. Uncle Harv was one of the first passengers to disembark, looking sprightly in his suit, top hat, and cane.

He seemed glad to see them all and hugged her first. Then Breanna. And Matilda after she put the lei over his head.

One of his first questions was to Breanna. "What's this about you getting married?"

She promised to tell him how it came about. Mary Ellen wasn't too sure how he'd take that. But for the present, he was pleased when Breanna said, "I want you to give me away."

Mary Ellen was about to climb into the backseat of Matilda's car beside Breanna when she saw Clay's car parked on the side street. She looked back and saw him and a beautiful brunette hurrying toward each other.

He swung her around. They hugged like they didn't want to let go. And kissed. It was brief, like a gentleman might kiss a lady in public. Their faces were close together as his arm went around her waist, and they walked toward his car. They were happy. . .with each other.

Mary Ellen jumped into the car and shut the door. The brunette obviously was no stranger to him. He was supposed to be busy at the plantation, getting ready for the harvest.

But he was with a beautiful brunette dressed in Western clothes.

He must think her very foolish. Had he deliberately manipulated her so she wouldn't go to the authorities about Geoffrey, which would involve his name? She was just another Western woman who fell under the spell of Claybourne Honeycutt. Even before she met him.

She threw herself into the wedding plans. There was much to do, although the wedding was to be small and casual.

Uncle Harv became open and fun-loving, even laughed about the photo incident and seemed to enjoy Breanna's love story. He took a room at the inn but came to the house often. After hours at the shop, Pilar began to show up to help with the wedding. The wedding day came. As maid of honor, Mary Ellen kept smiling, determined she was not going to spoil this day for her sister. And the blue tea gown Breanna had selected for her was lovely.

Geoffrey and Clay wore blue suits with light blue shirts, open at the neck as Breanna had requested. She didn't want the outdoor, daytime wedding to be too formal. The musicians who had been at the beach party all those days ago played Hawaiian music while Mary Ellen stood at one end of the arbor. . .and Clay on the other, not ten feet away. The pastor wore a white robe.

Uncle Harv walked Breanna down the aisle between the few chairs. Only a small group of people had been invited. Geoffrey's parents came from Oahu, along with Clay's sister and brother with their families. They were joined by the pastor's wife, Akemi, and a few of Matilda's special friends from church.

Mr. Hammeur and his wife were delighted to have been invited. Pilar came. Breanna looked perfect in the dress she'd chosen. A couple of Geoffrey's and Clay's friends came. And a photographer.

Uncle Harv had paid for the bridal suite on the cruise ship they would take around the islands on their honeymoon. Clay drove the bride and groom down in his car.

Breanna and Geoffrey would change clothes at Matilda's before leaving for the dock. There would not be a reception, but there would be a cake and fruit drinks for the couple, along with Mary Ellen, Uncle Harv, Pilar, Matilda, Rose, Akemi, Clay, the pastor, and his wife.

They piled in their cars and carriages and drove past the dock and along the main street of Hilo to Matilda and Rose's house.

Mary Ellen didn't want to think it, but she couldn't help it. Where was Clay's brunette? She hadn't been invited to the wedding, so she might be at his house. Perhaps he didn't play games with brunettes, just took them seriously.

"Yes, the cake is delicious. Matilda made it."

"Wonderful punch. Have some more."

Clay would probably drive Breanna and Geoffrey to the dock. She would be expected to accompany her sister. But rather than having to make excuses, as soon as Breanna had changed, Mary Ellen said, "I'm going to say my good-byes right here, instead of at the dock."

They hugged.

Soon after the bridal couple left, the guests did, as well.

Matilda said, "This has been trying on you. Rose and I will clean up in here. You take it easy."

Mary Ellen nodded. "I'd like to walk out back for a while."

She walked across the yard, through the trees, and farther than she'd meant. Before long, she could see the beach and the ocean. What would she do now?

What should she do? She had no reason to stay in Hawaii. She could use her sister as an excuse. But her sister was now a married woman.

She had. . .Uncle Harv.

"Mary Ellen."

She jumped, not from fear but from recognizing the voice.

"What's wrong?" he said. "You've ignored me all day."

"There's nothing for us to talk about. I won't be just another blond in your game."

He stepped around to face her. "I thought you understood."

She turned away. "Oh yes, I understand."

He gave a short laugh. "I guess I was egotistical enough to think you cared about me, that our dinner at the hotel was special, and the night at the beach. It was for me. I'm sorry."

Special to him? Yes, enough for him to want to spend time with her. Maybe she would even call him back, but her throat hurt and her eyes stung.

He was already striding away.

Chapter 17

The next morning, Mary Ellen went down to the kitchen. Uncle Harv was there. Matilda and Rose were fixing breakfast. She said good morning as cheerfully as she could, but had one more action to take before she could turn her hourglass life right side up.

"Be right back." She walked out to the back porch and stood beside the trash can. She would look one last time before tearing it into little pieces.

"Could I see?" Matilda stepped out.

Why not?

"This is what started it all? The little flame in your heart?"

"Doesn't everyone say all the women fall for him?"

"True. But I've never known him to put forth the effort he has with you. If a woman isn't interested, he can simply have another."

"He has another. But that's his business. I saw him hug and kiss a woman."

"When was that?"

"When we picked up Uncle Harv."

"A brunette about your age?"

Mary Ellen nodded.

"Oh, honey. That's Leia. Jane and Mak's daughter. There're like sister and brother. He met her to take her to the ranch. She had only one day here before going to Oahu for an equestrian show. She's been on the mainland for several months. Rose said Leia is serious about a man she met on the mainland. He's coming here in a few weeks."

Mary Ellen felt her shoulders slump, and she returned the photo to her pocket.

"Come inside, Mary Ellen."

She gasped. "Uncle Harv. You heard?"

"You're my niece. I have a right to hear."

She hurried inside, and they hugged. Her puffy eyes probably hung to her chin by now.

"I want to tell you a story," he said. "Drink your coffee and listen."

She did, and he began.

"Mary Ellen, back in San Francisco, I believed you wanted the Hawaiian adventure but was afraid to take it. After I arrived here and Breanna told me about that photo, everyone laughed or smiled except you. You've always put what she wanted first."

"What kind of sister would I be if I hadn't?"

"Not nearly the sweet, wonderful girl you are. But sometimes, fear keeps us from reaching out. I've never told anyone this in my life."

Glancing around, he smiled tentatively but didn't ask Matilda and Rose to leave. They settled back against their chairs.

"I came to Hawaii on one of the first steamship voyages. On that trip, I met a lovely widow a few years older than I, and we were inseparable. My business was here, and she went on to Maui to see a brother. I didn't accept her invitation to visit, using work as an excuse."

Mary Ellen could feel his sadness as he continued. "After she returned to England, she invited me to visit. For a long time, I did not write. But I was miserable and finally admitted that I loved her and wanted to have a life with her."

He shook his head. "But by the time she received my letter, it was too late. She had married a good man and was in the family way. Since then, I've tried to stifle my emotions." He glanced around and smiled. "But the last time I came to Hawaii, Matilda and Rose cracked my shell. Now, I've been introduced to a widow and am trying not to fear what may or may not happen."

She thought he was talking about Pilar.

"I was afraid to love you and Breanna. Love requires so much of a person. And with it comes the chance of being hurt."

"Uncle Harv, I love you." She went to him, and he held her tight.

Then he let go. "Stop this, young lady. You're smearing my glasses, and I can't see a thing."

She moved away, smiling at him.

Then he admonished, "If you're going to err, Mary Ellen, err on the side of love."

≈

That morning, she went to the church to pray and think. As if the Lord Himself had spoken, Mary Ellen knew she had to do it. She needed to ask Clay's forgiveness for her attitude toward him. She'd been rude and judgmental. And Uncle Harv had made her see she had been afraid. Not of Mr. C. so much, but of her own feelings.

She hadn't wanted to be hurt.

But she was hurting.

"I need to see him," she said upon returning to the house. Rose said she and Matilda wanted Uncle Harv to meet Mak and Jane. They could all go to the ranch, and then someone would take her to the plantation.

After they reached the ranch, Mak chose a horse for her. "But I'll go with you. I need to talk with Clay."

She was grateful for his company. Without him, she might have felt fear since she hadn't ridden in a long time and never over such a long stretch of road.

Mak stopped at the mill near a field, and they dismounted. Mary Ellen was trying to converse with a woman walking with little children. They had to make a lot of hand motions and smile and nod to make themselves clear. The children began copying them, and they all laughed.

When Mak came out, he said Clay was at a field a couple of miles away where they were burning the cane. "You stay here at the mill. I'll get him."

"Maybe I should wait until he's not busy."

"He can usually get away if he needs to."

He rode away.

Mary Ellen began to doubt. Suppose he thought her apology trivial. She walked toward the miles of sugarcane, its leaves swaying like waves on the ocean.

A fanciful dream crossed her mind. Why not let the dream of walking in the sugarcane become a reality? If Mr. C. rode down, she could call to him and watch him stride toward her. That will be a memory to have with her forever.

She felt a tug on her arm and turned. The woman was saying no, no, and shaking her head. The children stood back at the mill, watching.

"It's okay. I won't go far." She stepped inside the cane, which came to her shoulders. She looked back when the woman began yelling and running toward the children. One of them must have done something wrong.

The cane became thicker. She was getting into stalks higher than her head. But all she'd have to do was go back through the row. When she turned, the cane was still higher than her head, and rows led in every direction. Which would take her out? How far had she come?

She smelled smoke. Turning, she saw that it was all around her. It wasn't just smoke. She could feel the heat, smell the sugar, see the flames, hear the crackling of the cane as it burned.

She could scream, but who could hear above the rush of flames overtaking the fields? Her throat felt dry and tight.

The air was thick and smoky. She felt. . .faint.

She thought someone called her name. That was probably her imagination. She'd heard that when people died they saw a light. She was seeing fire, and darkness. Yes, she heard her name.

"Here. I'm here."

"Mary Ellen." She heard horse's hooves, but it was too dark to see. She could barely make out a horse and rider.

She kept coughing out. "I'm here! I'm here!"

A horse and rider passed, and she screamed. It turned and came back. She was snatched up and thrown onto the horse. They were headed straight into high flames. Her skirt was jerked up over her head, and an arm held her close to his chest. She could hardly breathe.

"Hold tight."

She felt the fire as they went through it. Then she was being unwrapped, and water was thrown on her. She coughed and wheezed but managed to get a few gulps of breath down her raw throat. She was sitting on the ground. The woman who'd tried to keep her from the cane put something on her burned leg.

She was given something to drink. Then she saw Clay stretched out on the sand. What were they doing? Was he all right? Mak was smearing something on Clay's face and on his arms.

Japanese and Caucasians stared at her. They knew this was her fault. Mak glanced at her. "Aloe," he said. "It will help the burn."

"I'm all right," Clay mumbled.

"He will be," Mak said. "He was just scared out of his wits. He knew the men were on the horses, ready to burn this field. Fortunately, the woman ran into the mill and wired the next mill. But not in time to stop the fires from being set."

Clay tried to sit. He took the liquid offered him. Mary Ellen didn't know what it was, but it made her throat feel better.

Clay rasped. "I've never prayed so hard." He coughed.

"Let's get more of this on your face and arms," Mak said. "Then we have to get you to the hospital."

"Hospital," he croaked out. "Why?"

Why?

No one said it, but it was because the man who had women fall at his feet over his looks had a face as red as a crimson sunset.

Asking his forgiveness for her attitude seemed minor now. Mary Ellen was responsible for destroying the face of the best-looking man in Hawaii.

Chapter 18

They wanted to keep Clay overnight at the hospital. After everybody visited him, the one he really wanted to see appeared in the doorway. She knocked softly but didn't enter until he asked her to come in.

"The doctor said you'll be fine," he said.

She nodded. "The place on my leg is like a bad sunburn. Thank you for protecting the rest of me."

"I should have been more clear when I talked about harvest and burning the cane. I take for granted everyone knows the fires can be set at any time and they burn quickly."

"I thought the cane would be cut before it was burned. It never occurred to me the fields would be set on fire."

"Why did you go in there?"

She sat in the chair and told him the most fantastic story about the photo and about her dreams of him running toward her in the sugarcane fields.

She called that foolish.

"I've been a problem to Breanna and Geoffrey since I came here. And now look what I've done to you."

His throat was raw, and he wasn't supposed to talk, but he had to, if she would listen.

"For quite a while now, it's as if God was whispering to me, and then you came shouting at me."

As best she could, through her raspy throat, she said, "I didn't shout at you."

"Same as. You asked about the significance of things, like that church steeple being one hundred feet high."

She shrugged. "I was just curious."

"Right. But I kept thinking about it. I asked Jacob, and he told me to figure it out. In reading about the history of the church, something jumped out at me. The church is one hundred feet long. Before Jacob left for the mainland, I asked him again. He said he didn't know and hoped I'd tell him."

Clay started to laugh, but that hurt his throat. He was talking too much. He drank some water.

"Maybe you shouldn't talk."

"I know. But I need to. I want you to know." He waited for the water to soothe his throat. "I thought of the steeple being one hundred feet high, reaching toward God. The church is one hundred feet long. Reaching across the earth. One's reach on earth should not exceed one's reach for God. I have a lot of sugarcane on this red earth of Hawaii. What I have with God has fallen far short of that."

"You've mentioned God a lot, like you know Him."

"Oh, I do. I'm part of this group descended from the early missionaries. I know we each have to make the decision to follow Christ, but there is a faith that seems inbred in us. It's a part of us that we can't deny."

He told her about his giving his heart to Jesus when he was nine years old. "And no matter how much I've tried to ignore it, deep inside, it's like the little boy in me is on the rope in the steeple, ringing the bell, saying, look up, farther than the sugarcane fields."

Clay watched her look down. But she had spoken her heart. He wanted to do that. "It's as if God said '*Reach for Me.*' I did, and you know what? His hand was no farther than mine. I was already in His arms the moment my thoughts, my commitment went to Him. Maybe that's why He allowed me to become burned and ugly. What I had to attract anyone is gone."

She looked up quickly. "At this moment, there could be no man more appealing than you."

If his throat would let him, he'd scoff at that. "I don't know if I'll ever look the same. The skin may clear. It may be scarred. But it will take time before it's healed."

Mary Ellen spoke softly. "You've never looked better to me. You were my knight in shining armor, on a white horse, coming to rescue me."

"My horse is black."

"It's the perception that matters. You rescued me." She hesitated. "But I thought horses were afraid of fire."

"Mine are trained to run through fire and to jump over it. When fires are set, there's the possibility of someone being caught between fields. Things can go wrong."

"Well, I'm grateful. I'm sorry about your face. But what I see of you now is the inside. I respect and admire that. I know you're a good person. And any decent woman would not love someone just because they're good looking."

"Did you say *love*?" He reached and caught her hand.

"No. I said I could *not* love."

She tried to pull away, but he would not allow it. "Could you love someone who has been foolish, played a dangerous game, and hurt you in the process? Could you forgive a person like that?"

"I suppose I've been foolish in my lifetime."

"Really? When?"

"I've tried to run Breanna's life. I've judged you. I saw a photo and imagined impossible dreams. I also accused you of being a villain. Can you forgive me?"

"For thinking of me as a villain, yes. Although I'm afraid I have been. Not in a criminal way, but in toying with women's hearts, although that was not my intent. My pride and ego needed that to make me feel worthwhile. I know now that doesn't do it."

"What does?"

"What I've been taught. The Lord Jesus in our hearts and lives. I knew that.

But I got away from it. And. . .I heard you praying for me out there in the hall when you wouldn't come in here. I am eternally grateful. If forgiveness is due, I offer mine."

"I forgive you, too. You found Breanna for me. Because of your photo, my sister is in love with Geoffrey and these islands. I think they were meant for each other."

"Do you think I'm worthy to have a wonderful woman love me?"

"I know you are"

"Someone as wonderful and beautiful as you?"

"I'm not—"

"Yes, you are. Outside and in. I've had to ask myself, who and what am I? I want to start over. I know I can. In fact, I have by asking God's forgiveness for my not taking life and women more seriously."

"Don't feel too badly. If you had, then Breanna and Geoffrey might never have met."

"Nor. . .you and I?"

"Is that so important?"

"Next to learning how to live my life for the Lord, it's the most important thing to me. Could you, would you, consider giving me another chance? Like you did the day we met and gave me the chance to prove my innocence. . .which proved my guilt?"

"That's a little complex. I'd like to think about it."

Her hand left his. She stood. He watched her turn, and it felt like a knife turning in his heart.

Abruptly, she faced him again. "I thought about it. Yes, I'll give you a chance. If you give me one."

≈

Mary Ellen was afraid to hope Clay was talking about her in that hospital room. Maybe he meant women in general. But now, they could relate. She would not have unrealistic dreams, but she could keep her memories and relate to Clay as her sister's husband's friend.

But she could also relate to Akemi's having said it would be hard to live in the world with Jacob, but without him.

Several days passed, along with the talk about the fire and the close call she and Clay had. No one seemed to blame her for the trouble she'd caused.

A few days later, the postman delivered a letter for her to the dress shop. Inside was a photo of Clay. On the back, was a note:

> *Wanted: An American blond with blue eyes.*
> *If interested, come to the Matti-Rose Inn*
> *7 o'clock Friday evening.*
> *Mr. C. Honeycutt*

Mary Ellen wore the coral-colored holoku that she'd tried on in the dress shop the day Clay had seen her play-dancing.

Matilda led her into the dining room and to a table covered with a white tablecloth. On it was a beautiful floral centerpiece. Akemi brought two glasses with pineapple nectar in them.

After she was seated, Clay appeared in the doorway, dressed in a white suit and a colorful shirt, open at the neck. In his hand, he held a flowered lei. He came up to her and arranged it around her neck.

His face was splotchy and peeling, but that didn't matter. What mattered was the warmth in his deep blue eyes. She was seeing him with her heart, and he was beautiful.

"Thank you for coming," he said.

"Thank you for inviting me."

He held her hands. The man who had raced through smoke and fire to rescue her, now trembled in this safe, calm, beautiful setting.

She hoped she knew why.

He took a deep breath. "I never thought I would say this. But Mary Ellen Colson, I'm in love with you."

She closed her eyes. When she opened them, he was still there holding her hands.

She felt her body tremble. And her hands. And her lips.

"Will you marry me?"

She was nodding. Yes. Yes.

He took a little box from his pocket. Sitting on blue velvet was the ring she had admired when she and Matilda had looked at rings with Breanna.

He slipped it on her finger.

"I love it. It is so beautiful." Her smile trembled. "But what it means is the important thing."

"And it means I love you and want to spend the rest of my life with you."

"I want that, too. I love you." After a moment, she said, "How did you know the size?"

"Matilda said you had tried on a pair of gloves in the dress shop."

"So a lot of people were in on this."

He shrugged. "Maybe. . .only. . .the entire island."

"What made you think I would accept this?"

"You mean besides your eyes being the mirror of your soul? Your not being able to stay away from me although I often acted like a heel? Your keeping my old photo in your skirt pocket?"

"How—"

"People talk. And," he added, "Matilda told me that women ignore only men they're in love with. And one other thing. I prayed to God that He would make you love me. See, you didn't stand a chance."

"You'd better stop while you're ahead, Mr. C."

Akemi said, "Kiss your bride-to-be."

Mary Ellen saw him look at her lips; then he grinned. "No way. Not here."

She was grateful. He, too, must be remembering when they were swept away, like a wave disappearing over the ocean. Even though they had not kissed. His eyebrows lifted. "We need to set a date for the wedding."

Epilogue

Mary Ellen planned the traditional American part of the wedding. Clay added the Hawaiian touch. It seemed everyone else wanted to plan the reception. Finally, Clay settled it.

"Plan what you like. But not until we return from our honeymoon." He wouldn't tell her where they would be.

She couldn't have dreamed a more wonderful wedding. After the guests were seated, a Hawaiian love song was sung by Clay's friend who had been at the party. His sister, in a sleeveless, rose-colored dress and wearing a white lei moved her graceful arms and hands. Her body barely moved like a tide caressing the shore, or a palm frond swaying in a gentle breeze.

The beauty of it lingered, even as Clay and the pastor entered from a side door. Breanna and Geoffrey walked down the aisle together as matron of honor and best man.

Uncle Harv escorted Mary Ellen down the aisle toward the most handsome man in the world, dressed in a black tuxedo. His face had healed, but that wasn't what was so appealing. It was him, his heart, his soul, and she loved him. She would love him if he were not handsome.

Breanna and Geoffrey handed each of them a white lei, and they put them around the other's neck. Mary Ellen hardly knew what the pastor was saying but managed to repeat after him and say *I do* at the right time. She and Clay knelt while his friends sang "Amazing Grace."

They stood, and the pastor pronounced them man and wife. "You may kiss the bride."

Mary Ellen saw that challenge, that dare in Clay's eyes, and felt the rest of the world fading. His face came near. She lifted hers, her lips begging for his touch. She could feel his warm breath on her lips. He barely grazed them, then whispered in her ear, "Not yet."

The pastor introduced them as Mr. and Mrs. Claybourne Honeycutt.

After being showered with flower petals, they began saying their good-byes. "Uncle Harv, don't leave here before I get back."

"Who knows?" he said. "I may quit my job and work with Mr. Hammeur. After all, Akemi says she's going to college." He and Pilar smiled at each other. . . in that special way.

Yes, Mary Ellen had to admit, Hawaii was a paradise for love and romance.

"For now," Clay said impatiently, "it's time we left on the yacht."

"Yacht?" Mary Ellen said. "What yacht?"

"Your yacht."

"I don't have a yacht."

"It's your wedding present."

"That's. . .I mean, yachts are expensive."

His eyebrows lifted, and his eyes challenged. "Haven't you heard? I'm the sugar king."

Later on the ship, she said, "I fell in love with you the moment I saw your photo. When did you know you were in love with me?"

"When I first saw you through the window of the dress shop, sewing little pearls on a wedding dress. I resented each time you said it would be worn by Breanna. I didn't know that I loved you then, but I know it now. And here you are."

He started to touch the pearls and moved his hand away.

"It's all right to touch them now," she said. "They're yours. Everything I am and have is yours."

He touched them. He touched her face and her lips. "Now, I am going to kiss you." His fingers on her lips were replaced by his lips, and beneath the golden moonlight and cool breeze, the sound of gentle waves caressing the yacht, they kissed, a deep, long, meaningful, belonging-to-each-other-under-God's-heaven kind of kiss. His fingers entwined in her long blond hair, hanging loose.

She leaned back only a little. "I feel like I belong to Hawaii and you, Mr. C."

"You do, Mrs. C.," he said meaningfully, looking at his bride. "You are so beautiful. Just like I've pictured you."

LOVE FROM ASHES

Dedication

To the writers of articles in *Chicken Soup from the Soul of Hawai'i*, from whose stories I gained personal insights into those who have lived in and visited Hawaii. Aloha!

Author's Note

Historical fiction includes characters who express the diverse views of their day. Especially when the subject is controversial, those viewpoints may not correspond with what is commonly accepted today. But members of each generation face new situations where they must learn to apply biblical principles such as love and forgiveness to the choices they make. May observing how those in the past went through that process give us insights on how we can do the same today.

Chapter 1

Hawaii
April 1946

W ill you show me Hawaii as he saw it?"
That's what Luke Thurstan would ask the girl named Amelia—if he found her. No, this had to be *when* he found her. As the plane droned on and on over the vast Pacific Ocean, he told himself he needed to do this for his parents because his mother's inner war had not ended.

"Whoa!"

Apparently the plane hit an air pocket that took his breath away. He envisioned the plane doing a bellyflop or a nosedive into that cold, murky water. Then it leveled off, as if the sudden drop had never happened. He turned his head to see how other passengers had reacted. They wore smiles, seemed to chatter faster, perhaps convincing themselves the little scare was nothing to be concerned about.

It wasn't, compared with his having been exposed to near drowning that June day in 1944. He'd jumped off the warship into the sea with his military gear and begun to sink. Someone yanked him to the surface in time to be met with machine gun fire on the Normandy beach. He'd been fortunate. Some buddies had survived neither the sea nor the bullets.

Now, with this little airless bump in the sky, he reminded himself the war was over. This trip would mean closure for his family. But to be honest, he had a feeling his survival as a marine had been more than luck. He had a mission: to walk where his younger brother, Joe, had walked, lived, loved, and died for his country and. . .had died for Luke.

Before closure could ever come for Luke, he had to stand where Joe had stood and ask his brother's forgiveness.

The words of the song "Sentimental Journey" tripped through his mind. The line "Gonna set my heart at ease" wasn't all that convincing. But he would try.

He, too, had fought for God, country, Mom, and apple pie. Now was the time to pursue happiness. But first he had to say good-bye to Joe—at Pearl Harbor.

Sleep had been elusive, partly from anxiety and partly from the cramped quarters in coach. He flexed his muscles as best he could in the small seat. And like many others after several hours of flight above the Pacific Ocean, he walked up and down the aisle a few times.

After military training and the war then working with his dad in construction, sitting still didn't set well with his mind or body. But sailing from the States to the islands had been out of the question. He'd had his share of ocean voyages during the war. He'd seen plenty of death and destruction. Now he looked forward to a place Joe had written about—a place called Paradise.

As they neared the Honolulu Airport, Luke gazed down at a beautiful bay town on the island of Oahu. His mind contrasted the chaos on the Normandy beach with the peaceful picture below. Long canoes glided along the surface of the blue Pacific waters. Surfers rode the waves that gently rolled in rhythmic movement. Swaying palm trees dotted the white sandy beach.

Amid the peaceful setting were the many military bases, including Pearl Harbor, a reminder of the war and destruction that had destroyed such a setting as this.

Wanting to think of the good instead of the haunting memories of war, Luke welcomed the landing at the airport. He breathed in the clean, fresh air that held a faint smell of water and fish, reminding him of childhood days of sitting on a riverbank with his dad and Joe, enjoying fish tales.

He welcomed the feel of cool trade winds brushing against his face. The sky, he'd read, could turn crimson at sunset and was already changing from blue to golden orange. He welcomed the beauty and peace of this so-called paradisiacal place, but alongside it lay the memory of Joe having lost his life here.

Later that evening he dropped his bag onto the floor of his hotel room, stretched and flexed his tight muscles, and headed to the bathroom for a hot shower.

After dressing in clean clothes, he went down for supper. The hotel and dining room looked similar to what he might find in the States, except for the people. In the States, other nationalities were the minorities. Here, *he* was. The majority seemed to be Asians, or at least a mix of Asian.

The menu featured some entrées new to him—*bacaiau*, adobo, tempura, and *opakapaka*. He ordered steak, mashed potatoes, gravy, and green beans, food that he was familiar with. For now, he was simply tired and hungry.

"Your first time here," the waiter said, after he'd had a brief conversation with Luke about the area. "Then you must try the Kona coffee."

Luke sat at a table for two near a window. Darkness obscured everything beyond the grounds outside the hotel flanked by trees and bushes, reminding him of one's ability to see no further than the present moment. After accepting a refill of the coffee whose rich aroma and smooth taste were as good as the waiter had said, he sipped it, wondering if Joe had ever eaten here. He regretted he and Joe couldn't know each other as mature adults. Their teenage and young adult differences now seemed like childish spats compared with having faced world issues.

After dinner he went to the lobby and asked the desk clerk about going to the big island of Hawaii.

The young clerk took on a disturbed look. "A tsunami hit Hilo a couple weeks ago." Then she delivered some heart-wrenching stories about the tsunami taking the lives of more than one hundred people, including children, and the havoc wreaked upon businesses and a school.

Luke didn't relish the idea of seeing damage and destruction. "I was thinking of trying to see a Pastor Grant in Hilo."

Her eyes lit up, and she said there were several Grants in Oahu. She knew of one who owned a sugar plantation and had a brother who was a pastor in Hilo. Luke learned he would be able to take a boat from Oahu to Hilo the following day.

For exercise he took the stairs instead of the elevator and walked along the halls before ending at the door of his third-floor room.

He stripped down to his underwear, turned down the covers, and sat in bed, looking at the letter Joe had sent back in 1941, two days before the Japanese bombed Pearl Harbor. Luke hadn't read it until 1945 when he returned home.

After having served in the marines for three years, his term had been extended and frozen when war was declared against Japan. He'd been a firearms instructor at Camp Lejeune, North Carolina, before being sent to the Normandy beach, which was no place for letters.

Luke's fingertips touched the words written in Joe's hand:

Pearl Harbor
December 5, 1941

Hey Bro,

After your stint in the marines, you should come to this Paradise. You've never seen anything like it. It's like another world. But what I'm writing about mainly is, I know we weren't on the best of terms the last time we talked. Or I should say, when you socked me in the jaw. But you know how I am. I hope you're not still holding it against me.

Just to let you know, I met this girl. You've never seen anything like her, either. Amelia Grant. Her dad's a preacher in Hilo. Believe that? Me and a preacher's daughter?

Anyway, I want you to know I'm sorry about Penny. I'm not leaving her hanging. I let her know I'm not ready to settle down. I'm sure she'd come back to you now that she knows for sure you're a better man than I am.

Be seeing ya,
Yo Bro Joe

Not the greatest of bedtime stories, but Luke had studied the letter before and had given it a lot of thought. There wasn't much left to think about it. He laid it on the bedside table, switched off the lamp, and gave in to the fatigue overtaking him before he could even begin his intended prayer to the Lord, asking why exactly he had come here and how it was going to solve anything.

No matter how many times he read Joe's words *"Be seeing ya,"* that wasn't going to happen.

Chapter 2

Amelia froze. She couldn't make sense of another word her dad said after he asked the visitors to stand and introduce themselves.

Before that, her dad had talked about the tsunami that hit two weeks ago and wiped out so much of Hilo town in the bay area. Buildings and businesses could be replaced, but the worst was losing children. They had been laughing when a small wave pushed ocean water into the streets, giving them a delightfully different means of playing.

The ocean sucked back the water, and then the giant, mesmerizing tsunami flew over like a giant bird, and they were caught, unable to hold onto anything, unable to swim in the force of it. The laughter turned to screams. Adults were killed, too, but the thought of drowned children was so hard to bear.

Her dad told the attendees the town needed all the help they could get to clean up the debris. They would rebuild, just as they had rebuilt their lives after volcanic eruptions and after the war.

He made it sound like a long time had passed since the war ended instead of less than a year. But she knew about rebuilding. That had begun the day the war started.

All that had been on her mind until the visitor said his name. She must have heard wrong. She thought a strong male voice from the back of the church said, *"Luke Thurstan, sir. Visiting from St. Louis, Missouri, in the U.S. of A."*

Thurstan, sir.

Spoken like someone in the military—or someone who had been.

Her internal lecture of denial began. Just as there were numerous Grants on more than one of the islands, there would be many Thurstans throughout the world. She just happened to have known. . .one. Although wanting desperately to close her eyes and shut out that heart-stopping moment, she shivered.

Her eyes searched the face of her dad, who stood in the pulpit. He did not change expressions except to smile and nod. He didn't glance at her. He didn't turn as white as his heavy crop of hair. Her mother, sitting at the organ, ready to play, did not change expressions. But she wouldn't, regardless. Her mother was the most serene person imaginable. Her mother never had an adverse thought in her life. And she never condemned anyone who did.

But I. . .

No. She mustn't.

She'd heard wrong, that was all. Even if she had heard right, there were some things he need never know. Some things he couldn't know. He wouldn't even know her last name was Thurstan. When the service ended, she would

254

sneak out the back way.

But after the service, just as Amelia tried to do that, Tara Furness, her supervisor from the tourism company, called to her.

Amelia turned toward the aisle.

"Amelia Thurstan, meet Luke Thurstan." Tara gave a short laugh. "He came by the office yesterday and surprised me when he said his name. I asked him if he had relatives here, and he said no but that he was looking for a Pastor Grant."

Amelia allowed a glance at his suit. Not his face.

Reaching out to hold onto the back of the pew didn't help much. "Dad will be out front."

"I know." Tara acted as if Amelia had said a foolish thing. But Amelia knew there were so many foolish things she might have said. Disastrous in fact. "But Luke mentioned seeing the sights, and of course I mentioned you since you're"— she laughed again—"Jacob Grant's daughter, and your last name is Thurstan."

"Coincidence," Amelia said. She shrugged and ventured a quick glance at him. "There were no relatives."

Tara said, "That's what I told him."

What else had she told him?

Glancing up, Amelia felt his stare and studied look, but he covered it quickly. "I'm imposing," he said.

"No. I don't feel well. So much has gone on lately. It's not. . .you." Why was he looking for Pastor Grant? This man from St. Louis?

Tara spoke softly. "The tsunami has us all torn up."

"I'm sorry," he said. "In Oahu I heard about the tsunami, but I don't know enough people to have gotten details or how much damage or anything."

Amelia knew she mustn't do this. It was the shock. But she had to look at him.

With a plea to God and all the courage she could muster, she lifted her gaze to his eyes. They were blue but not filled with mischievous laughter. These were serious. His wavy dark blond hair was conservatively cut, with no golden curls tumbling over his forehead. And the lips were not smiling. A resemblance. . .somewhere—but different. Older. He would be. All that was five years ago. And this one would be the older brother.

"I'm sorry," Amelia said, forcing her eyes back to Tara. "I'll be fine."

"No, I should apologize," the man said. "With all that's going on here, I shouldn't be talking of touring the island. But I did come on a serious matter. Please excuse me." He nodded and turned to go.

Tara's mouth opened. "Get some rest, honey. You don't look well." She hurried up the aisle after Luke Thurstan.

Amelia slumped down into the pew. She leaned back, bowed her head, and closed her eyes, with her hand on her forehead. If anyone asked, no, she didn't feel well, and yes, she was praying. Praying Luke Thurstan would not say anything strange to her dad or vice versa. She'd told everyone Joe had no relatives.

She'd gotten through so much—with the Lord's help. Losing Joe. The war.

And she was getting through the tsunami trauma, helping where she could.

But now she was experiencing her own personal tsunami.

Yes, the Lord helped.

But that didn't exempt a person from having to face the consequences of their actions. Her dad had preached that all her life.

Were her consequences standing at the front of the church, shaking hands with Pastor Jacob Grant?

Maybe if she ignored Luke Thurstan, he'd go away.

Right. And when was the last time she'd had that thought?

Chapter 3

Luke mentally kicked himself for not being more sensitive about allowing Tara Furness to introduce him to Amelia Grant Thurstan. Yesterday when Tara had said Amelia had no Thurstan relatives, he'd said no more about it. But niggling questions remained. He had thought she might have married someone because close to five years had passed since Joe had written his letter mentioning her. But the last thing he expected was the implication that she had married Joe.

If she had, why didn't she say so?

If she had not, why did she pretend?

Or had Joe told her he had no relatives? Joe had a way of making up his own world truth. Sure, coincidences could occur, but he seriously doubted that two days before Joe's death Amelia Grant had been his girl, and after his death she had married a Thurstan.

He'd seen enough to know that anything was possible—however improbable—that another Thurstan came to the island after 1941. Was he living now? Did she not want Luke to meet another Thurstan? Was he killed in the tsunami? Was the spelling of their last names different? There were *Thurstones*, *Thurstens*, *Thurstons*, and even *Therstons*.

"Luke," Tara said, catching up with him in the foyer. "Since Amelia isn't feeling well, I could show you some places of interest in the morning."

"Thank you," Luke said, looking at the outstretched hand of the pastor standing by the front entrance. "But for now, the pastor has inspired me to help with Hilo's cleanup." Sightseeing was taking a backseat to his having been introduced to Amelia Grant. . .Thurstan.

He shook the pastor's hand and thought it best not to say he enjoyed the sermon, since so much of it had been about the town's devastation.

While gripping Luke's hand firmly, the pastor smiled, thanked him, and made a few remarks about meeting others on the main street in the morning and Luke would be welcome to join the cleanup. The friendly man gave no indication that Luke's name meant anything to him. Luke suspected it had been a shock to the pastor's daughter. More than four years had gone by since Joe's death. She'd never written to his parents, never sent a word of condolence. He wasn't condemning, just contemplating. Had she known Joe had a family? Or how to reach them?

With a war going on, all sorts of situations were possible. War changed everything. Relationships. Traditions. Actions.

Maybe she, like Penny, had been devastated by Joe. Or by his death. He didn't want to cause her or anyone else any hurt, ever. He'd seen a world and families, including his own, devastated. Now was the time to pick up the pieces and rebuild. That's what the morning's sermon had been about.

"Where might you be staying?" the pastor asked, withdrawing his hand.

"The Matti-Rose Inn was recommended by—"

"By me, of course."

Luke looked over at Tara Furness standing next to him. When the cab had taken him to the chamber of commerce yesterday, he'd been directed to the woman who insisted he call her Tara, and she had driven him to the auto rental where he'd picked up the black Ford he was driving. Because of the tsunami damage, he'd followed her along back roads to the Matti-Rose and rented a room in the quaint inn that smelled of disinfectant.

Pastor Grant chuckled. "The Matti-Rose is a fine place to stay."

"What can he say?" Tara laughed lightly. "His wife is the manager."

"No." The pastor shook his head. "Last week I would have said it wasn't fit for man or beast." His brow wrinkled. "The inn is close enough to the bay that the tsunami caused some damage. Looked like a giant fist broke some of the windows, opened the front doors, and slung a mountain-sized barrel of water onto the floor. Soaked some of the furniture, and there's still some stains. We have more cleaning up to do, but the structure is sound."

"We were so fortunate to escape damage." Tara's eyes lifted to the ceiling. "Thank the Lord." She immediately looked repentant, saying softly, "Many did not. Everyone has lost relatives or friends."

A rush of despair that Luke knew he must learn to deal with swept through him. In the past few years, many—including children—had lost adult loved ones. Now, many had lost children. His mom said there was no worse calamity than losing a child, no matter his age. And he knew that to say *Mom, I'm here. I survived the war* could not make up for her deepening depression. Sometimes he suspected his being there added to her grief.

His dad had told Luke a long time ago he could take out his frustrations by hammering nails into pieces of wood. Luke knew the feeling. Maybe he could help these people do that.

"Aren't you staying for something to eat?" The pastor's manner was welcoming. "The inn doesn't serve breakfast on Sunday, so I know you may not have eaten."

When Luke had registered yesterday, the young man at the desk in the foyer told him the church would be serving lunch since so many restaurants were damaged. He had thought he'd stay and talk to the pastor and perhaps his daughter. But now the pastor made no mention of Joe or Luke's last name. And Amelia. . .wasn't feeling well. "No, sir," he said, stepping away so others could speak to the pastor. "I want to drive around a little this afternoon."

He found a restaurant in a little town outside Hilo and ate a light meal and drank the Kona coffee like he'd had at the hotel in Oahu. It was the best he'd ever tasted. He mentioned it to the waitress, who smiled and nodded. "That's what all westerners say. It's Kona. Grown right here in Hawaii."

Westerners.

A while later, that word still rang in his mind as he parked away from the devastated street leading to Hilo Bay, from where the tsunami had come. He got out to walk around and survey the damage.

Many stores along the main street looked intact, although closed. Walking farther down Kamehameha Avenue, whose sign was still there, was like walking into a war zone. He saw the words HILO MACARONI FACTORY on the side of the building where boards were scattered beneath. Part of the roof of GENERAL MILLS SPERRY FLOUR BUILDING lay on the ground in front of its door. SUN SUN LAU RESTAURANT was devastated, along with JEWITT AWNING SHOP, which leaned on its side.

Standing on the beach of Hilo Bay, Luke wasn't amazed that such destruction contrasted with such a perfectly calm day, warmed by the trade winds that carried the scent of flowers. He'd seen beautiful settings before, although he'd had to look up, even as high as the sky, to be reminded, *Our God is still here.*

The unfathomable depths of the deep blue ocean stretched out before him. Above him in serene calm was the bright blue sky. Tall palm trees with their green branches high overhead waved *aloha*, reminding him of the hope instilled by such inspired words as "the star-spangled banner yet waves" and "our flag was still there."

Walking back to the inn along the deserted street, he wondered just what a *westerner* was doing here—why he ever thought this a good idea. But he would stick around long enough for an answer to some of these. . .coincidences.

A short time later, propped against the headboard of his bed, he searched the brochures. Perhaps he should tour the sights alone, although he dreaded the thought of approaching Pearl Harbor—a site he knew he could not avoid.

A knock sounded on the door of his room. Luke blinked open his eyes and looked at the brochures scattered across the bed. He must have dozed off. Surprise flooded him when he opened the door and saw the organist from the church holding a tray with a covered platter on it, along with a cup and small pot.

"I brought your supper. Everything is closed downtown."

This beautiful, middle-aged woman had a smile and kind eyes that could warm almost any heart. He'd stifled his surprise in church when he'd seen her, dressed as she was now in a silk kimono. Then he'd been reminded of what he'd read about the Americans of Japanese descent in Hawaii.

He knew Japanese men had fought in the war for America. Many had been honored and received medals; some had died. "And your name?" Luke asked.

"Oh, I'm sorry. I thought Jacob might have told you. I am Akemi Grant. The pastor's wife."

Luke's gaze dropped to the tray. He felt the tremor and for an instant wondered if the volcano had erupted. Then he remembered reading that the volcano never stopped erupting. "Here, I—" He stepped back, and she walked in and set the tray on the table along the wall.

Who was killed? Who survived? Who is friend, or foe? Maybe someday he'd stop fighting the war.

"Thank you," he said.

She nodded, and the calm on her face seemed to reach his soul. "Breakfast will be served at eight o'clock in the morning for guests. But there will be food in the dining room for any who want to leave earlier to help with the work in town."

He could think of nothing more to say than thank you again. Her brief nod resembled a bow, and then she walked with graceful steps out the door and along the hallway.

Standing with his back against the closed door, Luke stared at the tray, smelled the aroma of that rich, dark coffee. It beckoned him. But a realization kept his feet planted to the floor.

That woman was the wife of Pastor Jacob Grant. And she was unmistakably Japanese.

That meant Amelia Grant Thurstan, the lovely young woman with black hair pulled back in a thick roll, olive skin, deep brown eyes was. . .part Japanese.

The girl Joe wrote about was Japanese.

He could not tell his mother.

It would kill her.

Chapter 4

He came on a serious matter?
        The disturbing thought tiptoed across Amelia's mind each time she closed her eyes during the night. It might as well have shouted. She kept hearing her dad's voice on the phone Sunday afternoon. "Amelia, do you need to talk to me and your mother?"

"No, Dad. Everything's fine."

"Aren't you curious about the Thurstan fellow?"

"No. Tara introduced us. I told her the last name was a coincidence."

She felt the pause of silence before he said, "We're here, honey. We love you."

"I know, Dad. I love you, too."

She kept telling herself that was the end of it. A lot of people had the same last name. No need to make a big deal of it. She'd told herself that all night long.

On Monday morning Amelia kept putting a cold spoon over her eyes, but the puffiness remained.

Her sister-in-law, Wanda, managed to get all three children, who invariably woke with boundless energy, to the table for breakfast. Amelia kissed them all on the cheek then turned to answer the ringing phone on the countertop.

She picked up the receiver. "Oh, Tara. Hi. Yes, I plan to come in. I'm feeling better but didn't get much sleep." She listened for a moment along with watching six-year-old Parker and Joseph, almost four, grabbing for the syrup at the same time. Wanda, in her magical way, retrieved the bottle, saying, "Let me."

After thanking Tara, Amelia hung up. Now that the young ones had stuffed their mouths, she could speak for a moment without interruption—maybe. Nine-year-old Ellie rolled her eyes and tightened her lips in her little-mama way. Without these children, what in the world would she and Wanda ever do?

Panic washed over her. That was not something to think. Children lost to a tsunami must be what triggered the thought. Oh how she and Wanda had hugged these children! "Amelia?"

Amelia lowered herself into a chair and took a sip of the orange juice that sat beside her empty plate. She and Wanda had the same kind of conversation after church yesterday that Amelia had had with her dad. Wanda had heard the visitor introduce himself.

"Tara says I can come in later. Word has gone throughout other countries about the tsunami, so the tourism business has slowed considerably. She said. . . ." Amelia hesitated, not wanting to say his name in front of the children. "The man who wanted a tour has canceled. He volunteered to help in town."

"That's nice. Want some more coffee?" Wanda offered.

Amelia saw the glance Ellie gave her. That little girl was nine going on nineteen. She could pick up on tension in a heartbeat. Amelia and Wanda's clipped conversation would have the wheels turning in Ellie's head.

"No thanks. But I just might take Tara up on going in late. I'd like to see Matilda."

"Good idea," Wanda said. "She'd like that."

All the children turned their cheeks to Amelia for her accustomed goodbye kiss. Resisting the urge to take Joseph in her arms and never let him go, she said to the children, "*Aloha au ia 'oe.*" Each one responded, "Love you," as usual.

The drive from Wanda's house to Matilda's was little more than a mile away. Amelia wanted Matilda to tell her which was best—to ignore Luke Thurstan or tell him the truth and face the dreaded fear she felt when she heard his name. No, the fear went even deeper. Each time visitors came from the mainland, she feared that someday someone would come and ask about Joe. Now her fears had materialized.

She had survived the war.

She had survived the tsunami.

But could she survive the likes of Luke Thurstan?

She parked in front of the two-story house Matilda had called home for more than fifty years. Even a tsunami dared not touch the house where Matilda lived, so it seemed. It had come to the edge, even into her yard, but not inside.

Matilda stood at the screen door before Amelia could knock. Matilda was everybody's friend. She knew everyone's secrets and told none.

Some said she was in her nineties, but she seemed ageless. Amelia remembered when she was a child and thought Matilda looked like she was on fire with her head of red hair. After her friend Rose died, her hair starting turning. Now it was pure white, as if smoke were coming from the fire that still raged inside her.

She had a mind as sharp as a tack and a tongue to match if a person showed disrespect or unkindness. People talked about her having a heart of gold, like the gold pieces she'd acquired in California when the real Gold Rush had long before ended. She was known for giving out the gold pieces as tips and to people who pleased her. Rumor was she'd given them all away. She was a legend. When anybody asked why a woman with such good posture would carry a cane, Matilda said it was to keep the snakes away.

A native Hawaiian knew there were no snakes in Hawaii. But nobody doubted Matilda would wield that cane against a two-legged snake if necessary.

"Come in," Matilda welcomed, holding open the screen door. The green fringed shawl enhanced the color of her brilliant green eyes, which spoke of intelligence and warmth. Amelia knew she was being welcomed into Matilda's heart. It wasn't the first time.

"You remembered the name," Amelia said, closing the screen behind her as they made their way inside.

Matilda walked over to sit in her timeworn recliner. She patted a leatherbound book on the table next to her chair. "All the names of my boys I've met or heard about are in this prayer book."

Amelia sat in a chair near her. "I'm afraid."

Matilda's voice challenged. "Of what?"

Amelia sighed. "Seems you asked me that before. More than once."

Matilda nodded. "There is only one answer when it comes right down to it."

"I guess I just need to hear it again."

"All right. Let's examine why you're afraid. And while you're thinking about that, I'll go on out to the lanai." She rose from the chair and adjusted the shawl so that the fringe fell gracefully along the flowered silk blouse she wore with dark green slacks. Matilda had been the first person on the island to wear pants for occasions other than work. But she had been a fashion setter in her younger days when she'd owned a dress shop in Hilo. Everyone had made do with their clothing during the war, and Matilda had shared much of hers.

Matilda picked up the prayer book. "Pour us a cup of that pineapple herbal tea, will you? The pot's on."

Amelia poured the tea. Being near Matilda and breathing in the fruity aroma of the tea were already having a calming effect. She took the cups to the lanai and set them on a small table in front of a wicker couch and chairs.

Looking out at the lush foliage with its sweet-smelling flowers, Amelia knew Matilda had brought her out here for the purpose of causing her to think of the beauty and perfection of this setting. Beyond the lawn, as green as Matilda's eyes, stood stately palms with their fanlike branches swaying gently in the bright blue sky. Many times in her young life, Amelia had played on that lawn, and she knew the closeness of the narrow beach to the wide blue ocean, calm and peaceful today.

After a long moment, Amelia propped the pillow on a rounded side of the wicker chair so she could better observe Matilda. She'd done that, too, as a child and had drawn her feet up. She'd always felt safe around Matilda. Even fallen asleep at times. She took a sip of the tea and set the cup on the saucer and leaned back.

Amelia struggled with what to say. "I've been afraid something like this might happen. Involvement with those people from the mainland can only mean trouble. I'm afraid this Luke Thurstan knows. . .something."

"What makes you think that?"

"Tara said he asked about Pastor Grant in Hilo."

Matilda looked at her for a long moment over the rim of her cup and then set it down. "And that's never happened before?"

"Quite often." The realization made her smile. Before and after the war. Many who had gone to seminary with her dad or heard him lecture on the mainland had visited him on the island. She had to consciously will her head to quit bobbing.

Fear quickly overcame that moment of relief. "But Tara told him my last name. He asked for my dad but didn't seem to have any particular business with him. I think he was looking for me."

"And what could he know about you?"

If Joe had written home about her, what could he have said? She shrugged. "My name? But this Luke said he came here on a serious matter."

Matilda nodded. "And for what serious matter do most people come here from the mainland?"

The answer was obvious. "To see Pearl Harbor. Oh, Matilda, after Joe died, I tried to make the right decision for all involved." She blinked away the moisture threatening her eyes. Crying wouldn't help anything. "Do you think God is getting ready to punish me?"

Matilda's kind gaze held a reprimand. "God doesn't want to hurt you. He loves you. Now, let's get back to this Luke person. What is the most logical reason he's here?"

"Tara said he wanted a tour, so I think he probably wants to see where his brother died."

"You're sure that's his brother?"

Amelia nodded. "Joe mentioned him. And. . .there's a resemblance."

"All right," Matilda said. "Reason this out. Luke wants to feel close to his brother. Do you think he believes the name of Thurstan is coincidental?"

"I wouldn't."

"So you're afraid of the truth coming out."

"Oh Matilda. I don't want anyone to be hurt more than they have been already."

"All right," Matilda said in her forthright way. "You're afraid of doing and saying anything. And you're afraid of not doing and not saying anything. So tell me your greatest fear."

Amelia had known that was coming. Matilda had said it almost five years ago. And of course she knew what she feared. Luke Thurstan had already volunteered to help with the work in Hilo. Was he so generous with his time? Or was he curious about her?

What would he learn if he began to ask questions?

What would he think if she told him. . .nothing? It wasn't as if she'd been asked anything.

And who in their right mind would ask the kind of question she would need to lie about? If someone asked, that meant they weren't in their right mind, so she wouldn't be obligated to answer.

Her thoughts had not been so muddled since just after the attack on Pearl Harbor. But Matilda was waiting for her answer. What did she fear?

"Fear itself?" Amelia whispered.

Matilda smiled. But Amelia felt the ocean waves churning in her stomach. "Like you told me before. You don't run and hide. You face life head on, and those who oppose you can just step out of the way."

"Yes. And what's the first thing to do?"

Amelia knew. She slipped from her chair and onto her knees and grasped Matilda's hand. A hand that was not the hand of an old woman. It was the hand of comfort.

Matilda prayed aloud, as she had so many years ago, that Amelia would make the right decisions. Amelia's tears soaked the rings on the dear woman's fingers.

Amelia tried not to fear. She knew God was in control. But war came. Tsunamis came. And so had. . .Luke Thurstan.

Chapter 5

Luke raised the window of his upstairs room. The lace curtain fluttered against his bare arm. The fragrant breath of morning greeted him with the sweet scent of flowers. Rain had fallen during the night, but the sun was rising with a smile across the sky like pink lips and a golden tongue. A damp landscape stretched out in many hues of green, meeting a sparkling, deep blue ocean and giving evidence that this island was a jewel in the sun like the brochures promised.

Wearing a short-sleeved cotton shirt and the denim pants he'd packed for possibly hiking, he went downstairs for breakfast long before eight o'clock. He knew many workers would have been on the job before sunrise.

The buffet table looked impressive with cereals, fruit, juice, coffee, and breads. Two young girls came into the dining room to take orders as if this were a restaurant, but the small group was more like a large family.

He met a couple of brothers, Ted and Frank, who were visiting from the mainland. They'd come specifically to help relatives whose restaurant had been damaged by the tsunami. They had no particular training in building and showed interest in Luke having studied architecture and worked with a developer for a short while before joining the marines.

"But I'm volunteering to work with my hands, just like you," Luke told them. "That's what I was doing along with my dad before coming here."

After a hearty breakfast of an omelet made with eggs, peppers, onion, and cheese, topped off with fresh island fruit, fresh-baked bread, and Kona coffee, Luke and the men left their vehicles parked at the back of the inn and walked down to the main street of Hilo.

A farmer's market was being set up at one side of the street, and farmers were putting all kinds of fruits and vegetables on the stands. People made purchases while crates of produce were still being taken from trucks and car trunks.

Ted and Frank knew where to go since they had arrived last week. Luke walked over to where Pastor Jacob stood with several men.

Jacob introduced them. The others were newcomers, too, who had attended the church service yesterday. "Glad you men joined us," Jacob said. "Some who helped on Saturday had to go back to their jobs. And of course, we don't work on Sunday." He took them around to a couple of buildings, and before long, Luke was using a crowbar to pry up damaged flooring and throwing it into a trash pile that he or someone else would get rid of later.

He was surrounded by a rainbow of nationalities, mostly Asian, primarily Japanese. Around midmorning, a man questioned him about his abilities so he could determine if Luke could best be of help by mopping out a muddy basement, repairing a broken window, or restoring a roof.

Before long, Luke was given some tools and placed in a somewhat supervisory capacity helping rebuild a restaurant to replace the one that had been destroyed. He was pleased to learn the restaurant belonged to John, the uncle of Ted and Frank.

He wanted to help, to be of service, lend a hand. Now he felt like a foreigner in a distant land. At times he worked alongside Japanese men, and his hand had even touched theirs. It was all he could do not to draw back.

A reflex of war. A mindset one had to have in order to fight a war, to kill—not a man but the concept of the enemy.

How many times did he have to remind himself the war was over? It was easier when it was a concept. . .not individuals.

Strange how the mind wasn't always the winner over emotion.

His crew broke to visit the farmer's market for lunch. Jacob Grant came up to him and praised his work and said he should get paid for all he was doing.

"Pastor Grant, I'm not looking for a job."

"Most people call me Pastor Jacob or just Jacob." He looked around at the new buildings whose frames were in place and the foundations being dug for others. "As you can see, there's a need for skilled labor and dirty work."

Luke nodded. "Like you said in your sermon yesterday: this is the time for rebuilding."

"You apparently didn't come here planning to work, since you volunteered."

"No, I came to see the place my brother called Paradise that became his grave when the—" Luke forced a cough before the next words could come from his mouth. This was neither the time nor the place to use barracks talk. This man's wife was Japanese. He quickly completed his sentence in another way. "When Pearl Harbor was bombed."

Luke half expected Pastor Jacob to ask about his brother, but instead he nodded. "Many people visit from the mainland and Japan. It's still shocking to think any nation dared attack a part of America. It's as if they must see this paradoxical place called Paradise where a war began. You haven't seen much, but is it what you expected?"

"No," Luke said immediately. He didn't say it, but he would have expected the pastor to at least acknowledge his name being the same as his daughter's.

After a pleasant nod, the pastor walked over to others. Then Luke saw the beautiful, middle-aged woman in a silk kimono who had brought his dinner to him—the preacher's wife—and an older woman. They brought baskets of sandwiches for the men.

Their frequent glances his way indicated they might be talking about him. The women laughed easily with each other.

Luke joined others who found anything and more than a person could want at the farmer's market.

The two women came up to him. "Now that we know you," the pastor's wife said in the musical voice he'd detected last night, "and you help build our town back, you call me Akemi. This is my friend Matilda. She is mother and grand-mother of all." With her free hand, the beautiful woman made a wide, graceful sweep as if encompassing all humanity.

"Ha," came from the older woman, who was quite attractive for someone her age. "She's being kind. I am the most critical, outspoken person on the island."

Akemi was nodding. "But in a good way."

Matilda touched his arm. "You're invited to my house for dinner. Right after sundown. Mine is the only house, back from the street a ways but opposite the Matti-Rose."

Luke hardly knew what to say, going immediately from an introduction to a dinner invitation. And that was just the beginning of his surprise. Next she said, "By the way, Amelia will join us."

Amelia Grant. . .Thurstan? He didn't mean to glance at Akemi, but he did and watched her turn to offer someone else a sandwich. His glance back at Matilda revealed her green gaze knew exactly what had crossed his mind, as if he'd said aloud, *Joe's girl?*

But he couldn't know that. It was just his mind trying to make sense of things. Others began vying for Matilda's attention, and she gave it to them. He'd heard that Hawaii once had royalty. He couldn't help but wonder if this woman was a descendant of such. Everyone seemed to know her, respect her. Her glance back at him made him realize he stood staring at her.

She hadn't really asked if he'd come to dinner. She had told him he was invited. What was it about this woman that. . .commanded his attention? He almost laughed, thinking, *As if she were my superior officer.*

She knew who he was. Apparently Akemi or Amelia had told her about him. Otherwise, why would she want him at dinner and say Amelia would be there? He'd never seen her before in his life.

Why had Amelia said their having the same last name was a coincidence, and now they were to have dinner together?

But she'd been Joe's girl. Or had she? Joe wrote that he *met* her. What did that mean?

Did Amelia know how American servicemen felt about the Japanese? He could almost laugh ironically at that. Of course. The American servicemen killed all they could of them. He'd never before thought about how a Japanese might feel about an American.

What was he supposed to feel now? How can you be ready to kill a person of another race one day and the next be ready to embrace them? One day an enemy, the next a friend. The answer was not as simple as right or wrong. Or like the song he'd learned in church as a boy: *"Jesus loves the little children, red and yellow, black and white, they are precious in His sight."* Yes. The little ones. He'd believed it then. But they grow up.

Was Amelia afraid he would hold against her that the Japanese had killed his brother? And yet her dad was obviously white.

Why did Amelia need Matilda to be present? Would he have to contend with another woman who couldn't get Joe out of her system? His first thought was that by now she should have accepted what happened. But Penny still had the scars. His mother still felt the pain. This was not what he had expected when he planned this trip.

While he was examining a fruit, but hardly aware of what he was doing, he heard her voice again. "Was that a yes?"

The woman was standing nearby. Looking into her green eyes that held a world of wisdom—perhaps knowledge he wasn't sure he wanted—he nodded. "Yes, ma'am. Thank you."

"Matilda," she corrected.

He smiled. "Matilda."

"Luke?"

He turned at the sound of a male voice saying his name. Frank stood with a man whose clothes and hands revealed he wasn't an everyday carpenter and hadn't been involved with the trash and debris.

Frank introduced them. The man was a developer. They shook hands. "Frank says you're an architect." When Luke confirmed that, Philip asked if he'd look over some plans.

For most of the afternoon, Luke talked with the developer and others about a park they were planning in the area the tsunami had destroyed, even washing away some businesses. Soon Luke was discussing the blueprints laid out on the board across the sawhorses.

As evening approached and the sky turned red, Luke headed back to the Matti-Rose. Looking across at the house where Matilda lived, he did not think this was just a dinner invitation from a kind, elderly woman. The prospect of learning more about his brother did not bring with it a feeling of elation but dread.

Chapter 6

In spite of the anxiety she tried to hide, Amelia liked preparing dinner with Matilda. She'd survived her shock at the arrival of Luke Thurstan in Hilo, but he didn't seem intent upon leaving.

"I will tell him about his brother," she said to Matilda. "And if he has any questions, he can ask me instead of snooping around, asking other people. I don't have to say anything personal, do I?" Amelia gave a quick nod as if punctuating that sentence instead of asking.

Matilda smiled. "You know I won't tell you what to say. Some things can only be decided by you, without anyone's influence. That is, unless I see you endangered and warn you."

"Check him out carefully tonight. My thoughts are as jumpy as dolphins playing in the sea. Except mine aren't playing."

"Now Amelia," Matilda scolded. "That young man is here about his own life, not yours. Stop fretting."

"Okay." But she grimaced as the cup on the saucer rattled when she picked it up from the counter to set it on a tray near the pot.

"You could turn on the living room lamps. He may think we aren't here."

Rather than say that might be a good idea, Amelia did as Matilda suggested. She would face him. She had faced worse. She had to remember he knew nothing except what she might tell him. Joe had been the type who wanted to see everything, do everything, as if he couldn't get enough of life. This brother might be the same way, so the best thing to do was tell him about Joe, and then he could return to the mainland.

The light knock on the screen door might as well have been any of those hammers pounding nails into boards, which was a constant sound in Hilo. Her heart picked up that rhythm. Automatically, however, she turned on the last lamp at the edge of the couch and, at her mental command, moved one foot in front of the other until she reached the door.

"Come in," she said, placing her hand on the door frame to open it a few inches.

Luke took hold of the handle and opened the door wider to enter as she stepped back.

"Nice to see you again." He stepped inside. "I trust you're feeling better."

"Yes, thank you." Her glance appraised him. His words had sounded. . . polite.

"Something smells good." His voice was friendly.

"Matilda's a wonderful cook." Her voice was monotone.

With lifted eyebrows, he asked, "Could I. . . ?" and gestured toward the kitchen.

"Sure." Her voice didn't sound sure to her ears.

He strode across the room. Joe wouldn't have asked. He would have bounded across that room, pulling her along with him and making everyone laugh.

But everyone wasn't here. And that was before the war.

She thought of Joe in his white navy outfit. So handsome, so happy.

This brother was wearing a short-sleeved white shirt and dark blue pants. He'd dressed as conservatively as she, who wore a white blouse and a simple tailored skirt that she often wore to work.

Matilda, however, wore pearls and a cranberry-colored dress she'd covered with a striped apron. Not ready to enter the kitchen, still uncertain about what this evening might bring, Amelia stayed in the living room but close enough to hear their conversation.

"Aloha," Matilda said in her welcoming voice.

"Good evening," Luke replied. "Or should I say *aloha?* That seems to be the greeting of everyone I meet."

Matilda's laugh was soft. "*Alo* means center of the universe, and *Ha* is the breath of God. When Hawaiians say aloha, it's not just a greeting. It conveys the *Aloha Spirit* of being bonded with a community or people."

Amelia noticed that Luke did not respond with aloha. But perhaps Matilda's actions prevented that, for now she was saying, "What brought you to our beautiful island, Luke?"

"Besides the airplane?" They both laughed. Joe would have quipped something like that. Then Luke said in a serious tone, "I wanted to see the place where my brother, Joe, died." He quickly added, "And lived."

Amelia heard Matilda say, "Open that prayer book on the table, Luke. Where the bookmark is."

He apparently opened it. What would he say? After an eternal moment he almost whispered, "Joe Thurstan. October 1941."

"That's when I first met him, along with several others from the base and their friends. He came here a couple of times after that. All those who came here I considered as my boys."

Amelia didn't move, except her chest with that errant heartbeat. She remembered those times. The group had come to see Matilda. Another time Amelia and Joe had eaten dinner with Matilda. Another time they'd stopped by to say hello. No one seemed to come near Matilda's house without stopping in to at least say aloha.

Amelia listened, as Luke was apparently doing, while Matilda stated her favorable impression of the outgoing, charming, appealing Joe Thurstan. "Yes," Matilda said, "he was one of my boys."

"I'm glad he had you as a family away from home, Matilda," Luke said. "Here, let me do that. Mmm, smells good."

Amelia expected Luke would ask how she fit into it all. But he didn't.

Hearing their voices talking congenially about food, Amelia walked into the kitchen and stood at the doorway, watching.

Luke took the pot holders from Matilda. He lifted the roast from the oven and set it on top of the stove. Matilda handed him a knife and meat fork. He sliced the roast and arranged the pieces on a platter, which he set on the table.

Glancing over at Amelia standing in the doorway, he waved with the fork. "My mama always told me, if you don't work for your supper, you don't get any."

She walked on in. This Luke was behaving as if they were new friends who, coincidentally, had the same last name. But he would know better. No, he wouldn't really know anything definite. Only speculate. And since the war started, a lot of different things had happened, and people didn't seem too inclined to speculate.

But he was displaying a trait she knew was typical of Americans from the mainland. They were confident and bold, which gave her more reasons to be afraid. She walked over to help.

She did not want to look at him. Did not want to think of Joe's face, his eyes, his lips, his way of having made everything else seem unimportant. . .except the two of them. A quick glance at Luke's left hand revealed he wasn't wearing a wedding band. But all men didn't wear them. What if he was married and—

He was talking about his dad being a builder. Luke had studied to be an architect and had worked with a developer and his dad. As the war worsened in Europe, his mind turned more toward enlisting.

"After the war, I worked for a while with my dad building houses in the suburbs."

"You would fit right in here," Matilda said. "Construction is booming throughout Hawaii. Has been since the war ended."

Amelia was setting the table, but she held the plate in front of her. No, Matilda should not encourage him like that. She'd heard so many people express a wish to live in Hawaii if they could. But Matilda rattled on.

"Hotels are springing up all over. Tourism has increased. Oh, it dropped off here because of the tsunami, but the visitors will come again. The airplanes are now used for travel instead of war."

Luke glanced Amelia's way a few times as if she were actively involved in the conversation.

She went about getting the silverware, the napkins, and the glasses of fruity iced tea more carefully than normal, lest she drop and break something.

She took the fish cooked in taro leaves and put one on each plate then removed the tossed salad from the refrigerator.

Luke watched Matilda as they set the fried rice and sweet potatoes on the table. Amelia arranged the fresh pineapple, papayas, and passion fruit in a bowl.

The bread was last, taken from the oven, sliced, and covered to keep it warm.

"Looks fit for a king," Luke said.

"Matilda does nothing halfway." Amelia's words surprised her. That was the first she'd spoken since coming into the kitchen. Luke's glance was quick, and then he smiled again at the table laden with colorful, aromatic, tasty food.

Finally everything was ready, and Luke pulled out a chair for Matilda, who removed her apron and laid it aside on the countertop before sitting.

Amelia sat before he could get to her chair.

Matilda asked the blessing. "Dear Lord, thank You for this bounty and for everyone involved in the growing and preparation of the food. Thank You for making it possible by giving us this good earth and all that's in it. May we treat it responsibly. Bless us who partake of this food. Guide our conversation during this dinner, and thank You for our guest. Amen."

Amelia did not find the last part of the prayer consoling. That brought the attention back to the reason for this dinner, and it wasn't just for the food.

Chapter 7

Luke reached for the pork platter and helped himself to another piece. "This Aloha Spirit sure tastes good."

Matilda laughed at his remark, and Amelia even smiled and took more sweet potatoes. He thought she'd relaxed some. "Best food I've ever had."

"Oh, there's plenty like it—and even better," Matilda said, "and cooked by people from every country imaginable."

He and Matilda kept the conversation going. Matilda had apparently traveled the world many times.

Luke had gone to several countries but not for pleasure, he told them. "That's one reason I wanted to come here. I want to enjoy the beauty of a place."

"I've visited the islands, of course," Amelia said, "but never gone anywhere else."

"Well, dear," Matilda smiled at her. "You were quite young when the war started. That was no time for you to travel."

Quite young. Luke figured she was in her early twenties now. She would have been five years younger when she knew Joe. A teenager? He chewed quickly and swallowed.

Although he wanted to ask about Joe, wanted to hear anything they might say about his brother, he instinctively knew that had to wait until the women decided to tell him.

"I was in my second year of college," Amelia said but seemed to have nothing more to add.

At Amelia's pause, Matilda spoke. "Life changed drastically after the bombing here in the islands. Some of the Japanese were taken to camps and held for most of the war."

Luke's gaze flew to Amelia. He knew the Japanese living on the West Coast had been forced to leave their homes, taking only what they could carry, and live in camps throughout the western states. Had her mother been interned? Had Amelia?

As if knowing what his glance meant, Amelia said, "I quit college. Studying music didn't seem to be the thing to do at the time. I kept Wanda's children."

"Wanda?"

"Wanda is my brother Andy's wife. When the war started, she returned to her job at the hospital. I kept the children. For about a year now I've been working with the tourism department."

Luke felt his appetite being sated not only by the amount of food he ate but also by the thoughts he had. When he'd first heard of the internment, his

274

thoughts had been that the Japanese deserved such treatment. . .or worse. Now he was sitting across the table from a girl who was half Japanese.

After a deep breath, he took another sip of iced tea to wash that down. It didn't cool his insides. Rather, they felt quite warm.

Matilda pushed away from the table. "Let's have coffee and dessert on the lanai."

He helped Matilda take the food from the table and put it in the refrigerator while Amelia put the dishes in soapy water in a pan. She washed them, rinsed and stacked them in a drainer.

Luke lifted the vase of fresh flowers to his nose and sniffed the sweet aroma then set it in the middle of the table, realizing how easily he'd become like one of Matilda's boys. He'd felt like one of her boys from the moment he stepped into her kitchen. Something about her made him feel confident he could tell her anything and she would understand.

After the tray was filled, he took it to the lanai. Matilda sat at one end of the wicker couch. Amelia sat in a chair. Luke put the tray on the coffee table and took a seat next to Matilda, wondering if they had deliberately meant for him to sit between them. He thought that normally two women would take the couch and leave the chair for the man. But this evening wasn't exactly normal, regardless of how welcome Matilda made him feel.

Luke felt completely sated and thought he would forgo the dessert. One bite changed his mind. He'd never tasted anything like the macadamia coconut cake.

He didn't even wait to swallow. "Mmm. This is wonderful."

"Thank you," Matilda said. "And I had help making it." She smiled at Amelia.

It was delicious, and of course, so was the coffee. Luke said so and commented on the pleasantness of the lanai, the scents of Hawaii.

By this time he'd decided Amelia wasn't going to mention Joe. She surprised him when she said, "How did you know to ask Tara about me and my dad?"

"Joe wrote me a letter that I didn't get until after the war ended. He said he'd met a girl named Amelia Grant and that her dad was a pastor in Hilo."

"Yes," she said, leaning over to put her coffee cup on the tray. That's when he saw she wasn't wearing a ring, so she must not be married now. Would she say she and Joe met and that was all? She leaned back. Her glance didn't reach his face, and she focused on her hands folded on her lap. "I knew Joe. Yesterday in church I was shocked when you said your name."

He didn't know what to think, what to ask. He'd been stymied since Tara Furness said, *"What a coincidence."*

He stared at his coffee for a long time. Long enough for it to grow stone cold had the weather not been warm. It then occurred to him that he could have assumed too much. When Joe said he met Amelia, perhaps that's all he'd done. His mentioning her implied more. That could have been his intention—seeing her again. After all, the letter was dated only two days before Joe was killed.

Luke didn't know anything about Amelia's personality, but her physical appeal would certainly attract Joe. She seemed quiet, and he felt she was checking him out, perhaps the way he was doing with her.

Joe's name had been entered in Matilda's prayer book in October. Luke had no idea what to make of this except to wait until they revealed something, or he could find out on his own.

Then Amelia asked, "Did he say anything else? I mean, about me or my dad?"

What *else* was she thinking? "He mentioned this being a beautiful place and that I should see it."

The previously talkative Matilda remained silent.

He sipped his coffee until Amelia spoke again. "You said you came here on serious business."

"Yes. Joe and I weren't on the greatest of terms the last time we were together." Luke didn't easily talk about his deeper feelings. Penny was a good listener, but he wasn't comfortable talking about his and Joe's differences with her. He placed an ankle over his knee and looked out into the shadowed foliage beyond the lanai.

"I need to be here, where Joe was, and reconcile things inside myself if I can. After I read his letter mentioning you"—he turned his head and watched her—"I thought you might be able to tell me something about his life here. He was my little brother. I didn't really know him as. . .a man."

He heard Amelia's intake of breath. "Like I said, I was shocked yesterday. And I didn't know for sure if you were related to Joe." She did not look at him when she said, "You see, Joe is. . .our having the same last name isn't a. . .coincidence because. . ."—she paused to clear her throat—"I'm Mrs. Joe Thurstan."

Her last words were a whisper. Her stoic look reminded him of a statue. He lifted his hand and caught his chin between his forefinger and thumb. This made a lot more sense than their last name being a coincidence.

What should he say?

I'm sorry? Congratulations?

To say *So you and Joe married* would sound asinine. She had just said she was Mrs. Joe Thurstan.

His sister-in-law.

Now what was he supposed to do?

Take her home to meet Mother?

Heaven forbid.

In the heavy silence, his gaze fell on his cup. He stood. "I could use another cup of coffee, if you don't mind."

Amelia stood, too. "I need to leave." She walked around the chair.

Leave? He thought her declaration should be the beginning of a conversation, not the end.

"Amelia," he said. She stood still. "I would be pleased to have you tell me about Joe and accompany me to Pearl Harbor. Perhaps this weekend?"

She lifted her hands to the back of the chair and grasped it. Luke wondered if she was still grieving after all this time. She might be. His mother was. And he didn't have everything settled in his mind. "Or do you know any of Joe's friends who are around? Anyone who might tell me something about him or who knew him?"

"No," she said quickly. "This weekend? Yes, I think I can do that. I'll get back to you."

He wondered if she meant as a tour guide or as the widow of his brother. He also wondered if all Joe's friends had been killed at the same time. That would be likely.

Matilda walked over to Amelia. They hugged. "Aloha, darling," Matilda said to her, and Amelia said, "Aloha," and glanced at him.

"Good night," he said.

After she'd gone inside, he turned to Matilda. "I should go. Don't want to overstay my welcome."

"No no," she said. "Get your coffee, and we'll walk out back. I know young people don't like being cooped up inside when there's all that nature out there to be discovered."

He nodded. The group. . .and Joe. . .would have walked out there. He felt sure Matilda would tell him as much as she could about Joe. He also felt she'd tell him nothing about Joe and Amelia.

That would be up to Amelia, who was obviously reluctant to talk about Joe.

Amelia had said, "I'll get back to you."

Maybe this weekend, if Amelia didn't change her mind about Pearl Harbor, he'd find the answers to questions he wasn't even sure how to ask.

Chapter 8

Amelia drove past William's car and pulled into the driveway. Her first thought was that something might be wrong and Wanda had called him. He was the best friend of the family anyone could have, but he didn't usually drop by without a reason or invitation and not late in the evening.

She hurried from the car and knew why he was there the moment she stepped onto the porch of the small bungalow. Joseph's demanding whine sounded through the screen door.

Likely William had returned the toy truck Joseph had broken. William had said he'd fix it.

Amelia opened the door and stepped inside. "You know the rule," Wanda was saying. "You threw that truck because you were angry. It's your fault it broke. So you can't have it back for a week. That's to teach you a lesson on how to control your anger."

Joseph's lower lip came out, and defiance filled his eyes. He looked at Amelia, but she tried to appear impassive.

Even before Joseph was born, she and Wanda had talked about raising the children together with one set of rules as much as possible.

Amelia knew some parents disagreed on how to raise their children. The children she and Wanda were responsible for, however, had no dad, and nothing could make up for that. But they would have two mothers. There hadn't been any big disagreements. Wanda was more experienced as a parent than Amelia, and she was glad for that.

This incident with Joseph didn't require any interference from her. He knew the rules. She glanced at William, who smiled, then looked back at the scene of the defiant little boy. Parker was watching intently, and Ellie in the recliner focused not at the book on her lap but around at each of them.

"You do understand this, don't you?" Wanda said.

Joseph lowered his head and extended his lower lip, but he nodded.

"Aren't you going to thank William for fixing your truck?"

He shook his head. "Not till next week."

"At least tell him good night."

"Night, Uncle William."

"Now," Wanda said, her dark eyes bright with mischief, "it's time for your tickle and good-night kiss."

She stuck out her hand. He jumped back, screeched, and headed for the bedroom, followed by Parker.

"Time for bed, Ellie," Wanda said and left the room.

Ellie closed the book slowly, pulled the lever on the recliner, and leaned back with her eyes closed.

Amelia laughed. "You know better."

"One minute," Ellie begged.

"Okay, till I get back from the boys' room." Amelia turned to William. "Can you wait?"

"Sure." He crooked his arm to stare at his watch then at Ellie, who gave him a playful scowl. The two of them laughed. The children had a good relationship with William. For that, Amelia was grateful.

After kissing the boys good night, she and Wanda came in to give Ellie her hug. The girl told them good night and went to her room. William said he needed to leave, and Amelia walked outside with him.

She leaned against the car with him standing in front of her. "Thanks for fixing the truck."

"No problem. Now tell me what's on your mind." Without giving her a chance to reply, he said, "This Thurstan fellow?"

"Yeah. Big time." She looked into his kind eyes. Dear, sweet William. She'd been just a girl when he was best friends with her brother, Andrew. After Andy married Wanda, they still ran around with William and his girlfriend, Nell. Then both men went off to war.

Andy didn't come back. William returned with his left leg shot up. He had scars and a limp that was noticeable if he did too much physical activity.

Worse than that, Nell had married a sailor, and the last they'd heard, she was living in Norfolk, Virginia.

After a long time of his seeming to be in another world, William had begun to come around. Without asking, he would mow the lawn. He'd notice anything that needed to be repaired. He pointed out the worn tread on tires that neither she nor Wanda would have noticed.

His greatest pleasure seemed to be filling in for Andy.

"This Thurstan fellow," she said finally, using William's words, "is Joe's brother."

William nodded as if not surprised. "So he knows about you and Joe?"

"I told him tonight that I'm Mrs. Joe Thurstan."

"He didn't know?"

"He couldn't."

William nodded, looking at his shoes. After a moment he lifted his gaze to her again. "How did he take it?"

Amelia sighed. "Like everybody has taken any kind of news or announcement since the war started. People don't ask too many questions, you know."

"Yeah." And he didn't question. She'd told him what she told others. That she was Mrs. Amelia Thurstan.

She told William about Luke's saying he came here to see where his brother died. "I said I might take him to Pearl Harbor. You think I did right?"

"As his sister-in-law—"

Amelia drew in a quick breath. She wanted to be rid of Luke Thurstan. Not. . .related.

William waited a moment. "You have to do something. Is that all you told him?"

"Yes. I won't tell him more."

William laid his hand on her shoulder for a moment in a comforting gesture. "That's your decision, Amelia." He took his hand away. "But how did he know to come here? Coincidence?"

That word again. Her dad preached there were no coincidences.

"Joe had written about me in a letter to Luke. It seems he only said my name and that I was a preacher's daughter." She groaned. "I don't want to be his sister-in-law or be involved with any part of his family."

William was shaking his head. "You don't have to be. Listen to me, Amelia. He would want to know about anyone close to his brother. I know, because that's how I feel about Andy. I was Andy's closest friend. I want to be of help to his wife and his sister in any way I can." He looked into the distance. "Maybe it's selfish, but it helps me deal with Andy's being gone, like I'm doing something for him."

Amelia could understand that. The fear she was supposed to let go of had a way of creeping in. She smiled. "So I should. . .let him. . .know me."

"Some. It will help if he knows you're all right. I couldn't even talk about Andy for a long, long time. But when I could, it released the pain. From what you've said, this Luke sounds like he has a lot of pain. I don't have any regrets about Andy. Regrets with grief would be unbearable."

Amelia found a grain of consolation in that. "So you don't think he's going to try and interfere with my life—just. . .get on with his own?"

"I'd say so. If you had a need, he'd probably want to help."

She shook her head vigorously. "I don't need his help. I mean, you know perfectly well how to fix a little boy's truck."

His smile was kind. "Would you like for me to befriend him?"

She felt helplessly unsure. "I don't know, William. I don't want anything underhanded, and at the same time I don't want him to know anything about my private life."

William shrugged. "Have you ever told me anything about your private life?"

"No."

"Then what could I say?"

She lifted her shoulders.

"He wants to know that you're all right, and he needs to talk about his brother. Maybe I can be of help."

"But don't mention the children."

"I won't."

"You're so good to me, William. Like Andy would be."

"I hope so," he said seriously.

A thought struck Amelia. "But you're not exactly like Andy would be. I think if he talked with Luke, he'd likely think Luke owed me something on behalf of his brother."

William agreed. "You may be right there. I want to think Andy would be pleased about my involvement with you and Wanda. But I'm not Andy. I'm William."

Chapter 9

Amelia thought William said that on a sad note, and he exhaled a discordant breath. "Oh, William. We've been doing so well going forward and letting go of the past the best we could. Why did this Luke Thurstan have to come and stir it up again?"

"Well, Amelia. Your dad would say there's a reason for everything."

"Sure," she said. "And sometimes that reason is because we make a mess of things."

Concern leaped into his eyes. "Is your life a mess?"

"My life is beautiful." As soon as she said that, doubts returned. "And I want it to stay that way." She took a deep breath and exhaled slowly. "I want to do what's right, but I don't always know what that is."

"Let's get to know him," William said with a comforting smile. "And take it from there."

"Okay," she conceded. "Thanks, William." She gave him a hug, and he patted her back briefly.

Then he stepped back. "You have nothing to worry about. All your friends and family are right here. You think we're going to let anybody get to you?"

She poked his upper arm. "Matilda and you, with your great advice. Why don't I listen?"

He shrugged. "Young and foolish?"

"No," she said, although she knew he was kidding. "Those days are gone forever."

He gave her a long look. "Good night, Amelia." He walked around the car and got into the driver's seat.

Amelia leaned down to the window and lifted her hand. When she turned toward the house, the flutter of a curtain caught her eye at the left bedroom. Ellie's room. The wind didn't likely move only one side of a curtain. Inquisitive little girl. Well, that was normal.

Going inside, she saw the kitchen light on and went there. Wanda was putting away dishes.

"You want to talk?" Wanda's glance shifted toward the bedrooms. "Just remember, little pitchers have big ears."

Amelia nodded. Her thoughts turned to Ellie, who seemed to question everything lately. Maybe that was part of growing up, paying more attention to adult life. She'd been through so much, losing her dad, now knowing adults and children who were killed in the tsunami. Amelia felt less confident than ever to help Ellie. She couldn't even help herself. But yes, she wanted to talk. "Any more of that lemonade left?"

Wanda headed for the refrigerator. Amelia took glasses from the cupboard. They sat at the table with their lemonade, and Amelia told her about the evening. "I told him that Joe and I married and that I might take him to Pearl Harbor on Saturday. I hate to ask you to watch the children without me, but—"

"No, Amelia, that's perfect," Wanda said. "William has already asked if he might take us all on a picnic this weekend."

"You guys will be fine without me," Amelia said, but she needed to hear Wanda agree.

"We'd all have fun, you know that. But it's okay if you don't go." She paused. "Oh, Amelia, William is so good about trying to be a male influence on the children."

"He seems to be doing more of that lately."

Wanda nodded. "I think he's more concerned about Ellie, since she knew some of the children in the tsunami. The boys, of course, have heard talk about it, but it's not as personal to them."

Amelia was thankful for that. It was bad enough that Joseph had never seen his dad and Parker had been only a year old when Andy died.

"You know, Wanda, we've talked about how the grief and memories seem to come at unexpected times. Last night I was afraid that being around Luke would bring all that back. But instead I felt like he was the one struggling."

"We never completely get over it." Sadness appeared in Wanda's eyes. "You know that."

"Yes, and since Luke said his name in church, I've been thinking about myself. But tonight I felt Luke's deep sadness. He said he and Joe weren't on good terms the last time they were together."

Wanda nodded. "Andy and I were glued together the day he left. I'm so glad the last thing we said to each other was 'I love you.' It would be so much worse to have regrets. And I'm so blessed to have you and Mom and Dad." Her finger traced a line down the glass. Amelia wondered if Wanda was thinking about the boating accident that took her parents' lives when Wanda was fifteen. Even before she married Andy, Wanda had become like part of the Grant family.

Amelia and Wanda had become a happy family, as happy as one could be with no male in the house but with three wonderful, lively children. They tried not to complain or be overly negative around the children. And to count their blessings. Trying to think positively now, Amelia said, "We're fortunate to have Mom and Dad and William to help out."

"I know," Wanda agreed. She called them Mom and Dad, too. Just like Amelia's mom often said "Mama Matilda."

"I thought things would settle down enough after the war that William might find someone." Wanda spread her hands in a helpless gesture. "But now it's the tsunami, and he is grieved over the loss of schoolchildren."

Amelia nodded. "From things he's said, I think he feels guilty for being alive when so many of his friends are not." Memories of the past flooded in. Every time she or Wanda saw a returned military man, one or the other would say, "Why not mine? Why didn't mine return?" But they also knew they had to get over it.

Wanda sighed. "Sometimes I've wondered if you and William might—"

After a mouth-opening moment, Amelia began to laugh. "That's what I thought about William and you."

"Oh no." Wanda began to shake her head. "Every time I've told him he does so much for us and the children, he always says he was Andy's best friend and that Andy would have done it for him if the situation were reversed. And it's not out of duty; it's out of love and respect for his friend. He sees me as. . . well. . .sort of like a sister." Her gaze shifted to her glass again. "He's probably still grieving over Nell."

"Like you're still grieving over Andy?"

"I miss Andy terribly. Death is so final we have to accept it." Her voice lowered. "But Nell is in Norfolk."

"Don't you think William has let that go? He's an educated, intelligent man, Wanda."

"Yes. But sometimes we don't know what or how to think. He'd have to wonder about her." She shook her head and heaved a sigh. "But we're getting down. Let's stop this." She picked up her glass and took a sip of the lemonade. "Now, what about this Luke?"

"Oh Wanda. This scares me so. If he finds out the truth, that could turn our lives upside down."

"It won't be easy, will it, Amelia, being open about some things and not others?"

"No, but if I'm the one with Luke, I don't have to worry about what somebody else might say."

"Can you handle this all right?" Just as quickly, Wanda answered her own question. "Of course you can."

Amelia wasn't so sure. "I don't know. I can't even let my thoughts go to the worst scenario."

"I thought you worked through that when you visited Matilda."

Amelia nodded. "I did. That's why I decided to associate with Luke. That's why I gave it to God."

"Then?" Wanda's eyebrows lifted.

Amelia sighed. "I keep taking it back. And have to give it to God all over again."

Wanda smiled. Of course she knew. How many times had they cried and prayed about. . .everything?

After another sip of lemonade, Amelia pushed back from the table. "I need to go give this to God again and try to sleep."

"I'll be praying for you, Amelia."

"Thanks." She could never have too much of that.

A short while later in her compact but adequate bedroom, which had been converted from the lanai, Amelia thought and prayed. She knew she had to face what she could. Keep praying for God to get her through this one day at a time.

She had watched the grief in her own family. She had grieved for Andy. That was the way she would relate to Luke Thurstan. Not dwell on the past or talk about her life since the war.

Yes, like Matilda had said, most of her fear was of fear itself.

Luke Thurstan wanted to know about his brother, not about her. She would take him to Pearl Harbor, which would be the hardest for him. It had been for her—returning where her brother, Joe, and friends and coworkers had been killed, the ships torn up, and the *Arizona* sunk with the men in it—trapped.

Yes, they would get that over with.

She could tell Luke good things about Joe. Then Luke Thurstan could return to the States with stories for his parents of how happy, carefree, well-liked Joe had been.

She shuddered suddenly and pulled the covers up to her chin, realizing how impossible her situation was.

She'd told Luke that she was Mrs. Joe Thurstan. She mustn't allow him to return to the mainland with that statement. Then his parents might want to see her. That would be a worse tragedy than having Luke Thurstan here.

She couldn't say that she had lied about being married to Joe.

Because then he would ask, "Why?"

Chapter 10

Luke's first thought as he descended the stairs was that the man with light brown hair and a pleasant face would be checking in at the Matti-Rose. He was tall, thin, wearing light pants and a short-sleeved, button-down shirt and tie.

When the man said "Aloha" to him, Luke reconsidered, thinking the man worked in a nearby office and had stopped in for breakfast.

"Good morning." Luke shook the man's outstretched hand, while getting the feeling that the stranger had been waiting for him to come down the stairs.

"William Honeycutt."

"Luke Thurstan." The man might be a contractor wanting to talk with him about building plans. He wouldn't be surprised if Matilda had sent someone who was building hotels, after their conversation a few evenings ago.

"Going in for breakfast?"

"Yes," Luke said. "Join me?"

"Thanks."

They found a table for two in front of a row of windows.

"Aloha, William," the young waitress said, taking her pencil from behind her ear and getting ready to write down their order.

"Those blueberry pancakes, Delia," he said, giving Luke the idea that William was no stranger around there.

"Same," Luke said, "and scrambled eggs."

She smiled without writing a thing. "And you want your coffee. . .what did you say? Lickety-split?"

"You got it," Luke said, and they laughed.

"Help yourselves." Delia smiled and glanced toward the buffet table.

The two men took their cups. They returned to the table with coffee, pastries, and fruit.

Luke was fast getting the idea that William was a local. His next words confirmed it. He looked across at Luke and said, "Just thought I'd come and introduce myself. I'm a friend of Amelia."

Luke started to say *I see* but realized he didn't really see. Was William implying he had a claim on Amelia? He didn't say *boyfriend*. He wasn't exactly a boy. He looked to be around Luke's age. He didn't say *fiancé*. Did he have some kind of message from Amelia? "Is she all right?"

"Oh yes. She's fine."

If William were bearing bad news, Luke supposed he wouldn't have ordered food.

"Sorry if I gave the wrong impression. Amelia told me about you and your brother. I'm sorry about that."

A discordant thought jumped into Luke's mind. Was William sorry that Joe died? Or sorry that Luke showed up, disturbing their lives? Not sure how to respond, he nodded.

"Amelia's brother, Andy, and I were best friends," William said, pouring cream into his coffee. "Andy died in the war, too."

"I'm sorry," Luke said and picked up his cup, watching William over the rim of it. He waited.

After William took a couple of sips of his coffee, he set the cup down. "Amelia told me a little about you, and I thought you, being new around here, maybe could use a friend."

Uncertain where this was going, Luke said, "A person can't have too many friends."

Delia brought their food. With a slight bow of his head, Luke looked across at William, who said, "I'll be glad to say grace." He said a brief prayer. After they took turns with the coconut syrup, William spoke again. "I suppose I should start by telling you something about myself."

Luke listened with interest as William talked about teaching, the children killed in the recent tsunami, the building taking place. "Everybody appreciates your pitching in to help."

After taking another bite of the delicious pancakes, Luke responded. "It seemed the thing to do, my having a background in construction. But I'm not the only visitor to the island who has pitched in."

William acknowledged that with a smile. "Many visitors have said there's something in this Hawaii air that makes you feel at home." After another bite he added, "Some never leave."

"I admit the people are friendly." Luke thought of Pastor Grant, who had made it a point to speak to him in the mornings on the streets of Hilo. Akemi had brought his dinner on Sunday night. Matilda invited him on Monday. And now William sat across from him at breakfast.

"I'm apparently a surprise to everyone. It's as if no one knew Joe had a brother. Perhaps he didn't talk about us."

"It's been close to five years," William reminded him. "I didn't know your brother. When I returned from Germany, wounded and depressed over what had happened to Andy and others here in Hawaii, I was in deep trouble emotionally for quite a while. When I finally came out of it with the help of friends and especially Pastor Grant, I began to go through the motions of life again."

Luke held out his cup for a refill when the waitress came near with a coffeepot. He set it in the saucer. "I didn't mean to stir things up."

William held up a hand in a conciliatory manner. "No, I'm not here to make you feel guilty about anything. I look at it this way. It's like I tell my students at school: A review is to help you see what you've retained, what you remember, and reinforce what you need to work on."

Luke was getting the point but listened to William's conclusion. "If our memories bring back negative feelings, we need to be aware that we have things to work on."

"When your students are aware of the problems, what's the next step?"

"I invite them to talk it over with me. If they didn't learn the lesson in the first place, they need to begin again."

"You must have a lot of A students."

William shook his head. "It depends on where they're coming from. If a student is without confidence or has no one to believe in them or has bad study habits, he may only come up to a C. But he's accomplished something."

Luke gave a short laugh. "You sound like a counselor."

William held his gaze. "Where do you think I got my positive, let-go-and-look-ahead attitude?" He laughed. "I've had my share of counseling from a psychologist and from Jacob Grant. And Matilda."

Luke smiled and nodded. He'd figured he could handle whatever problems he had by himself, but William seemed like the kind of man he wouldn't mind talking to. William, too, understood the effects of war on a person from first-hand experience.

But he didn't think William came here just to offer friendship. "It must have been doubly hard on Amelia, losing her brother and Joe."

After a thoughtful moment William nodded. "I'm sure it was. But she moved in with her sister-in-law. Wanda is Andy's widow. They have the Grants nearby and friends, so that helps." He paused. "She. . .we all are surprised by your being here. I don't know if Amelia knew about you. I've never heard her mention Joe having a brother." He shook his head. "But it's been almost five years."

He seemed at a loss for words. Luke thought he knew what William meant. Maybe she was like a student who had taken the final test and graduated with a decent grade. "I may still be in the classroom," Luke said.

"In many ways, we all are." William smiled and glanced at his watch. "I have a meeting with school administrators."

Luke nodded, but he had to make one thing clear. "If Amelia doesn't want to go to Pearl Harbor with me, that's fine. If you'd like to go along, that's fine, too." He shrugged. "Or I can do as I planned when I came here and go alone."

"No," William said. "I've already promised to take Wanda and the three children on a hiking trip and a picnic." He looked pleased about that.

"Sounds nice."

Pushing his plate aside, William looked at him seriously. "I think Amelia wants to accompany you to Pearl. I think she needs to."

Luke stood when William did and shook his hand. "Thanks."

William nodded. "I'm in the phone book. William Honeycutt. Or I'll see you around."

Luke nodded.

He returned to his seat and watched as William disappeared from the dining room. He hadn't thought about needing a friend to talk to. Most people wanted to forget the war, not relive it. And all his close friends had lost their lives, moved away, or were married. Some were wounded in ways he didn't want to think about.

If he were planning to stay in Hawaii, he'd like to pursue a friendship with William.

He had a feeling William was sincere about being a friend to him. He said he was a friend of Amelia's. Was he also trying to make a statement. . .that he was more than just a friend to her? Or that he wanted to be?

Chapter 11

But Amelia." Her dad had a strained look on his face. "Why won't you let me and your mother invite Luke Thurstan over for dinner? Or at least an evening, just to talk?"

Amelia looked at her mother's expectant face then at her dad's concerned one. "Because this is a matter of the past. You and Mom promised not to interfere with my decisions. I tried not to involve you back then when you were dealing with your own grief over Andy. And I don't want to do that now."

"But he's family."

"Dad, you and Mom have told me to get on with my life. Maybe find a man and settle down. How could I do that if I'm going to be involved with some American family because of what happened almost five years ago?"

"We should at least be cordial."

"I am cordial. I'm taking him to Pearl Harbor because he wants to go there. I can tell him about Joe. Then he can return to the mainland, and I can return to my life as usual."

"It doesn't seem right, Amelia. And do you know how hypocritical I look? I see him in downtown Hilo, and I speak. But I make no further overtures toward him."

"Well, Dad, is this about you or about me? What would you feel like if you brought him in like family, knowing that's against my wishes, knowing that's going to turn my life upside down?"

He sighed. "I don't think that would happen."

His calm incensed her. "What do you think would happen? That his parents would come, and they all would have a nice visit and just go back home, and we would write letters or make phone calls?"

He shook his head. "I can't see the future."

"Well, I can." Hot moisture stung her eyes. "And this is not the same as when Mom was sixteen. I know you think she could do no wrong. But she did as she pleased. Me? I'm in my twenties, and you don't trust my decisions. I'm always wrong."

Amelia watched her mother bend her head in that demure way. If only her mother would argue with her or take her side, but she didn't. Following Amelia's gaze, her dad turned to look at the hurt on his wife's face. He reached over and touched Akemi's hand. "You should not. . . ," he began. Amelia felt a reprimand coming. He would want an apology. Why didn't her mother speak up? No, she was too nice.

Akemi raised her head, looked into her husband's eyes, and gave a slight shake of her head. That small gesture was enough to render her husband speechless. Their shared gaze held a world of love in it, and for a moment Amelia felt like she was intruding.

They had so much. They had weathered public ridicule by some for not only their age difference but also their cultural and race differences as well. They'd weathered the loss of a son. And a disappointing daughter.

Oh, why did Luke Thurstan have to come and stir up what was supposed to have been over, forgotten, let go of?

Her mom took hold of her husband's arm. "We will abide by your wishes." She looked up at him. There was no mistaking their affection for each other.

Looking down at his wife, he said, "Of course we will. I was just making a suggestion."

Her mother's face and eyes took on that ethereal appearance that Amelia often resented. Resented because she was jealous of it. Her mother was so beautiful and perfect. If she had been at the bay the day of the tsunami, she might have been able to calm even that.

"*Kipa mai*," her dad said, asking Amelia to come to him. He held out his arms and took a step toward her. Amelia went to him, and they embraced. She snuggled her head against his chest for a moment, breathing in the natural odor of her warm, wonderful dad. She felt close to him. He understood and forgave anything and everything. She knew he understood because he preached about anything and everything.

Amelia looked over at her mom, who stood calmly by, her hands folded in front of her. She smiled and nodded at Amelia. Amelia loved her mother but didn't feel that closeness like she did with her dad. She couldn't confide everything to her mom, who was so good and so perfect. She'd never understand.

Feeling reasonably assured her parents wouldn't go against her wishes, she felt calmer and stepped back. "Dad, it's fine if you're friendly with Luke. Just don't. . .talk about me. Except. . ." His eyes brightened, until she added, "You can tell him I will meet him at the Matti-Rose around 7:00 a.m. on Saturday."

He nodded and squinted slightly, causing little lines to appear at the corners of his eyes. Her mom looked at the floor. Amelia was right: Her mom would never understand her. At least Amelia could talk to Matilda and Wanda.

～

On Saturday morning the children were up, jumping around, eager for William to come and take them on the outing. Ellie came up to her. "We're going with Uncle William. He's just like a daddy, isn't he?"

Amelia had never heard Ellie say anything like that. But now the young girl wore a smug expression on her face. Amelia wasn't sure what to say. "He's a fine man."

"He loves us," she said.

"He sure does," Amelia agreed.

Ellie's shoulders rose with her deep breath. She stared for a moment then turned abruptly and went outside. Amelia didn't understand that little discourse. Was Ellie upset that Amelia wasn't going with them, as family? Maybe she feared her family would be torn apart again, like some of her friends.

She wouldn't be having these problems if Luke Thurstan hadn't shown up so unexpectedly. But he had.

It would be to her advantage to know what he was really after. Had Joe said anything more than her name and that she was a preacher's daughter? Why would he describe her like that? Had Joe written anything in that letter to imply she. . .didn't live up to the standards one would expect of a preacher's daughter?

That moment of guilt was immediately replaced by the lecture she'd given herself many times. The message her dad had preached over the years. The comforting words of the Bible that God forgives and people can start over.

No, she knew too many people who lived in the past. She wouldn't. And she would make her future the best she could.

Amelia and Wanda had prayed and talked and cried and explored everything and questioned God and self and others after Joe and Andy died. They ultimately decided, after a very long time, to do as Matilda advised.

Matilda had said, "Don't live in the past. Learn from it. Start becoming today what you want to be tomorrow. You can't change the past. You can't question God to death. And you can't understand Him. Otherwise you'd be God, and you're not. He allows evil in this world. We fight our battles. The war is won. Now face the present. Each day is a present."

Amelia and Wanda had learned to take joy in the present and rejoice in their blessings. They could still remember the past and cry and wail and hate it but know that would pass after a few minutes. It was not the state of being in which they lived.

After that internal lecture, Amelia determined she would not be morose or fearful around Luke Thurstan. Just. . .cautious.

Right after daybreak, while the grass was still wet from the night's rain and sparkling with the morning light, she drove up in front of the Matti-Rose. There he was, sitting in a rocking chair on the front porch, talking to an older couple.

He lifted his hand in a wave to the couple and, with a spring in his step, came up to the car, looking like a tourist who hadn't yet bought an aloha shirt. He wore casual pants and a short-sleeved dress shirt, untucked. "Aloha," she said.

"Good morning," he returned. "Would you mind if I drive and you be the copilot?"

With his head bent down toward the open window, the light breeze lifted his wavy hair, and she remembered Joe bemoaning the fact that the navy had cut off most of his curls. Joe's blue eyes always danced and sparkled and teased. Luke's were waiting, and. . .he'd asked something. Now his eyes seemed to question.

The only thing she could think to say was, "You have something against women drivers?"

He held out his hand with his index finger pointed as if to say *wait*. She watched him hurry past the front of the car, go around and open the passenger side, jump in, and slam the door shut. "Now, just watch me trust you enough to ride with you all the way to the parking places at the back of the Matti-Rose." His smile faded, and his voice became serious. "Unless you're required to drive."

"Required?" Then she realized what he meant. "No, I don't work on Saturdays. This is my. . ." She wasn't sure what to add. Certainly not say it was a friendly thing. And she didn't want to say it was her pleasure. For want of a more appropriate word she said, "My personal decision."

Decision? Well yes, that's what it was. She'd decided to do this.

As a tour guide, she would have driven a company car or a van. But this was her personal car, and of course she wouldn't take any pay. Instead of the black skirt and white shirt typical of tour guides, she wore a colorful sundress with a matching short-sleeved jacket that she'd worn only to church.

It dawned on her that she rarely went anywhere but work and church, except as a tour guide around town and the Wednesday-night Bible study at Matilda's. She couldn't remember the last time she'd been in a car with a man driving.

Hoping she wouldn't wreck the car on the drive around the building, she kept her nervous fingers on the wheel. Yes, maybe it was best that he drive.

She didn't know if he didn't trust her to drive or thought it wouldn't look manly for a woman to haul him around. She doubted he would care about that.

A man just usually drove.

She couldn't help but remember what Joe had done one time. He'd opened the driver's side and said, "Let's go."

She's started to slide over, and he grabbed her arm. "Stay where you are."

They both had laughed, and she knew he couldn't drive with her that close. Still, she hadn't slid all the way over to the passenger seat but sat close to him. He never asked again. That was just the way they rode together.

"You don't mind, do you?"

Amelia looked at Luke quickly, realizing she'd been rather lost in that thought. "No, I'd like for you to drive. It will be a treat for me." She saw that he held a camera. "Would you like for me to keep your camera in my purse?"

"Yes, thank you," he said and smiled.

He had an engaging smile, she noticed as they exited the car to get into his rental. Joe seemed always to laugh. He'd been happy. She thought she'd made him happy.

She wouldn't even attempt such with Luke Thurstan. He might even have a wife.

"Are you married?"

"Married?" After a long moment he said, "No."

She wondered why not, then as quickly reminded herself he'd been fighting a war until a few months ago. He probably had a special girl. But she didn't need to ask that. It would be getting too personal.

She would be cordial and hope he would soon return to the mainland.

Chapter 12

The silence wasn't exactly a comfortable one. After Amelia asked if Luke was married, he considered asking if she had found anyone special since Joe, then he reconsidered. She seemed wary of him already, and he didn't want to add to it by seeming to pry.

At the appropriate time, if that ever came, he might ask her about William. Or how her family felt about Joe—or about his own showing up for that matter.

She only spoke to say *turn here, left over there, just go straight* as they headed for the airport. She probably was as dumbfounded as he at how to talk to an in-law you didn't know you had until a few days ago. Did she or her parents expect him to. . .do something? Visit them? Had she wanted to do this, or did she feel obligated?

He decided to talk about the work at Hilo. "Although it's not my town," he said, "I'm excited about the plans for Hilo. A park will be built along Hilo Bay instead of businesses."

The turn of her head toward him and the interest in her eyes encouraged him to continue. "The government and commercial life will be relocated farther back from the ocean. A large park will enhance the beauty of Hilo, and a roadway can help absorb any future tidal waves and help protect the town."

"Oh, and that will complement the banyan trees that circle the Waiakea Peninsula," she said. "We'll go along the drive on the way to the airport."

"That sounds like the word I've heard," Luke said and laughed at his ineptness with the Hawaiian words. "But I do recall a discussion and the name written on the plans we discussed—and talk of the banyan trees."

"But the interesting thing," she said with enthusiasm, "is that the park commissioners thought it would be a good idea to have celebrities plant banyan saplings."

He drove along the road, which she said was made of crushed coral. "The commissioners decided to make that road when Franklin Roosevelt was to come here in 1934."

"Ah, the president," Luke said with a lift of his eyebrows.

She laughed lightly. He thought she had forgotten he was Luke Thurstan, someone of whom she seemed wary. Now she was a lovely tour guide, simply giving information about a place she loved.

Then she surprised him by saying something more personal. "I was twelve years old at the time. We were let out of school to see him and stand on the beach and sing."

"What did you sing?"

" 'Aloha 'Oe.' Our national song written by our princess." His glance followed her gaze out to the vast, calm, blue ocean that melted into a brighter blue sky. "That was the beginning of my realization that the mainland and its people were special in some way."

"You said *the beginning*. . . ." He wanted to know more of how she felt and what was inside her.

She nodded, a reflective look on her face. "Yes. And I began to take more interest in history and what the missionaries have meant to these islands."

He could add a little to that. "I've read that the missionaries were so strict they almost destroyed the Hawaiian culture."

"Matilda has helped me understand that. And William, too, since he is a history teacher. Perhaps the missionaries were extreme. But that extremism caused the Hawaiians to take seriously the Christian way of life. Our Hawaiian culture is important but not as important as the salvation message." Her serious tone turned playful. "Do you know who was the first Christian in Hawaii?"

He looked over at her as he rounded the curve of the drive, heading back to the main road. "Have no idea," he confessed.

"Keopuolani."

The heel of his hand tapped the steering wheel as he shook his head. "How could I have forgotten that?"

She laughed. He hadn't heard that before. Nor had he seen that twinkle in her dark brown eyes. Yes, he thought after his brief glance at her. He'd just seen a glimpse of the kind of girl Joe liked. "Who was that Keo. . . ?"

"Keopuolani. Our queen mother. That was in"—she hesitated only a moment before saying—"in 1823. She was the first Hawaiian to be baptized in the Protestant faith. She received the baptism on her deathbed, but it made an impact throughout Hawaii."

Luke didn't feel it was the time or place or person with whom to contemplate his own faith or lack of it. Perhaps there was a better way than destroying a culture in order to bring the salvation message. Perhaps there was a better way than war to make a young man realize the extent to which evil could take over. But fighting in the war was when he accepted his own vulnerability, his own lack of control over his own life. He'd entrusted it to the Lord in a more serious way than he had previously known possible.

He deliberately changed the subject. "Who else has planted trees there?"

She named several celebrities. "Cecil B. DeMille and his wife planted trees when he was here filming *Four Frightened People*. Some of the actors in that movie did, too. Also, Amelia Earhart and George Herman Ruth."

"George Herman Ruth?"

His glance at her brought a smile. "You probably know him as Babe Ruth."

"Ah yes."

"And little Shirley Temple. She was five years old. And of course trees are planted by our own leaders and those known for their achievements."

"Tour guides plant any?" he jested, wanting to hear her laugh or see her smile.

Her eyebrows lifted. "Not yet. But tourism stopped when the war started. Only last year did it start again. Last year we had around thirteen thousand tourists. Tour guides are becoming quite important."

She began talking about the many changes that had taken place in the past year since tourists had again begun coming to Hawaii.

"Are the people pleased with the changes?"

"We're dependent on it," she said. "In times past, we were dependent on the whaling industry for oil. Then it became the big cattle ranches and beef transported throughout the world, followed by the sugar plantations. Now, our greatest industry is becoming tourism."

He nodded and inadvertently mumbled, "Paradise."

"Tourists say this is the most beautiful place they've ever seen."

From the moment he'd arrived in Hawaii, Luke had become increasingly aware that the colors, the feel, and the smell of the islands were exceptional. "Perhaps akin to the Garden of Eden."

"Except we have no snakes," she replied.

His quick glance saw her smile fade, and she turned her head as if looking out the side window. Perhaps she had the same thought as he. No snakes, but just as in the Garden of Eden, in this and every other place was the serpent, the god of this world, trying to destroy the goodness and beauty of people and creation.

Chapter 13

They arrived at the airfield in time to get the last two boarding passes on one of the interisland hourly flights from the island of Hawaii to Oahu. Amelia led the way down the narrow aisle of the plane, which had room for sixteen passengers. Quite different from a military transport, he observed.

"You might want the window seat," she said when they came to their row. "I've seen the islands from the air many times."

"Thank you." He slid in ahead of her.

After they were settled in their seats and the propellers took the plane into the clear morning sky, Luke leaned over and looked out the window and down at the land below. The propellers whirred, and he thought this was more like a giant bird, flying close enough to land that one could even see people milling around in various places.

"So much water and so little land from up here," he said.

"Jewels in the sea, we are."

He glanced over his shoulder at her and smiled. "That's what the brochures and tour guides say." He looked down again. "And that's what it looks like. The ocean seems to be sprinkled with diamonds, and the land below is like emeralds."

He settled back against the seat. "Did you and Joe do this?"

"Yes," she said, looking past him at the window. "He was most interested in flying over the volcanoes."

Luke almost laughed at that and was about to say that sounded like Joe, but Amelia went immediately into a discourse about the volcanoes. She faced straight ahead as she talked. Trying not to let her think he stared, he nevertheless studied her profile. The first time he'd met her in church, she'd been shocked and pale. The second time, at Matilda's, she'd seemed tense and flushed. Now she seemed like a detached tour guide, offering interesting information.

"Streams of lava flow down into the sea continually," she said, "so our island is still growing—about ten feet a year because of the volcanic eruptions."

"Ah," he said, half playfully but in truth. "That's how it should be with lifetime commitments. That spark between a man and woman that never dies."

Her quick glance made him wonder if she might think he was flirting with her, talking about sparks. Come to think of it, if he allowed himself or if she allowed it, he could pursue that. He cleared his throat and took another route. "Someday we may be able to hop over to these islands from the States."

She gave him a quick glance, and he thought a grin played about her lips. "Possibly, in a few thousand years."

Luke remained silent for a while, listening to the drone of the plane, glancing down occasionally at the sparkling water, the sailboats floating along, and ships far in the distance. He couldn't figure Amelia out. Why didn't she want to talk more about Joe? Offer any information about him? He felt some unease at the thought of seeing where Joe was killed. Perhaps Amelia felt that way, too. Perhaps it was still too painful for her to talk about.

Luke wanted to hear that Joe was happy. He almost smiled thinking that when Joe was on a plane like this, he wouldn't have been silent. Probably wouldn't have been still. Luke could almost see him dancing in the aisles and having everyone singing or laughing at his jokes. Amelia must have been immensely happy with him. Perhaps that's why she was so distant now. Her life had changed so drastically.

Soon the shape of land caught his eye then the activity. He leaned forward. "Surfers down there."

She nodded. "That's a common occurrence."

"I've never done that." He glanced over. "Have you?"

Her laugh was soft. "Here, we surf before we walk." Her expression changed. He felt his brow furrow. "I just remembered something," she said. "Joe said that in America many people are born with a silver spoon in their mouth, but here they're born with a surfboard in their mouth."

Luke laughed. "Yeah. That's Joe."

She nodded, a tight smile on her face as she looked down at her hands. At least she had finally shared something about Joe. He would try to be patient. This couldn't be easy for her.

Before long, they landed at Oahu. Luke rented a car and followed Amelia's directions to Pearl City. He viewed the coast as Amelia explained the four traditional Hawaiian land divisions. "*Waiawa* is the word meaning 'from the towering mountains to the brilliant sea.' *Manana* is 'bitter water.' *Waimano* is an 'area where lava flows meet,' and *Waiau* means 'swirling beautiful waters.' "

Luke marveled not only at the scenery of towering mountains and brilliant sea but at how easily the musical Hawaiian words rolled off Amelia's tongue. She had said she'd studied music. He wondered why she hadn't returned to finish her studies. But he didn't want to disturb this camaraderie he felt with her and with his surroundings.

"As in Hilo," she continued, "much has changed through the years. Cattle raising on the mountains caused denudation of the forests, and the oyster population waned. Then there was the sugar industry. Now, as I mentioned before, we look to tourism."

Luke knew she was a good tour guide, being adept even with exact dates as she talked about Hawaii's history. She and William would be compatible that way, with his being a history teacher.

She told the stories of the Polynesians coming thousands of miles in their canoes and discovering Hawaii. In 1778 Captain Cook discovered it and later was killed by the natives. She told of the missionaries coming in 1820, the days of the kings, and the palace in Oahu.

"I'll probably take a day and see that," he said.

"It's worth seeing."

As they neared Pearl City Peninsula, she spoke of its being established as a navy base in 1913. "It was a popular place for military families after the army-navy airfield was built on Ford Island in the 1920s." Her voice changed from tour guide into regular conversation. "Oh, I guess you know of the writer Jack London?"

"Doesn't everyone?" He smiled.

"Well, we maybe knew him first," she said in the playful manner he'd detected a few times.

"We?" he joked back. "I read that he and his wife planned to sail around the world. If I remember correctly, you wouldn't even have been born when Jack London stopped here."

She gave him a look. "When I say *we*, I mean we Hawaiians as a group."

It occurred to him that she likely didn't think of herself as part Japanese and part white. She was Hawaiian.

"I stand corrected." He felt himself relax some, now that he knew he didn't have to be careful of every word he spoke, and she instinctively knew when he tried to joke.

"Pearl City Peninsula was his first port of call in 1907," she informed him, "when Jack London and his wife, Charmian, were on a two-year cruise to the South Seas in the *Snark*."

"Ah, his yacht."

She nodded. "Many wealthy families had yachts and recreation vessels. They sailed along in the midst of fishing and ferryboats. In 1924 Pearl Harbor Yacht Club was established. Yacht club members had Carol Lombard and William Powell as their guests when the couple honeymooned on the peninsula in the 1930s."

Luke took in the breathtaking view of the sapphire blue Pacific. With the windows rolled down, he felt the warmth of the tropical, sunny weather accompanied by soothing winds that Amelia said this area provided all year-round. "I can certainly understand why visitors from America came here."

"When President Franklin D. Roosevelt was here, he stayed at the house of his friend George Fuller, vice president of the Bank of Hawaii."

Luke sped along a five-mile stretch of flat land beside the calm ocean. Amelia explained that Pearl City was one of the busiest ports of Oahu Island. "And the most popular tourist stop," she added. "Most American tourists come for the reason you did, to see Pearl Harbor. It's like they have to see it to believe it could really have happened."

Luke nodded his understanding. Yes, there was shock that any nation had dared attack any part of America.

He listened with interest as she related the changes that had taken place, from the pearl industry to the raising of cattle and then sugar production. "My dad's closest friend, Claybourne Honeycutt, had the largest sugar plantations in

Hawaii. And my dad's brother, Geoffrey, started with a small plantation that grew to be very productive in Oahu."

"William is a Honeycutt," he said.

"Yes," she said. "They're related."

Luke thought he would like to meet people like that, find out more about this different, intriguing place so full of history. But Amelia didn't mention having him meet any of her family. He probably needed to rid himself of the ideal family concept. Perhaps that didn't exist anymore. He'd never had family other than his parents and Joe.

"Sugar was our most productive industry," she said. "But the war changed that. Most sugar plantations and refineries in Oahu closed down."

"I assume it's called Pearl City for an obvious reason," he commented when she had him stop there. He smiled over at her.

"You assume rightly." She returned his smile. "Oysters bearing pearls were bountiful in these waters, particularly in the Pearl River. That came to the attention of King Kamehameha I, who expanded a lucrative pearl trade."

Listening to her, watching her, Luke knew Joe had found a rare pearl in Amelia. His brother apparently knew that since he had thought enough of her to mention her in a letter. It was as if Joe had said, *I did something right, Luke.*

Chapter 14

Luke could readily see that this paradise had everything to offer. One could enjoy nature or walk into stores that spoke of Hawaii's cultural diversity. Stores and markets with local produce reminded him of the farmer's market in Hilo. Other stores carried handcrafted items, many of which depicted Hawaii's past and culture.

He'd seen, too, the hotels being built and thought of Matilda's saying his profession would be an asset here. The terrain became steeper.

"I was living in one of those houses with a girlfriend," Amelia said, "until the bombing."

Luke looked at the single-level homes that stood on a steep hill. There were small yards. He could understand that single young people might be able to rent those at an affordable rate.

"Below is Pearl Harbor," she said.

Luke found a parking place and looked down on the harbor, a spectacularly beautiful and peaceful setting. "Could I have my camera, please?" He wanted to take pictures of the beautiful harbor below.

She took it from her purse and handed it to him. "Don't take my picture."

At first he thought this might be one of the many times when a person needed to be coaxed before they relaxed and smiled for the camera. But the look on her face was serious, and her eyes held determination.

"Promise," she said. "I don't want you going back to your parents with stories about how close Joe and I were. I don't think they should think about me as someone they might want to see. It's been almost five years. We need to get on with our lives."

"I think they want to know everything and anything about Joe's life here."

She shook her head. "There's no place in my life for. . .them."

Luke tried to let that register. Maybe she was right. Close to five years had passed, and she was still single. If she and William were planning a life together, she would need to let go of the past. It wasn't the same with parents or a brother. They would want to keep the memory alive.

He reached for the camera and said, "I promise," as he exited the car.

She stood behind him as he stood on a hill and took pictures of the harbor below.

Uppermost in his mind, however, was the realization that no matter how much this area had been rebuilt, how appealing, how normal it looked, how happy the people seemed, the beautiful harbor was where the Japanese had bombed. This was where Joe had been killed.

A short while later, standing on the beach at Pearl Harbor, Luke did not get the feeling of Paradise. They met up with a group, some Japanese, some Hawaiians, and several Americans. An American man engaged him in conversation immediately. "I'm Fred, and this is my wife, Marsha."

"Luke and Amelia." Luke knew the reason for the informality. They had a bond. A bond of death.

The first words from Marsha were, "Did you have a loved one killed here?"

"My brother."

"The worst part," the man said, "is knowing that forty feet below the surface, where you can see it plainly in that clear water, is the *Arizona*. Over a thousand men are trapped in there." He drew in a breath and said in a shaky voice, "Our son is down there."

Marsha wiped her eyes with an already soggy handkerchief. Luke could imagine his mom and dad here. His dad wasn't one to show a lot of emotion. His mom overcompensated for it. No, he doubted they would ever come here.

Luke hated it. Hated the feelings inside him. At the same time, he was glad he had come. Right now it was all emotional. His insides whispered, *Good-bye, Joe.* But he needed to have more conversations than that with his brother.

"Here." He heard a soft voice say. Amelia held out a tissue. He took it and wiped his face. She took another tissue and wiped her own. "You want to be alone?" she asked.

"No," he said. "Thank you for being here with me." It seemed right, being here with someone else who loved Joe. But it still didn't seem real. Something inside him wasn't able to accept or absorb it all.

Neither seemed inclined to talk very much, but this time the silence wasn't uncomfortable. A trip like this would be taxing for anyone, mentally and emotionally. He was glad he hadn't done it alone.

Luke reminded himself the war was over. Yes, the physical war, but what about all those emotional ones? Joe had thought enough of Amelia to have written home about her. He mentioned her dad but not her mom. Had he known Amelia was part Japanese? But that was before the Japanese bombed Pearl Harbor. How would Joe have felt about Amelia then, if he had lived?

Just as quickly, Luke answered his own questions. Amelia was a lovely, appealing woman. And Joe had known how to appreciate her.

Amelia didn't look away this time when Luke gazed at her. He could honestly say, "I'm glad Joe's last days were spent being happy with you."

Her whisper was barely audible. "So am I."

Chapter 15

Amelia led Luke into the airstrip coffee shop to wait for the flight back to Hilo. After a sip of the coffee, she watched him as he seemed to study a Japanese couple nearby. When he looked at her again, he asked, "During the war, were you interned?"

She hesitated, and he quickly apologized. "I'm sorry. I know some things are hard to talk about. We don't have to."

"No, it's all right." She tried to smile at him but felt the tension inside her, remembering all the uncertainty of that time. "There was much suspicion and many accusations that went on after the bombing. There was fear and shock and not knowing who to trust. I lost my job on the base. The building was bombed, and I was told I wasn't needed. That may be true, but full Japanese lost their jobs because of their race."

Amelia noticed he didn't seem surprised.

"Was your mother put into a camp?"

"Not her. Everyone knows my mother is trusted beyond anyone else." Why did she always have to feel that niggling resentment of her own mother? "She came here as a picture bride when she was sixteen."

"Picture bride? What is that?"

"In the early 1900s, Japanese men came here to work. And sugar plantations needed them. After a while, the men realized they might never be able to go back to Japan, so they were allowed to send their photos and information to Japan, seeking a bride."

"I can understand that," Luke said.

Amelia nodded. "Japanese girls and matchmakers looked at the pictures and information and sent their own photos back to the immigration office. The ships would come in, the men would be waiting, and often they were married right there, the first time they'd ever seen each other."

"And your mother was one of them. At age sixteen?" Luke shook his head as if that were unbelievable. "How did she become the wife of a white man? If I'm not being too personal."

Amelia couldn't help but be amused at his surprise. She'd grown accustomed to visitors to the island and military men like Joe—and now Luke—never having heard of the picture brides.

"No, it's not too personal. Her story is famous. A man had sent a photo taken twenty years before. He was in his forties. Many of the brides, having traveled so far and with nothing to go back to but humiliation, would have thought they had no recourse but to marry the man."

Amelia sighed. "Not my mother. She is one determined, stubborn person. Straight as an arrow on what she wants to do."

Luke pushed his cup aside, planted his forearms on the table, and leaned forward. "I'd love to hear the story."

Their boarding was called. "On the plane," she said.

They boarded, and she again stepped aside for Luke to sit by the window.

After they were settled in their seats and had flown high into the clear night sky, alight with moon and stars, Amelia glanced at Luke, who was looking out the window and down at the land below. She leaned back against the seat, allowing herself to relax for a moment and release the tension she felt in the back of her neck. She hadn't minded the memories or the talking about the war and Joe or the camps. But she'd tried to weigh each word carefully, wanting to know how Luke felt about her and Joe. She hadn't learned a thing about that from him. His mind was probably doing the same as hers—evaluating.

He wasn't probing. In everything, he seemed to ponder yet be sensitive to her feelings. That was how it was with most people. They didn't ask too many questions.

Afraid the droning of the plane might put her to sleep, she turned her head to face Luke and found his head turned her way. He, too, had leaned against the back of the seat.

For a moment her eyes saw Joe. The resemblance. Luke's face was more mature, his lips fuller, his eyes more serious. Her gaze locked with his. She would like to know more about him. But there was no point in that. The less either knew, the better.

He seemed to study her as she studied him. Was it her imagination that his eyes always had a question in them? She looked down at her hands on her lap. What had they been talking about? Her mother? Picture brides?

"My mom refused, right on the spot, to marry that man. That had never happened before, and everyone was shocked. With few exceptions, the Japanese were laborers on the plantations. The women were needed to keep the men happy and have children. If Mom had been able to return to Japan, she would have been an outcast and humiliated. Here, she wouldn't be socially accepted by the whites."

"What did she do?"

"There was nothing she could do. She just stood there. Nobody knew what to do." Amelia laughed. "Except Matilda. She took her in, put her to work at the Matti-Rose, and got her a job part-time at the immigration office since she could speak both Japanese and some English."

"What happened to the man?"

Every time she related this part of the story, Amelia was in awe of her mom's audacity. "My mom wrote for her widowed aunt to come. She did and married the man who had sent his picture." She laughed lightly. "So that man became my mom's uncle."

Amelia liked the sound of Luke's laughing with her. She suspected it would have been nice to relate to him without all the tension.

"Fascinating story," he said.

"Oh, there are many. My mom fell in love with my dad when he was a teacher and she a student. He went away to seminary on the mainland. She waited for him. She said she would never marry if she could not have my dad." She turned her head toward Luke. "My mom gets what she wants."

Amelia faced forward again. Her mom always had an opinion. What would she want in this situation? The thought was disturbing. To try and dismiss it, Amelia began to tell Luke how her mom had been like an intermediary between the Japanese and the whites. She told of her mom going to the plantations and talking to the Japanese who had their own villages, their own temples, and their own gods.

"Through her and my dad, many have become Christians," she said.

"She sounds wonderful," he commented.

"She's perfect." Turning her head completely away from Luke, Amelia looked across the aisle and smiled at a little boy who looked her way. She knew those unwanted feelings weren't really against her mother but against herself. She fell so far short of perfection.

After landing and getting into Luke's rental car for their return to Hilo, Amelia told him how things had changed. People were being judged on an individual basis and not so much on race. Many Japanese had gone into business, owned land, and were a part of the culture of Hawaii.

The return trip seemed shorter, with Luke remembering the turns. He pulled into an empty space in the parking lot behind the Matti-Rose. Amelia wondered what he thought about her rambling on about her family, even though he'd asked. "I haven't given you a chance to talk about your family." She didn't really want to hear about them. She only meant to be polite.

"I already know about them," he said and gave a light laugh. "Anyway, their lives aren't nearly as fascinating as the people I've encountered here. This is. . . different."

When she reached for the door handle, he said, "Thank you for going with me today and putting up with all my questions."

"I don't think I should say I enjoyed it," Amelia said, "considering the reason and all the memories. But. . .it was good. I'm glad I went. And I hope it was helpful to you."

Luke had turned toward her with his left arm over the steering wheel. "That's what I came for, Amelia. To see what Joe had seen, where he'd lived, wanting to know he was enjoying life. Some things I can only work out within myself. But it helps, too, knowing he. . .knew you."

"We had good times together. I don't think he was ever sad. And when the bombs came, there wasn't time to be anything but shocked. He was killed instantly." Oh, the sweep of that emotion seemed overpowering. She blinked it away, looked away from Luke's moist eyes. She needed to get away.

She wished he would go, and she asked, "Are you planning to stay around?"

"For a while. The contractors are consulting with me about the park at the bay and a few other projects. I've told them I'm not working, not on a payroll that is. It's voluntary, and I can give as much or as little of my time as I want."

She put her hand on the door handle again.

"One more thing," he said. She kept her hand on the handle but loosened her grip. "Is there anything you need? Anything I can do? I mean, I am Joe's brother."

"No," she said quickly. "There's nothing. The past is over. I've dealt with it." It was the present she was having trouble with. "But. . ." She hadn't meant to say what she heard coming out of her mouth. "Did Joe write to your parents about me?"

"No, only to me."

"What did he say about me?" She didn't turn from his gaze this time, although she felt a tremble in her lips, and she saw that question in his eyes.

He repeated what he'd said before. That Joe had said he'd met a girl, her name was Amelia Grant, and her dad was a preacher.

He shifted his gaze to the dark foliage ahead of the car. "I have the letter in my room. I'll read it again to make sure."

She got the strong impression there *was* more.

"I'm sure touring the island is more enjoyable with someone than alone. Would you be willing to be my tour guide again, Amelia? To places that bring back happy memories, perhaps?" Life had so many ifs. *If* the past had been different, *if* the present were different. Luke was nice. He tried not to probe. He respected her feelings, even when he didn't know what they were. If. . .he were not Joe's brother.

But the ifs were there. "Today was good, as I said. But the past is gone. My life with Joe is over. I shouldn't go backward, but forward."

"Of course," he said. "But from my point of view, we have a common bond, and that's important to me. I just want you to know that if there's anything. . . like. . .listen to you, do anything. . . ?

"Thank you. But there's nothing. It's been nice meeting you, Luke. I hope your stay in Hawaii is a pleasant one. Be sure and stop by the tourist office to say good-bye before you leave." She opened the door. "I wish you well."

He was out of the car at the same time she was and walked her to her car. He stood there while she turned the key in the ignition. "Good night, Amelia. Thanks again."

She backed out, and in the rearview mirror, she watched him walk across the lot toward the back entrance of the inn.

His head turned, and he stood at the back door until she had rounded the corner of the inn and headed to her own home. She had no idea why her tears wanted to fall now. Relief that this was over? Fear that it would never be over?

Chapter 16

Luke felt tired, mentally and emotionally more than physically. He stretched, trying to relax his tense muscles, showered, and went to bed. He barely got up in time for church the next morning, and he did miss breakfast. One of the cooks, however, gave him coffee and a banana nut muffin. He sat at the back of the church, still rather amazed at the Japanese woman in a kimono playing the organ while the congregation sang hymns like he'd sung in the States.

The sermon was encouraging, again meant for those who had recently experienced loss or perhaps for those who had never quite dealt with it yet. He didn't see Amelia or William. He noticed Matilda, but as soon as the service ended, he hurried out and shook Jacob Grant's hand. Their gazes seemed to lock for a moment. "I hope things are well with you," the pastor said.

"Yes, sir. Thank you."

Luke walked out the door, wondering. A pastor who had so much wisdom and hope from the pulpit had nothing to say about his daughter's late husband, Luke's brother? Had they not approved of Joe? Or had Amelia and Joe eloped? Had the marriage been an impulsive moment? He mustn't allow his mind to wander.

Luke felt like there were unspoken things in the pastor's eyes, as there had been with William and with Amelia. Was he an unwelcome intrusion into their lives? A reminder of worse times?

Just then he saw Matilda, who seemed to be waiting for him.

"Come home with me," she said. "We can have salad and a sandwich and talk, if you like. If not, just eat and sit on the lanai."

"My car is at the side."

"Oh, I walked. Come on. Work up an appetite."

He laughed. "That muffin the cook at the inn found for me has long ago disappeared."

They walked together to her house, not too far away.

The food needed very little preparation, and he had the feeling Matilda had planned to invite someone for lunch. He expected anybody might walk in, but no one else did.

They worked together on the lunch and took it to the lanai. The talk was pleasant, about the weather, the sermon, the building in Hilo, the contractor he was to meet that evening for dinner.

After he poured their second cup of coffee, she said, "How was your trip to Pearl?"

307

He wondered if Amelia had talked to her about it already or before they went.

Without intending to, he found himself confiding in her as if she were a parish priest and he at confession, although he wasn't even Catholic. He spoke of regrets of not having known Joe, of not having tolerated him better. "I was five years older than Joe and the responsible one. But to be honest, I would love to have been like Joe, fun loving, happy-go-lucky, impulsive. I gave the impression I wasn't pleased with him, when I really was envious."

"Oh, that's normal." She waved a hand. "But you were made like you for a reason. And he, because his life was going to be cut short."

"By the Japanese," Luke said, giving her a steady look he thought she'd understand.

She nodded, and he knew she did. Then she said, "Maybe that's why you're here. To learn to see the Japanese as individuals and not a race."

"I know that."

"Your mind knows it," she said. "It takes longer for the heart."

He understood that, too. He didn't resent the Japanese. But the idea of them killing his brother, bombing Pearl Harbor were the facts in his life.

"Everything happens for a reason," she said.

He scoffed. "My brother's being killed?"

"Yes, and his impulsive nature knew it, even if he didn't."

Luke hadn't reconciled everything in his mind. "Some things happen because of evil in the world."

"Absolutely. All the terrible things happen because of that. But no one dies without the Lord's permission."

Luke winced. "That's hard to take. The things I've seen."

"I'm not saying the Lord causes those things. Combine the influence of evil with a leader's greed and sense of power, and the consequences are horrible. The Lord allows them. I can't explain it all, but if God doesn't want someone to die, nothing will kill them."

Luke looked out through the screen of the lanai to the peaceful landscape. The green grass, the tall trees, the lush foliage, the blue sky. Some of that made sense. He'd seen men walk away from impossible situations. He'd done it himself. He looked over at Matilda. Her smile at him and her green eyes were as warm as the light breeze caressing his face.

"I should be leaving," he said. "I have an evening engagement, and I should write to my parents this afternoon."

"And I should take my afternoon nap," Matilda said, rising from the couch. She walked with him to the front screen door. "Luke," she said when they reached it. "You don't need to feel guilty because Joe died and you're alive."

Her few words were better than a sermon. Perhaps they were a sermon.

❧

That afternoon Luke wrote to his parents, telling them he had visited Pearl Harbor. He described it as he thought Joe would have seen it, in its serene beauty. They didn't know about Amelia, and he didn't want to add to his mother's increasingly depressed state of mind the shock that Joe had married. He leaned against the pillow at the headboard, thinking what he should write.

Joe had been the baby, the one who brought them the most laughter, tears, and worries. This was not the kind of news to tell them. And, too, Amelia's reluctance to be involved with him or his family bothered him. It was not what he would expect. It was so far removed from Penny's attitude. She wanted to be near them as family. But the situation was different. Penny had been a family friend. His family were strangers to Amelia, and she didn't want to be involved with them.

He knew Amelia had been uncomfortable talking about Joe. She was very congenial and forthcoming about anything else, including herself and her family. He could readily see that Joe would be attracted to her. Once in a while he caught a glimpse of a fun-loving girl. But again the thought came that war changed people.

At first he didn't understand Amelia not wanting to know his parents and not wanting him to tell them about her. Then he supposed if she were planning a future with William, it might be awkward for her to be involved with Joe's family.

On second thought it might be nice if Amelia would speak to his parents, at least his mother, and say she knew Joe. She wouldn't have to say they had married. Joe had always had a girl, and they would like to know that.

But William might be the kind of man who didn't want Amelia involved with Luke's family. After all, he'd taken the time to come around. He'd offered to be Luke's friend. William might think he was protecting Amelia from. . . what? Memories?

Luke's thoughts returned to the letter he should be writing. He began to write about Matilda. Yes, they would like to know Joe had visited a woman like her as a mother away from home.

He told his parents about the tsunami and his part in the rebuilding. He threw in a few sentences about Hawaii being a rainbow culture of many nationalities. He included the postcards and a promise of some pictures soon.

The thought occurred to him to call William and see if he would like to go with Luke to see the sights of Hawaii. But if William and Amelia were dating, Luke didn't want to interfere with their time together.

He read Joe's letter again, wondering if Joe had put the wrong date on the letter. But looking at when the envelope was stamped, he thought the date was right. Two days before he was killed, Joe wrote that he had *met* Amelia. He didn't mention marriage. When did they marry? Was that another impulsive move of Joe's? It could be. He hadn't always thought of the impact his actions would have on others.

Something occurred to Luke. Joe's beneficiary had been his parents. Had there not been time enough to change important documents? Or had documents and records been destroyed in the bombing?

Finally he figured all the thinking and questioning in the world weren't going to bring him answers.

He had more questions now than when he'd come to this island. And he wasn't about to leave before some of them were answered.

Chapter 17

On Monday morning Luke felt he had to say something to Pastor Grant. He drew the man aside. "Pastor, you must know that I'm Joe Thurstan's brother."

"Yes," he said immediately. "I suspected it the first time you appeared in church. That afternoon Amelia confirmed it."

This was a mystery to Luke. "You might have said something."

"No," Jacob said. "That's Amelia's decision. It's not easy being a man, a dad, a preacher, a friend. One role doesn't fit all. A dad can't preach to his daughter. A dad can't always be a friend to his child. Roles often clash. As with you. You're Joe's brother, and yet you are your own self."

Again Luke had that feeling. "I'm not here only as Joe's brother. I'm here as me."

"And what exactly is *me*?"

Their gazes locked. Finally Luke scoffed. "I think you just took on the role of preacher."

"Friend, too, I hope."

Luke nodded. "Thank you." He took a deep breath. "In that case, did Joe do something to cause you concern?"

"Not at all. I met him only one time and briefly when Amelia brought him by to introduce him to me and her mother. I had nothing against him. But he is Amelia's subject, not mine. You see, Luke, we each have our scars. Some wounds heal slowly. I have to let Amelia make her decisions and leave it up to her and God. I had to let go of my son. He was killed by the Japanese. The bomber could even have been a relation of my wife, whom I love more than life. I had to let Andy go, forgive. Oh, I have my scars. But I go on. I preach as much truth as I can. I know God's presence and the presence of evil more completely than ever before."

Luke nodded. He understood.

The pastor added, "I'm most blessed to be able to comfort others. I couldn't in the same way if I hadn't lost Andy, our first child. Oh how I've prayed to see the war over in other people's eyes! It's still in your eyes, Luke."

Luke couldn't dispute that. His emotions were still at war. He accepted Joe's death, but he didn't like the memory of their last time together. The memory of his own immature reactions to Joe's stealing Penny from him. In reality, Joe didn't and couldn't steal Penny. She went willingly.

༒

At midweek Luke called the tourism office. Tara was glad to hear from him and said Amelia had taken a van of tourists out for the day but that she'd be back. He stopped by at lunchtime.

He saw Amelia through the glass window, looking businesslike in a black skirt, white shirt, and her hair pulled back as usual with a few strands along the sides of her face in a casual manner. He wondered how long her hair was.

She looked up and saw him through the window. She seemed surprised, and her fingers stopped typing. He went inside. Tension seemed to settle about her. Was she afraid he was there to pay for a tour? Had she thought she wouldn't see him again?

She finally said, "Aloha," which she would be paid to say.

"Good afternoon," he said and tried to give her a pleasant smile. "How are you today?" *What a question.*

"I'm fine."

"Didn't see you in church. I was afraid Saturday's excursion wore you out."

She gave a skeptical look. "No. It was a long day. But I'm glad we went."

"Yes, so am I. And I read Joe's letter again. He did say something else. Or at least implied something."

"What—what was it?" she almost whispered and looked toward a doorway as if fearing someone might hear.

"Well, I wondered if you would take pity on this poor lonely fellow and have dinner with me one evening, and I'll tell you. Except next Thursday." He tried to sound as playful as he could but knew he couldn't hold a candle to the way Joe would have done it.

The front doorbell jingled as a couple came in.

"Here, I'll give you my phone number."

"I'll just call the inn. They'll connect me." Her eyes held a hint of laughter. Before they changed to something else, he decided to leave and stepped aside for the couple to step up to the desk. With a lift of his hand, he left.

He figured that was an in-lawish thing to do. If she called and said she wouldn't be able to have dinner, then what?

He had no idea.

Amelia hadn't called by the following Thursday afternoon when Luke returned to his room after work. He'd been invited to the preopening night of the American restaurant since he had helped work on it. They'd asked if he'd come and take photos, since he'd done much of that as projects were being finished.

All who helped with the cleanup and repairs would be there, along with invited guests. Luke decided to go. Perhaps he might see Pastor Grant or Matilda and talk with them. He walked down to the restaurant just as the brilliant sunset faded and lights shone from the glass windows.

Before he went inside, he saw William, and. . . Then he realized the woman was Amelia, with her hair hanging below her shoulders, pushed behind one ear and revealing a gold earring. The other side fell along her face as she bent her head slightly and laughed at something William had said. Had she sat like that with his brother, laughing, talking? Joe would have been delighted with her. No, Joe would not have cared about the beautiful girl having a Japanese mother, even after the war.

If Joe had lived.

Luke felt a sinking empty spot in his stomach to think of what Joe had missed. What Joe would never have.

Then Amelia looked through the glass window into his eyes. The laughter left her expression. Her eyes now held that reluctance again. But she lifted her hand in acknowledgment of him. For a moment he simply stared until he realized William was motioning to him.

Luke turned toward the entrance, stopped for a moment to inhale the cool, fragrant air, then went inside to be immediately greeted by the owner of the restaurant, along with Ted and Frank. "We have a special place for you," John said, "with other contractors."

"Thanks," Luke said with a nod. "I need to speak to a couple over there first."

"You can sit wherever you like," he said. "I just want you to know we do have a particular place for you."

Luke walked over to the table in front of the window, having no idea why he felt awkward. Perhaps it was his intrusion on a couple. But William had motioned for him.

"Fill your plate and join us," William said.

Luke didn't care to be a fifth wheel. He looked at the inviting buffet bar. "I think there's a place reserved for me back there." He tilted his head toward another area of the restaurant. "This is a table for two anyway."

"No problem," William said. "A chair can be placed right here."

Luke glanced at Amelia. "If you can sit for a moment," she said, "I'd like to explain why I haven't called."

He started to say she owed him no explanation. Only in rare moments did she let her guard down around him and seem to react naturally. But he would like to hear her explanation. "I'll get a cup of coffee," he said.

When he returned, William had placed a chair at the end of the small table.

"First," she said, "I'd like to thank you again. I didn't know I needed to go back to Pearl again. But I did."

Luke stared at his coffee. Yes, that visit had been much more meaningful being there with another person.

"The reason I didn't call you," she said, "is that Wanda has taken the children to Oahu for a week to be with relatives. I've been busy at work and at home, helping Wanda with packing and making preparations for their trip. They'll be staying for Lei Day and on through the following weekend, at least."

He opened his mouth to ask what Lei Day meant, but she surprised him by quickly adding, "So Luke, if you'd like, I can take you to some of the places where Joe and I had happy times. I can tell you what he liked to eat, to do."

He looked from her to William, who simply watched him, waiting for his answer. "Will you join us?" Luke asked.

William held up a hand. "No no. I think you two need to do that alone. Joe is a common bond for you. Besides, I have to be ready to resume my teaching as soon as all the repairs are finished on the school, which should be soon."

William was a very understanding man. Luke was glad Amelia had someone like him. Apparently he wasn't jealous of Amelia's relationship with Joe. Or with Luke. But of course there was no relationship with Luke. Like William said, Luke and Amelia had a common bond. And that bond was Joe's death.

"Thank you," Luke said to Amelia, with a brief nod at William. "I would like that, and it's something I can take back to my parents, the good things Joe enjoyed while here."

She smiled. "Come with me. I can give you a lesson about Hawaiian food."

"But this is an American restaurant, isn't it?" Luke countered.

"It's in Hawaii," Amelia said, bringing his eyes back to her hair, which moved softly along one side of her face as she tilted her head and lowered her chin.

She led the way to the buffet bar. "Oh, you must try these." She named island fish, fresh vegetables, fruit such as mangos, papaya, lychee, lilikoi, and more varieties of pineapple and bananas than he had known existed. He returned to the table with a plate piled high with samplings of many foods.

William's eyes widened as if his appetite had been whetted again. "I think it's time I got seconds." He took his plate to the buffet.

Luke felt totally sated when William mentioned the newspaper reporter walking around taking pictures.

"That's what I need to do," Luke said. "Ted and Frank want some personal ones to send back to their family and friends in the States. I've already taken many as repairs were made."

"You know I don't want to be in a picture," Amelia reminded him as he pushed away from the table.

"I remember. And I promised not to shoot you."

William laughed. She smiled and looked away.

Questions again jumped into Luke's mind. Did she say that to assure William her past was over and done with? Or to reconfirm to Luke she didn't want involvement with his family?

For some reason not quite clear to him, she didn't want him to photograph her. He was definitely getting *that* picture.

Chapter 18

Amelia called Luke early Friday morning. His "Hello?" seemed to hold a note of anticipation, or perhaps surprise, as if he hadn't expected a call.

"Did I wake you?"

"No, Amelia."

He recognized her voice? But he probably received no calls unless they were from the mainland. Then he filled the moment of silence. "I was getting ready to go down to breakfast."

"I won't keep you."

"No no. I don't mind missing breakfast if I could accompany" —she heard his pause before he continued—"someone to dinner tonight."

That helped her feel a little more at ease, being unaccustomed to making a date with a man. She did wonder what he'd been about to say. A what? Or was he about to add *anyone*?

It didn't matter. Did men have as much difficulty making a date with a woman? But this wasn't a real date. "I could take you. I mean, we could go to an international restaurant tonight, if you like. Joe and I ate there once." She had to say that to make sure he understood why they were doing this.

"Sounds great to me. Is it a formal place? Should I wear a suit?"

"Aloha shirts are accepted as formal attire in most settings," she said. "I'm sure you've noticed that in church. A few tourists might dress more formally at the restaurant, but most don't."

"All right," he said. "Casual it is. And where shall I pick you up?"

She couldn't possibly let him do that. "I'll pick you up at the Matti-Rose." After they hung up, she called for reservations. Those were confirmed, and she hung up the phone, then held out her hand and looked at it. No, it wasn't shaking, but she felt shaky inside.

At the moment, however, she was glad Wanda and the children were not there. How could she explain the turmoil inside her?

Leaning back against the countertop, she reprimanded herself for those feelings. And yet how could she help it? Part of her wanted Luke Thurstan to leave the island and let her resume her life as usual. Another part of her longed for more. The trip to Pearl Harbor had been, for both her and Luke, a time of remembering the war and the loss of Joe. Being in the company of a man had been good in so many ways.

Now she was planning to go out with a man for dinner. Of course she knew it was all about Joe, but she hadn't had a date in almost five years. The only man who halfway interested her was William, her dear friend William. Last night

315

she'd gone with him to the restaurant, but it hadn't felt anything near to being a date. Of course this wasn't either. But it could be good practice in case anyone ever came along who she. . .might date. Maybe she shouldn't be thinking like that. For so long, the children, her work, her church, and friends had filled her life. She'd accepted it had to be like that. And her life was full. She was blessed far beyond many who'd survived the war.

Even while searching through her closet, Amelia knew she wouldn't wear any of the clothes in there. They were Sunday clothes, work clothes, casual clothes. People had dressed conservatively and casually during the war years. The war was over. Would it be so wrong to pretend this was a real date?

"Where are my clothes, Mom?" she asked after driving to her mother's house.

"In the trunk where we packed them."

Amelia waited stiffly for the question, but her mom merely led her into the bedroom. "Come, I'll show you."

The trunk was at the foot of the bed in the guest room. It wasn't locked, and her mother lifted the lid and stood aside. Amelia bent down and found the pink dress she wanted. "I don't know if it will still fit."

"Try it on," her mother said.

Amelia did. And it fit. She hadn't felt such soft material in a long time, and she liked the flared sleeves right below her shoulders. But was the V-neckline too low?

Her mother smiled. "You look beautiful. It's so good to see you in something like that again."

Amelia shook her head. She hated the emotion that welled up in her. "I don't know if I should. I'm not trying to. . ." She couldn't stand it, feeling she had to explain to her mother.

"You are trying to look nice," her mother said. "There's nothing wrong with that. No matter who you are with or where you are going."

Amelia shrugged. "I'm just taking him to a restaurant where his brother and I went. That's all." She hated feeling like a child who had to explain. And her mother was standing there nodding, smiling, being her sweet, nonreproachful self. But what was she thinking?

Amelia turned to change back into her work clothes.

"I'll make sure it's clean for you. Come by after work."

"Thank you, Mom." When she turned again, she saw her mother holding a box. "Your heels are in here. What about jewelry?"

"I'll just wear my silver chain with the heart."

She noticed her mother's eyes look at her hair. No, she would not wear her hair down as she had when she went out with Joe. She'd become much more conservative since then. So conservative she hadn't even gone out on a date.

That evening she picked up the dress from her mom's, went home to shampoo and shower, then assessed herself in the mirror as she fastened the silver chain around her neck.

"That's my heart you're wearing," Joe had said. He'd touched it, and he'd traced a pattern. . . . No. Amelia closed her eyes against the memory. But her mind could hear as plainly as if it were playing on the car radio. She and Joe would be listening to Glen Gray and his Casa Loma Orchestra playing "Memories of You."

She and Joe would sing along with Artie Shaw's orchestra.

Amelia took a deep breath. Neither of them could have imagined how true that would turn out to be.

Maybe she shouldn't wear this dress. But it really wasn't the dress so much. Luke was making her remember what needed to be left in the past. And she wasn't wearing the dress as a tribute to Joe. She just wanted to feel. . .pretty. Unlike the tailored skirts she wore to work, the soft folds of this fine material made her feel feminine.

She smoothed the long strand of hair that fell along the right side of her face, then she fastened a magenta orchid and a white camellia on the other side of her hair, which was in a French twist. She applied a soft red lipstick. Was this a terrible mistake? Old feelings were being awakened, and she began to long for male attention again. After almost five years of resolving to be a content, spinster old maid.

Not that she had any aspirations about Luke. She wanted him to leave the island. But she would like this memory. A night out on the town with a man. Yet she realized when she got into her car to go and pick him up that this wasn't exactly how a date should go.

This is not a date, she reminded herself again.

She had thought, perhaps even hoped, she would have to explain everything to someone, someday. But not to Joe's brother. Not to Joe's family.

Those ifs again. *If* things had been different, would she have met Luke Thurstan under different circumstances? *If* she hadn't taken the name of Mrs. Thurstan, then Luke would have known her as Amelia Grant. What then? Anything? But if things had been different, would Joe have mentioned her in a letter? She'd made her choices—some bad, some good—and now she lived with the consequences.

When she arrived at the Matti-Rose, Amelia felt rather foolish. She'd been taught a fellow should never toot the horn for a girl. Should she toot the horn for Luke? She wouldn't be comfortable doing that—nor going into the lobby and asking for him. She sat, waiting, wondering if she was going to perspire.

Would he be at the back, expecting to drive his rental? Oh, this could be embarrassing. Then the front door opened, and out he came. He was not wearing an aloha shirt, with its square hemline that didn't have to be tucked in. He wore a white short-sleeved shirt tucked into dress pants and a tie.

The pretend side of her realized what a handsome man he was. Of course there was nothing wrong with knowing that. Facts were facts, that was all. The breeze lifted the waves of his dark blond hair that now had golden highlights. His face was tan from working in the sun.

He came up to the car. "My coach or yours?"

"We can go in mine."

He motioned for her to slide over, which she did. He smiled over at her after getting into the driver's seat. "Your wish is my command, pretty lady."

That sounded like an offhand remark, so she didn't say thank you. "You didn't take my advice on your attire," she said playfully.

"Well, it's like this." He turned toward her with a playful look in his eyes. "I figured you'd be all gorgeous, and I'd feel uncomfortable in a flowered shirt."

"You look nice."

His right arm was propped on the back of the seat, his fingers very near her shoulder. His fingers lightly tapped on the seat, then he exhaled, smiled, and said, "Where to, my lady?"

My lady! She straightened in the seat. "Banyan Drive."

She watched his thoughtful face. A fleck of gold appeared in his blue eyes, and he made a loop with his finger, tracing an invisible arc. "FDR, Babe Ruth, Shirley Temple—"

He faced the steering wheel and turned the key. "Now all I need to know is how to get there from here."

"You forgot?"

He laughed lightly and looked at her, and a swift glance seemed to take her in. His mouth opened as if he were about to say something; then it closed, and the teasing look left his eyes. "The last time I did this, I had a tour guide."

He pulled out into the road.

His manner for an instant had reminded her of Joe. She'd almost thought Luke had been about to flirt with her. But she knew he seemed to sense her moods. If she were serious, he was. If she relaxed, he did. She glanced over at Luke's arm, extended as he held onto the steering wheel. It was muscular and tanned; the hairs were golden.

By this time Joe would have complimented her profusely, taken her in his arms, and kissed her soundly, smearing her lipstick and wearing it himself.

But those were the days when she'd been young and foolish.

Those days were gone. . .forever.

Chapter 19

Luke marveled at the conversation he and Amelia were having, as if they were casual acquaintances on an evening out, getting to know each other. "What kind of music do you like?" he asked.

"Hawaiian and American," she said.

"I don't know anything about Hawaiian music," he admitted, "but I love the big bands and orchestras."

They talked about the songs that had been so popular all during the war. "Guy Lombardo," she said.

He nodded, adding, "Glenn Miller. Oh, and she's not a big band, but she has a big voice."

They both said, "Kate Smith," at the same time and laughed.

"I'll have to introduce you to Hawaiian music," she said, and just as quick as his glance toward her, he saw that her shoulders rose with an intake of breath, and she looked away. He felt sure she hadn't meant to say that.

Although he knew where to turn to get to the restaurant, he asked directions anyway to fill the moment of awkward silence. She began to talk again. "The restaurant is known for having the best soup in the area and a huge salad bar. And of course, since it's an international restaurant, there's any kind of food you could want."

After parking and going inside, Luke saw that most patrons were dressed casually, as Amelia had said. A couple of men wore suits. Luke felt he was in between. That thought almost brought a scoff. Around Amelia he often felt in between a rock and a hard place. He felt squeezed between wanting to ask about her personal relationship with Joe and holding back so as not to scare her away.

"The reservation is in the name of Thurstan," she said.

That jolted his mind for a second. Why, he wasn't sure. Perhaps because he'd thought of her as Amelia Grant, Joe's girl, from the time he'd read Joe's letter. Her being a Thurstan was still new to him. Had she and Joe come here as Mr. and Mrs. Thurstan?

They were led to a small table by a window, reminding him of the evening before when he'd stood outside and looked at Amelia and William on the inside.

Feeling as he did the first night in Oahu, Luke thought he would not sample Hawaiian or international cuisine but would order the Black Angus beef.

At Amelia's suggestion, with a challenge in her eyes, however, he ordered the same as she, the opakapaka that she said was a prized fish. Accompanying the kind of conversation he hoped to have, fish might be easier to swallow than steak.

They filled their plates at the salad bar and again sat at the table. "So," he said, "you and Joe came here?"

Had he not been looking for it, he wouldn't have noticed the minute stillness of her fork above her salad before she said, "Once. In fact, I wore this dress." Added color seemed to come into her cheeks when she added, "I hadn't worn it since. Until now."

Feeling his eyes widen, he forced them to narrow but not stare at the dress that so complemented her in ways he tried not to notice except to appreciate. "It's a lovely dress, Amelia. And I'm sure Joe must have told you that you're very beautiful."

There, he'd said it. It came from Joe, not Luke. Joe would have been fascinated by her. That went without saying. They had married.

"Do you have anything. . .of Joe's?"

She stared at him a long time as if the question were inconceivable. Finally her head moved slightly. "You mean his belongings?"

He nodded. "Pictures? Rings?"

He couldn't imagine that was a difficult question, but she didn't seem to know how to reply. Her lips opened slightly, and he could hear her soft breathing. Finally she lowered her eyes to the table. "Memories."

Memories. That she was keeping to herself. Joe had been shot. She had not. So they hadn't been together when the attack came. Or somehow she escaped being shot. Or had she? And recuperated? He came here for answers, and instead he was getting more questions. He had an uncanny feeling he wasn't going to get any answers either, not from Amelia or her dad.

He wouldn't mind having dinner with a beautiful woman—just the two of them. But they were here because he wanted to know more about Joe, and she had come because she could, if she would, tell him about Joe.

Hoping to lead her into being more open, he began to tell her about Joe's early life and later as a teenager. "Everyone loved him, no matter how mischievous or cantankerous he was," Luke said, and she smiled over at him. "He could steal a road sign or come in having partied too much or gotten a speeding ticket, and the reprimand would be there, but also the approving chuckles as if he'd done something others wanted to do but were afraid to."

She nodded. "He wasn't afraid of anything. He learned to surf and was becoming really good. He would do the hula at beach parties as well or better than the girls." They both laughed. Then she said quietly, "Everyone. . .loved him."

"You loved him very much, didn't you?"

He almost wished he hadn't asked. Of course she had. But the way she began to respond surprised him.

"I was nineteen. I fell for him hard the first time I saw him, because. . .he was so cute in his white navy uniform."

Wow! That took him aback like someone had hit him right between the eyes. That was called raw honesty. She looked away as if embarrassed. He wondered how many people would be so honest, even with themselves.

He was grateful for the distraction of the waiter setting their fish in front of them. After bites and comments, he decided to let her contribute information about Joe, instead of his asking.

"My first true love was in the first grade. It was her pigtails that got to me. They hung halfway down her back and were tied with ribbons. The blue ones with little sparkly stars were the prettiest. Perhaps the stars were just in my eyes."

"Oh," Amelia said, her dark eyes dancing. "My first true love was before I started to school. Georgie built me a sand castle. A wave came in closer and washed it away. He didn't just cry, he boo-hooed, and I had to console him. He didn't stop until I kissed him on the cheek."

"What did he do then, build another one?"

"No. He ran to his mother, who was sitting on a blanket, and he peeked out at me from behind her back."

They laughed. "Puppy love, I think it's called," Luke said.

"Yes. But it was serious."

"It always is. Especially in high school. The cheerleaders, you know."

"Careful," she said in a mock-threatening voice. "I was one of those."

"Oh." Luke cleared his throat. He probably shouldn't say what he was thinking. Most of the women and men he'd seen in Hawaii had great physiques. He assumed that was from surfing and swimming. All the moves of cheerleading would fit in with that, too. He observed, "So that's where you got your"—her chin came up slightly—"good, strong voice."

Mischief appeared in her eyes as if she knew what he was thinking. She smiled. "I think singing does that."

He nodded. "We young people used to sing at home. At church and around the piano sometimes. Joe always came out with a different version and made us laugh."

"He did that at our beach parties. He was fun."

That seemed to have brought them full circle, back to Joe. In the silence Luke felt the words. *Don't feel guilty.*

Another unexpected thought occurred. *Don't feel envious.*

Chapter 20

After dinner Amelia strolled with Luke beneath the massive banyan trees, with the deep blue ocean stretching into the horizon and the sun beginning to paint the sky with a gold and crimson glow. Others walking seemed to be families, probably tourists, and couples absorbed with each other.

She was conscious of her blessings of work, friends, family, and children. But a different kind of consciousness came to the forefront. Only now did she realize how much she missed having someone special in her life. There had been the thought of *someday*. The desire for that seemed more present in this romantic setting, walking with a man she could be interested in if the circumstances were different.

She liked the feeling of being alone with a man who said she was beautiful. For a moment she didn't want to think of him as just Joe's brother.

He gestured toward a bench. "Shall we sit and watch the sunset? I've never seen anything as spectacular as these."

She watched him relax against the back of the bench, looking content as he loosened his tie while gazing out at the reddening sky. The ever-active trade wind lightly teased the hem of her pink dress. She crossed her legs and laid her hand on her knee.

Luke's tie fell in two long strands down the front of his shirt, and he unfastened the top two buttons. He looked over at her. "I look like an islander now?"

"Not quite." She laughed and turned to loop the ends of the tie. "There, now it looks like a lei. Very Hawaiian." Aware of the warmth of his chest against her fingers, she returned her hands to her lap.

He smiled, and his gaze seemed to linger. She was aware of the reddish gold of his wavy hair and the flecks of gold in his eyes. "What are you thinking?" he said softly.

She hadn't been thinking at all, just aware. But a thought did occur. "I suppose you have a special girl back home."

His thoughtful hesitation made her wonder if his looking again at the sky was about the sunset or the question. The color of the sky deepened, and so did his voice. "No, not at the moment."

That piqued her interest.

"Oh there were special girls in college, but generally we related in groups. At Camp Lejeune, I had time for dates." He turned his head and glanced over at her. "Later, my being on the front lines vastly curtailed my social life."

"Undoubtedly." She gave a short laugh at the irony of that statement. "My dad says we're on the front lines of life in many ways, facing trials and adversities."

With a slight turn of her head, she saw Luke nod. "So true."

Just as she expected that conversation was over, he said, "After I reenlisted and knew I'd be sent into combat, I asked a girl to wait for me."

So there had been someone very special. "What did she say?"

His shoulders lifted as if the answer were obvious. "She said yes."

"Then you *do* have a special girl?"

"No."

Amelia could only surmise his girl must have died. She felt a chill and realized the sky had darkened and now they sat in the shadows. "I'm sorry," she said. "You still love her?"

"I always loved her." He spoke matter-of-factly. "She was a friend of the family. We were great friends. But before I was to go away, we became serious. Looking back, I think that seriousness was the fact that I was going away. We would be apart, and what we felt for each other was threatened by war." He heaved a sigh. "She said she'd wait for me forever."

Amelia felt like crying. "What happened to her?"

"Her affections switched to another."

She gasped, having trouble switching from sympathy to wondering how fickle his girl must have been. But that's what happened with William and Nell. "Was that sudden?"

He shrugged and turned his face toward her then. "How long does it take?" A fleck of silver lighted his eyes, and she realized the moon was beginning to cast a glow on the ocean. Stars began to appear in the sky.

"Sometimes it takes only a glance," Amelia said. She knew the first time she saw Joe that something clicked between them. Soon afterwards they spent every moment they could together.

"It wasn't really sudden. She'd known him as long as she'd known me. But he joined the service, came home on leave, and was—" His nostrils flared as he inhaled. Then he grinned. "He was real cute in his white sailor uniform."

How long her mouth remained open, she didn't know. Finally she closed it and gulped. A light seemed to come on in her mind, just as the moon was now lighting the landscape. "Was it. . .Joe?"

"Yes." He added quickly, "But in the letter he said he broke off with her and had met you. That's why I mentioned there was more in the letter. You've seemed reluctant to say much about Joe. I thought you might need reassurance of his love for you."

"Do you have the letter with you?"

He nodded and reached into his back pocket and brought out his wallet. He opened it and took out a thin sheet of paper and handed it to her. Amelia walked from the shadow of the trees onto the brightly lighted beach. She read it. The elation she might have felt that he gave up another girl for her was diminished by his saying he wasn't ready to settle down. Had he meant he hadn't been until he met Amelia? Or he hadn't been. . .at all?

She turned and saw Luke standing near her, looking down at his shoes lightly scuffing the sand. She handed him the letter. "So have you forgiven him?"

He stepped closer. "Oh yes, I've forgiven him. Joe couldn't help being the way he was. He attracted everyone to him. Always the life of the party."

Amelia nodded. She did know that. She'd been attracted to him. Did that make her shallow? But at age nineteen she was doing what young people did, dating boys on the base, having fun, getting to know each other. There were deeper things between her and Joe. Weren't there?

"But yes," Luke was saying. "I forgave them both. First, however, I had this big blowup with Joe. I punched him in the jaw. I wanted to fight him, my little brother." He inhaled deeply, now looking beyond her. "But he didn't hit me back. He said I could beat him up, but it wouldn't bring Penny back to me. I called him some dirty names and said neither of them was worth fighting about."

Amelia knew that had to have hurt.

Luke paced a couple of steps one way and then back. "He tried to talk to me before I went back to the base, but I wouldn't listen. I considered myself the mature one. And a marine, tougher than a sailor. I was the responsible one and Joe the fun one." He stopped and faced her again. "But my actions that day were those of an immature guy, not at all like an older brother should be."

He sounded forlorn. She knew he was hurting about that. "In his letter he didn't sound angry with you."

"That makes me feel worse."

She closed her eyes for a moment and nodded. How well she knew those feelings. She looked up at him again when he continued talking. "His not hitting me back made me angrier. But that anger and resentment helped me get through a lot of battles. Spurred me on because I couldn't take it out on Joe—he wouldn't fight me. But it wasn't because I lost my love. It was because I was humiliated. My pride and self-esteem had diminished. My little brother took my girl. That's what I told myself, and I decided neither of them were worth fooling with. I only saw him once after that."

"Were you still angry?"

He paced again. "Humiliated, I think is the word. Joe came to the train station. Penny was with him. They both wanted to talk, but I wouldn't. When the train pulled away, I did lift my hand in a good-bye gesture. You see, Mom and Dad were there, too. And friends. I told myself the wave was not to an unfaithful girl and double-crossing brother." He stopped and looked out at the ocean, shimmering silver in the moonlight.

She walked over to him, and they faced each other. He shook his head. "I've never told that to anyone before."

"I'm glad you did."

"So am I." He grinned then. "Nor have I ever said what I'm about to say. Unknown to others, I was somewhat of a romantic, too, wanting that special girl back home waiting for me. I visualized getting letters and cookies and red lipstick kisses on paper."

His glance seemed to rest on her lips for a moment, and she hoped the warmth that sprang into her face wasn't visible although the moon was bright. Was he remembering that she had refreshed her lipstick after dinner, before they'd gone for a walk?

His next words seemed strained. "Although I didn't want them to know it, my wave was for Penny and Joe, too. I knew I'd be sent to the front lines. I knew I might not come back. I never thought Joe. . .wouldn't."

She wanted to reach out and touch his hand. Maybe walk with him that way. Let him know she felt for him. She spoke softly. "Do you think you and Penny might become serious again?"

"No."

His blunt reply left his mouth almost before she finished the question. As if trying to cover it, he hugged his arms across his chest. "Getting chilly. We should go back."

They began to walk back across the sand. Amelia clasped her hands behind her back. Was he sorry he confided in her? Was he still angry? Hurt?

Or was it that he didn't take kindly to the concept of getting his younger brother's. . .hand-me-downs?

Chapter 21

Luke had mainly two things on his mind as he drove back to town. One, how much he'd enjoyed what seemed like just him and Amelia together during dinner for no other reason than two people on a date. He had become so vulnerable he'd opened his heart to her. The sharing felt right and good at the time. Afterwards he felt he'd told too much, and it made him realize how Amelia might feel talking about the past.

They'd seemed to relate as a man and woman on a date. On the beach, however, there was again the reason for their being together and memories of the past that weren't all pleasant.

He was sorry if he'd focused too much on himself and not enough on the reason for being on this island and with Amelia.

Maybe he could get her back to pleasant memories. "If you're not busy tomorrow," he said when they returned to the Matti-Rose, "is there somewhere we might go?" He expected a no.

She looked away from him and through the windshield. The moonlight lay softly on her face. "Since Wanda and the children are away, it would be the perfect time to clean house."

"I could help," he said. "I'm a decent volunteer."

Her gaze slid in his direction, and the warmth in them held a glimmer of mischief. "Or we could go see the Kona nightingales," she said, her eyes widening.

"What a choice," he mused. Watching the smug look on her face, he thought she was playing a game. "Kona," he said. "That's the best coffee I've ever tasted. Let's see. Nightingales are birds. Ah, the birds that sing at night in the Kona bushes?"

Her eyes lifted to the roof of the car for a moment then back at him. "Like Joe said, you have to see them to believe it."

That brought them back to Joe. Him, anyway. After all, that is what these excursions were about. Although there had been moments when he felt it was just him and Amelia, how could a guy—supposing he wanted to—compete with a dead war hero?

He reviewed that thought. No, it had not been vindictive. Regardless of what was to be or not to be for himself, he could not begrudge his brother any kind of happiness he might have had in his short life.

Don't feel guilty.

Don't be envious.

No, thank God that Joe *met* a girl like Amelia. And wrote to him about her.

"So," Amelia said, "have Delia make us some omelet sandwiches in biscuits, and we'll be on our way around eight o'clock."

"Is that a.m. or p.m.?" Her look of confusion made him laugh. "Night. . . ingales."

"Oh no. They're out in the mornings—eight o'clock a.m. And this is casual. You will definitely need an aloha shirt. And a bathing suit."

"Is there a place where I might buy those?"

"Many places."

He started to get out of the car and turned back. "Could I pick you up?"

She shook her head. "No. I'll be here."

He suspected her living quarters might leave something to be desired since she never let him pick her up there.

She grinned. "In the morning."

"Fantastic."

And that was the thought jumping into his mind when he saw her the following morning—fantastic. She walked into the dining room while he was drinking a cup of coffee and waiting for Delia to box up their breakfast.

She saw him immediately and strode toward him, wearing a red-lipstick smile that matched the red open shirt she wore over what appeared to be a brightly flowered bathing suit top. Her mid-thigh green shorts, matching the green leaves in the top, revealed what he'd already recognized as lovely, shapely legs. Her sandaled feet sported red toenails. She came up to him with a smile and held out a bundle.

"I called William last night, and he brought over some clothes this morning that might fit you. You two seem to be about the same size. I shouldn't have said you'd need to wear certain clothes."

"No?" He pretended to be insulted. "Then what's this bundle?"

She shook her head, and her long ponytail swished from side to side. "I mean, I shouldn't have made you think you would have to buy clothes."

He grimaced. "You mean, I could swim in my denim hiking clothes?"

She scoffed then. "Ha. You do that, and I might lose you in the ocean."

Would she mind. . .losing him?

She quickly turned her head toward the buffet bar. "If you want to try these on, I'll have a cup of coffee."

He took the bundle, drained his cup, and went upstairs to his room. He thought he was more muscular than William, but William was a couple of inches taller than he. He'd never worn a bathing suit that skimpy, but he knew he'd look weirder on this island in a boxer-style suit. He thought he looked to be in pretty good shape, if he didn't compare himself with some of those surfers he'd seen.

The tan-colored shorts fit well and reached to his knees. He'd seen many men in town and even in restaurants with their shirts open and their chests showing. He laughed at himself in the mirror as he buttoned the white shirt that had green palm leaves all over it. At least it wasn't flowers. Then he unbuttoned a second button. Yes, showing a little bit of masculine chest would be all right on a day like this.

He brushed his teeth and looked at himself again. His face had tanned, and his hair had grown longer than his conservative style. He'd been a soldier for so long he felt a little strange looking like a man, a carefree one at that. But he was dressed like William, and the day's excursion was in memory of Joe.

Would he ever be just Luke? He wasn't sure who or what that was anymore.

When he returned to the table, he felt he'd blushed for the first time in his life when Amelia gave a low whistle and looked at him with a teasing gleam in her eyes. "You no longer look like a tourist."

"I no longer feel like one." He picked up the cardboard box from the table.

"Okay," she said after she was in the passenger seat and he beneath the steering wheel. "We'll drive along the west side, along Queen Kaahumanu Highway."

At a certain point she said, "Pull off the road when you can."

He did and switched off the engine.

Her eyes scanned the landscape. "We might as well eat while we're waiting." She got the box from the floorboard and handed him a sandwich.

He stared at her.

"What?"

"Are we going to sit here and watch coffee bushes grow?"

"You object?" She took a bite of sandwich.

His glance swept over her as she ate. "Not at all." He took a bite of the sandwich.

He'd finished his breakfast, and she had only a little left when she pointed and spoke with a mouthful. "Umh. There."

He stared. "All I see is some kind of animal. A couple more are coming this way."

She swallowed and licked her lips. "Those are the Kona nightingales."

"In the States I believe we'd call that a donkey."

"Well," she said saucily, "in the States they don't carry coffee across the rocky terrain to the coffee mills."

"They do that, huh?"

"No. They used to. Since the war, the coffee is taken by jeeps."

The handsome animals came closer. They had long floppy ears, brown satiny coats, and big soulful eyes. "Why are they called nightingales?"

"Thought you'd never ask," she said. "There is a sweet, musical sound to their braying that you can hear in the quiet night. So they're called Kona nightingales."

They gracefully and slowly made their way across the road to the other side. "Beautiful animals," he said appreciatively.

She agreed. "But you see how dangerous it is for them. There is much debate about putting fences up or putting them in zoos. They have caused accidents at night when they're crossing the roads." She smiled at him. "Joe liked Kona coffee, too."

"We seem to like many of the same things."

Her tongue came out and touched her lower lip. And he saw her blink slowly. Did she think he was talking about her? Was that allowed? "Hmmm," he said, leaning toward her and peering out the window beside her. "I never would have imagined my brother and I would both like donkeys."

She gave a little laugh. His being the brother of Joe and wearing William's clothes didn't endear him to her in the slightest.

Not that he wanted it to.

It just reminded him of what might have been if he'd had a normal life without a war. But he wasn't the only person who thought those things. After all, it had been a world war.

"Next stop"—she pointed ahead—"the beach."

Chapter 22

Luke liked the playful manner in which Amelia threw down the blanket on a secluded part of beach near some boulders and threw off her shirt and shorts, revealing her bathing suit. She took the fastener from her ponytail and took off running down the beach. Her beautiful dark hair rippled in the wind like ocean waves, soft, revealing a blue black sheen beneath the sun. He shucked down to his suit.

She ran into the ocean, and he followed. He stopped at the edge, aware of the sand washing out from under his toes and the water rising and falling over his feet. Despite a twinge of uneasiness, he walked on in. When he neared her, she scooped up water and threw it into his face. She swam farther out. She could duck beneath a wave and come up still standing. He was hit with each wave and came up trying to swim.

"You fight the water," she said. "This is the way." She showed him how to be one with the ocean waves, not fight them but become a part of them, a part of nature, moving with the rhythm of ocean music. She was like music.

They swam far out, and Luke realized he had not swum since he'd almost drowned while trying to reach a foreign beach. He lay on his back and let the ocean rock him. Had she not said they mustn't go too far, he might have let the ocean take him where it would.

They swam back to shore, and she picked up a shell, held it to her ear and then to his. "This is what children do," she said.

His hand covered hers at his ear. Her eyes held a question. Why? Was it like a child wanting to know if he heard the ocean in the shell? He heard it, along with a warning voice, a cautious voice, a voice of reality saying she was showing him a child's game—this widow of his younger brother.

The swell of the waves seemed to be in his senses, and he forced the thought that a child would be waiting for his response. Do you like it? Are you intrigued? How should he answer the unasked questions?

He wanted to take something back to his parents. Would they want a shell? Could he take a shell and say, *This is from the beach where Joe ran and played in the ocean and had a girl, and they were happy and in love?*

"May I keep it?" he said. He wasn't thinking of his parents but himself. He would like to remember this day. It had felt like two people just enjoying the sun, the sand, the water, and. . .each other.

"Sure," she said, and he felt her hand move beneath his. She laid the shell in his open palm. He looked at the intricate markings and the color. The sound of the ocean was no longer in his ear, but the sounds of the entire ocean seemed to fill his being.

With a shell in his pocket, a camera in his hand, and Amelia by his side, he delighted in the afternoon of visiting Kona and the coffee plantation, seeing outrigger canoes gliding along the bays, and watching natives fish with spears on the coral reefs while Amelia told tales of the past, such as the king flinging a lock of hair into a stream of lava to appease the goddess of volcanoes.

He experienced the mixture of past and present and a strange kind of calm belonging to the magical place. He easily felt at one with others walking and running along the beach and hearing the laughter of children as they played on the sand and frolicked in the water.

He snapped pictures, careful to avoid Amelia. Finally he asked, "Could I have you in some pictures? Just for me? No one else would ever see them. I promise."

To his surprise, she consented. Perhaps she, as he often did, thought only of the fun time they were having together, without the intrusion of past memories. Or perhaps she'd begun to trust that he wouldn't mention her to his parents without her permission.

She led him to a luau taking place on green grass beneath swaying palms, with a view of the ocean.

"Are we crashing a party?"

"Sure." Then she grinned. "Kidding. A restaurant provides this for tourists or locals, for a small fee."

Pigs were roasting. Yellow tablecloths covered long tables, their edges dancing in the breeze. Pineapples and coconuts formed the centerpieces. Amelia and Luke stood in line and filled their plates from the buffet.

Before long, a man blew into a conch shell and announced entertainment while pretty girls in colorful dresses placed leis over each of their heads. A male quartet sang Hawaiian songs, while others strummed their ukuleles during the spectacular sunset.

"Now the hula," Amelia said, leaning toward Luke. She kept smiling at him as he alternately watched and glanced at her. Soon he knew why. The male and female hula dancers came around and invited everyone to dance, but they took the arms of him and Amelia and led them up front.

As the sky darkened, his spirits lightened. Luke followed instructions but saw that Amelia was as adept with the hula as she had been in the ocean. He felt it wasn't dancing but a gentle sway of the arms and body in rhythm with the ocean waves and the palm branches in the trade winds. Hawaiian air was flowers and music, and he felt lost in its spell.

Amelia's eyes were soft. Her face held an ethereal expression as if only this moment mattered. Was it at a luau that she had fallen in love with Joe?

"Enough for me," he said, feeling suddenly in Joe's shadow. "You keep on. I'll take pictures."

After he snapped a few, she came to sit beside him. Darkness fell, and they were entertained by a fire-sword dancer, athletic yet graceful as the fire made

ALOHA BRIDES

circles in the star-spangled night.

She sang some Hawaiian songs on the way back. He sang a few American ones she didn't know, and they sang together "I Got the Sun in the Morning and the Moon at Night."

They playfully challenged each other as they took parts in "Anything You Can Do." In the middle of "Zip-A-Dee-Do-Dah," Amelia stopped singing. "Look, Matilda's lights are still on. Should we stop and see her?"

"I'd love to," Luke said and pulled into the drive and parked in the clearing beneath the trees. He took his camera inside.

Matilda held open the screen door and welcomed them warmly. Soon they were sitting on the lanai, happily talking about the day they had spent together.

"Could I get a picture of you to take back to my parents?" he asked Matilda.

"Oh yes," she said. "If you like. I wish I could meet them. Here, take one of me and Amelia. I'd love to have that for my photo album."

"Sure," he said and gave a look at Amelia as if to say he'd keep his promise. She smiled. He snapped the pictures.

"Let me take one of you two," Matilda said and added, "For my album."

With the night as a background, they stood at the screened wall. Luke's arm went naturally around Amelia, and he felt her ribs move with her breathing as his hand touched her waist. But to move it away would seem awkward.

"All right," Matilda said, lowering the camera. "You two think about how Luke looked doing the hula." She lifted the camera as they both laughed, and the bulb flashed.

"I really need to go," Amelia said. "It's late."

Matilda bade them good night, and they walked out into the night. He tucked the camera into the deep pocket of the shorts. "I'll walk across to the Matti-Rose," he said.

Standing in the shadows beneath the trees, Luke again thanked her for the day. "It was wonderful. I'll never forget it," he said.

"It was for me, too," she said. "But—"

Before she could say more, the hand that had touched her waist came up to her lovely face, felt her smooth cheek, and her lips parted slightly with her soft intake of breath. Her shoulders rose slightly, as if she needed more breath. He did. No thought entered his mind at the moment but the beautiful girl standing so close, the feel of her skin, the soft parted lips, the questioning that gazed deep into his.

His errant fingers moved to her chin and tilted it as he bent to touch her lips with his. So soft, so sweet, and then he felt hers responding; he drew her close, felt the wild beat of his heart and the touch of her hand on his neck.

For a moment he yielded to the feel of this Jewel in the Sea being in his arms and his lips tasting paradise.

She was pushing him away, her hands on his chest and her head moving from side to side as she looked at the ground.

"I didn't mean. . . I'm—"

332

"No," she said. "Don't apologize. It wasn't just you." She backed closer to her car and put her hand on the handle. "I can't see you anymore," she said.

"Please." He held out his hand. "Forgive me. I promise it won't happen again. I'm sorry if I've offended you."

"No," she said. "It's not the kiss. I kissed you, too. If you apologize for that, then I have to apologize, too. I. . .wanted you to." Her shoulders rose again, and she drew a deep breath. "But I've shown you where Joe and I went, what we did. There is no more." He saw a tear glisten on her cheek and wanted to wipe it away, kiss it away.

He looked up toward the tree limbs that shadowed them. He saw her move and watched her turn the handle of the car door. Before he could find the words, she was in the driver's seat and had closed the door.

He leaned down to the open window as she started the engine. "One question," he said.

She looked at him, and he saw the sorrow in her eyes.

He heard the huskiness in his voice. "Was it the memory of my brother you were kissing?"

Her eyes closed, then they opened, and she stared straight ahead as she gripped the wheel. She nodded and whispered, "Yes."

Luke felt like a fool and stepped back. There he was feeling. . .something. . . for Amelia, only to find Joe had already been there, done that. He couldn't blame Joe. Amelia was a beautiful, desirable woman. And fun. But the fun day had been the memory of Joe and not because of Luke Thurstan.

He stood back and stared at the car as it backed into the street. Soon the red taillights disappeared.

The warmth of the day, the heat of the kiss disappeared, too, as if someone had dumped a pail of ice water over his head.

Chapter 23

On Sunday morning Luke felt uneasy and could hardly keep his mind on Pastor Grant's sermon. He felt as guilty as if he were the young boy who had pulled the pigtail of the little girl in school. He shouldn't have done it. It turned out all wrong. Now it was as if Pastor Grant and his organist wife and the congregation singing hymns were accusing, *You shouldn't have done that.*

He didn't see Amelia in church. Had he upset her so much she didn't even want to see him? Had it been *that* much of an indiscretion? Perhaps he shouldn't have, but it had been done because he'd forgotten in that moment they were anything other than a man and woman who had spent a wonderful day together. It was a caring gesture. Impulsive, yes, but not out of some disrespectful or selfish motivation.

William was there, and after the service ended, Luke walked across the aisle to him. "I thought I might see you here. I have your clothes in my car." He felt guilt again. Not only had he kissed his brother's wife, but he'd also kissed William's girlfriend. He forced his words. "I washed them last night."

"If you don't have plans," William said, "want to go out for lunch?"

"Sure. Shall I drive?"

"I will," William said. "Just leave your car here, and I can pick up my clothes when we get back."

Luke wondered if Amelia had told him about. . .the indiscretion. If so, William was doing a good job of keeping a pleasant "in church" expression on his face. If William wanted to sock him, the way Luke had socked Joe, then Luke wouldn't hit back. He'd feel a lot better if somebody did hit him.

While William drove, Luke told him about the day—with one omission—that he and Amelia had spent together: the dinner, the beach, the luau, the stopping by to see Matilda. "I appreciate her giving me a glimpse of what Joe might have done and seen." Luke told the facts, not the emotion. He told himself he would throw away that seashell and he'd give all the photos to Amelia and Matilda.

Luke did add, "I hope it's not a difficult time for Amelia, a stirring up of memories that may be best forgotten."

"I don't think so," William said. "It's best to face things, rather than push them aside."

A short while later they were eating at a table on the porch of an open-air restaurant, shaded by a roof and entertained by the rhythm of the ocean and happy voices from other tables.

Apparently thinking about the past, William began to tell Luke about Nell, and Luke shared about Penny. William said he wouldn't face it for a while. Then he made himself do it, and there was pain in the facing of it. He talked with Matilda, and that helped. "You can tell her anything. I know you can tell God anything, but Matilda talks back in an audible voice. And I think maybe it is the voice of God through her. She's discerning. When you feel so old and like life will never be good, she makes you realize you're young. Enjoy what you have. She says each loss helps you appreciate more whatever comes your way."

"It's worked out that way for you, hasn't it?" Luke said, thinking of William and Amelia. At least Amelia hadn't been thinking of William when she kissed him, but of Joe.

"The loving someone else, yes," William admitted.

Luke nodded. "You and Amelia have history in common. Your being a teacher and she a tour guide. I've learned more in a few days than I would have in months sitting in a classroom."

William laughed. "One-on-one teaching is always more effective than in a classroom of twenty-five to thirty. Amelia and I don't talk much about history. We both know it." His smiled faded, and he glanced toward the ocean. "What Amelia and I have most in common is Andy."

"I suppose you two have future plans."

William looked at him with a furrowed brow. Then it smoothed. "You mean, together?"

Luke halfway shrugged and nodded.

"No. She's always been Andy's little sister to me. Always will be. If anybody, it's Wanda." He grimaced and covered his mouth with a couple of fingers then seemed to play with his chin. "I shouldn't have said that. I've never said it. I refuse to think and try not to feel it."

"Not a chance there?"

"I don't think so. She was Andy's girl. Then his wife. That was not even thinkable then. Maybe it shouldn't be now. Be friends. But somehow it seems taboo for me and Andy's wife. She's Andy's widow. She was always a great person, for Andy. Wouldn't I be dishonoring him to even consider anything other than friendship?"

"William, I think he'd be pleased."

"It's something that had never crossed my mind and wouldn't have if Andy were alive. One just doesn't go there. Then, it was as if she were a sister."

"But that's changed."

"For me," he admitted. "We went through loss together. I help any way I can, and we do things with the children. We talk about Andy."

William stared at Luke for a long moment then said slowly, "Like you and Amelia are remembering Joe."

Luke tried to cover his momentary discomfort by keeping the attention on William. "Sounds like you're in love with Wanda."

He nodded. "I didn't mean to be. We've relied on each other. Helped each other cope, become familiar with each other. I can't even consider anyone else.

But she's my friend's widow."

Luke's fingers played with his glass of fruit drink. But he saw a beautiful young woman with big brown eyes, a smile on her relaxed face, her cheeks plump with a smile from the lips he had kissed.

My brother's widow.

What was protocol? What was ethical? Having no idea how much time had passed since William's remark, Luke nevertheless said, "I know what you mean."

William held his gaze for an instant, and then he looked out over the ocean. His solemn expression seemed to say, *And I know what you mean.*

Chapter 24

Luke felt he had no reason to remain in Hilo except to wait until his pictures were developed. He could have William pick them up. Had he not met Amelia, he might have enjoyed touring the islands with a group or alone. He might have met someone else, and they could have enjoyed the time together without the kind of memories that kept them apart.

But *what if* didn't exist—only *what is*. With so many feelings about Joe, Amelia, himself, Luke couldn't simply turn around and be a fun guy. He needed to get back to the States instead of this magical place. In the States he would face the reality of everything.

In the meantime he needed to do what he had come here for in the first place. For himself, he needed to act like a responsible adult, not like some kid running away from some foolish happening. He hadn't done anything so terrible, just a normal, natural thing that couldn't be reciprocated.

Luke didn't see a need to explain anything to Pastor Grant. They had left everything up to Amelia, so Luke would leave it there. He did feel that the pastor's eyes followed him speculatively on the work site.

"I'll be leaving soon," Luke told him.

The pastor seemed to accept the news with a nod, and he expressed heartfelt thanks for Luke's help in Hilo. At one point Pastor Grant looked off into the distance and briefly shook his head as if he'd like to say something. But he didn't. Except to wish Luke well. "I am sorry things didn't work out so you could stay around, at least for a while."

"So am I," Luke said truthfully. "But it's time I returned. My parents are anxiously awaiting any word I have about Joe."

The pastor's eyes seemed to ask if he had a lot of good things to report. But his tongue didn't ask it. Their eyes locked for a long moment before Luke looked away. He nodded to the pastor and walked off. What word could he report about Joe? That a friend had taken him to eat in a restaurant where Joe had eaten, had taken him to a beach and a luau like Joe had gone to? At least he could talk about meeting William, although William hadn't known Joe. He could tell them about Matilda. It would please his mom to know Joe was acquainted with a woman like her.

He could say he met a pastor who remembered Joe.

But no girl.

Joe had always had a girl since he was a toddler.

Luke doubted he could speak happily about his time in Hawaii. But then, his parents probably wouldn't want him to have had happy times in the place where Joe lost his life.

Luke returned to Pearl City and parked on the hill overlooking the harbor. He stood alone, looking down at the clear water, remembering the news releases of Japan bombing Pearl Harbor. He could see it, hear it, feel it. And experience the loss.

He emptied his heart to Joe. Forgave him for taking Penny from him, although he'd come to realize that relationship had been a fantasy. War itself couldn't be a reality; it had to be a concept of courage, bravery, freedom, self-defense, survival.

Then Luke did what he'd really come for. He asked Joe to forgive him. Forgive him for any and every childish meanness he'd shown, every word, every attitude, every jealousy, anything negative. Those times had been few and not really serious. He and Joe had loved each other, but Luke longed so much for Joe to be alive.

Forgive me, Joe, for my immature behavior toward you when I thought I was a grown-up teen and you a brat. Forgive all the petty things I said or did or felt. I'm sorry our last time together wasn't pleasant.

From your letter I know you forgave me. That's how you are, how you were. You were a great guy. I wish we could be together now. Forgive my attitude about Penny and about you giving her back to me. You picked great girls, Joe. The best.

Without realizing what he was doing, Luke found himself on his knees, and his words were sobs. "I miss you, Joe. I love you. And I'm sorry if I dishonored her memory of you, that I gave her something to regret instead of having respect for your older brother. You see, I'm not that good, responsible, serious older brother you thought I was. I've made my mistakes; I've sinned. But I love you, Joe."

If you had lived, would you have given Amelia to me? I think you would have kept her. I can't ask you to forgive me for how I've come to care for her because that has nothing to do with you. It's my own private business. I always loved you, Joe. I always will. But this is good-bye. Aloha.

Luke began to tell Joe how glad he was that he'd known Amelia, the good times they'd had together, and that he was glad Joe and Amelia had enjoyed even better times because they were in love. "I can understand how happy you must have been with her. And I'm glad. I'm glad you had that." He took a shaky breath. "God, forgive me." At that moment he realized Jesus had died so that Luke Thurstan's sins could be forgiven. Luke only had to accept that and forgive himself.

Finally he looked up and had to wipe away the moisture before he could see the blue sky clearly. His face was soaked, soaked with the release of guilt, the thanking of God for His presence and for sparing his life, and the tears from praying he would live in a way—like he'd promised on the front lines—that would honor God.

Standing, Luke wiped at his face, smiled down, and waved as if Joe were there looking up and, as Amelia had said, looking cute in his white uniform, smiling—no, he'd be laughing and waving and beckoning.

A strange feeling came over Luke. He looked around. He felt as if an arm had come around his shoulders. The wind seemed to whisper, "Hey, bro. Welcome to Paradise."

Luke felt the breeze on his face, drying the tears. He felt the burden gone. God had forgiven Joe, too, for everything wrong he'd ever done or said. Luke remembered when a young Joe had given his heart to Jesus and the look of wonder on his face when he came up from the baptismal waters. Luke spoke aloud with confidence as he looked into the clear blue sky. "Thank You, Lord, that Joe is in a place even better than Paradise. He's probably entertaining the angels."

He decided if he were going to get on with his life, he needed to start in this place Joe called Paradise. He took a helicopter tour over the volcanoes and to the other islands, striking up conversations with a couple of guys from Scotland who had come for the sole reason of enjoying the islands. Luke spent an entire day on Maui with them. The following day they left, and he had conversations with others on the tours. He enjoyed the scenery and slept well a couple of nights in hotels. No, his life wasn't settled, but he felt at peace.

Luke reasoned away any guilt about kissing Amelia. He was a man attracted to a lovely young woman with whom he'd had some extraordinarily good times in a fantastic place. He'd been without female companionship for several years except the times he'd had leave from his duties, and his behavior had not been exemplary. With Penny, it had been out of his need for someone back home to wait for him.

He knew what to do. He'd pick up his photos and then he'd make flight reservations for returning home. He'd take brochures and memories of the place where Joe had been happy, even though he'd promised not to tell his parents about Amelia. But he could say he met a girl who knew Joe. And he could say she was a preacher's daughter. They'd like that.

Luke picked up the pictures from the drugstore and stopped by to see Matilda and say good-bye. "I'll be leaving soon," he said.

"Leaving? Then you have everything settled within yourself."

"For the most part, but I may have added something else to feel guilty about."

He didn't say what, and Matilda didn't ask. She just looked at him with compassion and smiled.

"So," Luke said, "perhaps it's time I returned to the States and settled in my own life."

"Settled?" Matilda questioned.

Yes, he was thinking. Maybe it was time to forget about. . .sparks. . .and settle. And there was no reason for him to stay in Hilo. He had left Joe and Penny in anger before he went off to war and had never seen Joe again. He'd left buddies on a battlefield. He didn't ever want to leave anyone like that again. He didn't want to harbor ill feelings. He wanted to tell Amelia good-bye and wish her well.

"Can you tell me where she lives?"

"I'm sorry," she said. "I can't. You'll have to find that out for yourself."

What was this? If Amelia lived in a run-down shack and didn't want him to know, he'd help even if he had to do it anonymously.

Like a lightbulb going on, he knew what he had to do. Matilda wouldn't divulge confidences or anything she thought another person wouldn't want her to. But even the desk clerk or Delia would probably simply say where Amelia lived if he asked.

After returning to his room at the Matti-Rose, he opened the drawer and took out the phone book. There it was. The only Thurstan listed in the book. Amelia Thurstan. The phone number and street address.

Going downstairs, Luke asked the clerk where the street was.

"About a mile away," he said and gave simple directions.

On the short drive Luke reminded himself he was at peace about everything. He prayed for his calm to last. He would simply give all the photos to Amelia, thank her, and say he enjoyed knowing her. He would leave anything else up to her if she wanted to say anything. If not, he'd say good-bye and return to the States with his newfound sense of calm. He didn't need to take any of the pictures home with him. He might even leave the shell in his room at the Matti-Rose.

After the short drive he turned onto the right street and began looking for the house number. The houses were small cottages but appeared to be nicely built. The neighborhood was nothing to be ashamed of as far as he could tell.

He slowed and came to a complete stop outside the house. He picked up the packet of pictures. When he exited the car, he saw a dark-haired boy roll a rubber ball to another boy. It was the other boy Luke couldn't take his eyes off.

Capturing his attention was a little boy with a beautiful tan and a flock of blond curls spilling over his forehead. He was playing ball with the dark-haired boy who looked to be a couple of years older.

Any calm he had felt was gone. Truth hit him in the gut like a tsunami.

And the dark-haired boy confirmed facts when he said, "Catch it, Little Joe."

Chapter 25

The older boy ran toward the house. "Mom, some man is here!"

Luke's gaze was locked on the little towheaded boy named Joe, whose eyes were as clear as the bright blue sky. Luke had seen, had known such a boy before.

"You wanna play catch?"

Luke nodded. It was like hearing that many years ago. The boy threw the ball. Luke tossed it easy to make sure the boy wouldn't miss. His hands moved automatically, but his mind had stopped.

Then it started again. He was in his own backyard. He was teaching Joe to catch. He'd become impatient. Joe had cried. Now Little Joe was making Luke cry.

Luke felt the ball hit his leg. All he could do at the moment was turn to a nearby tree, lean his head against it, and let the tears flow.

Feeling a tug on his pants, he looked down at the soulful eyes of the boy.

"I'm sorry," the boy said.

"It's okay." Luke forced the words out. "It's my fault. I haven't learned to catch well yet."

The boy's hopeful gaze met his, and he smiled broadly. "I'll teach you."

"Okay." Luke dried his eyes as best he could, and they tossed the ball back and forth.

"You're doing good."

"Thank you," was all Luke could think to say, and he didn't know if he could take his eyes off the child, not even when he heard the screen door open and someone make a sound like a gasp or a wail.

He kept tossing the ball, not wanting to look away, afraid the boy might miss. . .or disappear.

A voice said, "Amelia, you have to say something." The same voice then said, "Parker, you play ball with Joe. Go on. Over there at the side of the house."

Luke watched the boys move several yards away and begin chattering as they threw the ball. Finally he turned his head and saw the pale face and fearful eyes of Amelia. Beside her stood a dark-haired woman who put her arms around a young girl's shoulders and said, "Let's go inside, Ellie."

That woman would be the one with Andy Grant's last name.

Amelia had Joe's last name.

Why?

Why had she not told him? He was more confused than ever about Amelia's reticence. The little boy was his brother's son.

341

He managed to take a few steps closer to Amelia, now alone on the porch. He could hardly breathe. His mouth moved before his voice. Finally he choked out, "Little Joe?" But she didn't need to say anything. Her trembling lips, glistening eyes, and the boy himself said it all. "He's. . .your son?"

"Yes, he's mine. And you have no right."

"No right?" This was unbelievable. Fighting the urge to shout and frighten the children, he ground out, "My brother's son. My nephew. My parents' grandson. And you weren't going to tell me?"

Her voice was a sob. "I couldn't."

His voice threatened. "You will."

She paled and appeared to shrink as if the life had gone out of her. His mind seemed to echo with that one word—*why*?

Looking around helplessly, he saw the packet of photos he didn't know he had dropped. He'd brought them for Amelia. Photos she didn't want his parents to see. He snatched them up and stared at the woman he had thought he'd begun to know. He didn't know her at all.

In the shock of it all, he hardly knew what he was saying. But he knew one thing, and he said it to her: "All promises are off." He strode to the car and returned with the camera.

He heard no protest from her this time. But it wasn't her picture he was taking.

He snapped pictures of Little Joe and Parker as they played ball. Little Joe, with his twinkling blue eyes and laughter, became an actor, posing, making faces. . .like his dad would have done.

This surely had to be a dream. He didn't even know why he felt compelled to take pictures. Maybe because he had to do something that appeared ordinary in this unbelievable situation.

His attention finally turned back to Amelia, who was holding onto the post at the front porch, fear all over her face. She whispered, "Let's go somewhere and talk."

"Yes," he said ironically. "Let's."

After telling Wanda, she said, "I'll drive." He thought she was in no emotional shape to drive. Come to think of it, neither was he. They rode in silence up the curving road until she parked in a clearing and got out of the car. She led them to a secluded spot in the shade of trees, high above a rocky part of the beach where angry waves pushed and retreated and pushed again. Off to the right, a long waterfall plunged for about a hundred feet into the churning water below.

Amelia sat on a smooth, flat-topped boulder, facing the ocean. Luke sat near her with his knees bent and his arms around his legs as he watched her expressions. Why would she bring him to a place like this? He needed a setting of peace to calm his frustration, which matched the churning water.

He waited for some reasonable explanation from this person he had wanted to know.

Finally she began to speak. Her tone was sad. "Joe and I were not married.

We were dating. We climbed those rocks after having a beach party with friends. That night we didn't leave when the others did." Her voice lowered. "Neither of us planned what happened."

This was not the part he needed or wanted to hear. Did she mean that's why she and Joe had a hasty marriage? "You don't have to tell me—"

"Yes I do." Her voice was shaky, but she seemed to draw strength from somewhere. "You came here to learn about Joe. I'm part of that." She paused and began again. "I was overwhelmed by Joe. He was all a girl could want: a handsome American in a white uniform. I was the most envied girl on the base. He was fun, the one all the girls liked, but he chose me."

Luke wanted to get up and walk away. Not hear any more. But he needed to know. What had happened in this secluded place at night? Had Joe taken advantage? So he listened while the waves splashed and pounded the rocks below as the story began to do in his heart.

"We were on a blanket beneath the stars, above the city. Our inhibitions were lowered just by our being alone up here, no longer with the gang. He said he might be shipped out. The thought of being separated seemed unthinkable. We didn't talk of marriage, just the possibility of being apart."

Luke knew that story. He'd lived it. "Before you say any more, Amelia, I want to tell you something." She had confessed to him as if he were a priest or something. "After Penny broke off with me, I used that as an excuse. But I would probably have done the same things even without an excuse. I dated girls every chance I had. I sinned. I didn't pretend it was in the name of love. You're far from the only one."

She was nodding. "I know that. But when I stand before God"—her lips trembled—"I am the only one."

"Yeah." He agreed with that. "You know, when the Lord forgives, it's like the sin is cast into"—he gestured toward the water—"the deepest ocean."

She slid a glance his way. "I'm a preacher's daughter, remember? I know all that. And when I look at Little Joe and all the good that has come from it, I've counted my blessings for a long time now. Then you came and stirred it all up again."

This muddled his mind. He could almost understand that neither Matilda nor William would blurt out that Amelia and Joe had a child. Matilda had encouraged him to stay in Hawaii. William had offered to be his friend. Maybe they had wanted him to know. "Your parents," he said. "How could they not tell me?" He scoffed. "Your dad—the preacher."

She was shaking her head with her eyes squeezed shut. "I made them promise. From the very beginning that was easy because they had their problems and grief."

Promise? Not to tell that she and Joe *had* to get married? "Okay," he said. "Let's leave them out of it. Why did you not want me to know? Why did you not want—"

He had to take a deep breath and try to control the emotion inside him before saying the little boy's name. He wanted to see him, hold him, know him. His brother's son. He tried again. "Why didn't you want me and Little Joe's grandparents to know about him?"

Was she ever going to answer? Finally she did. "At first, it was just dealing with the situation. Joe was gone, and I was having a baby. I lost my brother, and Wanda lost her husband." She glanced at him and away again. "There was a war," she said as if he had forgotten. "Everything here was changed. My baby became the good thing in the midst of all the awful things going on."

"You didn't think it might have been that way for my parents?"

"Not when my entire world had turned upside down. Time passed before we could think like that. My dad asked. But I didn't know how to get in touch with a last name in Somewhere, USA."

"But after I came here—"

"I was afraid. I am afraid."

That was incomprehensible. "Of what?"

She bent her head and looked down. "Of what is happening. Your anger. Your determination to make Little Joe known to your parents." Her voice grew softer. "Of what you all can do to me and my son."

He grimaced. "Do? What do you mean? We don't want to. . .hurt you."

"When you know the truth."

"Truth?" he questioned.

"You weren't listening close enough. I said when Joe and I came up here, we weren't married."

"I got that, Amelia. So you thought you had to get married."

"No." She jumped up. "I lied. Even my parents don't know I lied. You and your parents could undo the life I've made for myself and Little Joe." Misery was written all over her face. "I have a child," she said on labored breaths. "And I'm not married." She was sobbing now. "Joe and I were not married." She put her hands over her face.

Startled, Luke stared as she turned and ran away, toward a steeper part of the cliff. She reached the edge as if she intended to fling herself down the waterfall and into the rocks and fierce water below.

Chapter 26

Horrified, Luke pushed himself up and darted after her. He grabbed her, turned her, moved away from the edge, and held her close while she cried against his chest. He felt her suffering body, her hurting heart against his own.

Not married?

She was not Joe's widow?

That cleared up a lot of questions about her and Joe. Why a hasty marriage didn't seem to fit in the time line along with the letter. Why she had taken Joe's last name.

Hardly aware that his hand was in her hair, gently caressing, he tried to comfort her.

Her voice was muffled. "When I knew I was going to have a baby, I planned to tell Joe that night. But that morning the bombers came."

Luke knew he couldn't even imagine what it must have been like for a teenager to be with child and learn the one she loved had been killed in that sudden attack. Then all chaos broke loose.

Joe had been little more than a kid, too, in his early twenties. He hadn't had a lot of practice in self-discipline. Did he take advantage? Then Luke heard himself groan. How could he even attempt to place blame? This was not a time for that, and he wasn't the person for it.

Amelia was no longer sobbing but taking deep breaths. He felt her warm body against his and knew desire and temptation could easily erase anything else from the mind. If he had been here alone with Amelia, at night, and if she loved him. . .

Moving his hand away from her hair, he stepped back and placed his hands on her shoulders. When she lifted her face, he held it in the palms of his hands and gently wiped her tears with his thumbs.

The expression in her eyes seemed to say she needed, wanted him not to think ill of her. What did she think he'd do?

Condemn?

No one in the world had any right to do that.

Reality began to replace the shock he'd known from the moment he realized who Little Joe was.

A part of Joe. . .was alive.

Luke felt. . .joy.

He even felt the irony of the situation bubbling up in his throat, and it came out as a laugh.

345

Looking at her puzzled face, he tried to explain his reaction. "No one can blame you for taking Joe's name. You were trying to make things easier for your son."

She looked away. "Not just for him. For me, too. I felt such guilt. It was a shame. And a sin." She faced him again. "I know God has forgiven me. But for such a long time, I felt unclean anyway. I'd disappointed myself and my parents and everyone. And I've lived with the lie of making myself known as Mrs. Thurstan."

"Now you've told me. Now I know, and"—he looked up—"the sky didn't fall."

She grinned, and color touched her pale cheeks. "I feel better saying it. Telling you. But. . ."

He waited.

She took a deep breath. "That's only the beginning of what I'm afraid of."

There was more?

He looked around. This was her and Joe's place. "Could we go somewhere else? Have a cup of coffee or something?"

She nodded. They walked back down to the car, and he got into the driver's seat. She handed him the keys. He tried not to speculate what more there could be. Earlier they had passed a small restaurant on the edge of a town, so he stopped there. They sat in a corner booth, away from any window and from the few other patrons scattered about the room.

Luke ordered coffee for them both while Amelia went to the restroom— "to repair my face," she said.

Her face hardly needed repairing. He hadn't noticed or cared if there were any makeup smudges. What he'd seen were the heartfelt, soul-wrenching tears of a young woman feeling guilt and pain and remorse for living with secrets. He saw a courageous girl who had kept her baby and had raised him without a dad.

She'd held all this in for almost five years. He was glad she'd confided in him. His thoughts stopped. But she hadn't confided as friend to friend. Or as if he was someone special. She'd felt compelled to tell him.

But she'd also said. . .there was more.

The waitress brought the coffee. Soon afterward Amelia returned. Her face was still as beautiful as ever. He felt a smile seeing some wetness at her hairline. She must have splashed cold water on her face.

He stirred cream in his coffee then took a sip. "Now," he said, hoping he was ready for whatever other disclosures she might make. "You want to tell me the rest?"

She nodded. "First I want you to understand my keeping all this from you was nothing against you or your parents. I thought I was protecting my child. I was afraid you would find out about him."

He had seen that reluctance, that fear in her. "You were afraid we wouldn't accept you or Little Joe?" He looked around and lowered his voice. "Because you weren't married to Joe?"

She shook her head. "I was afraid of how you could disrupt our lives."

Many questions jumped into his mind at that, but he needed to let her talk. He picked up his cup and sipped his coffee.

She poured cream into her cup and stirred then took a sip. "I told everyone, except Wanda and Matilda, that Joe and I secretly married. I don't know if they believed me. I thought that was best. We had lost Andy. We were all grieving over that. Everyone's lives had been turned upside down, there was so much uncertainty after the bombing, and I thought it best for the baby to have his father's name. I thought of the shame I would bring on my parents. I mean, I'm a preacher's daughter. And my mom is as perfect as anyone can be."

Luke nodded. "I can understand that. You did what you thought best."

She nodded. "And while I'm being honest, I might as well say I did it for me, too. I didn't like the idea of being Miss Amelia Grant who has a child. I preferred being Mrs. Thurstan."

Luke thought that had a nice sound to it. He looked at his cup and took another sip.

"You see, I didn't know what kind of person you were. And you talked about your parents, especially your mom, having a hard time coping with Joe's death. Sometimes people do wrong things for the right reason."

He felt his brow wrinkle. "What do you mean?"

She took a deep breath as if the conversation were getting more difficult. "I mean, sometimes people don't know what the right thing is to do. Like, I don't know if it's best I took the name of Thurstan. Did I do the wrong thing for the right reason, or the right thing for the wrong reason?" She shrugged.

"But what does that have to do with being afraid of me and my parents?"

She took a deep breath. "I was afraid they might try. . .to take him."

"Take him?" He frowned. "What does that mean?"

Her reluctance to speak was obvious. "I've been afraid if your family knew about Little Joe they would try to get him, to give them a reason to hope. That happened to a girl here. She thought it would help a family if they knew there was a baby. But there was a court case, and they tried to take the baby, wanted to raise it on the mainland."

"Did they succeed?"

"No. But it was an awful time. Her reputation was ruined. She did have enough people speak up for her so that she got to keep the baby. I've been afraid that my life would become public and feared what that would do to my family. And me. And Little Joe."

"My parents would never do anything to hurt you or Little Joe."

She was nodding. "I think your parents are good people. They must be, to have raised Joe. . .and you." She paused, a troubled look on her face. "The people who brought that court case were good Christian people, too. She didn't have family. Their only son had been killed. They believed they were doing what was best for the baby."

Luke didn't know if he should say what was on his mind. But she had been honest with him, so he would try. "Amelia, believe me. My parents would try and help anyone in need, but the problem here is my parents, especially my mom, might not be able to accept. . ."

His voice trailed off. He saw the dawning in her eyes of what he was about to say. He hated to say it but added, "A mixed-race child. It's not you," he hastened to say. "It's that concept. The Japanese killed Joe."

She was quiet for a long time. "I didn't think of it that way." After another long moment of thought she traced the rim of her cup with her finger. "Do you think, if Joe had lived after the attack, he could have accepted the Japanese part of me?"

Luke wouldn't have known the answer to that if he hadn't come here, hadn't met Amelia. But he knew it now. "I had to be trained to hate the enemy. They weren't individuals. Joe's loving and accepting you came naturally, came easily. He would have known you weren't the enemy. He would have felt the same after the bombing."

She spoke softly. "I'm not sure. . .he loved me."

"I am," Luke said.

She scoffed. "You can't know that."

"Yes I can." He heard the revelation in his voice. "It's all in the letter. Your name, his letting Penny know. Mentioning a preacher's daughter. Saying that I'm the better man."

Something strange dawned on him. "Remember Matilda saying Joe wanted to live all of life quickly? He had to know he could be sent away and could die. Maybe he had a premonition. He might have suspected you were with child. Maybe that letter was a way of taking responsibility, just in case anything happened to him."

Her soft brown gaze met his. She spoke slowly. "You really believe that?"

He hadn't thought of the letter in that way until now. But yes, he was beginning to believe it. Whether it was Joe or God, he didn't know. But it was no coincidence he was here and having this conversation with this young woman.

The waitress was approaching with a pot of coffee. Their cups were empty. But they needed to be filled with something more than coffee. Luke lifted his hand in a gesture to ward off the waitress. His hand reached over and took Amelia's in his. "Let's pray," he said.

Although surprise leaped into her eyes, she extended both hands, and he held them. He'd never asked to pray on the spot with anyone like that. Prayer was in a group or in private. He did know his most heartfelt prayers had been an awareness while confronting the enemy and at Pearl Harbor.

Holding her hands, he took a deep breath, bowed his head, and closed his eyes. "Father God, thank You that the answers to our deepest concerns lie with You. We ask You now to look at this situation. Thank You for the blessing of this child we're talking about. Help us accept Your forgiveness of our sins. Wrap Your arms around Amelia and give her peace. Let her trust You. You brought me here for a reason far beyond our understanding. Help me to be a comfort to

Amelia and her family, not a hindrance. Thank You for intending good to those who love You. Show us how to love You and trust You. Amen."

She whispered "Amen," and looked across at him and smiled. "Thank you."

He wasn't sure he could take his eyes off the softness in her face, the tenderness in her eyes. For a long moment he held her hands and didn't realize the grip he had on them until he felts hers move from his.

It dawned on him that was how a relationship should be. Two people praying together. Not being selfish about what each wanted and having his own way. Seeking God's way. He wasn't even sure what he'd said. But it felt good, praying for her, with her.

Looking around, he saw the waitress steal a glance their way so he motioned her over. She came and refilled their cups. After adding cream, he stirred his coffee then glanced over at Amelia. "I came here thinking we might be able to donate to some cause in Joe's memory. My parents want to do something memorable with the insurance money. Joe's son has a right to his father's inheritance."

"No," she said. "He's never lacked for anything."

"That's not the point. I will try to do what I feel is right. Your boy has a right to know his family. They have a right to know about him. But you don't have to fear my parents doing anything to harm the relationship between you and your son. I would fight against my parents if they tried."

He almost added, *I promise*. But she might remember his outburst in her yard when he'd said, *All promises are off*.

This one was not.

Her voice held awe. "After all my secrets and lies and trying to keep you from knowing about Little Joe, I'm astounded you would do that for me."

He might have said, *I want you to like me, Amelia, trust me*. Instead he said, "It's the right thing."

Her tender expression touched his heart. Rather than put his self-interests ahead of what God had in mind, he repeated what she had said when he'd held her in his arms and they had kissed. "And I'm thinking of Joe."

Chapter 27

D ad, I need you!" Amelia sobbed when she entered her parents' home. "I don't know what's going to happen."

He led her into his study, along with her mom, and closed the door, like he often did when a church member came to talk about a problem.

"I've lied to you," she began. "Joe and I never. . .married." Seeing their steady gazes, she got the distinct impression they had suspected that and weren't surprised. She expected scripture from her dad and condemnation from her mother. But both remained silent, perhaps waiting for her to say. . .more.

She looked down. "I've lied to others, too. I've been believed when I said records were lost in the bombing. You know that happened to so many. I'm sorry. I—"

Her dad interrupted. "Amelia. That was a difficult time for all of us. You are our daughter, and you always will be. We're here for you, regardless."

She looked at her mom, who rarely had any expression on her face other than kindness and goodness. The only time Amelia had seen anything else was when her mom opened the front door to two uniformed officers. She'd known her son was dead.

She'd sympathized when Amelia told her Joe had been killed. They had cried together. She hated seeing her mother cry. Two months later she told her mom and dad that she had secretly married Joe and she was pregnant.

Now what would her mother say? That she was a liar? That she had fooled them all? She hadn't been honest. She didn't deserve. . .Little Joe?

"I thought it was best for Joe to have his daddy's name." She closed her eyes and felt the sting of hot tears on her cheeks. "I thought it best. . .for me."

"Honey," her dad said. "It's okay. Everything's okay."

She felt a soft hand on hers and looked. Her mother's graceful hand, with the long tapered fingers and rings she wore, lay on Amelia's bare one. "Come with me, Amelia."

Her mother sounded so calm. Did nothing ever touch her except the death of her son? Was she strong? Or. . .unfeeling?

They walked out into the backyard, in the midst of her mother's flowers. Amelia waited.

Her mother sat in a rattan chair, so Amelia sat across from her, looking at her mother's folded hands resting on her lap.

"I want to tell you a story," her mother said.

What? Amelia wondered. The story of David and Bathsheba, whose sin led to the loss of their first child? David had been a man after God's own heart. God forgave him as he forgave Amelia. But David paid the consequences. Is that the story her mother would tell her?

"I failed you, Amelia."

Amelia's mouth dropped open. That was the last thing she expected to hear. And she'd never seen her mother look so uncertain.

"I have felt inadequate. Andy was easier, being a man, and Jacob taught him men's ways. But you were my little *Haole*. My little white girl. I learned Haole ways. But inside, I was Japanese. I felt I wasn't good enough. I blamed myself any time you were unhappy or different from me. Amelia, I always felt I didn't measure up."

"No, Momma," Amelia said. "I thought the same about me. Momma, you're perfect."

"Oh my child! You're more than perfect. I love you more than air. I thought you might be ashamed that I am Japanese."

"I never thought that," Amelia said. "Even once. You were just my perfect mother, more beautiful than anyone, and I felt ugly, less."

Her mother was shaking her head. "I have been accepted because everyone knows my story of turning down the man in the days of the picture brides. And Matilda taking me in as if I were her daughter. And then I married a Haole preacher. And I had two beautiful Haole children. It is others who have made me accepted. Not because of me. And here, in Hawaii, being a Haole is better than being beautiful." She touched Amelia's face. "But you are both a Haole and beautiful."

Amelia was stunned that her mom was being so open and frank with her. Had Amelia ever given her the chance to be so honest with her?

Her mom spoke softly. "I was sixteen when I crossed an ocean for endless months as a picture bride to marry a man I didn't know. If he had not been a middle-aged man, I would have married him. But he was too old for me, and he had lied about his age."

Amelia closed her eyes at that. She knew her mother's story.

"I did not love the man I would have married if he had been of a reasonable age for me. Later I fell hopelessly, helplessly in love with Jacob. If he would have let me, I would have done anything he asked of me. I would have traveled with him to the mainland while he went to seminary. I was nineteen then, your age when you and Joe were together. If Jacob had come to me the night before he left for the mainland, I would have done anything he would allow me to do. It was your father's goodness that kept us pure before marriage, not mine. So I cannot condemn you."

"You're good, Mama. You're kind and caring."

Her mother shook her head. "Amelia, many things I do are because I am a preacher's wife. I want to do them, yes. I'm grateful for the opportunity. I want to be a good influence and help the Japanese, and I can because I understand them. I want to comfort the sick and grieving. I want to teach the Bible. But that's not what makes me good. I am good because I am forgiven of my sins. I am forgiven of my sins because Jesus Christ died on the cross for them. He became the sacrifice. He paid the penalty."

Amelia could hardly believe what she was hearing. She felt as if her world were silent. This woman was Akemi Grant, a person separate from Amelia Grant. Of course she had known that, but this was a new awareness. Her mother was not just a woman with titles or descriptions but a person with all the feelings Amelia had experienced. She wasn't sure she wanted to know her mother that way. It was safer just seeing her as Momma and Grandmomma.

But she was her mother. She had tears on her face. She was crying about. . .Amelia. Her mother whispered, "You think less of me now?"

Amelia leaped from her chair and fell at her mother's knees, like she had done many times with Matilda. She held her mother's hands. "Oh, Mom. That's what I thought you'd feel about me. I felt you would think me some awful person. I've felt it for years."

Her mother's hands were on her hair, smoothing it back, comforting, soothing. "No, my darling. The Lord gave us such strong emotions so we can love and share our bodies in marriage all of our lives. But when we're young, we don't always control those emotions. Yet the act of not waiting for marriage, although done as an act of love, is condemned. Abstinence is best. But you acted out of emotion and need and wanting to give to another person."

Amelia could hardly believe her mother could be so human. Now she knew she was the one who set her mother up on a pedestal. Her mother never pretended to be perfect.

"I do need you, Mom. Forgive me for lying."

"You did what you thought was best."

"I've been afraid something might happen like—"

Her mother stopped her. "Like that young girl whose life was dragged through the mud. I remember."

Amelia nodded. "Luke has said his family isn't like that. He prayed with me, Mom."

Her mother's eyes teared up. "I think he's a fine young man. I don't think he will hurt you."

Amelia said something she never thought she'd say. Holding out her hands, she said, "Mom, will you pray for me?"

Her mom nodded. "But first. . ." Her mother opened her arms, and they hugged. Amelia was glad to know her mother was not perfect but that she prayed to the One who was.

Chapter 28

At almost the last minute Luke reconsidered and stuck the shell in his duffel bag just before he left for the airport. A shell that didn't represent anything—except perhaps his own outward appearance. He probably looked intact, but inside, he felt hollow and empty.

He thought about Penny. He couldn't blame Joe for breaking off with her. If Luke had been the one in Hawaii, he, too, would have—if things had been reversed. He would have written, *I met this girl.*

But Luke had not met a nineteen-year-old girl. He had met a twenty-four-year-old woman who had a child and was a beautiful person. One who was loving and responsible and had never intended to hurt anyone. A woman he'd shared his heart with, who showed him fun and laughter and courage. At Pearl Harbor, she had said there was no place in her life for his parents.

Now she was willing to find out how they would react to her and Little Joe. He knew there was no place in her life for him, except as an uncle to Little Joe.

He could easily fall in love with her. But it was not him who Amelia loved. Maybe he would take that shell to the Ohio River and throw it in. Turn around and settle down with Penny.

Settle?

Matilda had questioned that.

He and Penny shared a spark of friendship. He'd told Amelia he wanted a spark in his life, knowing a spark could become a flame. But a spark could also become a dying ember, could it not?

Penny picked him up from the airport.

On the drive home he told her about the places he'd gone.

"When Joe wrote and broke off with me," Penny said, "I knew there had to be more to it than his not being ready to settle down. Did you find out if he had a girl there?" She laughed at her own question. "He always had a girl."

Luke didn't want to tell her about Amelia's private life and Little Joe. This was a family matter.

But he told her about the Amelia he'd come to know, the tour guide, the lovely fun girl, the preacher's daughter. He told about Matilda.

He kept talking, wondering how he could tell Penny that she was a wonderful person but he knew he couldn't love her like she deserved. He had been selfish to think of settling down with her.

When they arrived at his parents' home, he started to get out, but Penny sat with both hands clutching the wheel.

"Are you coming in?"

She shook her head. "I don't think so, Luke. Do you have another minute?"

"Sure." He took his hand off the door handle.

"You're different."

"How's that?"

She shrugged a shoulder and smiled sweetly. "I see something in you I've never seen before. A wistfulness, if a man can be wistful. Always before, you knew exactly who you were and what you would do. You became a marine to please your dad, an architect to make a good living. You had a desire to have a girl waiting for you. Everything right." She looked over at him. "From what you've told me, you've settled things with Joe. But something is bothering you."

He shook his head. "My time in Hawaii was good in many ways. But it was difficult, too."

She nodded. "This may not be the time, but I want you to know I've gone out with a teacher at the school a couple of times."

She deserved someone who wouldn't just settle for her. He nodded.

"He loves me."

He was glad.

She touched his arm. "I've always loved you, Luke."

"I know. I hope we'll always be friends. And you," he added, "you still love Joe."

Her smile was sweet. "Don't we all?"

Yes, Luke was thinking. They all did. That was something he'd been jealous of a few times. Now he wanted everyone to love Joe, the young man who had lived life fully, who was never mediocre, never did things in a small way. He begrudged Joe nothing now.

His mom had cooked one of his favorite meals—chicken potpie. The coffee wasn't as good as Kona, but it was fine. During the meal, he talked mainly about the tsunami destruction and his helping with rebuilding and planning in Hilo. He told about the beauty of Hawaii and how he would show them pictures later and bring out the more serious parts of his visit to the islands.

After they settled in the den, he described how peaceful and beautiful Pearl Harbor looked now. He'd never before told them what Joe had written in his letter, but now he shared that with them as a lead-in to Amelia.

They were glad Joe had spent his last days with a special girl. Luke's mom, with misty eyes, smiled at his saying she was a preacher's daughter.

He began to show the pictures. They thought she was beautiful. After they agreed on that, he dropped the first bombshell. "She's part Japanese."

He felt his dad's stare, and his mom looked at the pictures again. "I wouldn't have known." Her worried brow smoothed when she looked up. "Did Joe know that?"

"Of course, Mom. Her mother is a beautiful Japanese woman." He told her what he knew of Akemi, but it didn't seem to impress his mother. Finally, after a long look at him, she said slowly, "But he knew her before they bombed Pearl Harbor."

Luke shook his head. "That wouldn't have mattered to him afterward, Mom."

She huffed lightly as if he'd said something ridiculous.

"And there's more." Luke knew he had to tell about Amelia's private life because their grandson was a part of that.

"She goes by the name of Amelia Thurstan."

They stared at him for a long moment. His dad's lips tightened, and he looked down at his hands resting on his knees. His mom's eyes squinted. "They. . .married?"

"No, Mom. She had his child."

She repeated, in a raspy voice, "A. . .child?"

Luke drew in a deep breath and tried to control what he feared would become a heated discussion.

Her eyebrows rose. "Without the benefit of marriage?"

"What is that song you taught me? 'Jesus loves the little children, all the children of the world. Red and yellow, black and white, they are precious in His sight.' Did He stop when Japan bombed Pearl Harbor? Does He stop loving me—or any of us—when we sin?"

He looked at his dad, who had fought in World War I but didn't talk about it. His dad spoke forcefully to his wife. "Betty, you and I need to lay down our weapons and put on the armor of God that we've read about, talked about, and said we believed in."

His dad was a soft-spoken man most of the time, but that was said with the ring of authority. His mom lifted her chin and looked as if she might challenge him, but his fixed stare was unwavering.

She looked at Luke. "Is the child a boy or a girl?"

Luke scoffed. "Does it matter?"

"Well yes. I need to know if I should give my grandchild a doll or a baseball."

A flood of relief swept over him. Luke realized anew the kind of parents he had. They were fair and good, and their lives were ruled by right living.

He pulled out the pictures of Little Joe. His mom and dad passed them back and forth. They both were disbelieving.

Finally his mom shook her head. "Joe?" Her eyes questioned him. "But what is this? This is. . .Joe."

"That is Little Joe. Your grandson."

Her head turned to her husband. "We have a grandson." The awe in her voice matched that in his dad's eyes as he reached for her hand and held it in his.

"Not just a grandson," Luke said. "A whole other family."

They both nodded slowly.

He wasn't surprised at his mom's flooded face. He'd never seen his dad cry before, but he knew the feeling, like he'd done in that yard with his head against his arm, crying against that tree.

Luke went over to them, knelt before them, and they shared the pain, the grief, the joy, the unknown.

The three of them and the mother and child in the pictures, were a family.

Chapter 29

Luke hammered nails into boards during the next month with his dad as a way to pass time until he would return to Hilo with his parents. At first the phone calls his mom made to the island were short and polite. They became longer, and he breathed a sigh of relief when he heard her say, "Thank you for loving my son. I can hardly wait to see all of you. Your picture is lovely, and I know you are."

"Mom," he said, after the call, "if you don't stop that crying all the time, we're going to have to get a boat to take us out of this house."

She laughed through her tears. "This is happiness, Luke. Don't begrudge me that."

He hugged her. "No, Mom. I don't. I've done my share of crying, too."

She stepped back. "Thank you, son. You've given me a new lease on life."

He nodded, thinking how amazing it was what good could come from situations sometimes thought hopeless.

He wrote long letters to Amelia, helping her know his parents better. She in turn wrote about having an honest discussion with her parents and that her mom turned out to be human after all.

She also wrote that Little Joe asked about the man who didn't even know how to catch a ball. "I'm telling him about you, Luke," she wrote. "That you're a fine man and the brother of his daddy. I'm telling him about his mainland grandparents. Send more pictures."

She was sending pictures of her mom and dad to his parents. He caught his mom staring at Akemi's picture more than once. Finally she spoke about it. "Luke, I never thought I would say this. But she is a very beautiful woman. I think I'm going to get a new hairstyle and start exercising again."

His dad said, "Betty, you're beautiful enough for me."

"Well," she said, "looks like I trained you right."

Luke loved seeing their playfulness again. There had been too much somberness in that house for much too long.

Through letters and phone calls, arrangements were made for their visit to Hilo. His parents would stay at Matilda's. Although she invited him, Luke opted to stay at the Matti-Rose.

There was anticipation on their flight in early July, and that increased when they reached the Hilo Airport and Luke picked up the rental car. He remembered the turns, although he had his dad look at the directions Amelia sent, in case he had forgotten. He didn't think he'd forgotten anything—or anyone—on that island.

He slowed at the Matti-Rose, explaining that to them. "Across the street is Matilda's."

"Oh," his mom said, and he heard the snap of her purse. She would be getting a tissue to mop her face.

As soon as they parked at Matilda's and before Luke and his dad could take the luggage from the trunk, the screen door opened, and out ran Little Joe with leis around his neck.

"Wait," a familiar voice said. Amelia was standing in the doorway. She shook her head. "He's too excited to listen."

So was Luke. He searched Amelia's face for some sign she was glad to see him, but she was looking at Little Joe.

"You're my new grandparents." He looked up at them, from one to the other.

"Is that okay with you?" Luke's dad asked.

Little Joe nodded vigorously. Apparently he had been coached for this meeting.

Luke watched his mom's face, seeing the struggle he had felt, the shock, emotional tsunami—and then, "Joe," she managed to whisper through a trembly smile.

"Aloha," Little Joe said and took off one of the leis and held it up. His mom bent down, and he placed it over her head and kissed her cheek.

"Could I have a hug, too?"

Luke feared she wouldn't be able to let go or would weep all over him. Quite the contrary. After the hug, she stared at Little Joe with wide-eyed wonder as he stepped over to Luke's dad.

His dad knelt to be at the same level as the little boy with the dancing blue eyes, who wore a confident smile as if loving being the center of attention—like Big Joe had.

"Aloha."

"May I have a hug?" his dad asked.

Joe held out his arms.

Then it was Luke's turn. He, too, knelt for the lei to be put over his head.

"I already saw you," Little Joe said, "but Mom said to say aloha."

Luke opened his arms, and they hugged. He basked in the aroma of that warm little boy smell mingled with flowers.

After the hug, Little Joe said to Luke's dad, "He can't catch good."

"But we're going to practice, remember?"

Little Joe nodded. Then he reached up and held onto Luke's hand as they all walked to the adults who were standing on the porch. Matilda, Amelia, Akemi, and Jacob spoke to Luke, then they all began to introduce and welcome each other.

"You have a big family now," Luke said, looking down at Little Joe.

The boy looked up. "I have a bigger family."

Luke laughed. No matter how one expressed it, he was glad to be a part of this family. Then and later during dinner, he could readily see his parents wanted to know as much about Little Joe's family as the islanders wanted to know about these new grandparents and the mainland.

Amelia hardly glanced at him, but in watching her, he knew when her tension eased and she accepted the friendship of his parents as genuine.

He could tell they were fond of Amelia, and when Little Joe said his new granddad had written that he would take him fishing, Luke's dad replied, "Just as soon as your mother says it's all right, we'll sure do it."

"Well now," Jacob put in. "I think I need to go along to show you the way to the best fishing spots."

"You haven't been fishing in a long time," Akemi said.

"I just realized that," Jacob said, and they laughed.

Yes, this was just the beginning, but Luke had a strong impression there would be many good times to follow.

This far exceeded what he wanted when he came to Hawaii. He'd expected to take back some bit of information that would comfort his parents. He'd wanted to see his parents have an active, enjoyable life again. They had it now, and he thanked God for that.

In spite of his good feeling about it all, he couldn't help but wonder where that left him. Like William, who was a good uncle to Wanda's children? Was he going to turn out to be good ol' Uncle Luke?

Or should he return to the mainland and hammer some more nails into boards?

Chapter 30

His dad insisted Luke go along when he and Jacob took Little Joe on his first fishing trip. It was Joe who showed his quick mind when the first fish bit on Luke's line. He pulled it out, and they all laughed at the sight.

Joe's eyes widened in wonder. "You can catch. See, you catched a fish."

Luke and the others laughed with him. "Right," he said. "I can."

That was wonderful, and so was eating the fish later that evening after the women cooked them at Matilda's. Luke liked this family life—even more when Wanda and her children joined them. But it was a week later when he found out what Little Joe had meant when he said he had a bigger family.

A luau, held beyond the parking spaces at the back of the Matti-Rose, was planned for Joe's fourth birthday celebration, and Luke was in awe at the number of family and friends who came.

He was glad to see William and watched him tend the roasting pig. Children played on the small playground that Luke figured had been put there for Akemi and Jacob's grandchildren. It was a nice touch for guests, too.

Amelia took him around to meet all the family and friends who had been somehow related for generations. She gave snippets of their history as she introduced them. There were the MacCauleys who had been in horse racing and still had small horse and cattle ranches. There were the Honeycutts and Grants who had sugar plantations. They represented many countries and nationalities. That rainbow again, and it was beautiful. Luke learned that many of their ancestors had come from the mainland and had married someone they met in Hawaii.

Luke suspected his parents would change their residence to Hawaii. His dad could work in construction. Luke could do the same and someday tell his own children and grandchildren about buildings and homes he had designed and helped build. Already there was the restaurant in Hilo.

But one couldn't tell his children or grandchildren anything if he wasn't married. For now, he needed to count his blessings. And he did. He prayed he would be a responsible example to this extraordinary nephew.

During the next couple of weeks Luke got to practice being an uncle. William already knew how, and since school was out for the summer, the two of them planned outings for Amelia, Wanda, and their children. Luke saw a different side to Amelia and thought her an excellent mother to all three children, as was Wanda.

His parents had become like grandparents to Wanda's children, too. His mom was fast friends with both Akemi and Matilda. The three were constantly exchanging recipes, and Luke was glad he was staying at the Matti-Rose, except to go over and eat dinner with them.

One Wednesday evening when the Bible study group met at Matilda's, his dad and Jacob had plans. Amelia called and asked if she could see Luke after the study, which would last about an hour. He was standing outside Matilda's at the end of the hour when Amelia came out.

"They'll be awhile," she said, "but I'm not having any refreshments right now. Will you walk down to the beach with me?"

"Sure." He walked with her around the side of the house, across the backyard, along a path surrounded by lush foliage, and down to a narrow stretch of secluded beach. The sun was just beginning to cast its farewell glow across the sky.

He tried to imagine what Amelia might say. He'd seen a difference in her without her fear that some relative from the mainland might come and upset the life she'd built with her child.

They walked along the sand for a while, she with the breeze lifting her long hair that fell below her shoulders, and he with his hands in his pants pockets. He remembered something Wanda had said in what he'd thought was jest. One day after he and William had done some repairs on the front banister, she remarked, "You guys ever going to get a life of your own or just help us all the time?"

"It's our pleasure," William had said.

Luke had smiled then looked at Amelia, who turned and went back into the house. He'd taken that as a compliment and gratitude.

Now he wondered if she and Wanda were really thinking of getting a life of *their* own. They would have more time for that now that the children had another set of grandparents. But it might not be easy for them to have a social life with two uncles around all the time. Was Amelia going to say it was time for him and William to back off?

Amelia stopped and looked at him for a long time, as if pondering how to say what was on her mind. Finally she spoke. "I want to thank you for what you've brought into my and Little Joe's lives. Not just the obvious—you and your parents. But this feeling of being free. I don't have that burden of guilt and fear anymore."

He nodded. "I've seen that. I think it's something like I feel now that I've forgiven myself for not having been a perfect brother or person. And being alive when my brother wasn't."

He gave a short ironic laugh. "Strange, isn't it, how we hold onto our own guilt and fear although God already settled it?"

She smiled. "I want to ask you to forgive me for lying to you. For not being more forthcoming. You would never have known about Little Joe if you hadn't stopped by that day."

"Don't be so sure," he could honestly say. "I needed to return to the States, but I might have returned. There is much about Hawaii that is. . .unforgettable."

She drew in a breath and looked down at the sand. He saw the reflection of the deepening crimson sky against her face. Or was it a blush of wondering how to thank him one moment and reject him in the next? He really didn't want to hear that she could not be interested in him because he reminded her of Joe. But he didn't want to endanger his role of being a friend and uncle.

"Is everything all right between us now?" he asked.

She moistened her lips, as if they'd gone dry, and seemed uncertain. "There is one more lie I need to confess."

Not wanting to continue looking into her worried eyes—or was that the reflection of his own?—he dug his clenched hands deeper into his pockets and looked out at the ocean. The sun had dropped below the horizon, but the sky was still ablaze with color.

She'd told him that the night before the bombers came and killed Joe was the longest night, waiting, because of what she had to tell Joe.

Was this going to be one of his longest nights?

Her voice was soft. "There is another time I lied."

Through parted lips, he took a deep breath. Would this never end? Was she a compulsive liar?

"You remember the night. . .we kissed?"

He faced her then. Did she want an apology. . .now? He watched her swallow hard and glance away. "Vaguely," he said. He could lie, too.

Her eyes met his then, and she gave a small gasp. Then she started to turn as if ready to walk away. But wait a minute. She had lied?

He took hold of her arm then let go as she stood in front of him. "Tell me."

"You remember when I said I was thinking of Joe?"

"Yeah," he said slowly, afraid to hope what she might have lied about. He took a step closer. "What were you thinking?"

"I. . .wasn't thinking."

"Oh? Just caught up in. . .a kiss?"

She shook her head. "I wasn't thinking of Joe. I knew it was you."

His heart beat fast. "And?"

"And I kissed you back."

She took a step toward him, her eyes never leaving his nor blinking.

He forgot to breathe. "You knew you were kissing me. And you wanted that?"

She nodded.

He could already hear his heavy breathing and knew each word would be accentuated with it. "One of those romantic, under-the-stars moments?"

"No. It was the first adult, deliberate, real, meaningful kind of kiss that I'd never had before. Never knew I wanted. With Joe, it was all fun and new and young and wonderful."

"I'm not as charming as Joe."

"No. But you're real. You have the depth that hurt and grief and life bring. And that makes you so. . ." She took a deep breath. "How shall I say it? Sparky, to me?"

"Sparky?"

"Yeah, like the volcanic eruption."

"Oh, one of those little things."

They were so close he could feel the warmth although they weren't touching.

"That's when I felt it," he said. "All along, I told myself there wasn't a chance for you and me, because. . .you could never love me."

Her gaze didn't waver. "I could."

And he saw it in her eyes as if they reflected the glow of the moon now brightening the darkening sky. He frowned. "You think we can be sensible about this?"

She shook her head. "I don't think so."

He began to laugh. "I agree." His arms went around her, and he swung her around. Then he kissed her. And she wound her arms around his neck, and he felt this was what he'd been waiting for all his life. "This is too good to be true. I resisted falling in love with you, but it happened anyway."

"I knew right away you were the kind of man I wished could love me. But I felt. . .guilty and thought—"

"No more of that. I do love you, Amelia."

"I love you, Luke."

"I've been afraid to hope," he said. "Will you keep convincing me for the rest of our lives?"

"I will start now." She lifted her face.

"Yes," he said against her lips. "I love you."

When they moved apart, she looked up at him. "That was one of those beneath-the-stars romantic times."

"Well," he said and looked up, "that's putting it mildly."

She smiled and linked her arm through his.

As they walked back, Luke said, "Is there a Hawaiian custom? Should I ask your dad for your hand?"

"Maybe we should ask Little Joe."

"Good idea."

"But about my dad. He and Mom already said they approved if anything like this worked out for us. They told me they thought from the day you showed up in church and said your name that was the beginning of something good. Not a coincidence but a miracle."

"I can go for that." He smiled and held her hand.

"They always wanted me to have a church wedding."

"Sounds good to me. As long as I'm the groom."

Chapter 31

The Bible study group had already left Matilda's when Amelia went inside. Luke had walked on to the Matti-Rose. She slumped down into a kitchen chair.

"He. . .he loves me. He wants to marry me." The reality of it began to sink in.

Matilda nodded. "Yes."

"You knew?"

"I knew all the makings for it were there. You're two wonderful, attractive people just ripe for a lasting relationship. And you're perfect for each other."

"Do you think. . .I should wear white?"

Matilda shook her head. "No, my dear. You should wear black and paint a scarlet letter on your forehead."

Amelia groaned.

"Unless," Matilda said, "the Lord Jesus is in your heart. He died for every sin we have committed or ever will commit. If that's so, you're as pure as the driven snow. Now, get on with the blessing God has brought into your life."

Yes, she would do that. "I wouldn't mind having a small ceremony. But I want to give my family and Luke's family this time to remember. A happy, beautiful time."

Matilda nodded, and they hugged.

To Amelia's astonishment, no one was surprised that she and Luke were in love and would be married. Wanda said, "I can't think of anything better than an uncle becoming a dad. Or a friend becoming a husband."

Amelia agreed. She and Luke talked to Little Joe together. She told him the two of them would move into a home together.

"We won't live with Parker and Ellie and Aunt Wanda?" he said.

"Parker and Ellie will be going back to school soon. You know, when they're in school you don't see them much anyway. We will still have special times together. And you have your new grandparents to do things with."

He was nodding.

Luke ventured to ask, "Would you like for me to live with you and be your dad?"

Little Joe said, "Okay," but he turned and ran from the room.

Luke looked at Amelia, but she shrugged.

Little Joe soon returned with a truck. "This broke again. Uncle William fixed it, but you can fix it if you want to."

Yes, he was a fixer. He could build things. And he would do his best, with God's help, to build the right kind of relationship with his wife and his son.

"If I can't fix it, I'll build you another like it."

Little Joe didn't express an inkling of a doubt. "Okay."

Luke winked at him.

Little Joe scrunched up one side of his face and blinked both eyes.

Amelia smiled when Luke looked at her and said, "That's good enough for me."

Often she felt it was all too good to be true. But the big day finally arrived. It was a formal evening wedding for family and friends. Amelia stood in the foyer in her traditional white dress with the long train and fingertip veil fastened on her hair, which was pulled back in a chignon and with tendrils alongside her face.

Peeking into the sanctuary while her uncle, Geoffrey Grant, sang "Dearly Beloved," she saw her family, who had come to Little Joe's birthday party. Matilda was the first to be escorted down the aisle as Amelia had requested. Her mother, in a green satin kimono, sat at the organ.

Luke and William stood at the front of the church in their black tuxes, green cummerbunds, and bow ties.

Wanda, in a green silk gown draped with a flowered obi, carried the bride's bouquet down the aisle. Even from that distance, Amelia could see the longing in William's eyes as he watched her ascent to the front of the church.

The pleased reaction could be heard like a delightful breath as Little Joe and Parker carried rings on small pillows and stepped carefully down the aisle. Amelia smiled. That was one of the few times those boys ever walked.

Ellie was a lovely little lady in a gown similar to her mother's as she spread rose petals on the aisle.

Amelia thought her heart would beat out of her chest when her mother began the rousing rendition of "The Wedding March."

The congregation stood and turned toward Amelia. But from the moment she put her arm in the curve of her dad's and they started down the aisle, she saw no one but Luke and his eyes of love.

Her dad took his place in front of her and Luke and spoke the words that bound them for life. She could not have imagined God would bless her so wonderfully. But before she knew it, she and Luke had exchanged white leis and wedding rings and were pronounced man and wife. They sealed it with a kiss.

The reception was held in the Matti-Rose dining room where most of the adults remained, and love songs were sounding from the record player. It was all too confining for the children, who opted for the playground and lawn.

After all the congratulations and photography, holding their plates of cake, Amelia and Luke finally walked over to a table where William had taken a seat. Wanda came over, too.

With "Until. . .You Love Someone As I Love You" sounding in the background, William glanced at Wanda holding the bridal bouquet then at Amelia. "Aren't you going to throw your flowers?"

Wanda answered immediately. "I told her I'm not chancing anyone else catching it. If she can do this, I can, too. My children need a dad."

William paled. "Is that. . .all?"

"No. I need a husband. For a while I've been ready to move on. I intend to."

"Anyone in particular you plan to move on. . .with?"

"Well, I should hope. I guess I'll have to see who catches Amelia's garter when Luke throws it."

"Oh no," Luke said. "That garter is mine."

Wanda sighed. "Well, I guess I'll have to throw the bouquet. Catch."

William jumped back as the bouquet struck him in the chest. He fumbled around, breathing heavily, but grasped it and finally held it up by the white ribbon tied around the flowers.

"Good thing you didn't drop that," Luke said.

"Not a chance. I almost missed it, but if it had hit the floor, so would I." He addressed Wanda. "Well. . .okay. I guess this is settled."

She patted her left hand. "Not until this hand has a ring on it."

William spoke loudly. "Anybody have a ring I can borrow?"

She grinned. "That can wait till tomorrow."

"Could I seal this. . .with a kiss?"

"For now, a peck."

To the tune of "I Can't Give You Anything but Love," William held the flowers between them, leaned over, and lightly touched his lips to hers as she leaned toward him.

Neither seemed to know what to do next.

Amelia put her hands together. Others, who apparently had been watching, joined in with applause.

Geoffrey and Breanna walked up. Breanna hugged Amelia and Luke then held out her hand. "Here's the key to the house."

"Thanks again," Amelia said. The sugar plantation house in Oahu would be their honeymoon base for the next two weeks. Geoffrey and Breanna's children were all grown, and they had no grandchildren. They would be staying at the Hilo plantation with Breanna's sister, Mary Ellen, and her husband, Clay Honeycutt.

Just as "You'd Be So Nice to Come Home To" began to play, Luke said to Amelia, "We should leave soon. Don't want to miss our plane."

Matilda stood nearby. "When we get back to the house, I have one more gift to give. This one is for Little Joe."

Chapter 32

After Luke changed at the Matti-Rose, he drove his rental car over to Matilda's. Amelia had changed into an ivory-colored suit with a flowered silk blouse beneath. She'd let her hair down and was particularly breathtaking.

The two sets of grandparents were seated at the kitchen table with Matilda. Jacob called Little Joe in from the lanai.

Matilda handed him a gold piece.

His mouth opened wide. "Everybody says you're rich and give these to special people."

"I give them to special people," she said. "But this is my last gold piece."

Joe seemed torn about taking it. "You don't want to keep your last one?"

"I want you to remember me and that I thought you were special. I've kept this long enough, waiting for just the right person to give it to. You're that person."

"Thank you." He held it up for all to see. "It's gold."

"Yes," Matilda said. "And about my being rich. My father is. And where I will be going one of these days, I'll be walking on His streets of gold."

Luke felt the moment of silence. He also felt Amelia's hand slip around his arm. He looked into her face and smiled. No one could take Matilda's place in their lives. No one could take anyone's place. But they could be there for each other, to fill a heart and to love with all they had to offer. Amelia smiled back at him.

They drove to the airport and soon were seated on the plane, which lifted high into the air, but no higher than Luke's euphoria at having found a lasting love—with all the sparks he could dream of—with a beautiful, wonderful woman.

He took a moment to look out the window and down at Hilo and remembered that Joe had written in his letter, "Be seeing ya." Luke felt like his brother would be doing just that, through the bright laughing eyes of a little boy.

Thank You, God, for the good that comes from the worst of things. Thank You, God, and, Joe, for Little Joe. . .and a girl named Amelia Grant, a preacher's daughter, of all things.

My wife.

He moved back from the window and turned his head to face her. She smiled, and her eyes were bright with happiness.

"I love you," she said.

He touched her face and spoke in the language one uses upon feeling like a part of Paradise, one who has found a rare pearl among the jewels of the sea. "Aloha, love," he said.

A Letter to Our Readers

Dear Readers:

In order that we might better contribute to your reading enjoyment, we would appreciate you taking a few minutes to respond to the following questions. When completed, please return to the following: Fiction Editor, Barbour Publishing, Inc., P.O. Box 719, Uhrichsville, OH 44683.

1. Did you enjoy reading *Aloha Brides* by Yvonne Lehman?
   □ Very much. I would like to see more books like this.
   □ Moderately—I would have enjoyed it more if _____
   _____

   _____

2. What influenced your decision to purchase this book?
   (Check those that apply.)
   □ Cover   □ Back cover copy   □ Title   □ Price
   □ Friends   □ Publicity   □ Other

3. Which story was your favorite?
   □ *Aloha Love*   □ *Love from Ashes*
   □ *Picture Bride*

4. Please check your age range:
   □ Under 18   □ 18–24   □ 25–34
   □ 35–45   □ 46–55   □ Over 55

5. How many hours per week do you read? _____

Name _____

Occupation _____

Address _____

City_____ State_____ Zip_____

E-mail _____

HEARTSONG PRESENTS

If you love Christian romance...

$12.⁹⁹

You'll love Heartsong Presents' inspiring and faith-filled romances by today's very best Christian authors. . .Wanda E. Brunstetter, Mary Connealy, Susan Page Davis, Cathy Marie Hake, and Joyce Livingston, to mention a few!

When you join Heartsong Presents, you'll enjoy four brand-new, mass-market, 176-page books—two contemporary and two historical—that will build you up in your faith when you discover God's role in every relationship you read about!

Imagine. . .four new romances every four weeks—with men and women like you who long to meet the one God has chosen as the love of their lives—all for the low price of $12.99 postpaid.

Mass Market, 176 Pages

To join, simply visit www.heartsongpresents. com or complete the coupon below and mail it to the address provided.

✄- -

YES! Sign me up for Heartsong!

NEW MEMBERSHIPS WILL BE SHIPPED IMMEDIATELY!

Send no money now. We'll bill you only $12.99 postpaid with your first shipment of four books. Or for faster action, call 1-740-922-7280.

NAME_____

ADDRESS_____

CITY_____ STATE _____ ZIP _____

**MAIL TO: HEARTSONG PRESENTS, P.O. Box 721, Uhrichsville, Ohio 44683
or sign up at WWW.HEARTSONGPRESENTS.COM**